Hanna's Daughters

Hanna's Daughters

Marianne Fredriksson

translated by Joan Tate

ORION

Copyright © 1994 Marianne Fredriksson
Translation © Joan Tate 1998

The right of Marianne Fredriksson to be identified as the author
of this work has been asserted by her in accordance with
the Copyright, Designs and Patents Act 1988

Original title: *Anna, Hanna och Johanna*
Published by Wahlström & Widstrand, Stockholm, 1994

Published by agreement with
Bengt Nordin Agency, Varmdö, Sweden

This edition first published in Great Britain
in 1998 by Orion
An imprint of Orion Books Ltd
Orion House, 5 Upper St Martin's Lane,
London WC2H 9EA

A CIP catalogue record for this book
is available from the British Library

Typeset by Deltatype Ltd, Birkenhead, Merseyside
Printed and bound in Great Britain by
Clays Ltd, St Ives Plc

The sins of the fathers are inflicted on the children into the third and fourth generation. We learned that at school when Bible study was still on the curriculum. I remember thinking that terribly unjust, primitive and ridiculous. For we were the first generation brought up to be 'independent' people, people who were to take their destinies into their own hands.

Gradually, as knowledge increased of the importance of our social and psychological inheritance, the words of the Bible acquired weight. We inherit patterns, behaviour and ways of reacting to a much greater extent than we like to admit. It has not been easy to adapt to; so much has been 'forgotten', disappearing into the subconscious when grandparents left farms and countryside where the family had lived for generations.

There are no biblical words for the actions of mothers, although they are probably of greater importance than those of fathers. Ancient patterns are passed on from mothers to daughters, who have daughters, who then …

Perhaps this is an explanation for why women have found it so difficult to stick up for themselves and make use of the rights an equal society has to offer.

I am greatly indebted to Lisbeth Andréasson, superintendent of Bengtsfors Gammalgård, who has scrutinized the book about Hanna from a cultural-historical point of view, provided me with literature on Dalsland, and last but not least translated dialogue from high Swedish to Dalsland borderland dialect. I would also like to thank Anders Söderberg at Wahlström & Widstrand for his criticism, encouragement and enthusiasm for the project. My thanks also go to my friends Siv and Johnny Hansson, who came every time I managed to confuse my new computer. That was many times.

Finally, I would like to thank my husband for enduring.

I should add that there are no autobiographical elements in this book. Anna, Johanna and Hanna bear no resemblance to me, my mother or my grandmother. They are imaginary characters and bear no relation to what is called reality. That is just what makes them real to me – I hope also to you, the reader, and that you will begin to wonder who your grandmother was and in what way your inherited patterns have shaped your life.

Anna

INTRODUCTION

CHAPTER I

Her mind was as clear as a winter's day, a day as quiet and shadowless as if snow had just fallen. Harsh sounds penetrated, the clatter of dropped enamel bowls and cries. It frightened her. Like the weeping from the next bed slicing into the whiteness.

Where she was there were many who cried.

She had lost her memory four years ago, then only a few months later her words had disappeared. She could see and hear, but could name neither objects nor people, so they lost all meaning.

That was when she came to this white country where time was non-existent. She didn't know where her bed was or how old she was, but she found a new way of being and appealed for compassion with humble smiles. Like a child. And like a child, she was receptive to emotions, everything vibrating between people without words.

She was aware that she was going to die. That was knowledge, not an idea.

Her kin were those who kept her going.

Her husband came every day. With him it was a wordless meeting. He was over ninety, so he, too, was on the brink of death. But he had no wish either to know this or to die. As he had always controlled his life and hers, he was putting up a fierce struggle against the inevitable. He massaged her back, bent and stretched her knees, and read aloud to her from the daily paper. She had no means of opposing him. They had had a long and complicated relationship.

Most difficult of all was when their daughter came, the one who lived in another town. The old woman knew nothing of time or distance, and was always uneasy before she came, as if at the moment she woke at dawn she had already sensed the car making its way through the country, at its wheel the woman with all her unreasonable hopes.

CHAPTER 2

Anna realised she was being as demanding as a child. But that was no help, so as soon as she gave in, her thoughts slid away: just for once to a proper visit, perhaps an answer to one of the questions I never had time to ask. But after almost five hours' driving, as she turned into the hospital car park, she had accepted that this time her mother would not recognise her either.

Yet she would ask the questions.

I do it for my own sake, she thought. It makes no difference what I talk about to her.

But she was wrong. Johanna did not understand the words, but was aware of her daughter's torment and her own powerlessness. She did not remember that it was her task to console the child who had always asked unreasonable questions. But the demand remained as well as the guilt over her inadequacy.

Her desire was to escape into silence, to close her eyes. But she couldn't, her heart thumping, the darkness behind her eyelids scarlet and painful. She started crying. Anna tried to console her, there, there, wiping the old woman's cheeks, ashamed.

But she was unable to halt Johanna's despair. Anna was frightened and rang for help. As usual, there was a delay, but then the fair girl was standing in the doorway, a girl with young eyes that had no depth in them. Anna could see contempt in those blue eyes and for a moment she could see what the girl was seeing: an oldish woman, anxious and clumsy, by the side of the really old one.

'There, there,' she said, too, but her voice was hard, as hard as the hand that ran over the old woman's head. And yet she succeeded. Johanna fell asleep, so suddenly it seemed unreal.

'We mustn't upset the patients,' said the girl. 'You must sit there quietly for a while. We'll come and change her and remake the bed in about ten minutes.'

Anna slipped out through the day room to escape to the terrace like a shamefaced dog, found her cigarettes and drew the smoke deep down into her lungs. It calmed her and she could think. At first angry thoughts: damned bitch, hard as nails. Pretty, of course, and horribly young. Had Mother obeyed her out of fear? Was there a discipline here that the helpless old people sensed and gave in to?

Then came the self-reproaches. The girl was only doing her job, everything, according to the laws of nature, that she should be doing. But couldn't, *couldn't* bring herself to do, even if time and place had existed.

Last of all came the astonishing realisation that Mother had somehow been touched by the questions she'd asked.

She stubbed out her cigarette in the rusty tin at the far end of the table, a reluctant concession to the lost. God, how tired she was. Mother, she thought, dear wonderful Mother, why can't you show pity and die?

Frightened, she glanced out over the hospital grounds where the maples were in flower and smelling of honey. She drew in the scent with deep breaths, as if seeking consolation in the spring. But her senses were dulled. It's as if I'm dead, too, she thought, as she turned on her heel and walked determinedly to the ward sister's door. Knocked, had just time to think: please let it be Märta.

It was Märta, the only one she knew here. They greeted each other like old friends, and the daughter sat down in the visitor's chair. She was just about to start asking questions when she was overwhelmed by emotion. 'I don't want to start crying,' she said, then did so.

'It's not easy,' said the sister, pushing across the box of tissues.

'I want to know how much she understands,' said the daughter, adding her hope of being recognised and the questions she'd asked her mother, who didn't understand yet did.

Märta listened with no surprise.

'I think the old understand in a way we find difficult to grasp. Like newborn infants. You've had two babies yourself so you know they take everything in, anxieties and joys. Well, you must remember?'

No, she didn't remember. She remembered nothing but her own overwhelming feeling of tenderness and inadequacy. But she knew

7

what the nurse was talking about. She had learned a great deal from her grandchildren.

Then Märta talked in consoling terms about the old woman's general condition. They had got rid of her bedsores, so she was in no physical pain.

'But she's rather uneasy at night,' she said. 'She seems to have nightmares. She wakes up screaming.'

'Dreams?'

'But of course she dreams, everyone does. The pity is we can never find out what they're dreaming, our patients.'

Anna thought about the cat they'd had at home, a lovely creature leaping up out of its sleep, hissing, its claws extended. Then she was ashamed of the thought. But Märta didn't notice her embarrassment.

'Considering Johanna's poor condition, we prefer not to give her tranquillisers. I also think perhaps she needs her dreams.'

'Needs?'

Sister Märta pretended to ignore the surprise in the other woman's voice.

'We're thinking of giving her a room of her own,' she went on. 'As things are, she's disturbing the others in the ward.'

'A room of her own? Is that possible?'

'We're waiting out Emil in number seven,' said the nurse, lowering her eyes.

Not until the daughter was backing the car out of its slot in the car park did she take in the content of what had been said about Emil, the old priest whose hymns she'd heard over the years. She hadn't thought about it today, that there'd been no sound from his room. For years, she'd heard him singing about life in the valley of the shadow of death, the Lord waiting with his terrible judgements.

CHAPTER 3

Johanna's secret world followed the clock. It opened at three in the morning and closed again at dawn.

A wealth of images, filled with colours, scents and voices. Other sounds, too. The roar of the falls, the wind singing in the tops of the maples and the forest rejoicing with birdsong.

On this night the pictures she is seeing are trembling with excitement. It is summer and early morning, slanting rays of the sun and long shadows.

'You must be mad,' shouts the voice she knows best, her father's. He's red in the face and frightening in his agitation. She's scared and flings her arms round his leg. He lifts her up, runs his hand over her head.

'Don't you think, girl?' he says.

But her eldest brother is standing in the middle of the room, handsome, with shiny buttons and high boots, and he's shouting, too. 'To the cave, all of you, and today, too. They might already be here tomorrow.' Then another voice, resourceful. 'Listen now, lad. Would Axel and Ole from Moss and Astrid's lad from Fredrikshald be coming here now to shoot us?'

'Yes, Mother.'

'I think you've gone mad,' says the voice, but now it's uncertain. And the father looks at the soldier, eye meets eye, and the old man can't mistake the gravity in the young man's eyes.

'Then we'll do as you say.'

The pictures change, start moving. Feet stamp, burdens are lifted. She sees the earth cellar and store emptied. The great barrel of salt pork carried out, the herring barrel, the potato bin, the cloudberry jar, the butter in its wooden tub, the hard round slabs of crispbread, all out on the ground. Down towards the boat. Sacks filled with blankets and clothes, all the wool in the cottage going the same way, down the slope towards the lake. She sees the brothers rowing. It's heavy going towards the headland, easier back.

'The oil-lamps!' It's the mother calling out on her way indoors.

But the soldier stops her, calling too, 'No, Mother, we'll have to do without light.'

The child is wide-eyed and anxious. But then a brimstone butterfly lands on her hand.

9

The picture changes again, the daylight is miserly and she's perched on her father's back. As so often, she's being carried up the slopes to the mountain lakes, so secretive and introverted they are, quite different from the great lake with its light and blue glitter. But just above the mill, the largest of the dark lakes breaks the stillness and would hurtle down the falls with all its strength had the dam not been there.

Father checks the sluice gate as always in the evenings.

'Norwegian water,' he says, with weight in his voice. 'Remember that, Johanna, that the water that gives us bread comes from Norway. Water,' he says, 'is much wiser than people, it doesn't give a damn about borders.'

He's enraged. But she's not afraid as long as she's on his back.

Dusk is falling. Laboriously, heavily, he makes his way down the slopes, goes to the mill, feels the locks. The girl hears him muttering wicked swear words before he goes on along the path down towards the boat. It's quiet in the cave. The brothers have fallen asleep, but the mother is moving uneasily on her hard bed.

The girl is allowed to sleep curled inside her father's arm, as close as she can get. It's cold.

Later, new pictures. She's bigger, she can see that from her feet running towards the mouth of the cave, in clogs, for it's slippery on the slopes now.

'Father!' she calls. 'Father!'

But he doesn't reply. It's autumn and soon it'll be dark. Then she sees the light in the cave mouth and grows anxious. Someone's shouting in the cave and Rudolf is there, the blacksmith she's afraid of. She sees them staggering about, him and Father.

'Get on home, brat!' he yells, and she runs, crying, running and falling, hurting herself, but the pain from her grazed knees is nothing to the hurt in her breast.

'Father!' she screams. 'Father!'

The night sister is there, worried: 'There, there, Johanna. It was only a dream, sleep now, go to sleep.' She obeys, as she usually does, and is allowed to sleep for an hour or two before the voices of the day shift explode in her body and race like ice through her veins. She's shaking with cold but no one sees it, the windows are flung open, they change her; she's no longer cold and feels no shame.

She's back in the white emptiness.

CHAPTER 4

Anna had a night of difficult and clarifying thoughts. They started with the feeling that had arisen when Sister Märta had asked her about her own babies. Tenderness and inadequacy. It had always been like that for her: when her emotions were strong, her strength ebbed away.

She hadn't fallen asleep until three in the morning. Dreamed. About Mother. And the mill and the falls hurtling down into the bright lake. In her dream the great waters had been gleaming and still.

The dream had consoled her.

Oh, what stories Mother had told. About elves dancing over the lake in the moonlight, and the witch who was married to the blacksmith and could conjure the minds out of people and beasts. When Anna was older, the stories grew into long tales of life and death of the people in that magical border country. Then, when she was eleven and more critical, she considered it all lies, that that amazing country existed only in her mother's imagination.

One day when she was grown-up and had her driving licence, she had put her mother into the car and driven her home to the falls by the long lake. It was only a hundred and fifty miles. She could still remember how angry she had been with her father when she had measured the distance on the map. He had had a car for many years and could well have driven Johanna and the girl for those few hours, the girl who had heard so many stories about this country of her childhood. If the will had been there. And the understanding.

But when they reached their goal, she and her mother, that sunny summer's day thirty years ago, her anger had blown away. Solemnly and with surprise, she had stood there and looked. Here it was, the land of fairy-tales with the long lake at the bottom, the waters falling twenty metres, and the still Norwegian lakes up in the mountains.

The mill had been pulled down and a power station built, disused now that nuclear power had taken over. But the lovely little red millhouse was still there, long ago turned into a summer place for some unknown person.

The moment was too great for words, so they had said little. Mother had wept, and apologised for doing so. 'I'm so stupid.' Not until they had taken the picnic basket out of the car and sat down with coffee and sandwiches on a smooth flat rock by the lake had Johanna begun to speak, and her words came just as they had when Anna was small. She had chosen the story of the war that never happened.

'I was only three when the Union crisis came and we moved into the cave. Over there, behind the headland. Perhaps I think I can remember because I'd been told the story so many times as I grew up. But I seem to have such a clear picture of it. Ragnar came home. He was so handsome as he stood there in his blue uniform with its shiny buttons and told us there was going to be a war. Between us and the Norwegians.'

The surprise was still there in her voice, a child's amazement when faced with what is incomprehensible. The three-year-old, like everyone in the borderlands, had relatives on the other side of the Norwegian lakes, where Mother's sister had married a fish merchant in Fredrikshald. The cousins has spent many summer weeks in the millhouse and she herself had gone with her mother to spend a month or two in that town with its great fortress. She remembered how the fish merchant smelt and what he had said as they stood there looking at the walls of the fortress.

'We shot him there, the damned Swede.'

'Who?'

'The Swedish king.'

The girl had been afraid, but her aunt, a gentler person than her mother, had lifted her up and consoled her: 'That was long ago. And people in those days had no sense.'

But perhaps there had been something in her uncle's voice that had stuck in her mind, for some time after her visit to Norway, she asked her father. He laughed and said much what her aunt had said, that that was a long time ago when people let themselves be ruled by kings and mad officers.

'But it wasn't a Norwegian who shot him. It was a Swede, an unknown hero in history.'

She hadn't understood, but she remembered the words. A long time later, at school in Göteborg, she had thought he was right. It had been a blessed shot, the one that had been the end of King Karl XII.

They had sat for a long time on that rock on that day, Johanna and Anna. Then they had walked slowly right round the bay, through the forest to the school, which was still there but much smaller than Johanna remembered. In the middle of the forest was a large boulder, thrown there by a giant, thought Anna. Mother had stopped by the boulder in surprise: 'How small it is.' Anna herself had charged her childhood mountain with magic, so she didn't laugh.

Anna managed to remain a good daughter for the whole of that long Saturday. She cooked her father's favourite dishes, listened with no apparent impatience to his endless stories and drove him to the jetty where his boat was, then sat there freezing slightly as he checked the fenders and hoods, tried out the engine and fed the ducks with breadcrumbs.

'Shall we take a trip round?'

'No, it's too cold. And I have to drive to Mother.'

He looked scornful. Anna had never learned to sail or start an outboard engine. Probably because he … but she'd better be careful.

'You've never done anything in your life,' he said, 'but stick your nose in books.'

He had intended to hurt and succeeded.

'I've made a good living out of it,' she said.

'Money,' he said, scorn now dripping from the corners of his mouth. 'Money's not everything in this world.'

'That's true. But quite a lot to you, the way you complain about your pension and watch every penny.'

The mask of the good daughter had cracked then, she thought, cursing her vulnerability and hunching up against the inevitable quarrel. But he was as unpredictable as ever. That's what makes him so difficult, she thought.

'You'll never know what it is to be hungry and poor,' he said. 'I had to learn early to watch every penny.'

She managed to smile, saying, 'I was only joking, Dad,' and the cloud passed as she helped him ashore and into the car.

He has only two sides, anger and sentimentality, she thought. When he had let off steam with one, it was time for the other. Then she thought she was being unfair. He was right, anyhow: she had never gone hungry.

Things also went better at the hospital that day. Anna did as she should, prattled away with her mother, held her hand, fed her when lunch came. One spoon for Pappa, one spoon for Mamma, then she stopped in the middle, ashamed. It was degrading.

The old woman fell asleep after the meal. Anna stayed where she was, watching the calm face. When she was asleep, she was almost the same as she'd been before, and Anna, almost bursting with tenderness and helplessness, went out on to the terrace for a while for a smoke. Cigarette in hand, she tried to think about the difficult sides of her mother, her self-obliteration and burden of guilt. A stay-at-home housewife with one child and all the time in the world to worship it.

That was silly and no help. Nothing hurts so much as love, she thought. What's wrong with me is that I've had too much, that's why I can't keep myself in order, neither when it comes to Mother nor Rickard. And never when it comes to the children.

The thought of her two daughters also hurt. For no reason: there was no cause for her to worry about them. They had had an inadequate mother, too. And nothing done can be undone.

When she got back to the sick room, her mother woke and looked at her, trying to smile. It was only for a moment, and perhaps it had never happened at all. And yet Anna was as pleased as if she'd met an angel.

'Hello, Mother dear,' she said. 'Do you know what I dreamed last night? I dreamed about the Norwegian waters, about everything you told me.'

By then, the moment had passed, but Anna continued: 'It reminded me of when we were there for the first time, you and I. You remember, I'm sure. It was a lovely summer's day and I was surprised that everything was just as you'd told me. We sat on that big rock down by the lake, do you remember? You talked about the cave you fled to when you thought there was going to be war with Norway, how you lived there and how cold you all were. Except you, allowed to sleep curled up in your father's arm.'

Perhaps it was wishful thinking, but Anna thought she could see some life come into the old face as it shifted from surprise to joy.

She smiled.

I'm imagining things. It's not possible. But I can see it's possible. Keep it there, Mother, keep it.

She went on talking about the waterfall and the forest, then the face vanished again. But Anna went on: 'I've often wondered what it felt like, sleeping in that cave. When it was so damp and you couldn't light a fire and had only cold food.'

This time there was no doubt about it: her mother's face shifted again, this time towards amusement.

She was trying to smile at Anna. It was a great effort and she didn't manage it, so it became a grimace. But then the miracle happened again. The brown eyes looked straight into Anna's, steadily and meaningfully.

The next moment she was asleep. Anna stayed where she was for a long time. Half an hour later the door opened and the blue-eyed girl said, 'Time to change the patients now.'

Anna got up and whispered a thank-you into her mother's ear. As she left the room, the old woman in the next bed started crying out.

CHAPTER 5

Anna made a detour round by the shore and sat in the car for a while, looking out over at the headland where she'd learned to swim. Where hawkweed and sea campion, crane's bill and bird's-foot trefoil grew among the coarse grass there was a boatyard. Here there were simple once individually owned cottages now smartened up with Mexican tiles and such insensitive extensions that they were scarcely recognisable. Over towards the mountains where her childhood meadows had been, with their wild strawberries, corn-flowers and cows, were now rows of terraced houses like horizontal high-rises.

Only the lake beyond was unchanged as were the islands, their low profiles outlined against the grey horizon.

Lost country, lost childhood.

We once walked hand in hand across that shore meadow with towels and a picnic, sandwiches, coffee for you, soft drinks for me. I'm growing up, she thought, with grief. And anger. Why does it have to be so ugly, so barbaric?

Once upon a time her mother had been as beautiful as the landscape here. Now she's falling apart. I'm trying to learn to accept it. About time, for I'm old, too, soon will be.

Must go home.

But she needn't have hurried. Her father was asleep.

Silently, like a thief, she roamed through the house and finally found what she was looking for. The photo album. But the photographs aroused no memories and were largely a confirmation of how they had looked. Yes, that's what we looked like.

Cautiously, she opened the drawer to put back the old album. It got wedged and it took a moment for her to see why. Under the floral paper with which for years her mother had lined the drawers was yet another photograph, this time in a frame. Grandmother. Her mother's mother.

She took it out and looked in surprise at the wall where it had always hung beside those of her paternal grandfather and grandmother, their children and grandchildren. It was true, the photograph had been taken down and the unfaded patch on the wallpaper showed where it had been.

How strange. Why has he taken Grandmother away? Hadn't he liked her? But he had, hadn't he?

What do I know? What can anyone know about parents? About children?

Why was it so important? Why does it seem a loss not to remember, not to have understood? In me, it's like a hole that has to be filled. As if I hadn't had a childhood, only a story about it, about what happened, or perhaps didn't happen.

They were good story-tellers, Mother most of all with her talent for making pictures of everything.

Gilded pictures?

She had known since childhood that Pappa embroidered his stories, adding things for effect and avoiding anything complicated. She'd excused that because the drama was exciting and he was doing it for fun.

She crept slowly up the stairs to her old room and went to bed, realising how tired she was. On the borders of sleep, she thought she had made an important discovery. Perhaps she had so few memories of childhood because she had been living in a story in which she never really recognised herself.

Was that how a sense of alienation was born?

She was woken by the old man clattering about in the kitchen with the kettle. She hurried out of bed, guilty conscience sending her racing downstairs.

'Oh, there you are,' he said, smiling. 'I thought I'd dreamed you'd come to see me.'

'You'd forgotten?'

'I forget so easily these days.'

She took the kettle from him. 'You sit there on the kitchen sofa and I'll fix the coffee.'

She found cinnamon buns in the freezer, put them in the oven, watched the hot water bubbling through the filter paper, sniffed the smell of coffee, not listening to the old man, now far into some account of how he met a whale one day when sailing from Skagen. An old, old story she'd heard many times, with pleasure.

He'd lost the art of maintaining the tension and keeping the threads together. His story crawled on, made detours, got lost: 'Where did I get to?'

'Outside Varberg.'

'Yes, that's right,' he said gratefully, but the thread from Varberg was part of another story about a girl and a dance in the courtyard of the old fortress. He broke off in confusion in the middle of it, saying it was probably Kungälv fortress where he'd been dancing one light summer night. And had got involved in a fight with the girl's fiancé.

As he described his exceptional victory over the other man, he was quite clear and distinct, the story lifted and glowed, only to collapse into a muddle of other memories of fighting and winning, stopping a bolting horse and saving the life of a child who'd fallen into a harbour somewhere.

She took the cinnamon buns out of the oven, her despair unendurable. It was terrible, all this foolish boasting, a decayed mind blurting out jumbled memories.

Memories? Perhaps they were just tall stories that had simply become enlarged over the years.

I don't want to grow old, she thought, and as she poured out the coffee, How can I ever be truthful? But aloud, she said, 'Your oilcloth's beginning to wear out. We must go and buy another tomorrow.'

When he'd finished his coffee, the old man went over to the television, the blessed, loathsome television. There, in a sagging armchair, he fell asleep, as usual. She was able to prepare dinner and even managed a short walk through the oaks between the mountains and the house.

They ploughed through dinner, meatballs with cream sauce and cranberries.

'I only get food like this when you're here,' he said. 'The girls who keep coming haven't time to cook real food.'

There was reproach in his words. When she didn't appear to understand, he emphasised it again. 'You could just as well do your writing here.'

'I have a husband and children.'

'They could come and see you,' he said, and she thought that, actually, he was quite right. She could perfectly well finish her report up there in her old room. Truthful, she thought, smiling in all her misery, how do you become truthful? Supposing I said that I don't get a moment's peace in your house, Dad. I just don't know how I'll stand two more days without going mad.

'I wouldn't disturb you,' he said.

There was an appeal in his words and she felt tears coming. But she started talking about the computers she needed for her work, machines that couldn't be moved.

Truthful, she thought as she sat there, lying in the face of her father. When he got up and thanked her for the meal, his voice was frosty. I don't like him, she thought. I'm afraid of him. I can't stand him. I loathe him. The difficulty is that I love him.

She did the dishes. A neighbour came in, a man she liked, an amiable man. He was cheerful as usual, stroked her cheek and said, 'It's not easy, I know.' She felt an incomprehensible fear as her eyes met his, as if a shadow had flitted through the kitchen.

'You go on in to Pappa,' she said, hearing the unsteadiness in her voice, 'and I'll fix a drink.'

With fumbling hands, she laid a tray with the gin bottle she'd brought with her, tonic, a bowl of peanuts. Premonitions? No. I'm tired and an idiot. She said it half aloud and several times, tired and idiotic. He's still young, healthy and happy, the kind of person who lives long. As she served the drinks, she said, as if in passing, 'And how are you, Birger?'

He looked at her in surprise and said he was well, as always. She nodded, but didn't dare meet his eyes all evening.

They went to bed early, at about nine, when the old man suddenly tired. She helped him to bed, as gently and compliantly as she could. His dignity was vulnerable.

She took a cup of tea up to her room. That was part of it all. Her mother had insisted on it, a cup of tea with honey before they went to bed. As she drank the sweet liquid, she recalled her childhood: the smell of honey in tea, a blue flowery cup and the shriek of gulls falling from the sky in insolent *joie-de-vivre* outside.

She flung open the window and watched the screaming flock as it headed out to sea, above Asper Island and Köpstad Island. The next moment she heard the blackbird singing from the oaks where the may was in bloom.

It was too much, a melancholy of that kind was unbearable. She reached out for a sleeping pill.

CHAPTER 6

The golden light woke her early. Perhaps not just the light, for in her dreams she'd heard birdsong from the garden, as lovely and strong as the spring itself. For a moment she lay still, trying to distinguish the voices, the chaffinch's joy, the cheerful signals of blue-tits and the whir of swallows as they flew low towards the eaves.

The swallows have arrived and are building their nests under the eaves, she thought, for a moment able to feel that everything was as it should be.

She slipped down to the kitchen and, as soundlessly as a ghost, got herself a cup of coffee, stole a cinnamon bun and crept silently back upstairs, remembering that the sixth stair creaked and successfully stepping over it. The old man was snoring in his bedroom.

She meditated, the birdsong assisting her into her own silence. For a while, she succeeded in thinking things weren't too bad for her mother, that she had gone beyond pain. And that her father's memory was so short, he couldn't keep up his bitterness.

Then she took out the photograph of her grandmother and gazed at it for a long time. Hanna Broman. Who were you? I knew you, oddly enough, almost entirely from hearsay. You were a legend, magnificent and questionable. So amazingly strong, Mother said.

I must have memories of my own. You lived until I was an adult, had married and produced children. But the photograph bears no resemblance to how I remember you. That's understandable. The photo was taken when you were young, a woman in her prime. I saw you only as old, a stranger, tremendously large, enveloped in huge pleated black dresses.

So this is what you looked like in the days of your strength, when you walked six miles with a fifty-kilo sack of flour from the mill to the village on the border. There you bartered with it for coffee, paraffin, salt and other necessities.

Can it be true? You carried the heavy sack on your back, Mother said. But only in spring and autumn. In the summer you rowed, and in winter you pulled a sledge across the ice.

We were born into different worlds, you and I. But I can see now we are alike, the same forehead and the same jagged hairline. The same broad mouth and short nose. But you haven't my chin, no: yours is strong and obstinate. Your gaze is steady, your eyes keeping their distance. I remember they were brown.

We look at each other for a long time. For the first time ever, we're looking at each other.

Who were you? Why did we never get to know each other? Why were you so uninterested in me?

Suddenly Anna hears a question. The child who says, 'Why isn't she a proper gran? Whose lap you can sit on and who tells stories.'

And her mother's voice: 'She's old and tired, Anna. She's had enough of children. And there was never any time for stories in her life.'

Was there bitterness in that voice?

I must go back to what *I* remember.

Grandmother sometimes came to see us in the mornings when I was small and she was still able to walk the long way from the bus stop to the house by the sea where we lived. She sat on the kitchen sofa, in the smell of cakes and newly baked bun-loaf, and the table was laid with a fine cloth and the best cups. She brought comfort with her, like a cat settling in the corner of a sofa and purring. She purred too, I remember, creaked like a corncrake at night. When she wasn't talking.

Even her talk brought pleasure, a strange language, half Norwegian, easy-going, sometimes incomprehensible.

'Us here,' she said. 'Indeed, that's it.' She always succeeded in surprising herself and others because her words flew out of her mouth before she had time to think. Then she would look surprised and stop abruptly, shamefaced or laughing.

What had they talked about?

Their neighbours in the block. About children whose lives had gone badly, about men who drank and women who were ill. But also about weddings and new babies and parties, and food – and however could people afford it?

For the child, it was like lifting the roof off a doll's house and seeing crowds of people. Like a game. But for the two women it was reality, and serious. They had a living interest in the Höglunds' delicate children, and Johansson the master painter's boozing. Not to mention Mrs Niklasson's peculiar illness.

Gossip. Not malicious, or kindly. For the first time, Anna thought that the endless talk was an orgy of emotion. Her mother and grandmother wallowed in the misfortunes of others, tut-tutted and lived out their personal needs without ever becoming personal. Talking about yourself was impossible. Shameful.

Grandmother flushed easily.

'Don't you ever cry, Grandmother?'

'No. No point,' she said, flushing scarlet.

Mother was also embarrassed and scolded the child. There was a lot you couldn't ask Grandmother, who probably thought that impertinent children should be reprimanded and that Johanna's spoilt girl-child had no manners.

'You were so damned practical,' Anna said to the photograph.

Perhaps I'm wrong, she thought as she turned her eyes away from the photo to look beyond the window, past all those small houses where anonymous people lived wall to wall and scarcely even knew each other by name. Perhaps you both had a sorrowful longing for the village you came from. And you were trying to restore the connection and the village feeling when you came to the big city.

Anna could hear her grandmother snorting at that explanation. She liked the city, the electric light and running water, the nearby shops and the right to close your own door.

Grandmother came for Sunday dinner. Pappa fetched her in the car and she wore long black jet necklaces and white ruffles at her throat. At table she said nothing until she was addressed, and was always submissive to her son-in-law.

Anna suddenly remembered, a perfectly clear memory, she thought with surprise. All round the dinner table amazed voices turned over and over the schoolmistress's talk about Anna being gifted.

Gifted? That was an unusual word. The teacher had talked about high school. Grandmother flushed and snorted, finding the talk indecent. She took a long look at the girl and said, 'What use would that be? She's nothing but a girl. She'd get superior and she wouldn't get away.'

Perhaps those were the words that had settled Anna's future. 'Nothing but a girl' had aroused her father's anger. He would otherwise never admit to his grief that his only child was a girl.

'Anna'll have to decide for herself,' he said. 'If she wants to go on at school, she shall.'

How did I forget that Sunday, that conversation? Anna wondered, going back to bed and looking at the photograph again. You were wrong, you old witch, she said silently. I went on at school, I took exams, I was successful and moved in worlds you couldn't even dream of.

Superior I became, too, just as you said, as everyone said. And as far as you're concerned, you became a fossil, a primitive leftover from a vanished time. I excluded you from my life. You were a painful reminder of origins I was ashamed of. That's why I never got to know you and have no memory of you. But it's also why your photograph speaks so strongly to me. For it says quite clearly that you were a gifted girl, too. Your prejudices were different from mine, that's true. But you were right sometimes, especially when you said that I wouldn't get away, either. For me, too, a woman's life awaited me.

I didn't carry sacks of flour from the mill to the village, Grandmother. And yet I did.

Hanna

BORN 1871, DIED 1964

CHAPTER 7

Hanna's mother had two batches of children. The first four died in the famine in the late 1860s. Maja-Lisa marked time, daring to believe she would have no more.

But in 1870, spring came with rain, just as it should, the baked soil drank and once again there was bread on the table. There was no talk of surplus, but by autumn they had turnips and potatoes in the earth cellar and the cows had enough grazing once again to give milk.

And Maja-Lisa was with child.

She cursed her fate, but August, her husband, said they should be grateful. The bad years hadn't driven them from the farm and they hadn't had to wander the roads as vagrants in gypsy carts like so many other smallholders in Dalsland.

Hanna was born the eldest child of the new batch, then along came another girl and three boys. What the mother learned from previous deaths was never to get fond of the new child. And to fear dirt and bad air.

The latter she'd learned in church.

In the days before the famine years, they'd had a young gentle-eyed priest who did his best to live in imitation of Christ. He shared his bread with the old, and wherever he went he had milk with him for the children, although the parsonage itself was also short of food. In the daytime, he buried children and the old, and signed papers for all those fleeing west to Norway and America. At night he prayed for his poor people.

As his prayers had no visible effect, instead he took to writings he had been given by his brother, a doctor in Karlstad. That was how his sermons came to be about the importance of cleanliness.

Consumption thrived in dirt, and rickets in darkness, he told them. All children should be out in the daylight. They didn't die of cold, but of darkness and filth, he thundered. And they had to have milk.

It was a message his congregation would have scorned if times had been ordinary. But now the mothers listened with anxiety, and Maja-Lisa was one of those who took seriously his talk about cleanliness.

There was trouble at home before she persuaded her husband not to spit on the rag rugs. But she was relentless, for she found that the priest was right. The new children were unusually strong and healthy.

But the gentle-eyed priest left and was replaced by one given to drink. With the change of priest, worse came after the famine years. Fear had settled in, joy was in short supply, but there was plenty of envy. Distances between houses also grew, as the forest took over fields and meadows round abandoned farms.

And in winter the procession of beggars straggled through the villages, reminding them all.

When Hanna was ten, the new priest came to Bråten to hear their catechism and told them they ought to thank God for being allowed to live in such a beautiful place. Hanna looked with surprise over the lake and the high mountains. She didn't understand what the priest was talking about. Even less did she grasp what he meant when he assured her that God took care of his children. God helped only those with hard hands and who learned to save every crumb.

At twelve, the girl was sent into service at the farm on the river mouth. She had been at school long enough to be able to write and do sums. That was enough, her father said.

Lyckan, as the farm was called, was ruled by Lovisa, a mean woman known for her harshness and arrogance. The farm was considered rich in these poverty-stricken areas. Down towards the plain, it would have been a pitifully small holding. Lovisa was unlucky with her children, two daughters crushed to death in

28

infancy, a son dead, shrunken and crippled with rickets. Now there was only one left, a handsome boy, used to having his own way. He was not like ordinary folk, even in appearance, dark and black-eyed.

Malicious tongues talked about the gypsy tribe that had come through the district the summer before he was born. But sensible people reminded themselves that Lovisa's grandfather had been Spanish, a shipwrecked sailor rescued off the coast.

The farmers were related. Joel Eriksson at Lyckan was brother to Hanna's mother. The maternal grandfather still lived at Framgården, but had shared his outlying farms between the children. Joel, the son, was given the freehold of Lyckan. Maja-Lisa and her husband had to be tenants at Bråten, a poorer and smaller farm.

Yet, as if there was some justice in life after all, Maja-Lisa had a good, hard-working husband in August Olsson, born and bred in Norway, while Joel had been landed with the difficult Lovisa from Bohus County.

Lovisa was pious. Like many of that kind, she delighted in keeping her fellow human beings in the good order of the Lord and with good conscience was daily able to indulge in cruelty.

By now, Hanna was used to long days, hard work and much abuse so she didn't complain, and never knew that the neighbours pitied her, saying that Lovisa worked her like a beast of burden. The girl had enough to eat and once a month she was happy. That was when she was allowed to go home to her mother with a bushel of flour.

When the darkness closed in in October, she menstruated. It hurt. She bled a great deal and was frightened, but didn't dare go to Lovisa. She took her most worn shift, tore it into strips and squeezed her legs together to keep the bloody rag in place. Lovisa looked suspiciously at her and screamed, 'You move like a knock-kneed heifer. Get a move on, girl.'

Not until she got back home to her mother on the Saturday could she cry. Only slightly, for her mother as usual said that crying never did any good. So she got help with proper crocheted towels and a ribbon for round her waist. Two expensive safety-pins were found from her mother's sewing-box. She felt wealthy. Then Maja-Lisa said, 'Now you have to know it's dangerous. Never let a man close to you.'

Then came the evening when she fell asleep in the hay. She had her sleeping place in the kitchen, but there was no peace there with all the quarrels in the evenings, which were usually about the son the mother spoilt and of whom the father wanted to make something. Hanna was so tired she would probably have been able to sleep despite the bitter words that flew over the straw mattress in the servant's box-bed. But that evening, her master and mistress were fighting in the bedroom, and the sound of heavy blows and screams penetrated to the kitchen. Hanna thought, Now Joel's killing her. But then she heard dark Rickard calling, a terrible agitated cry like a bellow from the underworld.

They've woken him, God help us.

That was when she slipped out into the barn, frightened that the boy would begin to pinch her the moment his mother's eyes were elsewhere.

She was sleeping in the hay like an exhausted animal and didn't wake until he was pulling at her skirt. She tried to scream, but he gripped her by the throat and she knew that she was going to die. Faced with that, she lay still. He was as heavy as a bull as he hurled himself on to her and when he thrust inside her and she broke, in all that hideous pain, she was able to pray to God for Him to receive her.

Then she died – and was surprised when she woke an hour or so later, bloody and torn. She could move, first her hands, then her arms and last her legs. Finally, she was able to make a decision, or at least shape a thought: home to Mother.

She walked slowly through the forest, leaving a blood-stained trail behind her. She crawled the last bit on all fours, but when she called outside their door, her voice was loud enough to wake her mother.

For the first and only time in her life, Hanna saw her mother weep. The girl was put on the kitchen table and the mother washed and washed, but was unable to stop the bleeding.

'Dear Lord,' said Maja-Lisa, over and over again, before pulling herself together and sending her eldest boy for Anna, the midwife who had helped Maja-Lisa through her many deliveries. She was also good at stemming bleeding.

'Hurry, hurry!' she yelled at the boy.

Then when she was about to take off the girl's ripped clothing, she stopped. In her wild fury, she had remembered that Anna was not only a midwife, but was also the one who went from cottage to cottage with all the wicked secrets of the village.

Hanna was asleep or unconscious, Maja-Lisa couldn't make out which. The kitchen looked like an abattoir and she called upon God even more earnestly to show mercy, while the children around her put their hands over their ears and eyes.

Then at last Anna came, sturdy and calm. She had brought finely grated wild parsley and mixed arnica into it, then she greased the girl's loins with the ointment.

The treatment woke Hanna and, slowly, she began to weep. The midwife leaned over the child and said, 'Who?'

'Black Rickard,' the girl whispered.

'Might've known,' said Anna harshly. Then she gave the child a concoction of mistletoe and white deadnettle. 'That should stop the bleeding and make you sleep like the dead,' she said. 'But God knows if you'll ever be able to have babes. And you'll never be married.'

Maja-Lisa didn't look upset, nor had she any idea that Anna's two predictions would come to nothing. She sent the children off to bed in the other room, put on the coffee, cleaned up the kitchen, then noticed the shotgun had gone from the wall and August had vanished.

She screamed again. The children came racing out of the other room, but Anna had seen what Maja-Lisa had seen and snorted. 'Men! Calm down, woman. There's nothing we can do.'

'He'll end up in the fortress,' cried Maja-Lisa.

'I don't think he'll succeed.'

She was right in that prediction. When August got to Lyckan, the son had disappeared. Both farmers calmed themselves with strong drink and decided that the boy should be forced into marriage as soon as Hanna was of marriageable age, and until then she was to be respected as a daughter of the house.

But nothing much came of the agreement. Hanna said she'd rather jump in the river than marry Rickard. Maja-Lisa said nothing, but Lovisa sent secret messages to her son to say, for the sake of Jesus Christ, that he must keep away from the farm. Anna the midwife was talking about the policeman, saying that when she was small there'd been talk of a man condemned to death for despoiling a servant girl.

But neither August nor Maja-Lisa wanted to cause such trouble to the relatives at Lyckan.

Tongues wagged in the cottages. People began to avoid Lovisa and Lyckan. Until it was clear one day that Hanna was with child and more and more came to the conclusion that the girl hadn't been entirely unwilling. All the talk about her being so badly hurt had been lies. Anna's tongue had run away with her as usual.

CHAPTER 8

When her bleeding didn't come twice in a row, Maja-Lisa must have said to herself a hundred times a day that it was because the girl was so badly torn down below. But then one morning the child began to vomit.

Maja-Lisa took the girl to Anna. The midwife felt her abdomen, threw up her eyes and said she could make nothing of God's ways. Then she went up to a clearing in the forest where the wild parsley grew and made a potion with it, but it had no effect on the babe in Hanna's belly.

''Tis gone too far,' she said.

At scarcely thirteen years old, on 5 July, Hanna gave birth to her bastard, a strong healthy boy with black eyes. He found it difficult to let go, so the birth was long drawn-out and difficult. Although the baby was like his father, Hanna was seized with a strange tenderness for him when he at last arrived.

The feeling was so surprising that it made her bow to the decisions that had to be taken. She knew that her parents' land couldn't feed two extra mouths. She had to go back to Lyckan. The master there solemnly promised she would be treated as a daughter and, as far as he was able, kept his word. He was fond of the boy, who grew quickly and laughed at the world. He was a happy and energetic child.

Hanna worked just as hard as before and Lovisa was no friendlier, although she had talked a great deal about compassion ever since she had been saved by the Mission Society preacher, who came once a month and assembled his flock in the neighbouring barn.

All three of them were waiting for Rickard, but not a word was said about the vanished youth. Then village rumour had it that he had been seen in the district.

That was when Hanna decided to go to the rune-master in the forest up-river behind the Devil's Ravine. She'd thought about it for a long time, but had been frightened by evil whispers about the old man and his troll wife.

She asked her master to look after the child. It was Sunday, and she had to go to church, she said. He nodded encouragingly and said it was good that someone from the farm sought out God in His own house, and gave his wife a malicious look. Lovisa screamed after her that she wasn't to forget the whore-cloth if she was going to God's house.

It was fully six miles to the church by the riverbank, then up the steep hill past the waterfall. But there, in the calm water, she found the ford, and then it was only half an hour's walk through the forest to the cottage on the ridge at the end of the path. She found her way, for she had been there as a child with her mother and had been made to swear never to tell anyone. Her heart was thumping with fear, but the two old people received her with no surprise. So, she wanted a rune-staff, did she? The girl didn't dare speak, but nodded, looking in terror towards the corner of the cottage where, the local

33

people believed, the rune-folk kept the amputated member of a murderer hanged many years ago on the gallows.

She saw at once that it was no man's member. No, it was from a stallion and couldn't frighten her. She'd seen things like that before, in secret corners of cottages where the wife was childless.

The old woman laid her hands on Hanna, on her forehead first and then over her heart, meanwhile speaking to her husband in a wild, alien language. He nodded, whittling away, the one rune added to the other on the little staff. When he'd finished, he looked pleased and smiled as he told her she must take care of it, so that her shame would leave her.

She paid with the meagre few coins she'd saved, curtsied low and ran the whole long way home with the secret rune-staff hidden between her breasts. She had her ears boxed for being away so long, accepted that without complaint, even swallowing the comment that maybe she was on heat again, for she was a whore, she was, Lovisa said: she had seen a strange gleam in Hanna's eyes.

Two days later, Rickard came home, brilliant as a rooster in high boots and uniform with shiny buttons. He swaggered around, laughing at his parents' surprise, bragging in the way soldiers do. He talked loudly, particularly loudly when he announced that he'd never be a smallholder, wearing himself out on this miserable farm. Hanna could forget him. He wasn't going to marry a whore.

Only once did he waver and that was when his four-year-old son appeared at the kitchen door and laughed straight in his face. But then the soldier turned on his heel and left.

Lovisa's weeping turned into loud wails. But the farmer looked at the child and then at Hanna. Both found it hard to conceal their relief and neither said a word of consolation to Lovisa.

Hanna hugged her rune-staff to her under her blouse. From that day on, she woke every morning with a feeling that something singular was going to happen to her.

CHAPTER 9

At midsummer, a man came to the village, a man from Värmland. A miller, said people who'd talked to him, a miller with plans to put in order the old mill at Norskvattnet. Already old, the young ones said. A man in his prime, the older ones said. But they all agreed he was taciturn, silent about his own life. Only to old Anna had he said that his wife and child had died way up there in Värmland. And he couldn't stay at the mill in all that loneliness.

He also said he drank to escape his memories.

He was going round the farms to find out what they needed. He was received everywhere by smallholders who assured him they would grind their corn at Norskvattnet as they and their fathers and grandfathers had done before. In the end he decided that if he restored the mill, it would give them all new heart.

Yet he hesitated. These people were more burdened and grim than he would have liked. There was little joy in the cottages, and the coffee they offered him was like dirty meltwater and tasted of burnt rye.

He came from a richer, more sociable place. But one of the shadows that had frightened him at home was envy, which had led to him being observed, measured and compared. Here, where the countryside was meaner and the poverty more severe, the same awful disease had struck harder, nourished by the famine years and poisoning every encounter.

Then there was the mill. A great deal of work was needed to put it in order. The railings along the channel were ruined, the landing stage rotten and the inner stairway in an appalling state. But the oak drum had held, as had the wheel and the sluice gate up by the lake. The two pairs of millstones were new, of natural stone from Lugnås, and looked as if they had a good edge. He calculated the height of the falls to be about thirty metres, which promised sure running.

The storehouse and the barn were still standing. The dwelling house was in fair shape, sturdy with the living room facing the lake, a small bedroom and large kitchen.

He had seen many fine landscapes in the forests of Finnmark and along the banks of the Klara river, but never before an area of such wild beauty. He gazed at the mountains rising against the sky, saw the peregrine falcons' nests in the cliff walls and the eagle's flight over the precipices. He listened to the thunder of the falls and the quiet rippling in the dark Norwegian lakes, and looked thoughtfully at the soft hills where the sheep grazed. He did not close his eyes because the fields were poor and the forest neglected, impenetrable in large parts. As if it had not been touched since primeval days, he thought.

And yet it was magnificent.

He was a man with a keen ear and could hear the mountains and lake, the rapids and the tall maples on the mill site speaking to him with secretive voices.

A close neighbour was the blacksmith, who seemed a good man. And access to a forge was necessary for the mill workers.

Money was the main reason for his hesitation. He had sold his own mill in Värmland and he would have to rent this one. Like all peasants, Erik Eriksson at Framgården was careful with his money, but had reluctantly agreed to contribute to the necessary repairs.

Old Anna, the midwife became his confidante. She made decent coffee, too, so he was seen more and more often in her kitchen. She was the one to put into words what he had long thought but had also rejected.

'Man, get yourself a woman, a hard-working and tolerant one. You can't manage with no woman up there in the forest.'

After she'd spoken there was a long silence. He suddenly realised how exhausted he was. And old, far too old to start again.

'I haven't got the right urge no longer,' he said, in the end.

'You're a young man.'

'Over forty.'

'A man in his prime.'

'I've had bad luck with my womenfolk.'

When he came back the next evening, Anna had done some thinking. She was cunning and, as if in passing, she began to talk about Hanna, the poor girl who'd had such a bad time in life.

36

Shame, it was, she said. The girl was the grandchild of Eriksson of the big place at Framgården.

The miller was horrified by the story of the rape, she could see it in his face, and understood when he interrupted. 'I suppose you haven't a drop?'

He was given his drink and was probably slightly unsteady on his legs as he made his way home in the dark. He said nothing about what he was thinking, but Anna, ashamed, felt he had seen through her.

When John Broman got back to the abandoned millhouse, he saw for the first time how filthy it was in the rooms and the kitchen. The discovery gave way to practical thoughts. Mm, indeed he needed a woman. When he had gone to bed, his need grew into desire; the blood throbbed in his veins and his member stiffened. Dear Lord, how long ago, how long ago it was since he'd had a woman.

He thought about Ingrid and his desire deserted him, his member slackening. Things had not been good either in bed or in the kitchen. What had she looked like? He could remember only her eternal nagging about money and how she couldn't make it go round. And about the drink he allowed himself on Saturdays.

If the picture of his wife was misty, the memory of Johanna was as clear as if she were before him now. He had had a daughter and consumption had taken her when she was eight. He still missed her.

When he woke the next morning, practicalities were still on his mind. The girl would be grateful. He could reckon on keeping her in order. That she had a child was good. He liked children but wanted no more of his own. And it was no bad thing that the girl was related to the big farm.

Later that morning he steered his steps towards Lyckan.

CHAPTER IO

Hanna woke as usual with that strange expectation, clasping her hands round the rune-staff, as if in prayer. Then she woke the boy on his straw mattress beside her in the box-bed in the kitchen.

'Ragnar.'

She was pleased with the name and that she'd had the strength to insist on it. On both farms there'd been objections, for no one in either family had ever been called that. Then they'd said nothing, thinking that it was as it should be, the bastard not to bear a family name.

But Hanna remembered a boy at school with her.

She knew now she'd succeeded with her intention. For her son resembled her schoolfriend, sunny and good-tempered. Even now at dawn and just woken, he was laughing.

She tidied the kitchen and made breakfast. Her master came in as soon as the porridge was ready, sat down heavily and ate, she standing behind him by the stove, eating as she usually did, the boy on her arm. One spoon for Ragnar and one for Mother.

Both she and Erik Eriksson enjoyed this morning moment. Lovisa did not take part in it, for she had so many prayers to recite.

An hour or so later, the stranger came. The girl observed him, thinking him handsome with his broad shoulders and short, squared-off beard. A gentleman. He was looking at her. It was awful the way he stared.

He found her good to look at, and her eyes were awake too. An observant girl, she sees, he thought. Strong, too, amazingly undamaged through that shameful darkness.

So young, he thought, seventeen, not much older than Johanna would've been, if she'd lived.

He was suddenly ashamed of his dreams of the previous night and the thoughts of the morning. But he emerged from his confusion as the child rushed into the kitchen, a small boy, eyes wide, inquisitive and unafraid. He looked at his mother and laughed. A big laugh, so unusual that it seemed challenging here in this poor district.

The miller squatted down and held out his hand.

'Good-day to you. My name's John Broman.'

'Good-day, good-day, good-day,' said the boy, putting both hands in his.

It was the first time anyone had been polite to the child, and Hanna's eyes glowed.

Then Joel Eriksson came stumping into the kitchen. 'Hurry up with them turnips, now. Take the boy with you.'

The next moment Lovisa was there, shouting for the coffee Hanna had forgotten to put on. The girl vanished through the door and John Broman watched her go, noticing how upright she was as she walked across the field, holding the child by the hand. It was then that he decided that both she and the boy should be away from this farm.

He drank the dishwater coffee and was assured that Lyckan would also grind its flour at the mill at Norskvattnet.

He went home via Anna, and told her briefly that no doubt she'd have her way, 'But you have to make sure I can talk to the girl.'

That was not easy to arrange, as Hanna was never free. But Anna went to Maja-Lisa, who sent one of the boys with a message to Hanna that she should come home at the weekend to see her parents.

CHAPTER II

On Saturday morning, Broman got up early and cleaned the house. He hadn't much furniture, a table and a box-bed was all, so that was soon done, and it *was* clean, even if it looked rather bare.

There was an old clay pot by the stove. He picked it up and scrubbed it, then went out to pick some flowers. It was already September, but he found some clumps of white and pink yarrow, cut a branch off the birch by the porch and went up to the Norwegian lakes where he'd seen clumps of blue and white campanulas. They were rather far gone but he removed the dead leaves and flower-heads.

By the time he'd finished he was really pleased with his flowers.

At midday on Saturday, old Anna took the girl to Bråten. To Maja-Lisa, she said that the two of them, Anna and Hanna, were to go into the forest as Anna needed plants for her medicines. Maja-Lisa looked surprised, but Hanna was pleased. She liked roaming round the countryside.

When they came to the millhouse, John Broman was waiting. Anna had to go and look for belladonna in clumps by the north stream, she said, and disappeared.

He showed Hanna round. To her, the house was magnificent, with its kitchen, bedroom and the living room with two windows facing the lovely view over the lake. There was an upper floor, too, for overnight visitors and storage.

John spoke. Maybe she wasn't listening very attentively to his words, but his intention was clear. He needed a woman in the house and, secretly, she clasped the rune-staff under her blouse.

When he started talking about marriage, she turned rigid with surprise.

'But the boy …' she said eventually.

He nodded. He'd thought of that. The boy's to come too. He liked children. As soon as they'd decided, he'd arrange to take over responsibility for the boy.

She didn't understand, and he explained patiently that he would speak to Hanna's father and the priest, it would be put in writing that John Broman was the boy's guardian: 'We don't know each other,' he said.

Then she smiled for the first time and said there was time enough.

'It'll be a hard life,' he said. 'A lot of work.'

'I'm used to that, and I don't eat much.'

She seemed to be afraid he would change his mind, he could hear that, and he said, rather curtly, 'You and the boy'll no doubt have enough to eat.'

Then Hanna smiled for the second time and thought about the talk she'd heard as a child. They said they were never short of bread in the miller's house. But then she looked at the rotten bridge and remembered how the old miller had died. He'd gone through it one night and drowned.

Then Anna was back, telling them how secret it all had to be. Not a word to anyone until the banns were read in church. By that time, the papers would be ready and Eriksson of Lyckan would have no chance of finding Rickard and getting him to claim paternity.

'You must hurry and talk to August,' she said. 'He's not a talkative man.'

Hanna walked home through the forest with a dizzy sense of it all being too much. She'd be mistress in her own house, a house as big and fine as at Lyckan. The boy would be like a son, Broman had said. It's the end of the shame, she thought. No one will call us bastard and whore any longer.

Too much, she told herself. For she knew good fortune was measured out and was costly if you were given too much. But then she straightened up, tossed her head and thought she'd already paid.

'Justice,' she said aloud. 'I'd never have believed God could be just.'

She was troubled by the lack of furniture in the house, and the rugs and towels and all the other things she didn't possess. She gave not a thought to the man with whom she was to share her bed and life.

When she got back to her parents' home to fetch the boy, she felt like blurting out her amazing secret but she had to get away, quickly, back to the hell of Lyckan.

There, it was easier to keep her joy to herself, and when she had made up the bed on the straw mattress in the box-bed in the kitchen and got the boy to sleep, she took out an advance on her triumph. She even swore. 'Christ,' she whispered. 'Christ, how I'll laugh the day I can say what I think to those high and mighty beasts.'

Then she was frightened and prayed earnestly to God to forgive her for such sinful thoughts.

Before she fell asleep, she wondered about the flowers. She'd never before seen or heard of a man picking flowers and putting them into a vase. It was strange, but important too, she could see that. She'd have to see to it that there were flowers on John

Broman's table. At least in the summer.

That night she dreamed of geraniums, flowers in a pot she'd once seen in the parsonage window.

CHAPTER 12

A few days later it was rumoured that the miller had gone back to Värmland and nothing would come of the mill at Norskvattnet.

They're lying, thought Hanna.

But when the week had gone by with no message from John Broman, she gave up, and for the first time in her life, she despaired. This was harder than the shame, and she saw that it was hope that made people vulnerable. You shouldn't hope. Or believe that God is just.

'Get a move on!' shouted Lovisa. 'You're as white as a ghost. If you're going to be ill, you can go back to your mother.'

But Hanna hadn't the energy to walk through the forest with the child.

Autumn came early, storms whipping the leaves off the ash trees. On Sunday morning, the leaves rustled underfoot as she went to the barn to do the milking. August was waiting for her there in the dark.

'Father,' she said, 'what're you doing here so early in the morning?'

He pointed at the house.

'They're asleep,' she whispered.

Then she was told that John Broman had been to see her father on the Monday, had told him about the marriage, and had asked August to take the message to Hanna. Then he'd gone to the priest to arrange for church papers for the boy.

'I signed, so when the banns are read, Broman is guardian,' said August, the sweetness of revenge in his voice.

Then Broman had gone back to Värmland to fetch furniture and other household goods for the millhouse. He would be back in a few weeks, then he and Hanna would have the banns read.

'Why've you been so long telling me?'

'We haven't had a moment, Mother and I. Autumn's come so early, we daren't leave the potatoes in the ground.'

She nodded, unable to reproach him. She sat down heavily on the milking stool and nodded again as he stopped by the barn door and told her to hurry with the milking. But she wept, the tears rolling down her cheeks and mixing with the warm milk.

That week had taught her one thing: that she'd never again live in hope.

On his way home in the faint dawn light, August remembered he'd forgotten to tell her that both he and the boys would have work that winter. Broman had asked him to help with the repairs to the mill.

'Suppose you can work with timber?'

'Mm.'

August also had timber, matured timber felled before the famine years when he'd still thought he'd be able to build a proper barn.

Hanna did her work as usual. When breakfast was over, she said calmly to Joel Eriksson that she was going home to her parents and taking the boy with her. He nodded sullenly and told her to hurry so that she got away before Lovisa woke. 'Make sure you're back for evening milking,' he said.

It was bitterly cold as she walked along the path through the forest, but she was so warm with gratitude that she didn't feel the biting wind.

For the first time, she thought about Broman and how she could serve him. She was orderly and strong, had learned what was required of a mistress on a farm. She'd never handled money, but the teacher had said she was good at sums. She'd see to everything, so he could be proud of his home as well as of her.

Furniture, she thought. What kind of furniture would it be he was fetching from Värmland? Much grander than they had at Lyckan? Then she remembered she'd promised herself never to hope.

The boy whined. He was cold, so she lifted him up and wrapped her shawl round him as the path rose the last bit before the forest gave way to August's fields. They were already working in the potato patch, but her mother stopped and came over to her.

'So they gave you time off,' said Maja-Lisa, her tone of voice warmer than her words, and when Hanna looked at her tired face, there was joy there. And pride. This was so unusual that, after the first greeting, the girl was lost for words.

They brewed coffee, sat down at the kitchen table and sucked the hot drink through lumps of sugar that dissolved in their mouths.

Then her mother said those terrible words. 'Hope you get away with three or four children.'

Hanna straightened up, drew in her breath and remembered that she was a girl. John Broman would do to her what Rickard Joelsson had done. Every night, in the bed in the other room.

He had almost said so, said, 'Here we'll have the bed, my girl.'

She remembered flushing slightly, for a moment something frightening in the air. But she hadn't understood, or thought. Though she'd known.

The mother saw her terror and said calmly, 'Don't look so feared. Women just have to put up with it and you get used to it after a while. Think about being mistress in your own place, and that man of yours seems better than most.'

'Why does he want me?'

'You're young and pretty. And hard-working.'

Amid all her fears, Hanna looked at her mother with surprise. Never before had she had a good word for Hanna. Praise was dangerous, challenging fate. But Maja-Lisa went on: 'We must make sure you've decent clothes, new for everyday. For the wedding … I'd thought we might remake my old wedding dress.' She was looking uncertain. Hanna said nothing, and finally Maja-Lisa said, 'Don't know what he thinks. He looks a bit of a gentleman.'

She was appealing to Hanna.

I'm being respected. Even Mother …

But it was only a fleeting thought. Then the girl was back again with her fear of the mill bedroom.

'Mother,' she said, 'I can't do it.'

'Nonsense,' said Maja-Lisa, and that was the end of any respect. 'Why shouldn't you do what any decent woman can? You get used to it, as I said. It isn't the bedding that's awful, Hanna, it's giving birth.'

Hanna remembered when she had given birth. That hadn't been easy, but nothing like as terrible as death in the hay with black Rickard.

'You have to close your eyes and make yourself soft,' her mother said, flushing. 'It's not shameful once the priest's read over you. Now, let's go and try on my old wedding dress.'

But they soon had to abandon the idea. Her mother's wedding dress, folded away in tissue paper, was too small. They could see that without trying it on. Hanna was taller and stronger than Maja-Lisa had ever been.

'I'll have to hang my head in shame and tell John Broman how things are.'

Maja-Lisa was bitter.

'We never have any money.'

Hanna wasn't listening. Despite the warmth in the kitchen she was still rigid with cold. For the first time, when she got back to Lyckan that evening, she considered running away, leaving with the child and joining one of the bands of beggars that had roamed the roads since the famine. Then she looked at the boy, remembered those emaciated ragged children, and knew she couldn't.

Maybe you got used to it, as her mother had said. *Close your eyes and make yourself soft.*

Just before she fell asleep in her corner of the kitchen, she again tried to think about the fine furniture John Broman was fetching from Värmland. But it was too difficult and finally she had to give up and sleep.

The next morning her worst fears were gone. When she got up to light the stove and drag the heavy pans over to the barn, she tried to think about how different everything would be when she was lighting her own stove and going to her own cows.

She started milking. With her forehead against the sides of the big

45

animals, she made the decision. John Broman was never to know how frightened she was, never. She'd be submissive and soft, just as Mother had said.

When she came out of the barn it was snowing, great wet flakes. She stopped in it. It was only the beginning of October. A long winter had begun early and a primaeval terror was moving inside the girl.

Long winter, iron winter, starvation. Yes, she'd be good to John Broman.

By midday, the snow had turned to rain and a few days later the sun came out. Winter retreated, autumn glowed in the maples as it should, it turned warm and the old people talked with relief about Indian summers. As usual in the autumn, the women went out into the forest to pick the lingonberries. Hanna went too, saying boldly to Lovisa that she'd promised Mother she'd help. Then, with the furious Lovisa at her heels shouting abuse at her, she left.

Hanna turned round once, and laughed straight into Lovisa's face.

CHAPTER 13

To everyone's surprise, at the end of October, John Broman came back with a horse and a heavily laden cart, a man with him, too, a cousin from Värmland. The gossips were soon able to report that the two of them were repainting the millhouse both inside and out. White inside, red outside. That was altogether too much for them all. Not even the parsonage was painted red, and there was much talk of pride always going before a fall.

Two days later, Broman suddenly put in an appearance in the kitchen at Lyckan and told the Erikssons they now had to say goodbye to Hanna and the boy. On Sunday, banns for him and Hanna were to be read. For the first time in her life Lovisa was so astonished that she could find no words. But Joel Eriksson went into battle. 'The boy stays here. He's the grandson in the house.'

'The boy's mine,' said John Broman calmly. 'I've papers to say so.'

As they left the farm, Hanna wept. John was carrying the boy and didn't notice, and her tears were soon over. But Hanna herself was amazed, for tears of joy were new to her.

They went straight to the priest, who received them without surprise, wished them luck and even shook hands. As they went on, Hanna said, 'He didn't seem surprised.'

'He knew,' said John. 'I had to have church papers for the boy. Can you walk all the way to Norskvattnet?'

Hanna had to laugh. They went slowly, almost strolling through the forest as if both were thinking how much had been left unsaid between them. But it was hard to find words. Again and again, Hanna was about to ask, 'Why did you choose me?' but the words wouldn't come.

They stopped for a rest by the stream below Wolf Mountain and quenched their thirst. The cliff rose straight out of the ground, solid and ancient, still in its deep dark blue shadow. Golden strips of birch swirled below the precipices and peregrine falcons were gliding in the upward currents.

'It's beautiful here,' said Broman, and Hanna smiled as always when she didn't understand. Then she moved aside for a moment to wash her face and arms, came back and sat silently opposite him.

Then he started talking, a tentative story of the life he'd left, of his wife quarrelling over his drinking.

'I have to tell you I get drunk on Saturdays,' he said.

She looked neither frightened nor surprised. 'So does my father. And Joel Eriksson.'

He smiled at her, and went on to tell her about his little girl, who'd died and whom he'd dearly loved.

'A man can't put all his joy in a child like I did.'

'Consumption?'

'Yes.'

He couldn't bring himself to talk about the dark memories of his wife, how mean she'd been with food. But, as if reading his mind, Hanna said she'd learned that consumption took the young who didn't get enough food. And you had to be fussy about keeping clean, for the infection was in filth and bad air.

He nodded, thinking about his wife being so plain. Then he flushed, and said that Hanna should know it would be difficult to start again. 'Sometimes I think I can't,' he said.

Hanna was downcast, but swallowed and said, 'We'll have to help each other.'

Then he said he was pleased to have a new place for a wife who was so young and pretty.

At that Hanna was frightened.

None the less it was one of the happiest days of her life. The newly painted house was as handsome as the farm on the wall chart at school. When she saw it Hanna clapped her hands with delight.

The cousin from Värmland had left with the horse and cart, but the furniture was all in the barn. They could take it outside so that she could examine it. Then they'd put everything in order in the house, just as she wanted it. What she didn't want they could take up to the attic.

Her eyes widened in surprise.

He went into the kitchen and found the toys he had put aside for the boy, a small wooden horse and cart and a pile of building blocks.

'For you,' he said to him. 'Now you're to sit quietly while your mother and I get to work.'

But Ragnar went wild with delight and ran after Hanna: 'Look, Mother, look what I got.'

Hanna wept tears of joy for the second time that day, then pulled herself together and told him to stay in the kitchen. When they went outside again, John and Hanna, he looked round with a troubled air. 'There's lots of dangerous places for a young 'un here,' he said.

Then he saw Hanna's tears.

'You never usually cry,' he said hurriedly, clumsily running his hand down her cheek. 'Or only when you're pleased.'

The furniture was grander than Hanna could have dreamed of, some polished with brass fittings. There was a sofa with a rounded birchwood back and striped blue upholstery ... It just couldn't be true!

'Silk,' she said, stroking the material cautiously as if afraid it would split on touch.

But his face had clouded. 'Darned great monster,' he said. 'Can't sit or lie on it. Let's throw it out.'

'Are you mad?' cried Hanna, then slapped her hand over her mouth to stop her wicked words. 'I mean,' she went on, 'I've never seen finer, not even at the parsonage. We can have it in the best room.'

He laughed. 'You're the one to decide.'

He laughed again as they carried the furniture into the living room, the desk, his wall shelves, the chest of drawers and chairs with the same round backs as the sofa.

'Won't be room for people in here now,' he said. And, to her disappointment, Hanna saw that he was right. Some of the fine things would have to go into the attic.

The chest of drawers found a space in the bedroom and John said, 'Didn't bring the bed with me. Thought I'd make a new one. But rugs and towels are all in the chest.'

In the end the long benches, the drop-leaf table and the pull-out sofa all found a place in the kitchen. Hanna went through all the linen in the chest. There was a lot and it was good quality, but it had been packed damp and had ugly patches of mould on it. Dismayed, she decided to take it all home to Mother's to wash.

Then, last of all, she found the crate of porcelain, of a kind that yet again brought tears to her eyes.

He had bread and cheese in the kitchen, so they got something inside them before, heavily laden, they went back to Hanna's parents, John carrying the linen chest, Hanna the boy and the boy his toys.

Over the next week, Hanna's brothers hauled the dried timber through the forest to Norskvattnet, while Hanna and her mother washed and rinsed rugs, covers and towels. The neighbouring women scuttled like dizzy hens in and out of the washhouse, inquisitive and envious. On the Thursday, old Anna came and said that people hadn't had so much to talk about for years. She'd met Broman, who'd complained about the women making excuses to come to the mill. Maja-Lisa allowed herself a big toothless laugh and Hanna silently remembered the old saying about tempting fate. 'Your good fortune is another's misfortune, and don't you go thinking you're someone.'

But then Anna said, 'The old people are beginning to whisper that Hanna uses sorcery to bewitch the Värmlander.'

Both old Anna and Maja-Lisa had a good laugh at that too, not noticing that Hanna had left the washhouse and was standing outside, her hand clasped round her rune-staff under her shift. Fearful thoughts were racing through her head. Couldn't be possible, could it? Could the rune-master and his troll wife have such power?

Next day she was to go to the mill with food to celebrate their banns. Would she dare tell Broman about the rune-staff?

CHAPTER 14

On Friday afternoon, Hanna made her way through the forest towards Norskvattnet. The sun persisted, even at the end of October, the air was crystal clear and easy to breathe. But Hanna took no pleasure in the lovely weather, because of the rune-staff, and then there was what Mother had whispered as she had left home.

'You stopping overnight?'

Then she'd laughed. Hanna hadn't wanted to believe it, but her mother's laugh had been lewd.

She was walking past Wolf Mountain when she suddenly decided that this was where she would get rid of the rune-staff. She climbed up the steep cliff face, bundled the staff into oak leaves, bound it and then threw it into one of the great hollows.

'You've done what you were going to,' she said, adding just to make sure, 'for this time. If I ever need you again, I know where you are.'

Then she went on, crossed the stream and came to the rise. It was steep but not heavy going, as from here onwards there were negotiable roads to the mill. She could soon hear the roar from the falls.

It was quite a while before she noticed other sounds, almost drowned by the rushing water, yet audible. Someone playing a fiddle! Hanna stopped as if paralysed by fear, quite still for a long time. The wicked water spirit. It was out to lure John Broman to his death in the falls.

The thought made her quicken her steps. She ran until she was out of breath and had a stitch, so she reached the mill with her hand pressed to her side and there she found Broman sitting above the waterfall scraping away on his fiddle.

'You here?' he said, looking in surprise at the girl running towards him, her skirts flapping. She stopped and looked at him, trying to get her breath back. 'Something frighten you?'

'I thought it was the water spirit.'

He laughed loudly and put his arm round her. 'Oh, girl, I didn't think you believed that sort of thing. You're so sensible.'

She flushed, but heard the amusement in his words.

'I'm playing for the mountains and the falls,' he said. 'And for the trees and the lake. They play for me, you see, and I think I owe them an answer. But I can't find the notes.'

He was silent for a moment, then he said, musing, 'Finding the right tune is as hard as trying to remember dreams.'

He really is mad, Hanna thought. He's escaped from the asylum up there in Värmland. Help me, Jesus. What shall I do?

Then she saw the tankard of aquavit propped against a stone where he'd been sitting and realised with relief that he was drunk. Drunken men had to be humoured, her mother had taught her. Never contradict them. He followed her gaze, picked up the tankard defiantly and said, 'Here, have some to calm yourself.'

He poured out half a beaker and handed it to her, then raised the tankard to his lips. 'Here's to us, Hanna.'

She'd never tasted strong spirits before and she choked on the first gulp. But he urged her on and she took another gulp, then felt the strange warmth spreading through her body, in it an unfamiliar lightness. She giggled, then started laughing, right up into the sky, unable to stop. Nor did she want to. For the first time in her life, Hanna was free, with no worries. It's like in heaven when you don't have to worry, she thought. Just as the priest used to say. Then she noticed the tall trees swaying and said, 'Why don't the trees stand still?'

'They're doing a wedding dance for you,' he said.

She no longer thought he was mad now. When he carried her into the bedroom and undressed her, the lightness was still there in her body and nothing was either dangerous or shameful. She liked him caressing her breasts and her loins. Nor did it hurt when he came into her. In fact she thought it was all over far too quickly.

Then she must have fallen asleep and slept a long time, for when he woke her the autumn outside was quite dark.

'Got a headache?'

Hanna discovered that her eyes hurt when she moved them: that was a headache. She'd never had one before. She nodded, and that hurt even more.

'I'll make some coffee,' he said consolingly, but then she felt worse and had to go outside to vomit. Not until she'd turned her stomach inside-out did she realise she was naked. The shame of it overwhelmed her as she tried her best to hide behind her long hair as she slipped through the kitchen, where he'd lit the two pinewood sticks.

'You're as lovely as a siren of the woods,' he called after her. She slipped into the bedroom, where her long skirt and new blouse lay in a heap on the floor. As she pulled them on, she felt great relief. It hadn't been all that bad.

'I was right, then, about the evil water spirit,' she called through the door. 'You must be related to him.'

'A distant third cousin, if so,' John said jokingly, noting to his surprise that she had a sense of humour and wasn't as shy as he'd thought. He didn't know that that was the only time he was ever to see her naked.

Then he taught her how to make coffee as he liked it, clean kettle, fresh water that must boil then simmer before it came off the fire and the coffee was thrown in to sink slowly through the water.

'Heavens, what a waste of an expensive gift of God,' said Hanna. But when she'd tasted it, she had to agree it was better to drink strong coffee seldom than dishwater often.

'What did you come for?'

'Lordie me!' cried Hanna. 'My bag! I was to do some baking. In case people come for coffee after the banns.'

Then she heard the rain outside where she'd left her bag. At her cry of dismay, John went out to fetch it, but it was leather so most of the flour was still dry.

She sifted and mixed the flour and yeast, raisins and sugar for the big loaf, then she plaited it quickly into a wreath, put a cloth over it and left it to rise. He watched her, enjoying her quick clever hands and the way she moved confidently round the kitchen. 'Luck's been with me,' he said, but Hanna didn't understand what he meant. She lit the stove so that it would be warm for baking in the morning. She had cream with her too, and sugar and coffee were in the larder, with the crispbread and a bit of cheese.

They were hungry. 'If you've got some milk, I can make gruel,' she said.

Afterwards, they fell asleep side by side in the big bed. He didn't touch her and she thought maybe he didn't want it all that much, and maybe it wouldn't be all that often.

He was still asleep the next morning as Hanna put more wood in the stove to heat up the oven. She couldn't resist the temptation to lay the table with the fine china, and was pleased to think how surprised they would be, all those wretched old gossips. When Broman woke, he was heavy-eyed and surly so, familiar with hangovers, Hanna made coffee in the way he'd taught her. She'd put aside some dough for flat bread and when he'd eaten and drunk, he said, 'Went to market last week and bought a cow.'

She clapped her hands and he went on, 'A betrothal gift, too.'
A headcloth of silk, green with red roses.

'I thought it'd go fine with your hair,' he said. Now she knew she could go to church like everyone else. With this fine kerchief, in a housewife's knot. No more talk of a whore-cloth.

Those annoying tears dimmed her eyes again and John looked at her in surprise. It was to be some time before he got used to Hanna crying only from happiness, never from want or misery.

All that Saturday, they scrubbed out the barn, the privy, the storehouse and the earth cellar. She noticed he soon tired. Towards the afternoon, the heat of the oven was just right and she put in the huge wheatmeal loaf in the shape of a wreath.

They sat up very straight in the pew as the priest read out the banns, and never had Hanna felt such pride. The mill had a great many guests, just as she'd thought, eyes taking in all the grandeur of the house, and Hanna glowed. As was the custom, they brought gifts with them; her parents had four sacks of potatoes and old Anna three laying hens and a rooster.

Joel Eriksson appeared, too, his horse and cart laden with hay, and he told Hanna that old man Erik had said there was more at Framgården. She drew a sigh of relief for she had had many an uneasy thought about how she was to get feed for the cow John had bought.

Then came copper pans, a coffee kettle and a wall-clock from Aunt Ingegerd. They were all competing at being generous, for Hanna's marriage had given the family back its honour.

Hanna offered them all strong coffee and John produced drinks. It was a cheerful afternoon with a great many coarse jokes. Hanna had heard them all before without understanding them, but now she laughed with all the others.

Three weeks later, they were married at the parsonage. Hanna's sister was in labour in Fredrikshald, so couldn't come, but she had sent a fine shop-dress for the bride and Maja-Lisa was delighted.

Now she needn't be ashamed of her daughter going to her wedding in clothes that were not new.

John's sister from Värmland came to the wedding with her husband and daughter. Hanna was frightened when John got the message.

'What've you written about Ragnar?'

'I told her what happened to you.'

That was not much consolation, but when Alma came, Hanna calmed down, for she was a good person and kindly.

'He's given to melancholy, my brother,' she said. 'He's always been so.'

Hanna was surprised. Never before had she heard anyone talking like that about people who were present. But John just nodded and said maybe it was good that Hanna knew. 'So you don't go blaming yourself when I get down,' he said.

She didn't understand that either.

CHAPTER 15

Hanna left the beautiful wedding-dress hanging up long after the wedding.

'For the joy of it,' she said.

But there weren't many other joys for her. She had plenty of other troubles, the worst of which was the potato field that had to be turned before the frost came. She could haul, but Broman hadn't time to steer the plough now that the mill was working to the full. I could borrow Father's ox, she thought. But it'd take several days to trudge it here and back through the forest. I haven't time. The earth cellar has to be filled and we must have more hay before winter comes.

One evening, John looked at her and said, 'What's troubling you?'

She grew quite talkative as she described the field and all its weeds, the time it would take to get the old ox through the forest and, as so often recently, he thought what a child she was. 'I'll talk to your father tomorrow,' he said. 'He'll bring it over.'

She slapped herself across the mouth and said, 'Stupid of me not to have thought of that before.'

'It's not so easy with the cow,' he went on. 'That's to be fetched from market in Bøttlen on Tuesday. But I can't get away. Could you go on your own?'

'I should think so,' she said. 'I'll have to leave the boy with Mother.'

That's what she did. Hanna left the mill, in the dark before dawn, equipped with the receipt for the cow and a pouch of money hidden in the lining of her blouse.

'The money's in case the cow doesn't please you,' said Broman. 'Then you'll have to add to it to get a better one.'

The responsibility for such a major decision was great. When the morning light came, walking the long way seemed easier. She'd manage.

She'd never seen so many people as there were at the market. But she found Anders Björum and saw that the cow Broman had bought was young and had just calved. That meant milk for the whole winter.

'Expect you want a heifer calf, too,' the cattle dealer said.

Hanna was sorely tempted, but Broman had said nothing about a calf. And yet it was a fine creature. Hanna looked longingly at the calf, thinking she had plenty for the winter, and it would be just right if she could take the heifer to the bull next spring, have a calf for meat as well as fresh milk.

With two cows she'd always have milk for the boy and Broman. Before she had time to think it over, the question came. 'What d'you want for it?'

He told her the price, and she had enough money. Nevertheless she haggled, beating him down by a third. The dealer laughed and said she wasn't as foolish as she was young.

Then they met half-way, and Hanna started off home with two creatures and worries over what her husband would say. It took a long time, too, for the calf was difficult to manage and couldn't walk for long stretches at a time. They didn't get back until midnight and there was no mistaking John Broman's relief.

'I've bought a calf as well,' she said, to be rid of her fears as soon as possible.

'Probably right in that,' he said. 'You know more about such things than I do.'

That made her plump to the ground with relief, and she stayed sitting there in the yard while John took the creatures into the barn and gave them hay and water.

Hanna fell asleep almost the moment her head hit the pillow and she slept soundly all night.

'You must've been tired,' said Broman in the morning, and she nodded, her eyes as usual on something behind his head.

'Wasn't the tiredness that was difficult,' she said. 'It was the calf I bought with your money without permission.'

'Don't suppose you waste much.'

She smiled.

'Hanna,' he said. 'Look at me.'

For a moment, their eyes met. Hanna flushed and rose.

'Time for milking.'

John Broman had noticed, even at the wedding party, that she found it difficult to look people in the eye. She was just as he had thought at their first meeting, a wakeful observer, but only in secret. She averted her eyes the moment anyone looked at her.

By the time Hanna came back from the barn, August and his sons had arrived so there was no opportunity to continue the conversation. But Broman did not give in and asked again, at their evening meal, 'Why don't you look people in the eye?'

Her face and neck reddened as she thought, but she was unable to find an answer. 'Don't know,' she said finally. 'Never thought about it. Maybe because I've got no looks.'

'But you're pretty.'

Her flush deepened to scarlet. Silence fell while Hanna sought for words.

'You're the only one to think so,' she said at last. 'And you see things in a peculiar way. Like those horrid mountains you think beautiful.'

Now it was his turn to be at a loss for words.

Hanna cared for her cows as if they were infants, and everyone said her barn was so clean you could eat off the floor. The cow answered to the name of Lyre, but the calf was nameless until one day John Broman said they'd call her Star. That's good, Hanna thought, looking lovingly at the brown calf with a spiky white patch on its forehead.

As soon as the work at the mill was almost over, Broman had a letter from his sister to say that their mother was ill and wanted him to come and see her. He thought of taking Hanna with him but she begged so miserably not to have to that he gave in.

He was in a black mood when he left.

'Are you worried about your mother?' Hanna said in farewell.

'Not much. She's been dying so many times before,' he said curtly.

He got a lift with a carter as soon as he reached the main road, a man taking his sheep to slaughter in Fredrikshald. At the border, Broman was glad to be alone. He wanted time to think.

He had heard old men saying that the worst of a difficult wife was that you never got her off your mind. And it was the same for him as he pondered on his young wife. But Hanna wasn't difficult. As he took a short-cut through the forests up by the Värmland border, he found himself making a long list of her virtues. She was obedient and quiet, didn't run around gossiping, was a good cook and kept the stable clean. Best of all, she never complained or reproached him. And she was orderly, clever at keeping house and with money. Then she was good to look at and not unwilling in bed.

Then he remembered the night the boy had cried and she had opened her eyes in the middle of their lovemaking. They were so full of terror, he had had to stop. 'What are you afraid of?'

'Maybe that the boy's so uneasy.'

She was lying, and that was unusual in her.

58

It had taken him a long time to shake off the memory of her eyes that night. He had lost his desire and hadn't touched her for a week.

She was so full of mysteries, and he was the kind of man who had to understand. Like all this God business. Every Sunday she walked the long way to church. Occasionally he went with her, for he, too, might need the word of God. But the service simply increased the emptiness inside him, although the organist was good. Hanna sat bolt upright in the pew, apparently listening devoutly, not looking round. Yet he was almost certain she was as bored as he was.

On the way home he tried to talk to her. 'You believe in God then, do you?'

'Believe?' she said in surprise. 'But He *is*.'

She said it as if she was talking about the ground she was walking on, but he persisted. 'What's He like, then, d'you think?'

'The worst thing about Him is you never know where you are with Him. You have to submit whatever happens.'

'You mean … that God's cruel,' John had said, tentatively, as that seemed blasphemous.

'Just that,' she said. 'Blind and unjust. He doesn't care about us. That sort of talk's all rubbish.'

'Sounds as if you're talking about destiny,' he said.

She frowned, thought for a moment, then said, 'Yes. He's probably like fate because you can't escape Him.'

Surprised, John Broman asked what she thought the priest would say if he knew what she had said. She laughed. 'The priest's daft.'

John Broman laughed, too, as he walked through the wet autumn forest, remembering their talk. But it was no happy laugh, for there was something frightening in his wife's faith, something heathen and witch-like. Then he abandoned the thought. Hanna was no witch. She was just more honest than most.

Before reaching his native parish, he took a rest and ate his packed food. He found that Hanna had treated him to butter on the bread and a slice of pork. It was good, and he would have preferred to stay there by the stream in the forest. But then he sighed heavily and turned on to the road to his home farm. When he saw the farmhouse, it struck him that perhaps he'd been thinking so much about Hanna to avoid thinking about his mother. He stood for a while on the edge of the forest, trying to look at Brogården as a stranger would see it, thinking it looked grander than it was. In the end, he pulled himself together and walked up the gravel path to the door.

He was afraid of his brother-in-law who ran the farm, almost as afraid as he had been of his father. The old man had been dead fifteen years, but his mother ruled the family from her sick-bed. Both parents were of the kind to whom you were indebted, whatever you did.

His brother-in-law was not at home, but Agnes received him with her usual resignation, like greeting a dog you know is going to cause trouble.

'Alma wrote ...' he said.

'I know,' she said. 'But Mother's no worse. She's asleep now, so you've time to wash and have a cup of coffee.'

He rinsed his face and hands in the tub out in the yard and drank coffee as weak as Agnes herself. As he went towards his mother's room, his sister whispered, 'Don't wake her. It's best for us all if she sleeps at night.'

'How are things with Aunt Greta?' he said quietly.

'She lives with Alma and still has her wits,' whispered Agnes.

He sat there looking at his mother. She was panting, her breathing light and thin, as if a hair's breadth from death. She looked peaceful and, for a moment, he wished he could feel tenderness for her. But then his bitterness took over and he thought that, if God were merciful, she should die. I'd be free, he thought. To take out my inheritance. God knows, I need the money.

They were only thoughts, but his mother woke and looked at her only son with eyes so full of reproach that he had to look away.

'So, you've come, have you?' she cried, suddenly with air in her lungs. 'But not brought that new wife with you, the whore from the gypsy village down in Dal. Suppose she daren't come and see her mother-in-law.'

He didn't reply, knowing from experience that sensible talk simply made things worse. But this time his silence provoked her into raging, shrieking insanely.

Agnes came rushing in. 'I told you not to wake her.'

He got up and left, but turned in the doorway and said meekly, 'Goodbye, then, Mother.'

She shrieked at him again, the same old words about him bringing shame upon family and farm, just as his father had predicted.

John Broman hurried through the kitchen and across the yard to the path leading to Alma's farm. Alma had no share, and until her mother died she would live with her husband and children as tenant of the outlying farm up towards the forest.

'You look terrible,' she said, when he arrived. 'I can see it went wrong.'

They fell silent, as people do when faced with the inevitable. In the end, Alma spoke first. 'And yet she kept urging me to write. I thought she wanted to be reconciled.'

He could find no answer to that, and felt the melancholy descending on him.

But Alma started asking about Hanna, the boy and the mill, so for a while he could keep the darkness at bay by telling her how well things were going at the millhouse, how clever Hanna was and how fond he'd become of the boy.

He asked about Greta, their father's sister, to whom they had turned during their childhood years, the aunt with all the stories and delights.

'She's gone to sleep for the night,' said Alma, but when she saw the darkness in her brother, she hurried to say, 'Go in to her. She'll be glad to see you. But wake her slowly. She's in the bedroom by the baking-oven wall, where it's warmest.'

They crept in, but that proved unnecessary for Greta was awake. She sat up in bed saying she'd dreamed John had come home to see her.

'That was no dream,' said John, taking both her hands in his and looking at the toothless smile and her thousand wrinkles. She was just the same, strength pouring from her hands and into his body. They talked about old times and she didn't ask about his visit to Brogården, as if she'd known beforehand what would happen. Then she wanted some coffee, but Alma laughed and said there'd been enough madness for one evening. They would have their evening meal now and then the house would sleep.

To his surprise, John felt sleep coming the moment his head touched the pillow in the attic room. He slept all night, no longer brooding over his mother when he woke. As he walked home through the forest, he was laden with a new oil-lamp and an old gilt-framed mirror Alma had cleaned for him.

'A few more wedding presents for Hanna,' she'd said, and as he walked on he reckoned they would please his wife. But, most of all, he thought about the agreement with Alma's husband. Threatening his mother with the law, he was to take out some of his inheritance in advance. The next time John came home, the horse and cart would be his.

Where the road came to the long lake and the high mountains soared into the sky he took a rest. A goat track ran down the mountainside and he climbed a short way up it to look out over the land in which he now belonged, a valley down each side of the long lake with poor strips of soil along the shores. From there he could see about ten of the hundred or so lakes in the parish, all winking like mirrors flung out into the wilderness.

This was no farmland, but intended for wildlife and bold hunters. Yet the stubborn earth-bound peasants had stuck firmly to the poor fields, built a church and a school, married and had children. Too many children.

'It's always been a hard life here,' August had said, but real hardship came when people began to breed like rabbits.

On his long walk, John had seen the clouds roaming across the sky in the south, and now they were gathering on the horizon over where his house was and his wife was waiting.

62

He got up, humped on his pack and set off into the rain. He was soon soaked through before the clouds gave way and the sun used the last hours of the day to dry off forest and paths, people and creatures. John Broman was not surprised. He had got used to the weather here being as changeable as the landscape.

By the time he got home it was long into the night. But the stick of resinous pine was still burning in the kitchen and Hanna was ironing. Probably afraid of being on her own, he thought, and he called out before thumping on the door, 'Hanna, it's me.'

She flew towards him, and in the dim light he could see her wiping away those annoying tears with the back of her hand. 'Oh, dear Lord, am I glad to see you!'

'Were you afraid?'

'No. My brother's asleep in the attic.'

Then he remembered that he and August had agreed that Rudolf should sleep at the millhouse while Hanna was alone. His melancholy left him. For now.

'You ironing here in the dark?'

'Hours of the day are never long enough for me.'

They didn't touch each other, but their joy lit up the kitchen. That made Broman remember the oil-lamp.

'Put the clothes away and sit down here, Hanna.'

He didn't look at her as he put the lamp together and filled it with paraffin. But when he lit it, his eyes never left her face, and as he stood there in the clear light, he revelled in the sight of her surprise and almost unfathomable delight. Finally, she whispered, 'It's as light as a summer's day.'

It was so light it woke Ragnar, who sat up and said, 'Is it morning already?'

Then he saw John and ran straight into the arms of his stepfather, who hugged him as he had wished to hug his wife, but hadn't dared to.

Not until the next morning did John Broman remember the mirror. 'I've a present from Alma.'

He hung the handsome mirror on the wall in the front room.

Hanna stood beside him, gasping with delight, running her hand over the gilt frame, but not meeting her reflection in the glass.

'Look at yourself in it. See how pretty you are,' he said.

She obeyed, her face flushing, then covered her eyes with her hands and fled.

When she gave him his morning coffee, she said, 'How was your mother?'

'As usual,' he said, and that was all that he uttered about his visit to Värmland.

CHAPTER 16

The next week, the mill started up, the roar from the race grew more subdued and the wooden drum held the sluice gate. Broman was satisfied, pleased also that he had money over to pay August and his sons for the work they'd done.

But he had to tell Hanna that the last coin had now gone from the money pouch. And she replied, as he had hoped, 'we'll manage.'

She was sure. She considered herself rich. She had the cows, the earth cellar full of potatoes and turnips, lingonberry and cloudberry preserves. The hens were laying and a cousin had given her a pig. The beer was brewing in the brewhouse and Broman's aquavit was bubbling away in its keg. They would have more than enough flour, so there would be no shortage of bread in the miller's house.

Then there was the fishing. John Broman knew many arts that surprised the peasants of Dal, but the one most talked about was his ability to take fish from the lake. The village people seldom owned boats and not even during the famine years had they reckoned on fish as everyday food. Broman had acquired a flat-bottomed boat as soon as he'd decided on Norskvattnet, and he put out his fish trap every evening.

The only fish Hanna had ever eaten was salt herring, so at first she found it difficult with pike, perch and whitefish. But she believed

John when he said fish was wholesome food, and she soon learned both to cook and eat it.

The days were all work. Hanna hadn't known that the men would want coffee while they waited for their flour. And preferably a bit of bread or a bun with it.

'It's like an inn,' she said to her mother. But she liked having people round her with all their chat, joking and laughing.

With the snow came other visitors. As always in winter, beggars appeared at the cottages, standing at the kitchen door, their eyes so far back in their heads they looked black. Worst of all were the children. Hanna couldn't bear it. She baked bread and gave it away, then set about baking again.

'I can't turn them away,' she said to John, who nodded with understanding. But the more baking Hanna did, the further the rumour spread, and the stream of beggars increased day by day.

'It's hard work for you,' he said, watching her scrubbing the kitchen at night, the floor, table and benches. She wasn't only afraid of fleas, but truly believed that disease lived in the dirt left by beggars. Broman laughed at her, but said nothing. He knew he would never overcome her superstitions.

What was most difficult for Hanna that first winter when she was learning to be a miller's wife was seeing Broman wear himself out. He developed a cough from exhaustion and the dust from the flour, a bad cough which kept him awake at night. 'You'll work yourself to death,' Hanna said.

When things were at their worst, she helped him carry the sacks into the mill, although that embarrassed Broman, who said, 'You see to yours and I'll see to mine.' Then Hanna spoke to her mother and together they drew up a plan. Hanna's youngest brother was no longer needed at home so he could come and work at the mill. He was fourteen and strong and would be paid in flour.

Thus Hanna had to learn women's cunning. In passing, she said to Broman that her parents were worried about Adolf, who just idled around at home. At the same time, Maja-Lisa said to August that she

65

was worried over the flour maybe not lasting through the winter. 'I've every reason to,' she said.

So that's how August had his good idea and went to Broman to ask if Adolf could go into service as the miller's labourer at Norskvattnet. He was paid in flour as agreed, but he didn't have to sleep in the labourer's box-bed in the kitchen, for Hanna had plenty of firewood and put the attic room in order for him.

Broman was less exhausted, but his coughing continued at night and worried Hanna.

Then there was trouble with the flour. The peasants of Dal paid the miller in the old way, two bushels of flour for a barrel of corn. And the flour had to be carted the miles to the village on the border, where it was bartered for coffee, salt and sugar. And money. When the ice froze on the long lake, Hanna undertook the task, hauling the heavy sled to Alvar Alvarsson's store and returning home with the necessary goods and ready cash.

Broman was ashamed. It was hard work for a woman even if she was young and strong. But he was pleased when he was at last able to pay her brother one *riksdal* a month and the agreed flour. Every day he waited for news of the horse from Värmland; it didn't come, but Hanna said it was all right. They hadn't enough feed for a horse in winter.

After the early service at Christmas that year, they took breakfast with August and Maja-Lisa at Bråten. The table was laid with the Christmas pork and porridge. Hanna made the coffee, because Maja-Lisa had stayed behind for a while at the churchyard, where she'd laid spruce wreaths on the children's graves. John Broman went with her and perhaps it was his friendliness that made her speak about her dead for the first time.

On the long way home, she said, 'It's a heavy burden, for I was so fond of them. Much more than the children who came later and I was allowed to keep. They were Anders and Johan, they were almost like twins. So happy and lively. Then there was Elin, so weak I never got to know her. No point in that, though, for Death already stood right there by the cradle.'

66

She wept then and wiped her eyes on her best apron. He said nothing, but ran his hand down her back.

'Worst was Maria, losing her. She was such a bright one, fine both inside and out.'

Then she blew her nose in her fingers and flung the snot into the snow.

'I've never said that to anyone, but now it's come out of me. When Astrid was born, only a year after Hanna, she was like ... It was as if Maria'd come back. Things like that are called foolishness. But I think it's true, for she's like the dead one in both her ways and looks.'

They were nearing Bråten. Maja-Lisa went round the corner of the house to wash her face, while John slipped into the warmth and sat down at the Christmas table. He needed a drink. Hanna could see that and handed him a full tankard.

CHAPTER 17

One Saturday towards spring, when the snow was melting but the nights were still cold, Broman came back with the news that Rickard Joelsson had been shot accidentally on a bear hunt in Trösil.

'So he's dead now, Ragnar's father,' said John.

Hanna turned as white as a sheet and as rigid as a hayrack. 'Is it true, or just talk?' she whispered.

'It's true, all right. The policeman's been to Lyckan and told the old folks. Things are bad for them.'

Hanna's face flushed scarlet and she began to shake. Then she suddenly cried out, 'Serve them right, the Devil's arses.'

Broman looked at his wife in surprise, seeing all her shame running out of her and, with it, all her sense and dignity. She rushed out of the door and ran round the yard, shrieking and laughing alternately, like a mad thing, oaths pouring out of her mouth, words he would never have believed she knew.

'Hell and damnation, the Devil take them, that bloody Lovisa's got her deserts – Christ, how she deserves it. You had it coming, had it coming, dear Aunt!'

Then she laughed again, so loudly the birds rose from the trees.

'Ragnar, Ragnar, where are you, boy? You're free! At last you're free from that evil.'

Frightened, John went after her as she rushed off down towards the lake, crying, 'I'm free, Ragnar, we're free of all that horror. For now your father's sizzling in hell.'

Then she ran back towards the house and threw herself on to her back on the ground, her skirts flying over her head, exposing her loins, but either she didn't notice or she didn't care. When she pulled her skirt off her head, it was to clench her fists. Shaking them up at the sky, she shrieked, 'I'll never forgive you if you forgive him, you damned God. Do you hear me? Do you hear me?'

Then suddenly she quietened down, gathered her clothes together, turned over on her side, curled up like a foetus and started to cry. He went over to her and stroked her head, and she stopped sniffing and whispered that he knew she only cried when she was happy.

'I know that, all right,' said Broman. Then he said nothing for a long time before going on. 'I didn't know things were that bad for you.'

Her wild weeping had stopped and her voice was steady when she said, 'You, John Broman, are much too kind a man ever to understand.'

He was silent for even longer, then said, 'That isn't true. I was pleased when my father died.'

Her weeping stopped altogether. She sat up, wiped her eyes on her apron and said in wonder, 'Then we're alike, you and me. A little, anyhow.'

For the very first time, she looked him straight in the eye. His eyes met hers, and she did not turn away when he replied that it was true, all right.

He saw that she was cold and told her to go with him into the warmth before she caught a chill. She obeyed, and as soon as she was in the kitchen, she washed her hands and face. Then she went over to the mirror in the front room and for the very first time stopped in front of it and looked at herself in it for a long time.

'I look like anyone else,' she said at last. Then her shame caught up with her. 'Where's the boy?'

'Playing at the smithy.'

'That's good, then.'

'Yes, that's good.'

'I behaved like a madwoman,' she said, her voice uncertain.

'It was good you got it out of you.'

To his surprise, she understood what he'd said and agreed. 'Yes, probably was. You won't tell ...'

'Don't be silly.'

The next moment the boy came rushing into the house shouting that the smith had said Rickard of Lyckan had been murdered in the forest.

'No,' said John Broman, in a firm voice. 'He had an accident. The man who shot him thought Rickard was a bear.'

'Was he wrong?'

'Yes, things like that happen. It's called an accident.'

'I know,' the boy said quietly.

But when John said he was going out on the lake with the trap, the boy brightened. 'Can I go in the boat, too, Mother?'

'Yes, you can,' said John Broman, for her. 'Mother hasn't time to row for me so you can do that while she gets our evening meal.'

In the boat, the boy grew serious again, and finally found the courage to ask the question. 'He was my father, wasn't he?'

'Yes,' said John Broman. 'He was.'

For the first time, Hanna sought her husband in bed that night. Then she abruptly fell asleep, but John lay awake a long time, worrying about his wife. He had been more frightened than he cared to admit, and considered that she was perhaps a bit mad, and that anything could have happened. But he also thought about his own wild joy when the message came that old Broman had gone through the ice. John had caused some wonder because he had wept so loudly at the funeral.

Was he like Hanna, who had wept for joy?

In the morning as Hanna lit the stove, she was feeling a kind of sense of destiny. Now I'm with child, she thought.

After that day, the air cleared somewhat at the millhouse. And on the Thursday, when her parents arrived unexpectedly with the terrible news that Joel of Lyckan had strangled his wife, then gone into the barn and shot himself, Hanna managed to look decently horrified. But her eyes did not leave Broman's, and sought deep down into them.

He did not turn away, but in some strange way felt guilty.

CHAPTER 18

On the Friday, they cleared the potato patch. Hanna hauled the plough and John Broman felt shame as he walked behind his wife in the furrows. He had to get a horse somehow.

He had had a letter from Alma shortly after Christmas. Their attempt to acquire an advance on their inheritance with the aid of the law had failed and their mother refused to talk about it. 'She'll survive us all,' Alma wrote. He thought that that was probably true. His cough would be the death of him long before the old woman gave up.

There was no reproach in his sister's letter, but John could read between the lines. The fact was that if he'd stayed at home and, as the only son, taken over the farm, their inheritance would have been distributed and Alma and her family would have been better off. But he had left the farm when he was young, had apprenticed himself to a miller in the neighbouring village, then married unhappily.

Although suicide was much disapproved of, a great many people came to Joel Eriksson's funeral. And, as if everything was as it should be, husband and wife were buried alongside each other, beside them their son, whose shattered body had been brought from Trösil. Erik Eriksson stood as upright as a pine tree by the grave, and after the funeral coffee had been taken and the guests had left, he told them all of his plans. August was to take over Lyckan and his eldest son was to have Bråten. But for the first time in his life, the old farmer met with opposition. August said he didn't want Lyckan, but the deeds of Bråten. And his son said he'd decided to go to America.

Then they all said, with one voice, that none wished to live at Lyckan, haunted as it was by both Joel and Lovisa, not to mention the unfortunate Rickard. This talk frightened Hanna so much that she took a firm grip on John Broman's arm.

Erik Eriksson, never before opposed, crumpled as he sat at the table at Bråten, his back bowed, and suddenly they could all see that he was old and that this misfortune had affected him badly. As usual, Ingegerd was the one to find a solution: she suggested that the farms should be combined and transferred to August, who in his turn would have to decide on who was to inherit them.

'It'll be long roads for you to go if you insist on staying on at Bråten,' she said, to her brother-in-law. 'But that's up to you.'

August made a special effort not to show how pleased he was. This was the solution he'd hoped for. Hanna looked wide-eyed at Aunt Ingegerd and, as so many times before, thought how upright and handsome she was, Erik Eriksson's elder daughter. She was fifty now, and seven years older than Maja-Lisa, but she looked much younger.

People spoke contemptuously of daughters who stayed at home, but as far as Ingegerd of Framgården was concerned, people had little to say. It had long been known that Erik Eriksson had never made a decision without first consulting his daughter.

A woman can be like that if she escapes husband and children, Hanna thought. Then she was ashamed, for she knew that women had to bow to established custom and children had to be born.

After Erik Eriksson and his daughter had left in their cart, August, his sons and John Broman celebrated their victory. They drank so deeply that there was no question of John and Hanna returning home. With her mother, Hanna dragged the menfolk up to the attic, laid them out on the floor and covered them with quilts. Then the two women went down to the kitchen to clear up after the funeral and the wake. They talked about Ingegerd, who had been beautiful and clever when young.

'She never lacked for suitors,' said Maja-Lisa. 'They came in droves but she just laughed at them. And Father was pleased as he didn't want to lose her. Poor Joel had to keep hearing that he'd been born an old woman, that Ingegerd was the heir Eriksson and the farm needed, and it was the misfortune of his life that she was a girl.'

Grumbling, Maja-Lisa told her story, and Hanna thought she was referring to Joel and his unhappy life. But suddenly Maja-Lisa cried out that she would never forgive her brother, who'd taken the honour from the family, murderer and suicide as he was.

Five great maples grew in a clearing above the house, on the very edge of the shores of the Norwegian lakes. When they flowered that spring, there was a smell of honey all round the millhouse, and Hanna said it was a great pity they couldn't take the sweet juice straight out of the trees. But Broman laughed at her as he gazed at the pale green pointed flowers swooping down towards the dark water, and saw that she didn't mind.

'You must help me carry the best sofa up to the attic,' she said. 'I need the space for a loom in the living room.' He was pleased and said she knew what he thought of that sofa.

She snapped back that it was only temporary, this loom business, and she'd soon have her fine sofa back down again.

'Nothing but a showpiece a man can't even sit on,' he said.

At that she grew fiercely angry, saying there were better things in life than sitting. He looked at her in surprise. 'You're very short-tempered these days,' he said.

'I'm to have a child,' she shouted at him, then clapped her hand to her mouth. Here she'd been pondering over when to tell him for weeks, and this was the way she had chosen!

She could see he wasn't pleased, but he put his arm round her shoulders as finally he said, 'Yes, well, it's to be expected, isn't it?'

She managed to lift the potatoes in time and stock the earth cellar before the boy arrived in November. The birth almost frightened the life out of Broman, and it was made no easier when old Anna slipped out into the kitchen for a cup of coffee and said his wife had been so torn down below before that this was only to be expected.

'You get on out, Broman,' said the midwife. He obeyed, thinking it was lucky Rickard Joelsson was dead for today he could gladly have killed the man himself. Then he went across to the mill, pulled some sacks over himself and fell asleep on the floor.

At dawn, old Anna woke him and said solemnly that he had a son.

'How's it with Hanna?'

'She's sleeping and healing. She's strong, your wife.'

Relief washed over him and Anna's solemnity affected him. He washed thoroughly in the kitchen and put on a clean shirt before creeping into their bedroom. She was pale, his girl, but sleeping soundly, her breathing deep and even.

The baby was already in the cradle at the foot of the bed, an ugly little creature with a bright red tuft of hair. Broman gazed at the infant, recognising those features and thinking he would have trouble with this boy. Then he heard the first cart coming up to the mill and went off to the day's work.

Towards evening, Maja-Lisa and August arrived with Ragnar, whom Broman had taken over to Bråten when the birth pains had started. He'd not wanted the boy to be frightened, he'd said. Maja-Lisa had taken the boy, but thought it a strange idea. Children had to learn what life was like. When she told August, he'd agreed. He had long thought the miller was soft on the boy and was ashamed when Broman stroked Hanna's cheek.

Now they'd come to see their new grandchild. They soon found that he was nothing like anyone in the family, for none had a round face like that, a turned-up nose like that, or red hair like that. So

Broman had to say that the child was like his own father, Hanna the only one to notice that he looked miserable as he said it.

'Looks like a frog,' said Ragnar, and both Hanna and Maja-Lisa scolded him. But Broman sat the boy on his knee and said comfortingly that newborn babes often looked peculiar. 'He'll soon be as handsome as you,' he said, knowing it was a lie. This new child would never be as handsome as his brother. It was decided that the baby would be called John after his father.

'Next Sunday as ever is,' said Maja-Lisa, so decisively that no one dared say there was no hurry this time. Hanna was given a long list of things she must do. No uninvited guests at home for the next week. And Hanna must watch out for Lame Malin, the blacksmith's wife, as she was suspected of being on heat and might have the evil eye.

When his in-laws had gone, John made up a bed for Ragnar and himself in the box-bed in the kitchen. They fell asleep immediately, exhausted by all the excitement. But Hanna lay awake for a long time in the bedroom, looking at the new child and saying to herself: Ugly little thing.

She felt the same strange tenderness as she had for Ragnar. Then she gave thanks to God that it was over and that it was a boy. For a moment she thought with anxiety about what Broman had said, that he was almost insane with joy when his father died. Must have been an evil man, she thought, looking again at her newborn son. 'He won't be like him in his ways,' she said aloud, as if pronouncing an invocation. Maybe that helped, for the ugly infant grew into a good, compliant child.

The snow came at the end of the month but, thank heavens, gave way to rain from Norway. John Broman swallowed his pride and went to Erik Eriksson to borrow a horse and cart. The old man was in bed with high fever and pains in his chest, Ingegerd said, and John was ashamed of his relief.

He liked Ingegerd, who was one of the few in the valley to whom he could talk. She offered him coffee and they sat in the kitchen discussing all manner of things. About Rickard, she said that the wretched boy went mad when his father beat Lovisa.

'I tried to do something to help Hanna,' she said, 'but Father was against it. You know how the old think, that a whore is a whore whatever she's done. And there's something strange about Maja-Lisa's children.'

'Something strange?'

Ingegerd regretted saying it, he could see that. But he pressed her and she told him about Astrid, Hanna's sister, who had married well in Fredrikshald. 'She had fits,' Ingegerd said. 'Went clean off her head. Then she ran all the way to the churchyard and tore the flowers and crosses off the graves of her dead brothers and sisters. To the priest she said they weren't dead. They were alive and it was wrong to have them in the earth.' Ingegerd shuddered as she sat there, then took a sip of her coffee.

'You can imagine what was said in the cottages. But I made sure Father didn't hear it, and took Astrid in here. She was a good girl, and clever. Pretty she was, and she was never once mad here. I was fond of her and wanted to keep her. But the village tongues wagged and I was pleased when a job in service was arranged for her in Norway. I went to Fredrikshald myself, so I knew it was a good family she was going to, not a smallholding but a merchant's household. Then the fish merchant fell in love with her and there was a wedding in Fredrikshald. Her man is the kind with his feet firmly on the ground. He knows nothing of madness.'

'So it turned out well in the end?'

'That's right. Letters I get from her are happy. I think her peculiar thoughts went when she got away from Maja-Lisa.'

'Maja-Lisa says she's like one of the dead children.'

'That she is. But siblings are often as alike as peas in a pod.'

John was comforted by her calm voice and sensible explanation. He'd had some strange thoughts ever since last Christmas, when Maja-Lisa had told him about Astrid and the dead sister.

In the end, he told her what he'd come for. To his own surprise, he told her all about his mother refusing to die, the inheritance which couldn't be divided and how long and vainly he'd waited to get a horse from the farm.

'We can't manage without it,' he said. 'No one pays me in money, and once a month I have to go off and sell my flour. Alvarsson pays poorly. He knows how to make the most of the trap I'm in.'

'You could borrow the horse and cart and go to Fredrikshald,' said Ingegerd. 'Father needn't know. He won't be on his feet for the next few weeks. Meanwhile I'll think of something.'

He was surprised at her benevolence as he harnessed the horse, young and strong and not all that easily managed, to the cart. But when he said goodbye, he understood better.

'It's the same for us both – you, Broman, and me,' said Ingegerd. 'It must be hard to wish the life out of the old.'

Hanna was hugely surprised when he came back with the horse. But unease took over from her joy when he said he intended to go all the way to Fredrikshald with the flour.

'Then you'll be away for many a day.'

'You've got your brother here.'

'But that's not the same. He mostly says nothing.'

Broman thought that all the children from Bråten mostly said nothing, not least Hanna herself. But aloud he said, 'I thought you didn't like me telling my stories.'

'But that's only because it should be like that,' she said. Then he laughed at her but saw, too late, that she was saddened. 'Hanna, tell me why you pretend not to like what you like.'

'It's not necessary.'

'To tell stories to your boy?'

'Yes,' she said, and she was angry now. 'That brings no bread to the table.'

'I didn't think you lacked for bread,' he said, and he went out, slamming the door behind him with such strength it shook the house.

Then she was afraid.

But Ragnar, on the floor with his building blocks, looked thoughtfully up at her and said how stupid his mother had been.

She tried but, as usual, couldn't be angry with her son, so she just snapped at him that children should keep quiet about things they didn't understand.

'It's you who doesn't understand,' said Ragnar, and the thought that he might be right raced through her mind. Meanwhile the boy slipped out to John, who was now grooming the horse and making a place ready for it in the barn. Little John was yelling in his cradle, and Hanna calmed him by putting him to her breast. When husband and son came back, she heard them laughing outside, and she thought they were laughing at her. That hurt. But she would get used to it. All through her life, her sons were to make fun of her.

CHAPTER 19

Eighteen months after Little John was born, the next boy arrived and, as expected, was like the Eriksson family, large brown eyes, straight nose and dark brown hair. Maja-Lisa was as proud as if she herself had given birth to him and decided that he was to be called Erik after her father.

The birth had again been difficult, and when Broman saw Hanna's suffering, he solemnly promised himself he would never again touch his wife. But it was a promise he couldn't keep, for when Erik was two, their third boy was born and named August after Hanna's father.

The last boy was frailer than the other two. After the birth Hanna could see that at once, even before the midwife had washed the child. When she put him to her breast for the first time, she sensed there was little will in him to live.

Takes after his father, she thought.

She lived in constant anxiety over her husband as each year his cough grew worse. It was often so bad he found it difficult to breathe and had to go outside and gasp for air. When it was at its worst, old Anna came to put hot compresses on his chest and to speak soothingly to him. 'You should go to the doctor,' she said, and in the spring, when there was least to do at the mill, Broman and

77

Aunt Ingegerd travelled the long way to Vänersborg, where an ill-tempered doctor told him he had asthma and must stop working in the mill.

'Nothing about how I was to support my family if I closed the mill,' said John to his wife, when he got back. The medicine he had been given soon ran out, though that didn't matter much as it had been of little help.

As far as the horse was concerned, what Erik Eriksson had decided came about. August received two thirds of it and John Broman a third. Broman was bitter, but Hanna considered it a good agreement. They hadn't enough grazing for the great beast up there and they only needed the horse for one week a month, when the flour had to be taken to Norway to be sold.

As Ingegerd had predicted, living up at Bråten and looking after the Lyckan farm became too much for August. Cautiously, he took up the matter with Maja-Lisa, who immediately said she would never go and live at that place of misfortune. When John was brought into the dispute, he pondered for a long time and eventually came up with a suggestion. 'Let's pull down the old house and build another on the hill,' he said. 'It'd be better, a fine new house, with a view across the river and lake.'

But August had neither the money nor the energy to build anew. That meant a move to old Lyckan, where August, his sons and John Broman distempered ceilings and walls and whitewashed round the stove.

At midsummer, all their belongings were taken there. Maja-Lisa stopped complaining, but she never really liked their new home and some time went by before they noticed what was wrong with her. One day John told his wife that her mother was fading away up there at Lyckan. Hanna was shaken and frightened, whispering that the evil spirits were there again. Broman snorted and told her that what was troubling Maja-Lisa was a sickness of the kind that set in the body.

Hanna went with the children to see her as often as she could and each time saw that she was thinner and paler.

'Have you any pain, Mother?'

'No. I'm just so wretchedly tired.'

Housework went by the board. Hanna cleaned and did the baking, but soon had to tell August that he must get hold of a servant girl. 'You can see she can't manage.'

But it was no longer possible to get hold of servant girls. Young girls left in a steady stream for Norway where they got work in households and at guest-houses in Moss and factories in Fredrikshald. Some went on to America, some stayed and married Norwegians. Others sometimes came back on weekend visits in fine bought clothes and big hats with roses on them. That annoyed all decent housewives, who said what hussies they were, if not worse. For you could well imagine how much such fripperies cost.

Hanna did what she could for her mother, leaving the children almost every day at old Anna's and taking the infant August to Lyckan to make sure her parents and brothers at least had some food. One day the question slipped out of her, the question she had never considered asking: 'Is it true the dead walk again here, Mother?'

'Yes,' said Maja-Lisa, smiling. 'But it's not Joel and Lovisa who're here. It's the children, Anders and Johan. And sometimes little Elin.'

'But they never lived here.'

'They do now, anyhow.'

When Hanna got back home and told John Broman what her mother had said, he told her folk never got over grief. It's there to make inroads into life, taking from you a bit at a time. 'People with a lot of dead begin to lose the desire to live.'

August couldn't endure his wife's illness and sent a letter to Johannes, a well-known healer to whom August was related. He wrote, 'Now, Cousin, you must come, for I cannot manage without my wife.'

When Hanna told John about the letter, he was surprised and said he thought Johannes cured animals.

'People, too. You must've heard about the soldier at Piletorpet –

he was dying of cancer. Then Johannes went into his cottage and made a drink he got the old man to take. Then he told him to get up. Johannes said he would live to ninety. And he did.'

John hadn't heard that tale, but he had heard many others, each more amazing than the next, for Johannes's reputation was great even in Värmland. John had never believed the stories, but he said to Hanna that perhaps a visit might comfort August and Maja-Lisa.

But John was wrong. One Sunday afternoon, when the family were assembled at Lyckan, Johannes came, shook them all by the hand, and went into the room where Maja-Lisa lay. He took one look at her and said, 'So you're on your way now, are you?'

Then she could admit it to herself and to the others. 'I'm so weary,' she said. 'When will it be?'

'Probably this week. You needn't fear for torments. You'll go in your sleep.'

'Then may I see the children?'

'Expect so. All except Maria, but you know that.'

John Broman, in the kitchen, heard every word and couldn't believe his ears. Then Hanna came out, as white as a ghost, closely followed by her father, who looked as if he were the one sentenced to death. They couldn't bring themselves to speak, but finally Ingegerd said, 'Must send a message to Astrid.'

Although she whispered it and Johannes was still in with Maja-Lisa, he heard and said loudly, 'No, Astrid's not to come.'

'That's right,' said Maja-Lisa. 'Astrid's not to come. But I want the priest, if that drunk can stay sober for a whole day.'

Hanna stayed at Lyckan to cook for them all. But John went back to the mill where Ragnar, now ten, was alone with his younger brothers. John had a lift with Ingegerd, who was now hurrying back to old Erik, who'd been *in extremis* for over a year now.

In the cart, John said, 'What can one believe?'

'Johannes has great experience of sickness. It's not too hard to see that Maja-Lisa is on her way out.'

'But what Johannes said about Maria and Astrid?'

'Don't take it so seriously, Broman. Johannes has been in America for a long time and got himself a new religion. A strange teaching which says the soul leaves the dead and goes into the newborn. 'Tis all nonsense.'

She glanced at John but saw he wasn't convinced. 'Listen, now. Johannes stayed at Bråten all one winter when Astrid was small. That was when he put those strange ideas into Maja-Lisa's head, which sent the poor girl crazy later.'

John heaved a deep sigh of relief and agreed with her from the depths of his heart when she said that the dead were dead, 'And you know that, Broman.'

The priest was only half drunk when he arrived on Monday to give Maja-Lisa communion. She was calm, almost expectant. But August was rigid, dumb with terror, as if exiled to another country.

On Tuesday, Maja-Lisa had a pain in her chest and was finding it difficult to breathe. The family sat by her bed all night and things went just as predicted: she drew a deep sigh and stopped breathing.

John was not at the death-bed. Someone had to be at home with the children and he had just got them to sleep when there was a knock on the door and Johannes came in.

John made coffee and put out a bite to eat, moving about awkwardly, for he did not like his guest. They said nothing until they'd finished their coffee, then John spoke.

'D'you always condemn people to death straight out like that?'

'Only those who want to hear,' said Johannes, smiling. 'August hasn't long to go, either. But he wouldn't benefit from knowing.'

John thought about his asthma and his own tiredness, but he didn't dare ask. Nor was that necessary.

'Broman, you've several more years to go than you really want. And that's for a definite reason. Can I sleep up in the attic room?'

John was astonished. But as he was lighting the stove in the attic and preparing the bed, he felt happier than he had for a long time.

When Hanna returned she was pale and tense as she fed the hungry infant. As she sat there with the baby at her breast, she looked long and hard at John and said, 'Dear Lord, how I wish I could've cried.' She slept for an hour or so but, despite the sleepless night, still had the milking to do. As she'd expected, Johannes came to the barn, praised the creatures and told her she needn't worry about her husband. 'He'll live on a good bit into the nineteen hundreds. He'll be here, all right, when we've to write nineteen ten.'

Hanna was greatly relieved. It was still the summer of 1894, a long time until the turn of the century. She didn't have time to work it out until Johannes had left, and she found to her surprise that he'd promised no more than sixteen years. But that was enough, for by then Ragnar would be twenty-six, John nineteen and Erik eighteen. There'd be three hale and hearty men at the mill.

'Even you, poor wee thing, you'll be sixteen and grown,' she whispered to August, as she put him to her breast.

'You're looking a mite more cheerful,' said Broman, as he came in for his midday meal. She nodded, but pursed her mouth, Johannes's final words still ringing in her ears. One word to Broman, and he'd die out of sheer cussedness.

After they'd gone to bed, Hanna found it hard to sleep, despite her exhaustion, memories of her mother coming and going in her mind, some of which hurt.

'You look worn out,' said John at breakfast.

'Been having bad thoughts.' She couldn't stop herself flushing. 'Like that winter I was carrying Ragnar. Mother made me help with the slaughter, and she actually had me hold the blood pail. Then an old woman in a cottage by the river died and what d'you think? Mother told me to go and wash the body! All that so the boy inside me should be unhealthy and die.' Hanna smiled wryly and pointed at Ragnar asleep in the box-bed. 'Then he was healthier and finer than any of her own children.'

John could only shake his head. But as he reached the door on his way to work, he turned round and said, 'One thing we can learn from this. The old superstitions haven't any effect.'

In the middle of the busy harvest, August Olsson had a pain in his chest and lay down under a tree to rest. When his sons went to wake him an hour or so later, he was dead. They stood round him in silence, neither surprised nor frightened. Old August had not really lived since Maja-Lisa had gone into the ground.

There was no will, so the farms went to the sons. Robert had given up his plans for America and Rudolf was as hard-working as Hanna so established himself at Lyckan. But Adolf stayed at the mill at Norskvattnet for a few more years. When the miller's sons were old enough to take over the work, Adolf took out his share of the inheritance and went to America.

None of Hanna's brothers married.

CHAPTER 20

Astrid came to her father's funeral with her husband and children. John Broman often looked at his sister-in-law with appreciation, grand as she was in her bought floral dress. She was a sight to see – and friendly to them all, loved a good talk, sang lullabies to the children and farmyard songs to the cows.

In temperament, she was nothing like her siblings, yet had the same stature as Hanna and if you looked closely you could see the likeness in her features.

But her sister made Hanna seem heavy and countrified. While Astrid flew across the ground, Hanna plodded. Astrid's face reflected every emotion and was as changeable as spring weather, while Hanna's expression was closed. Astrid chatted and sang, Hanna said nothing, giggling occasionally, but at once putting her hand to her mouth, always embarrassed when it happened. John felt sorry for his wife, but sometimes angry: she could well have taken off her kerchief to show her lovely hair, and wear something else besides black and brown striped wool.

Astrid said so. 'Why do you have to look like some old country bumpkin? Come on. Try on my green skirt with this flowery blouse.'

'I'd never dare,' said Hanna, tittering, and Astrid realised that things were just as her sister said, she didn't dare.

One thing was unmistakable: the two sisters were fond of each other, not a scrap of either envy or distance in Hanna, though now and again she did speak of conceit and vanity. Astrid could smile at those words, tenderly and compassionately. 'You're too hard on yourself,' she said.

'Things went for me as they went.'

They never got any further than that.

John was attracted to his sister-in-law, entranced by her sunny nature. But she frightened him, too, so they never became truly intimate. Once he said, 'You're not really of this world.'

She laughed at him, but he saw that Hanna was frightened.

His brother-in-law agreed. 'My wife's an angel,' he said. 'When she's not being a troll. It's not easy, as you can imagine.'

They could all laugh then, all except Hanna, who flushed and bit her lip. She's remembering the madness, John thought.

He grew to like the fish merchant, a trustworthy man with a big heart and a good head. They became friends when out fishing on the lake in the early mornings. In the boat, Broman began to realise a crisis was blowing up, maybe something worse, between Norway and Sweden.

Arne Henriksen's voice rang across the lake with such force that he frightened the fish away.

'There's got to be an end to the Swedish lording it over us,' he said. 'Otherwise it'll all blow up. You can be certain of that. We've got both arms and men.'

John thought about his trips to Fredrikshald, where the poor peasants from Dal stood humbly in the market square to be rid of their sheep, their hay and tubs of butter.

'I mean the gentlemen in Stockholm,' Arne went on. 'Not you.'

'But we'd be the ones slaughtered if you come with arms.'

'You have to join the cause and get rid of the King, the damned old fox.'

John Broman was surprised at his own feelings. Never before had

84

he felt how Swedish he was. For a moment, he felt like flinging the loud-mouthed Norwegian overboard. But Arne noticed nothing of his anger and launched into a long explanation, talking of the law in Eidsvold which gave ordinary people greater rights than anywhere else in the world. Then he came to the consulate dispute.

Broman had heard about it but, like most Swedes, hadn't taken the matter seriously. Now he was told about the party of the left and its demands for a foreign minister of its own with power in Parliament, and that Norwegians were already taking the Union badge off the flags of their ships sailing round the world.

The miller listened without really understanding. But when Henriksen told him Parliament had bought new warships for eight million *riksdaler* and the new Norwegian defence minister, a man called Stang, a lieutenant-commander, was building forts along the long border to Sweden, John Broman was frightened.

'Stang's a bloody good man,' said Henriksen, then went on to say the defence minister had bought new German arms and that Fredriksten fortress had been given cannons with much greater range.

Henriksen gave John a long look before he rounded off his speech. 'We don't talk all that much about it, but every single Norwegian knows ... Arms first, then ...'

They went on talking about it over their evening drink. Henriksen was unusual: voluble and vociferous when sober but calm and factual once he'd a tot inside him.

'You must see it's sheer madness, Norwegian seamen sailing all over the world without their own countrymen looking out for them.'

Broman understood that.

'Parliament's decided on a consulate of its own,' Henriksen went on. 'We've allocated money for it. But the King in Stockholm refuses.'

John nodded.

'King Oskar's a shit,' said Henriksen.

The sisters serving their evening meal heard him. Hanna looked as if she might faint with shock, but Astrid laughed.

The Norwegian relatives were offended when they heard that John Broman visited Fredrikshald once a month. Why hadn't he let them know? John found that difficult to answer, but in the end said he'd probably been too shy.

'Nonsense,' said Arne, but Astrid laughed as usual and said there would have to be a change. Broman could stay overnight with them next time, and he had to agree to that. In a few months' time, little August would be weaned and then John would bring Hanna with him.

'Mother'd never let me,' said Hanna, then flushed when she remembered that Maja-Lisa was dead. 'I mean,' she went on, 'that if children are to be healthy you have to breast-feed them for two years.'

For once, Astrid was angry. 'It's time you got free of Mother and her awful superstitions,' she said. 'Times have changed, Hanna.'

Then Hanna said something that truly surprised John. 'Mm. I think I know that. But it worries me. What am I to believe in if all the old things are wrong?'

'You have to try for yourself,' said Astrid, as if that were the simplest thing in the world.

The two sisters gossiped their way through the local news. Astrid was horrified at all the changes, the Kasa people in America, only the old people left at Bönan, the forest growing over the big Kleva farm, Jonas dead, Klara dead, Lars dead.

'But they weren't old!'

'No. Neither was Mother nor Father.'

'What did they die of, Hanna?'

'They were worn out.'

'I reckon they died of grief after the famine.'

They went through all their schoolfriends. Where was Ragnar? And where Vitalia, Sten, Jöran and Olena?

Hanna replied, 'In Norway, in Göteborg, in America, at sea.'

Hanna hadn't thought about it before, how deserted it had become in the valley. Now it was put into words.

'Soon a wasteland,' said Astrid.

Astrid fell in love with Ragnar, the dark-eyed eleven-year-old with his quick smile and light-hearted nature. 'A Sunday's child,' she said. 'Life's incomprehensible, isn't it, Hanna?'

'He's like his father,' said Hanna, adding hastily, 'only on the outside. Ragnar's kind and good by nature.'

'Must be hard not to spoil him.'

Hanna had to admit that Broman had a soft spot for the boy and was much fonder of him than of his own sons.

But Henriksen told John he would have to look out for the boy. 'They find it difficult to grow up, the ones who can sweeten themselves to get what they want.'

John nodded. He'd thought about that.

When the Norwegians left to return home, it had been decided that John should stay with them whenever he took his flour to Fredrikshald, and that once every summer he would take Hanna with him.

'We'll buy you some fine new clothes and take you to the photographer,' said Astrid, and Hanna cringed with dismay. But with delight too, John noticed.

It was early morning, the sun low as the Norwegian wagon with their children asleep in it set off downhill towards the border. Hanna stood waving in the yard outside while Broman went with them to the gate. After their guests had disappeared round the bend, he turned round and stood still for a moment, looking at his wife, her shadow long in the slanting light, dark and sharply outlined.

Hanna's first trip to the busy town was a great event. She liked everything she saw, the crowded street life, the many shops, and best of all being surrounded by strangers.

'Just think,' she said to John. 'Just think, being able to walk the streets and into all the shops without having to speak to a single person.'

Pressed by her sister, she tried on clothes in the shops. It was painful to watch her, deeply embarrassed as she was, sweat pouring off her.

'I feel so awfully ashamed,' she whispered. But Astrid refused to give up. She got Hanna to try another dress and told her to look at herself in the big mirror, though she didn't dare for more than a brief moment, then clapped her hands over her eyes.

In the end she relented and bought a dress with flounces and green flowers on a white background. But when she was made to go to the photographer's, she put on her best dress from home, the brown check one, and once there did nothing but gaze solemnly straight into the camera.

She was profoundly taken by the photograph. Back at home she had it framed and hung up, and she often stopped to look at it, as if she couldn't have enough of those eyes meeting hers.

On their way home, she told Broman she had never imagined Norway like that ... so bold. She'd been there when she was small, but hadn't remembered that they were all so cheerful there.

John agreed. He'd also been across from Värmland quite often as a child and hadn't noticed much difference. But now there was a kind of rousing force in Norway, a liveliness and joyousness you could feel the moment you crossed the border. He understood it better since he had got to know Henriksen. The Norwegians had a common purpose and a great dream. But he didn't want to worry Hanna so he said nothing about the Union crisis. They talked about Astrid, and Hanna said she was like a whole lot of people in one.

'She's got lots of aprons,' Broman agreed, but Hanna was cross.

'She doesn't dress up, my sister.'

No, she didn't, he agreed. She was all of them at once, angel and troll, mother and child, grand wife and cheerful country girl.

He had wondered what held her together, thinking perhaps it was a secret, that the great secret was the core of her nature.

★

88

As soon as Hanna got home, she started making curtains with the thin white cotton material she'd bought in Norway. The little windows in the house looked softer.

'How fine, how fine,' she said, as if beside herself with delight.

The curtains were looked at askance in the district as new-fangled and the product of vanity. Hanna persisted, though and, the curtains stayed.

But she never dared put on the flowery shop dress.

CHAPTER 21

Hanna had a hand with butter. No churning failed for her, not even if a beggarwoman came into the kitchen and put the evil eye on the churn. But then one day the blacksmith's Lame Malin remarked that it'd always been said that whores had luck with butter.

Hanna lost her temper and shouted back, 'Get out, you lame bitch. And never show your face in the millhouse again.'

That had been a few years ago. But from then on, there was hostility between the two houses by the lakes. Broman was never told what had happened, but it was difficult for him as he was dependent on the blacksmith in many ways, not just because they drank together on Saturday nights: every other month the grind-stones had to be lifted for chaff-cutting. That was heavy work, and for cleaning the millstone ridges he needed sharpened cutters. He reproached Hanna. 'We have to keep in with the neighbours.'

But she was unmoved. Malin was never to cross her threshold again. 'Ask her,' she shouted. 'Ask her why I've a hand with butter.'

So Broman went to the smith's house with his question and Malin said it was probably just as Hanna had said, that she had luck with the butter because she kept both kitchen and barn clean.

That evening when he got home with Malin's reply, John was told what she'd actually said to Hanna. He was so angry that he went straight back to the forge and scolded the smith's wife. The men had to take their drink down to the big cave by the long lake.

Then Hanna regretted what she'd said, thinking she'd gone too far. Especially as she couldn't keep her sons away from the forge and the blacksmith's boys, who were about the same age as hers.

In the old days I didn't even blink when they called me a whore, she thought. Now I'm respectable I get so horribly angry.

She was disappointed with respectability. It hadn't come up to her expectations. At first she'd gone to church to sit among the other wives, even on an aisle bench so that the young had to squeeze by. But it had been no pleasure, and when Broman had asked her what consolation she sought in church, she was ashamed. Now it was many years since she'd been to divine service.

Then, one late winter's day, Ragnar came home from school covered with blood and bruises. Yes, he'd been in a fight. The others had come off worse than he had, he said, wiping the blood from his nose off his upper lip with the back of his hand.

Hanna sent for Broman.

He came, demanded hot water to wash the injuries, scraped the worst of the blood off the boy's face and asked what had happened.

'They say I'm a bastard,' said the boy.

'Heaven's above!' cried Hanna. 'That's nothing to fight over, is it? It's only the truth!'

Broman at once turned round abruptly and struck Hanna across the face with the flat of his hand, sending her flying across the kitchen floor until her back hit the long bench under the window.

'Are you mad?' she cried.

'No, that I'm not,' shouted Broman. 'But you'll drive me mad.' Then he went out and slammed the door behind him.

Ragnar was crying, but she could see his eyes were ice-cold behind the tears. 'It's you, Mother, who's crazy.'

Then he, too, disappeared.

Hanna was shaking all over but managed to pull herself together. She looked hard at her face in the mirror. It was swollen and bruised, but not bleeding. Her back was worse, aching from the blow against the bench.

Thank goodness the children are out, she thought, but then

remembered where they were, at the forge, where Malin gave them bread and juice.

She made their evening meal and her sons came home. She sent Erik to fetch their father and Ragnar. Broman appeared, looking miserable, but said not a word.

'You hurt yourself, Mother?' said Erik.

'Where's Ragnar?'

'Gone into the forest,' said Broman.

'Dear Lord,' whispered Hanna. 'We must go and look for him.'

She looked terrible, white as sheet beneath the bruises and swellings. He was ashamed but said, in a steady voice, 'He'll be back. He told me he had to be alone to think. I can understand that.'

Hanna moved with difficulty as she served at table and set about the dishes. When Broman noticed, she said apologetically that she'd hit her back on the bench. That made him even more ashamed.

Ragnar came in as they were getting the beds ready for the night. He did the same as Broman, said nothing.

Dear Lord, how can I explain? Hanna thought.

When they'd gone to bed, all Broman said was: 'I want to know why you can't forgive it when Malin calls you a whore but it's all right when Ragnar's called a bastard.'

She said nothing for a long while, then finally, 'I'm no whore. I was attacked. But Ragnar ... He's illegitimate and that can't be denied.'

'So you're innocent and he's guilty?'

'I don't mean that.'

In the morning, she could scarcely move, but Broman ignored her pain and tried again. 'Hanna. You're not stupid. You can think. Now you must explain to the boy and me.'

She thought about it all day, but could find nothing that would make her words understandable to others. To her it was obvious. At their evening meal, she said to Ragnar that her tongue had run away with her. 'I was that frightened, I didn't know what I was saying,' she said.

That was as near to asking for forgiveness as she could get, but not enough for the boy. His eyes were still icy and it was a ghostly, silent week in the house. They were all good at saying nothing, Ragnar, Hanna and Broman. The days went by. Her back got better and the bruises and swellings disappeared. But her eyes were dark with shame and grief.

Then one morning, before Ragnar and his brothers had gone to school, the boy said, 'You're a bit thick in the head, you are, Mamma.'

That was the first time he had ever called her Mamma. She sat quite still at the kitchen table, thinking she'd lost him and he was the most beloved she had.

Again she wished she could cry, but as usual she was dry to her very soul.

CHAPTER 22

Broman took his flour to Fredrikshald and Hanna worried whether he would tell her sister what had happened. She tried to calm herself with the thought that he didn't make a habit of going round gossiping and telling tales.

But when he came home late that night, she realised she'd been wrong. He said curtly that he and his brother-in-law had agreed that Ragnar could go to work in the fish trade in Fredrikshald as soon as he was thirteen.

When John saw her despair, he told her she must realise the boy was growing up and had to make a life of his own. At that moment, Hanna made a decision. 'I suppose he must choose for himself,' she said.

'Yes, he'll decide for himself.'

'He's needed at the mill.'

'No, it's enough with Adolf and the boys.'

'We'll ask him at midday tomorrow,' said Hanna, and Broman nodded.

As soon as the men had left the next morning, Hanna started to make a sponge cake, generous with both butter and sugar, and tasting until the mixture was smooth and sweet. Then she took the cake to the forge where Lame Malin almost swooned with surprise.

'I thought,' said Hanna, 'we neighbours must stay friends.'

Malin was so astonished that she never even got round to putting on the coffee. Hanna was grateful for that, for she found it difficult to bear the filth and bad air in the smith's house. She talked for a while about Malin's boys, who were growing up well, she said. And about the winter, which refused to let go.

Then she went home and said to Him up there in the heavens that now she'd done what she could. Now it was His turn to do something for her.

But at dinner when Broman told the boy what had been agreed in Fredrikshald, Ragnar went wild with delight.

'If I'd *like!*' he cried. 'You mad, Father? If I'd like ...'

Broman went on to explain that Henriksen had customers all over the town and needed an errand boy to cycle round with the orders. Some wanted fresh herring on Wednesday when it was brought in, others mackerel on Thursday. And then there was the cod that nearly everyone wanted on Saturday.

John was quite voluble as he described this trade, but Ragnar had heard one word only. 'Cycle?' he said. 'Father, d'you mean I'd have a bicycle?'

At that moment Hanna knew that, yet again, God hadn't listened to her.

After Ragnar had gone the house seemed empty, and Broman thought about how the boy had filled the place with his laughter. He was troubled about Hanna, too. She was so tired and upset, not at all herself. He tried talking to her.

'It was good you settled with the smith's wife.'

'It was useless.'

As usual, he didn't understand her.

By the time spring came, with the snow melting and the starlings, they'd got used to it. Even Hanna began to regain her old briskness and take a greater interest in her other sons. Broman looked at Little

John, their red-haired and smallest eldest son, and to his surprise he found the boy was filling the space left by Ragnar. He was full of ideas, had the same laugh as his half-brother and the same liking for what was light-hearted and amusing.

He was tender, too, noticing his mother's grief and doing what he could to console her. He'd never been close to his father, but now Broman had to admit what was obvious, that Little John was the son who worked hardest at the mill.

'You stick to things more than your brother does,' he said, almost reluctantly, one day. When the boy flushed with pleasure, Broman felt guilty. He had neglected his sons. Not only Little John, but Erik, too, and August, the youngest, a constant source of annoyance with sickliness and whining. Erik was good at school. Hanna had said, long ago, that he had a scholar's head. It wasn't long before the schoolmaster had taught him most of what he himself knew.

Broman started hunting out his old books in the attic, never unpacked since the move from Värmland. He found *Robinson Crusoe* and smiled wistfully as he remembered how the book had fed all his boyhood dreams.

'Not an uncalled-for word,' he said warningly to Hanna, as he brought down the book. As they sat down for their evening meal, he just said to the boy, 'Here you are, a present for you.'

Erik flushed just as his brother had, and disappeared up into his icy bedroom. Then he took to vanishing up there at every free moment. Hanna was troubled and took up blankets and jerseys so that he shouldn't die of cold. In the end, she gave in and lit the stove for him.

A few days later she told him his blood would rot in his veins if he lay there every evening with his nose in a book. But Erik laughed at her. She recognised that laugh, superior, just like Ragnar's.

Erik soon found his own way to the chest of old books.

August caught whooping cough that spring. Hanna walked round with the boy in her arms at night and gave him hot milk and honey. But that didn't help, and he usually brought up all his food. John

94

tried in vain to find some rest in the bedroom, but the boy's terrible cough started his own up again. Father and son were competing together at coughing.

'You've been so well for so long now,' said Hanna uneasily. And Broman realised that his cough had not really troubled him since Johannes the healer had promised him a long life. Henriksen was jealous. Astrid could always sense bad weather in other people's minds long before they noticed themselves, and she hadn't interfered with the decision to bring Ragnar to Fredrikshald.

She was fond of the boy, but she kept that to herself. She greeted him kindly but briefly when he arrived, then showed him the labourer's room up in the attic. He was to have no advantages just because he was a relative, she'd said to Henriksen.

'They've spoilt him at home,' he said.

'Yes, they have. We'll get that out of him.'

So Henriksen was more friendly to the boy than he'd intended, just to outweigh his wife's prejudice.

The first thing Ragnar had to learn was to rid himself of his Swedish words. He was to speak Norwegian. It wasn't that different, and in a week he had learned it.

'He's got a quick head on him,' said Henriksen.

But Ragnar never understood why he was to avoid Swedish words. Fredrikshald was not a big town and most people he came across knew that he was Swedish, nephew of the fish merchant's wife. People had nothing against ordinary folk from Dalsland and Värmland.

Much more important to Ragnar was that no one knew his origins. Here he was the son of the miller across the border.

He had to wait for the bicycle until he had learned his way round the town, so for the first six months he pulled the cart with the fish orders himself. At each door he smiled his warm smile and the housewives melted. He was soon able to tell Henriksen that he could sell more fish than just orders, and after a while the little cart had also become a stall.

'He's a clever businessman,' said Henriksen. When his wife didn't reply, he was angry and added, 'He's honest and hard-working. He never complains about long days and he accounts for every penny.'

One day, in one of the narrow alleys below the fort, Ragnar was confronted with something that coloured the rest of his life. A gentleman from Kristiania arrived ... in a car with a chauffeur! The incredible vehicle had to stop for the boy to pull his cart into a porch. Ragnar stood there for a long time, his eyes gleaming as he watched the amazing vehicle disappear down towards the market square. Father had talked about cars, and back home he had once read out a newspaper article about these vehicles that went by themselves, frightening people to death and making horses bolt with their noise and fearful speed. But words had never made much impression on Ragnar for he lived by his senses. He was now so astounded and happy that he dawdled that day and was late with his errands.

He asked Henriksen what a machine of that kind cost. 'About five thousand kroner.'

An inconceivable sum for the boy. He tried to imagine five thousand kroner lying gleaming in a great heap on the floor. Would it reach right up to the ceiling?

From that day on he saved every penny he earned.

CHAPTER 23

Over the years, John Broman kept his secret promise not to approach Hanna in bed. She was thirty now and the midwife had told him that another birth might cost Hanna her life.

Old Anna had been widowed, but still lived on at her holding. Her sons were in America, so she'd had to rent out her patch of land to her neighbour. When the winter was at its worst that turn-of-the-century year, John and Hanna had persuaded her to come and live at the mill. Both considered she brought good cheer with her, and they missed her when she insisted on going back to her own place.

When Broman came home after helping Anna move, he was gloomy, his old melancholy on him again. They were alone again now, and silence was to settle beneath their roof.

He had become more taciturn than ever over the years and had accepted that he would never be truly intimate with his wife. For weeks on end he spoke not at all, and when he said something, it was unpleasant. 'Your head's all sawdust.' Or 'You look like a crazy old hag.'

They also had worries over their living. Holding after smallholding in the district had been abandoned, so there was less and less flour, even in the miller's barrel. They grew increasingly dependent on the potatoes, the cows and the fishing.

John was also worried about the crisis with Norway. The newspaper he fetched twice a week from Alvarsson's store on the border was full of antagonistic and increasingly violent speeches. The hostility began to infect the people. Ragnar came home once a month and told them about insults hurled at every Swede across the border. When Astrid and her husband came to see them, they kept off politics. Henriksen was quieter than usual and Broman could see the Norwegian was also afraid of what might happen.

These days, Ragnar took the flour from the mill to Fredrikshald. Broman said he was pleased to be relieved of the burden, but he missed the trips.

That spring he was forced to take out a loan to survive. Ragnar contributed too, with what he had left over. Things were going well for the boy in Norway – so well that Arne told John that if he'd not been Swedish he'd have made him a partner.

That summer was cold and wet, keeping them indoors, chafing against each other more and more. Broman's cough grew worse than ever at night when desolation crept over him, and it was on such a night that he approached his wife.

She received him with warmth, as if even for her the loneliness had become too much. Their union softened them both. By the time late summer arrived, at last bringing with it the sun and warmth, they had made a habit of being together at night.

In November, old Anna moved back and was welcomed with coffee and newly baked bun-loaf. She brought with her great news. Anders Olsson, younger brother of August, and Hanna's uncle, had been to see her with an offer to buy her holding. He'd worked at the shipyard in Fredrikshald for many years, had saved his earnings and now wanted to return home.

'But this has never been his home,' said Hanna, in surprise. 'He was born in Norway, like our father.'

'I asked him about that,' said Anna, 'but he thought that, as things were now, Sweden was home for anyone Swedish.'

Hanna looked at John, her thoughts on Ragnar.

'There'll be another solution for Ragnar,' said John. 'He'll soon have to come back for his military service.'

'D'you think there'll be war?'

'We've new laws for national service.'

Was Anna going to sell? Another neighbouring farm would be important, bringing more life to them all. Anders Olsson had four sons and three daughters. The eldest son had already made enquiries about buying Svacken, the farm below Troll Ridge. It had been derelict for several years, but there was good grazing land there.

Anna sensed what the miller and his wife were thinking and nodded. She'd thought that, too. But she also knew what she wanted.

'I want a room and furniture of my own. And I'll pay well.'

'Payment'll have to be as it will,' said John.

'Your work does you justice,' said Hanna.

'I know how things are for you with money,' the old woman went on. 'And I've grown fond of you both. But I don't want to be a burden so it'll have to be as I've decided.'

As he rowed out on to the lake John was almost happy. He got two pike on the line. She's already brought me luck, he thought.

Their new joy lasted a few months. They preserved and made juice, the kitchen full of good smells and women's chatter. But as autumn came it became clear how things were with Hanna.

'You've another on the way,' Anna said to Broman, her voice and expression harsh, but when she saw how frightened he was, she softened.

'We must pray to God,' she said.

John went out into the forest, burdened with fear and guilt. 'Dear Lord,' he said, but couldn't go on. He hadn't prayed since he was a child, and then it had been no help.

On his way home, he thought perhaps they could go to the doctor and have the child taken away.

'Should be possible,' said Anna, after thinking for a while. They did things like that, the doctors, if it was necessary. And it was for Hanna.

They both looked at Hanna standing stiffly by the stove, a clenched hand over her mouth. Time and time again, she took away her hand and gasped for breath, but found it difficult to get a word out. In the end she cried, 'Never! Don't you see it's a sin that takes you straight to hell?'

'But, Hanna, if you don't get through it, the children will be motherless.'

'Then it's God's will.'

'You usually say no one knows that.'

'No. Then there's nothing to do but bow to it.'

Nothing more was said, for at that moment the sons came in, tired and hungry. They ate as usual, but when Hanna went to bed, she said to Broman, in a quiet but steady voice, 'Don't worry. Maybe I'll manage.'

For a moment he dared believe her and he brightened. 'How strong you are,' he whispered.

She was back to normal the next morning, brisk and active. As on every morning since old Anna had come, he heard her saying to herself that she missed her sofa that had ended up in the attic now that Anna had the bedroom and John and Hanna had moved their bed into the parlour.

Can she have forgotten? he thought. Or isn't she afraid of death?

She hadn't forgotten: that was quite clear when one day he happened to hear her talking to their sons, whispering advice to them, about keeping clean their clothes, bodies and way of life. And they must promise her to look after their father should anything happen to her.

He was moved, but the boys laughed at her.

'You'll live to a hundred,' said Erik.

'Maybe,' said Hanna. 'But if I don't, you're to remember what I've told you.'

Anna had worked out that the child would arrive in March. By the middle of February she was making Hanna stay in bed, to rest and gather strength. Anna mostly sat with her, talking away to make Hanna forget the shame of her, a healthy person, lying about in the middle of a weekday.

They talked about many things, about death as well.

'I want to go decently to the grave,' said Hanna. 'I've saved my butter money, what I've put aside, in the cupboard over there. You can take it and make sure the boys have black mourning clothes.'

'I promise.'

Hanna had to get up sometimes to go to the privy. On 15 February, she came back from it and told Anna she was bleeding. The midwife looked pleased and made an astringent herbal drink for her. 'Drink this down now so we can get it started. It's good it's come early, then it won't be too big.'

'You must send Broman away,' said Hanna.

But Broman refused to go, and he was never to forget the three days that followed. Hanna pushed and screamed but the child seemed to have grown into the womb. Anna tried all her old arts, and in the end had Hanna suspended from a beam in the ceiling, the pains coming at shorter and shorter intervals, but the child would not budge.

'I'll cut you now.'

'Do that.'

'Go on out,' the old woman said to Broman.

Anna had the sense to dip her sharp scissors into boiling water on the stove before she cut the mouth of the womb. The child shot out like a cork from a bottle and Hanna fainted, though she didn't bleed as much as Anna had feared. She couldn't stitch, but clamped the cut together as best she could and smeared it with mistletoe ointment.

Hanna slowly came back to life.

'You've managed, Hanna,' whispered Anna. 'It's over. Sleep now.'

The child was blue and bloody, but Anna got it breathing with a slap, cut the cord and washed the babe.

'It's a girl,' she said.

'God have mercy on her, the poor wee wretch,' whispered Hanna.

Broman had gone to sleep at the mill, curled up and as cold as ice. When Erik came with the message that it was all over and Hanna was asleep, at first he didn't dare believe it. When Anna brought him a stiff drink, the message at last sank in.

'You've a daughter,' said the old woman.

Her words touched on an old memory. But he tossed back his drink and the fiery spirit made him forget. Once he had washed, put on a clean shirt and was holding the babe in his arms, the memory came sharply back to him. 'She's to be called Johanna,' he said.

But the midwife objected. 'It never bodes well to give babes names of dead siblings,' she whispered.

The look he gave her said more clearly than words what she hadn't understood.

Hanna wept and whimpered alternately when she woke next morning.

'She's in pain,' said Anna, but she knew Hanna was grieving over having a girl, for the terrible fate that awaited all womenfolk. She'd had nothing against the name and both John and Anna took it for granted that she'd long forgotten the name of John Broman's dead daughter. They were wrong there. Hanna remembered, and felt great satisfaction at having borne him a daughter in place of the one he'd grieved over so long. With her own eyes, she could see that the newborn babe was like her father.

She also saw that she was an unusually beautiful child.

'Poor wee thing,' she said, as she put the babe to her breast.

CHAPTER 24

They never found out what old Anna put into the water with which she washed Hanna's torn body, but over the next few weeks there was a strong smell of secret brews in the kitchen. She made Hanna lie still in bed and drink her vile herbal concoctions.

Her labours all had a good effect. Hanna healed, and a fortnight later, she was out of bed, her legs weak and, though it took a while, she returned to running the household.

'I'll see to the house,' said Anna. 'You see to the babe.'

But that didn't happen. Broman looked after the child more or less on his own, changed her, rubbed in ointment, prattled to her and rocked her.

'Just like any old woman,' said Hanna, ashamed.

'He's old and tired. Why should we grudge him the child when he has such joy from her?'

'It's not natural,' said Hanna, glad they lived so far away from others. Lame Malin no longer came to see her, so there were no prying female eyes here, or tongues to wag bad talk all around. When their new neighbours came to see them, she made sure she had the child at her breast.

They were pleasant people, her aunt and uncle from Norway. Hanna was pleased to have relatives back again after the long, lonely years. Ragnar came home and was almost as attached to his little sister as Broman was. He brought gifts from Astrid with him, dresses for the little one and the finest bed-linen for her cradle.

He brought presents for Hanna, too, a jet necklace so long she could wind it three times round her neck. He had bought it when Astrid had happened to say that Hanna had always gazed longingly at the strings of jet beads when she was last in Fredrikshald.

As always when she was pleased, Hanna wept and the tall youth flushed. Never, he thought, never is she to know what Astrid and I get up to in the bedstraw when Henriksen is away on business in Kristiania.

Spring came early and was warm. Broman wove a birch-bark knapsack, lined it with sheepskin and then went walking along the banks of the lake with his daughter on his back. He taught her to look, to see the blue anemones cautiously appearing in last year's grass, the roach slapping the surface of the water, the first butterfly, and the clouds wandering across the sky.

Old Anna laughed at him. 'The babe's far too young to understand that sort of talk,' she said. But Broman could see from the glint in the child's honey-brown eyes that she understood.

He taught her to listen, too.

'Listen to the diver calling.'

At midsummer, at last, old Eriksson at Framgården died, after having lain for many years like a log in his bed with neither speech nor reason. Ingegerd herself came to them with the message, congratulated them on their daughter and asked Broman to assemble the family at the mill the following Saturday, when everything was to be settled.

'I suppose there was a will?'

Hanna was the one to ask, but Ingegerd shook her head and said the old man had never got round to writing one before his illness took away his mind.

On the Saturday, clearly and sensibly, Ingegerd described her plans. She was going to sell Framgården and share out the money equally between them and Hanna's brothers. Hanna would have her rights to the mill and the millhouse, and any articles she wanted from the old family farm. She was also to have whatever creatures she wanted from the barn, the stable and the pigsty. Astrid was to have all the old family heirlooms, jewellery from both their maternal and paternal grandmothers.

'I've had them valued, so I know Astrid's heritage is no worse than yours.'

They all found the settlement reasonable. Only one thing surprised them, and that was that the illegitimate boy, Ragnar, was to have a thousand *riksdalers*.

'He's family, on both his mother's and his father's side,' Ingegerd said.

Broman was pleased. It was good to have your own mill. And they could sell many of the creatures.

'But what about you? What are you going to do?'

Then they were told that Ingegerd had got work as housekeeper at a merchant's house in Stockholm.

Stockholm! That was a great surprise. Those who left Dalsland didn't go there, so far away as it was, almost at the end of the world. Ingegerd laughed and said it was a good deal closer than America, then added that she'd long wanted to go to the capital.

'I want to see the King,' she said. 'Seems right in these bad times.'

She had papers, and all of it was written down clearly.

'Read it carefully now,' she said. ''Tis important you've understood, because I want no family squabbles behind me.'

They read it and signed their names to the settlement.

Ingegerd was hardly out of the door before Hanna started wringing her hands. However were they going to find grazing for all those cows and the handsome horses? Broman said they would probably have to reckon on selling some in Fredrikshald. Ragnar could see to that, for he was a good businessman. Hanna looked miserable, but had to agree when Broman said they needed some ready money.

He reckoned he was going to miss Ingegerd.

★

That autumn they experienced a miracle at the millhouse. The diver called one evening as usual, and suddenly Johanna, sitting on her father's knee, said, 'Listen, listen. Diver.'

Her father and brothers rejoiced, but Hanna exchanged an uneasy look with Anna. She'd never heard of an eight-month-old child who could talk.

'I was terrified,' said Hanna, when the women were alone in the kitchen. 'Does it mean her life's going to be short?'

'No, that's only superstition,' said Anna. But during the autumn she'd thought about that old saying about God loving those who die young. The little girl was an unusually beautiful and clever child.

A few months later, when Johanna took her first steps across the kitchen floor, the two women had to agree in their delight.

'Never seen such a forward child,' said Hanna, torn between fear and pride.

That winter Broman was tired and spent a lot of time in the warmth of the house. But his cough didn't afflict him too badly and he was cheerful.

'Never seen him so happy,' said Hanna.

'Never imagined he had so many tales in him and such a good singing voice,' said Anna.

Johanna laughed as much and as often as Ragnar had, and Hanna thought it strange that the children she'd borne with the greatest pain were the sunniest of the lot.

CHAPTER 25

'Once upon a time there was a poor peasant woman who had a child. But no one would take the child to the priest, because, you see, they were so poor, people thought it shameful to have anything to do with them. So the peasant himself had to take the child to the priest.'

John was telling Johanna the tale of the peasant and Death in his broadest country accents. She kept asking him to tell it over and over again, so that in the end she knew it so well that if he changed a word or skipped a bit she at once corrected him.

'She can't understand that peculiar story,' said Hanna.

'She must do. She's always asking for it,' said Broman. He laughed when he remembered the first time he'd told Hanna the story about Death. She had been so taken by it, she'd dropped the kettle at the moment when the peasant was walking along the road and met God himself, and God asked to go with him to the priest. But the peasant had said, 'I don't think I want to have anything to do with you, for you're such an unjust Father. Some people you give a lot to, others so little, and to me you've given nothing. Nay, be off with you.'

It had caused a great stir when Hanna had dropped the kettle, then had to get down on her hands and knees to mop up the water. All the time she was wiping and wringing out the cloth, she kept laughing.

John was laughing, too.

'And then,' said Johanna, her eyes shining, 'then he met the Devil.'

'Yes, Satan himself, and he, too, asked if he could go with the peasant to the priest. "Nay, nay," said the peasant. "I'll not get myself caught in your claws. Nay, be off with you."'

'And then,' said Johanna, 'he met Death himself!'

'Yes, and Death asked if he could go along with the peasant to the priest. And, you know, he was allowed to, because the peasant considered Death a good man. "At least you're the same to everyone, whether rich or poor," said the peasant.'

John expanded on the story, making a detour through the forest until the peasant and Death were brought before the priest and they had the child baptised.

'Now comes the wonderful bit,' said Johanna. And it did, for Death invited the peasant back to his home.

'"Come back home with me and you'll see how fine it is."

'When they got to Death's house, the peasant was dazzled. For so many candles were burning there, one for every living person on earth. And one for the peasant's new child as well.'

'Wait, Father, wait,' whispered Johanna, for she wanted to stay on at Death's house to look for her own candle to make sure it was tall and burning steadily. Her mother's candle was fine, too. But she couldn't find her father's.

The fairy-tale ended with Death taking the peasant into his service and teaching him first how to cure people and then when to tell people that it wasn't worth extending life further. The peasant became famous and rich and lived well right up until his own candle burned down and went out.

'In Death's house,' said Johanna, shuddering with delight.

CHAPTER 26

'I think you should go,' John said to Hanna. 'No one knows when you'll see each other again, you and Astrid.'

'Is it that bad?'

'Yes. Take the girl with you, for she's something to show.'

Hanna nodded. What he'd said was so true.

Ragnar was home on a short visit before going back to Fredrikshald for the last time to say goodbye and pack his things. From Fredrikshald he was to go to Vänersborg, where he would be recruited into the Västergöt-Dals regiment for his twelve months of military service.

He was glad to be leaving Norway. It was now May 1905 and the Norwegian government had resigned. As the King in Stockholm had refused to approve it, Parliament had stated that as far as Norway was concerned, royal power no longer held good and the Union was dissolved. In Sweden that was called revolution. The Norwegians reinforced their border defences.

John Broman read in the papers that the Swedish people were full of righteous anger. But here in the border areas, they were terrified of what might happen, although there were some malicious comments about those loud-mouthed Norwegians.

Hanna hadn't taken seriously much of the talk about the Union crisis. As usual she had enough to do with her everyday troubles, but when she saw soldiers all over the place at the border and in Fredrikshald, she was frightened. Even more frightening was Astrid flapping round like a captive bird, far too nervous to sit still and talk. Relations between her and her husband were bad. He had come to hate everything about Swedes.

'Maybe I'll go back with you,' Astrid said to Hanna.

'Nonsense,' said Henriksen. 'You're Norwegian now and your home is Norway. If you're afraid of war, then you're safer on this side.' He was curt and unfriendly to Ragnar, but he took his sister-in-law and her little girl to Fredriksten fortress to show them how impregnable it was.

'That's where we shot him, the damned Swede,' he said.

Their visit lasted only two days. As they crossed the border, Hanna heaved a sigh of relief and said to Ragnar, 'Can't make out how you stuck it.'

'It hasn't been easy.'

To her surprise, Hanna noticed he was blushing.

Ragnar had a brief talk with John Broman before going on south to Vänersborg.

'Father, you must get the cave in order.'

But John shook his head.

In August, Ragnar came home on his first leave. Negotiations were going on in Karlstad and the Swedes were demanding that the Norwegians should demolish not only the defences along the border, but also the old forts of Kongsvinger and Fredriksten.

'They're insane,' said Ragnar. He was able to tell them that other countries agreed with Norway, that England had said that the country should be recognised, and that Russia and France had stated that they 'highly disapproved' of the demands made by Sweden regarding the two forts.

That was when he got his family away to the cave.

Only a few weeks later, agreement was reached in Karlstad. The border forts disappeared, people on both sides sighed with relief, and

Broman's conservative newspaper quoted what Hjalmar Branting had already said in the *Social-Democrat* in the spring: 'On 27 May 1905, the Royal Union between Norway and Sweden died at the age of ninety years six months. All that remains is the funeral and the inventory. We must part in peace like brothers.'

'We should've taken the *Social-Democrat*, then we'd've had a more peaceful summer,' John said to Hanna.

'You're mad! People would think we were socialists.'

'Well, for me, that isn't far wrong.'

Hanna stared at her husband before she could bring herself to speak.

'So you both renounce God and would kill the King!'

'Where do you get all that nonsense from?' laughed John.

Johanna was sitting on the floor with her doll. She was always to remember that exchange of words.

CHAPTER 27

John Broman was not the only one to spend all his free time on the girl. Old Anna also took care of her, taught her women's things and told her all the strange local tales.

So as a result there was little room for Hanna in her daughter's life. All that was left for Hanna was to teach the girl to behave and obey. Johanna did both willingly, but there was no intimacy between them.

Johanna was five when she learned to read and write. When Hanna found out, she was very angry. What would people say? She knew how tongues wagged when it came to anything different and precocious. And what would the teacher do with her when she went to school?

Broman told her to be quiet. But he realised there was something in what his wife had said. As he was on a friendly footing with the new teacher, he went to see her and explained about Johanna.

The teacher was still young enough to believe in her work. She just laughed and said having a girl who could read would be a pleasing problem. She was a good enough teacher to be able to keep the child occupied while she hammered the alphabet into the beginners.

'She can draw and paint,' she said. 'And I'll look out some books she can read for herself in school hours.'

John was pleased. But neither he nor the teacher had reckoned with the other children. Johanna had a bad time, was ignored and disliked, so exposed to bullying. The talk also got round, just as Hanna had predicted.

But the little girl said nothing about the torments of school. Mother would be angry and she could bear that, but Father mustn't be sad.

When Johanna was just seven, old Anna died. Death came peacefully. She had had a pain in her chest, and one Saturday evening Hanna saw her concocting some medicine to relieve it. Hanna watched with some surprise as she mixed large quantities of belladonna and henbane in the drink.

'Don't you go taking too much, will you?'

'I know what I'm doing,' the old woman said.

In the morning, they found her dead. White and rigid, Hanna stood by the bed, the boys sobbing and snivelling. John Broman's eyes were glistening and grave as he stood with Johanna in his arms.

'She's gone to God, now,' the child whispered, and John nodded, glancing sternly at Hanna, afraid she might take the consolation away from their daughter. Hanna didn't notice; her mind was full of strange thoughts. But she said not a word to anyone about the drink the old woman had made the night before.

One day in the thaw, the millhouse family experienced an event not one of them ever forgot. They were at their midday meal when Broman suddenly crashed his fist down on the table and roared, 'Quiet!' In the silence that followed, they could hear a rumbling, growling, screeching sound. John and the boys rushed out, fearful of what might have happened at the mill.

The sluice gate!

But there was nothing wrong with the dam. They just stood there, but then realised that all the noise was coming from far away down the road.

It was getting closer.

Hanna took the terrified Johanna into her arms and thought about the Devil himself, the one who came on the Day of Judgement in his chariot of fire to take the wicked to hell.

It was a kind of fiery chariot. They could see that as the monstrosity came roaring over the crest of the hill as fast as if shot from a cannon. But it wasn't the Devil at the wheel, but Ragnar. He drove straight in and braked with the screeching and tooting of a madman.

Then it fell silent and they all stood there, eyes wide and mouths open. Never had it been so quiet at Norskvattnet until that moment.

'An automobile!' said Broman. 'The little devil has got himself an automobile!'

Then he started laughing, and when Ragnar climbed down from the monstrosity, both father and son laughed and laughed until tears rolled down their cheeks.

In the end, Ragnar collected himself sufficiently to be able to speak. 'Now, Mamma, I want something inside me. I'm as hungry as a lion.'

Hanna took her trembling legs back inside to heat up the cooling food while the brothers buzzed like bees round the vehicle.

'Did you buy it with your own money?' said Broman.

'Yes. Saved up every *riksdal* since I started working for the fish merchant. And everything I've earned building in Göteborg. Then I got my inheritance. It's going to earn my living now.'

John didn't dare ask what it cost. A thousand? Several thousand?

Ragnar ate and explained, his mouth full, but Hanna didn't dare say anything about table manners. The town at the mouth of the river Göta was growing. Fredrikshald was nothing but a country village in comparison with the city by the sea. There were lots of people building houses and factories there, but there was a shortage of timber and tiles and bricks.

'Transport didn't keep up with development,' he said. Horses and carts blocked the roads. The motor vehicle was the solution. He could get as much work as he liked.

Hanna understood most of what he was saying, but the question wouldn't leave her. What on earth kind of language was he talking?

In the end, she asked, and Ragnar laughed again.

'Swedish, Mother. I've at last learned to speak Swedish.'

'You sound like it is in books,' said Johanna, profoundly impressed.

Ragnar decided they should go on an outing that afternoon. They had to take some old straw mattresses and make themselves comfortable on the open back.

'Mother can sit in the cabin with Johanna on her lap.'

But by this time Hanna had become herself again.

'Never, never will you get me into that monster. Not my girl, either.'

So it was John who got up into the cabin, while the brothers clambered up on to the back. Johanna forced back her tears, but Ragnar noticed and whispered in her ear, 'Another day, girl. I won't leave until you've had your ride.'

When they were back after an hour or so, they never stopped talking, all at once, about how people's jaws had dropped in amazement, and how the old women had screamed in terror, the children with delight. Alvar Alvarsson had raised his cap when Broman got out to fetch his newspaper, and the priest himself had come up to inspect the vehicle.

'I knew it'd come, even to these remote places,' he'd said. 'But I'd no idea it'd come so soon.'

It was clear all this pleased Hanna. And when Ragnar said that she and Johanna must go out in it with him tomorrow, she said, 'I'm no worse a person if I can change my mind.'

CHAPTER 28

The spring of 1910 came kindly and early to Dalsland, not the usual kind of spring with its great strides and changes of mind. No, it crept in so cautiously that not even the blue anemones felt the cold.

The starlings came early and found their home in the north friendlier than usual. It rained, the sun shone and white wood anemones replaced the blue ones. One May morning, the maples flowered and Norskvattnet was enveloped in the scent of honey.

John Broman was wearier than usual as he roamed the forest with his daughter. But it was his body that was weary, not his mind, which had never before been so clear.

Together, he and Johanna watched the migrant birds arriving and occupying their old places. By the time the swallows had built their clay nests on the ridges of Wolf Mountain, the diver already had a clutch of eggs and the peregrine falcon chicks had hatched.

He was happy, and the girl lodged that in her memory.

That was the spring when Johanna became religious. She was to remain so, even when she became a socialist.

Not until the summer did John draw any conclusion from the strange state of exhilaration he found himself in, life and death confronting each other within him. He imagined them drinking together like good friends, for the feeling spreading through him was like the slight intoxication felt from that first drink.

Once he'd understood what was happening, as he sat by the stream watching Johanna slaking her thirst in the rippling water, he wasn't afraid. He was relieved. And sorrowful. But not with the weighty kind of sorrow. It was blue like melancholy, just what gave the world depth.

In the following weeks, he often tried to summarise it. Occasionally he got as far as that life had been good to him and that he had largely done as he should have done. On other days, the final reckoning frightened him. Full of remorse, he thought about the mother he hadn't seen for twenty years, and about the sons he had neglected and pressed into work far too hard for their growing bodies.

Then there was Johanna, the girl scampering round him on the forest tracks and along the lakes. Perhaps his love had been selfish and the child was badly equipped for a hard life?

Johanna, now eight, was exactly the same age as his first daughter had been when she had died. This little girl would live, well fed and healthy as she was.

Thanks to Hanna.

He thought about Hanna. Surprised, he realised his wife was the only one to whom he did not stand in debt. Not that he had been a thoroughly good husband, no, things had probably happened that he regretted, but he was exonerated from any blame for there were no reproaches in her.

He pondered on that for a long time and came to the conclusion that anyone expecting injustice does not collect injustices.

Then, of course, there were all the worldly things that had to be arranged, and for that he could rely on Ragnar. The mill was worth quite a lot, although it was mostly silent now farms were being abandoned all round them, but John had had a surprising offer.

Then there was his inheritance from Värmland.

He was suddenly struck by a certainty that his mother would die as soon as she heard he had gone.

He must write to Ragnar. They needed to have a long and clarifying talk before it was too late.

How long had he got?

Ragnar came at the end of July, and he had a woman with him in the van, city-pale and shy.

'A shilly-shallier,' Hanna said.

But Johanna said Lisa was nice.

'She's got a haberdashery shop in Göteborg, so whatever she looks like, she can't be,' Hanna said to John. And John had seen from the start that Lisa's submissiveness was for Ragnar alone, and that she was one of those poor wretches who loved too much.

'Take care, Hanna,' he said, 'that you don't become a shrewish mother-in-law.'

John had put the upstairs room in order, pulled out the drop-leaf table and assembled all his papers. He'd told his wife he'd asked Ragnar to come and help him draw up a will, and that he wanted her to be there to go through everything. When he saw her eyes darkening, he tried to calm her. Every husband gone sixty-five had to do that.

She hadn't answered, her hand stubbornly covering her mouth, then she had turned and gone stiffly down the stairs.

She knows, he thought.

Hanna said little as Broman, Ragnar and she sat round the table for a whole afternoon, not even when Ragnar said that if the worst should happen, Mother and the children would have to move to Göteborg.

'What do you think, Mother?'

'I'll have to think about it.'

'There's no future for the boys here,' Broman said. 'They can't make a living out of the mill, you know that. And I don't want you to stay here alone in the wilderness.'

'Can't you try to live a bit longer?' she said, but at once regretted saying it. Ragnar stared at his stepfather. At that moment, it was clear to him that Broman would be gone before winter, and his cough had set in.

That stuck in Ragnar's throat.

But Broman went on as if nothing had been said. This was the moment to mention the offer.

The previous autumn, when Hanna had been in the forest picking lingonberries, an engineer from the electricity company in Ed had come to see him in Norskvattnet. He had stood for a long time by the falls, and had even asked John to open the sluice gate. Then he'd said he might buy the place. Five thousand *riksdaler* they would pay. Cash.

'Why've you not said anything?'

'Didn't want to worry you.'

Hanna was silent. Ragnar said he should contact the company in Ed, his tone revealing that he was relieved.

Then there was the Värmland business. John didn't know how much the farm might be worth.

'It's beginning to be a wasteland up there, like here,' he said. 'But Mother can't live much longer. She's ninety-eight. Ragnar, you'll have to keep in contact with my sister Alma. She and her husband are honest folk and they won't cheat you of your inheritance.'

He said nothing about knowing that his mother would give up the ghost as soon as she got the message to say her son was dead.

The next morning, Ragnar wrote out the will with an unaccustomed hand and poor spelling, for it was only the spoken word he found easy.

'We'll have to ask Lisa to write it out properly,' he said, and his parents nodded. Broman hesitated, but finally plucked up the courage to ask if a marriage was in the offing. Ragnar blushed and said things were probably heading in that direction.

Even Hanna had to admit the will looked very fine and that Lisa wrote like a priest. The blacksmith was summoned to witness the will with Lisa.

When Lisa was packing the van that afternoon, she noticed Ragnar standing there holding both his father's hands in his for a long time. John was bright-eyed and Ragnar weeping. Hanna was also looking at the two of them, remembering that day many years ago when the strange miller had held out his hand to her bastard child and said, 'Good-day, my name's John Broman.'

Just as the first autumn storms were ripping the leaves off the trees, John Broman coughed his last.

CHAPTER 29

It was the first and only time the child at Norskvattnet ever saw her mother cry. Hanna herself was surprised. She'd never imagined there

116

was so much water in her head, she said. She sobbed and wept for days and nights as she made all the arrangements for the funeral.

No one gave a thought to Johanna, who was going around in a strange way, feeling horribly cold.

'Hurry now, girl,' Hanna might cry when something was to be done. Only occasionally did she notice the girl was cold and feeling her hands, said, 'Put your thick jersey on.'

They never noticed the child said not a word.

It was obvious the moment Ragnar arrived.

'Johanna's gone dumb!' he cried. 'Haven't you noticed, Mother?'

Hanna was ashamed. Ragnar walked around with the girl in his arms, talking, tempting. She grew warmer but showed no desire to see either the lakes, the falls or the big lake, and he could not get her either to weep or to speak.

Indoors, Hanna was baking bun-loaf and cakes, while Lisa laid the table for the funeral meal. Ragnar went straight up to her with the little girl and said, 'Will you try, Lisa?'

Lisa couldn't carry the child, but Johanna took her hand as they walked across to the stable where Broman was lying in his coffin. Hanna was about to call out to them not to, but Ragnar snapped at her, 'Quiet, Mother!'

Lisa drew back the sheet from the dead man's face. 'Johanna,' she said, 'this person lying here isn't your father, only his shell. He's waiting for you in heaven.'

It was enough. Johanna wept in the stranger woman's arms and at last could whisper that she'd thought that, too.

They stood there for a long time. Then Lisa said she wanted Johanna to go back with her to Göteborg as soon as the funeral was over. The two of them would have a good time together while they waited for her mother and brothers to come later.

That is what happened. The day after the funeral, Ragnar drove Lisa and Johanna to the train, then went on to see the engineer in Ed. After that he was to return to his mother and brothers.

'To clear up the worst,' he said.

At Ed things went better than expected and the sale was to be completed by the spring. As Ragnar drove his wretched old vehicle northwards along the lake, he felt satisfied. But, most of all, he was thinking that now he understood what Broman had said at their farewell. 'You must promise me to take care of Johanna. You see, she's of a different kind.'

On the train, Johanna sat on Lisa's knee thinking that this terrible new life of hers was beginning right there in this carriage, rushing through the darkness and hooting like a monster.

The morning after John's death, Hanna had already sent Erik with a message to Alma in Värmland. He returned home wide-eyed as he described how magnificent Brogården was with its many fields and extensive grazing lands.

John had never said anything about that, Hanna thought. But, then, neither had she asked.

On the same evening that Ragnar left, there was a knock on the door and there stood a man she had never seen before, a Värmlander who said he was Alma's son-in-law. He had brought a message to say that the old lady of Brogården had died on the Sunday. Could they come to the funeral?

Hanna fried pork and put out bread while the stranger stabled his horse in the barn. Erik lit the stove in the attic room and Hanna warmed bedclothes for her guest. The next morning, she told him that she was going to send her two older sons to the funeral. She had no place there, she said.

The man nodded as if he understood and they parted friends.

After he'd gone, Hanna sat for a long time on the bench in the kitchen, thinking how amazing it was that the old woman had died on the very day a week after her son.

CHAPTER 30

On Wednesday, 22 April 1911, Hanna went to the neighbouring farm to say goodbye to the relatives who had moved in from

Norway during the Union crisis. With her she had the cows, the pig and five sheep. It was a dismal walk and it did not help much that the Olssons at Kasa paid honestly for the creatures.

From Kasa, she went on to the priest to get the moving certificate to Haga parish in Göteborg for herself and her four children. They exchanged a few words and as she was saying goodbye, she thought that the priest had shrunk since, to everyone's surprise, he had stopped drinking.

Last of all, she went to the forge. The smith and his wife were old now and had received the news about the power station with dismay. Hanna kept the visit as short as possible, but as she was leaving she said a few things would be left behind, things not going to Göteborg. She would put them in the store shed and they could take anything they could use.

The blacksmith's wife's eyes brightened, covetously and inquisitively, so as Hanna crossed the yard to the millhouse, she decided to make sure there wouldn't be much left for Malin. But then she remembered Ragnar's words: 'None of that old rubbish in the load. Just bring the bare essentials.'

That remark stayed with Hanna so clearly that she didn't grieve over her departure from Norskvattnet or worry about the future. What, in heaven's name, was all this she'd collected over the years?

She flung out all the rag rugs, Broman's clothes and the two box-beds in the kitchen, though she was to regret the latter.

She was to take the Värmland furniture with her. If he says a word about the best sofa, I'll have something to say to him, she thought.

But when Ragnar arrived, all he said was, 'It'll be difficult to find room for the sofa, Mamma. But maybe you could sell it and get a good sum for it.'

When everything was loaded and lashed on to the back, and the boys had made themselves as comfortable as possible, Hanna stood for a while in the yard, looking at the house, the falls and the long lake. Then she sighed heavily. As she took her place beside Ragnar in the cabin, she was sobbing.

'Not crying, are you, Mamma?'

'Course not,' said Hanna, the tears pouring down.

'We'll come back on a visit in a few years.'

'No, boy, I'll never come back here.'

After they'd gone quite a way, she asked after Johanna and how she was getting on in the city with Lisa.

'She's not as cheerful as before. But she's so fond of Lisa.'

'Can imagine that,' said Hanna briefly.

They said nothing for the rest of the winding road along the lake to Ed. When the church tower appeared, Hanna said, 'When're you getting married, you and Lisa?'

He flushed and his voice was cold when he answered. 'Mind your own business.'

That made Hanna angry. 'Hasn't a mother the right to know when her child is to marry?'

Ragnar was already regretting his remark, but said, 'It's different in the city, Mamma. They don't mind so much about when people who like each other live together without marrying.'

'Terrible lot I've to learn,' said Hanna, in astonishment.

'Mm, you'll probably have to relearn most things, Mamma.'

They left Ed and then Hanna was in unknown country. She had never been further than this. At Vänersborg, they stopped for a rest and ate the sandwiches they had brought with them. Hanna stared out across Lake Vänern and could see where the water met the sky, far away.

'Is that the sea?'

'No, Mamma. The sea's much bigger than that.'

He laughed at her, so she didn't ask any more questions. But she found it difficult to understand how any waters could be bigger than this. She said nothing all the way through the valley and didn't even answer when he said wasn't this lovely countryside, this too.

Not until they drove into the stone city did she get her voice back. 'I'd never even dreamed of anything like this.'

They inched their way between horse-drawn carts, people and

motor vehicles up to Järntorget. To impress his mother and brothers, he took a long, roundabout route to get to Haga.

'Is it market day as there's so many people?'

'No, it's always like this.'

'Heavens,' said Hanna, exhilarated rather than frightened, and when they finally drove in through an entrance gateway to the great building, she was glowing like the sun. 'So ... so grand,' she said. 'Where are we going to live?'

'Up there,' he said, pointing.

Towards the sky, she thought.

'Three floors up, with a view over the street,' he said proudly. 'Lisa's put up new curtains for you to hide behind.'

'That's very kind,' said Hanna, who'd been worried about curtains. The next moment, Johanna came running out of one of the many doors.

Hanna stood gazing at the girl, thinking, My girl, my girl. Then she said, 'How fine you look.'

'I've got new clothes, town clothes. Lisa made them.'

Hanna did not look pleased, but made an effort to think that she must learn to like her, that kind creature.

Inquisitive eyes were staring at them from windows and entrance porches as they carried up the furniture. We look countrified, Hanna thought with shame, wishing herself out of their sight. Yet she had to ask what kind of little houses they were under the chestnut trees on the great courtyard.

'They're privies and sheds. Each family's got its own key.'

'Mercy, how grand!'

You stepped straight into the kitchen and it was a fine kitchen with an iron stove, the kind Hanna had admired at Astrid's in Fredrikshald. Then there was a sink unit, drain and water. Hanna had heard about that amazing thing, running water, and now she stood there turning the tap on and off.

'Doesn't it ever run out?'

'No, Mamma, it never runs out.'

'Mercy me!'

There was a tiled stove in the living room and shiny pine floorboards, real gentry stuff, Hanna thought.

What was most amazing of all, and they were to talk and laugh about it for many years to come, was the light. Fortunately Hanna wasn't the one to make a fool of herself this time, but John.

'Getting dark, Mother. I'll run down and fetch the oil-lamp.'

'No,' said Johanna. 'Look – all you do is this.' She turned the switch on the wall inside the kitchen door and the light flooded down on them.

Once Hanna had recovered from her surprise, she was pleased that Ragnar hadn't seen her standing there with her mouth open. He'd gone out to buy food and fetch Lisa. They brought hot soup Lisa had made and bread and butter Ragnar had bought.

'Welcome to town,' said Lisa.

'You're kind,' said Hanna. 'Thank you for the curtains. And for looking after the girl so well.'

Lisa said it had been nothing but fun. 'Tomorrow we'll go and get some new clothes for you, too, Mother-in-Law.'

'I'll be needing all the help I can get,' said Hanna to Lisa, who didn't really understand what an incredible remark that was.

But the sons were scared. They'd never heard their mother ever say anything like it.

So they settled into a one-roomer and kitchen in the great block. The boys were given a pull-out sofa in the main room and August a modern folding bed that could be put away in the wardrobe.

A large round table stood in the middle of the room; it, too, was modern, and went well with the old chairs from Värmland, Hanna thought.

Hanna and Johanna slept in the kitchen. That was where the box-bed from Dalsland would have been of use, but Hanna consoled herself that the new kitchen sofa was also modern.

'An awful lot of money's slipping through my fingers,' Hanna said to Ragnar.

'You can afford it, Mamma,' he said comfortingly.

Once all was ready, Hanna invited the neighbouring housewives in for coffee and a horribly expensive shop cream cake. That was usual, Lisa had said. Hanna had on a new bought dress. Modern. They were people of all kinds, lamenting when she told them she'd just been widowed, and making no comments on her odd speech.

'You're from Norway?'

'Not quite,' said Hanna. 'We're Swedish, all right, but we lived right on the border. My father was from Norway and my sister is Norwegian.'

Hulda Andersson lived on the same hallway and was not unlike Hanna in her ways. The two of them were soon on good terms. The day after the party, Hulda said, 'Are you rich or do you have to work?'

'Of course I have to work.'

'They need people at Asklund's steam bakery in Risåsgatan. I work there myself. Can you bake?'

Hanna gave a great laugh and said that if there's anything you learn as a miller's wife, it's to bake.

CHAPTER 31

That was how Hanna became a bakery worker, heavy work, every day starting at four o'clock in the morning. But that was good, for she finished work at two, so had plenty of time to look after the home.

On May Day, she stood in Järntorget watching the red flags fluttering above the marching people singing ... Rise, ye slaves ...

Hanna was afraid.

'They're mad,' she said to Hulda. Hulda agreed.

Even more frightening was one morning when the two bakery women were crossing the market square and met some dolled-up females with their mouths painted red.

'What kind of people are they?'

'Whores,' said Hulda. 'Sell themselves to seamen in the harbour. They're on their way home.'

Quite a long time went by before Hanna could bring herself to say anything. 'D'you mean they have a different man every night?'

'Oh, no, they have to have several, otherwise they can't make ends meet.'

Hanna was speechless, her head quite empty.

But what made the greatest impression during those early days was the man who employed her at the bakery. Not that he was unpleasant, just supercilious, and he had a right to be that, fine gentleman that he was.

'What's your name?'

Hanna hesitated for a while before answering. 'Hanna, Lovisa, Greta … Broman.'

'Married?'

'But my husband's dead.'

'Widow, then,' said the man, noting it down.

'Date of birth?'

She was silent. She'd never heard anything so silly. He had to repeat it.

'When and where were you born, woman?'

She knew both year and parish, and then she had the job, was given a white coat and put to making plaited wreath-shaped wheaten loaves. That she did, and the foreman looked satisfied.

She soon came to enjoy the warmth and the women's chatter in the big bakery, where the gossip started the moment the foreman had left. There were many women like her there, farming and smallholding wives speaking dialects even cruder than hers, and whose situation was much worse than hers because they had small children at home.

But she never forgot the foreman's questions and repeated them to herself every evening for a long time afterwards. Name, married, born? To her it was as if she'd fallen into a gigantic hollow on Wolf Mountain. Where on earth was she that no one knew she was Hanna

Augustdotter from Bråten, granddaughter of the rich Erik of Framgården and who became the miller's wife at Norskvattnet?

Fortunately she wasn't given to brooding. But many a time over the next few years she had to fend off the feeling of having lost her foothold.

The bakery was as big as a palace and built like a fortress round a large courtyard. All four wings were three floors high, faced with brick and decorated with green soapstone figures. There were departments for the hard crispbread, ordinary bread, another for finer confectionery and the sweet-bread bakery for plaited ring-shaped wheaten loaves and Danish pastries. Finest of all was the big corner shop at street level.

It was an awful lot to take in and she often felt as if there was no room in her head for it all. One day Hulda asked the foreman if she could show Hanna the mill high up in the fortress where there were millers and a whole series of miller's labourers mixing and sifting flour for the different kinds of bread.

'Where do they get power from?' whispered Hanna, and was told about the steam engines growling away day and night and the dynamo turning the energy into electricity.

Broman would've fainted if he'd seen this, Hanna thought.

But most amazing of all was on the third floor, and Hanna was struck dumb. There was one huge dough-kneading machine after another doing all that heavy work done by women before.

They took the lift down, and that scared her, too.

The sons roamed round town doing nothing much and filling the emptiness with strong drink, just as their father had. But their fears were not driven out like that.

Ragnar got them jobs in the building trade, where they were scoffed at for their strange accents and soft miller's hands. They left the jobs and went home for another strengthening drink. When things got so bad that they never even got out of bed all day, Ragnar took them seriously to task. The brothers laughed scornfully at him.

There was a fight and Hanna's fine Värmland chairs were smashed to matchwood.

'Never!' shouted Ragnar. 'I'd never've believed you were so bloody spoilt. Have you no shame? Letting Mother keep you, grown men like you?'

Then he threw them out on to the street, left and locked the apartment door on the outside.

Hanna had never been so frightened as that night when she was locked in and alone in the apartment, trying to clear up after the fight. Ragnar had taken Johanna with him to Lisa. 'The girl's to live with us until you knock some kind of sense into those damned boys of yours.'

When he came back on the Sunday morning, he had calmed down. 'What shall we do, Mamma?'

'You can start by letting me out so I can set about finding out where they are.'

'Go to the police. I expect that's where they are. The police pick up all the drunks around town.'

'Oh, my good Lord,' said Hanna, shaking her head, knowing better than most that the Lord was not good. But she tidied her hair, put on her best dress and new hat, and went to the police station. There they were, behind bars. They had to sign papers before she could get them out.

They were to pay fines.

'If it happens again, it'll be prison,' said the sergeant as they left.

Ragnar eventually took John, the eldest and strongest, with him in the truck.

'Can't afford to pay much,' he said, 'but if you drink on the job, I'll kill you.'

The other two went to sea. 'They'll teach you how to behave there,' said Ragnar.

Hanna didn't dare protest, but she often whimpered in her sleep in her anxiety over her sons, worries that followed her for a whole long year. But they survived, returned home, coarser, heavier and more serious. They got steady work, married eventually and drank only at weekends.

Hanna's life had become lonely, for Johanna spent most of her time with Lisa. John was indeed still living at home, but they exchanged few words. She had her friend across the hallway, and to Hulda she said that if she hadn't had her, she would've gone mad.

But she never became intimate with Lisa, although she did have one opportunity to thank her daughter-in-law for her help, this daughter-in-law who wasn't really a daughter-in-law because Ragnar refused to marry.

Lisa was with child and came to see her mother-in-law in her distress. Hanna undertook to speak to Ragnar. What she said during their long talk in the kitchen no one ever knew, but it must have been about bastards and the awfulness of condemning your own child to a life of shame.

Anyhow, Ragnar said to Lisa that they might as well get married. 'But you'll have to take me for what I am and you know I'm not to be relied on when it comes to women.'

Lisa was grateful.

CHAPTER 32

Hanna grieved over her lovely chairs but, with Hulda's help, managed to install her sofa. There wasn't really room for it, but both she and Hulda thought it was rather grand.

When her sons came home, they simply flung their filthy clothing on to the silk-covered sofa, making Hanna moan and scold Johanna for not picking things up after her brothers. Johanna grew more and more silent, but Hanna didn't notice, closing her eyes to the fact that there was little comfort in the home with all these quarrels and drinking every weekend. Her back was aching.

The ache spread from her shoulder blades down her spine. At first she thought it would pass, but then she heard that most of the women at the bakery suffered from the same affliction. And that it only grew worse.

You had to endure it, they told her. Not a word to the foreman, for then they would lose their jobs.

Lisa had given birth to a son and, amazingly, Ragnar was so delighted with his boy that he spent all his free time at home, so he had less and less time for his mother and brothers and sister.

The years went by slowly. The First World War broke out and the shortage of food was acute. In Haga, there were hunger riots and police and soldiers were brought in. People screamed their hatred at the Queen, who was German and was accused of smuggling food out of Sweden to give to the mad Kaiser. Hanna bit back the pain in her spine and gave thanks for her work at the bakery. She could take out her wages in bread so she and her children did not starve. Then the Spanish flu came, and again Hanna was grateful that none of her family caught the terrible disease.

Johanna had left school and was able to help with their keep. It was quieter now that the boys had left home, and more orderly. But Hanna and Johanna did not get on well together. The girl was insolent and uppity, not good and submissive like the sons. She reprimanded her mother for being stupid and uneducated, correcting her speech and telling her to shed her superstitions and begin to think. At first Hanna tried to defend herself with words. But Johanna had so many more words than she had, and a much clearer mind.

She's always been cleverer than the others, Hanna thought.

When Johanna joined the Social Democrats' May Day procession, Hanna almost died of shame.

'Have you gone out of your mind?' she cried.

'You wouldn't know for you've never had one,' the girl retorted.

Hanna's bad back got worse over the years. She grew bent and could only move heavily, but she stuck it until pension age, when for the first time in her life she was able to rest. She had definite views on the old-age pension that came every month. It was shameful to get money not honestly earned, she said to Johanna. But only once, for the girl was so angry that Hanna was frightened.

Johanna married. Hulda Andersson died.

Hanna had so many grandchildren, she couldn't tell them apart. The only one she recognised was Johanna's horrible girl, a child with strong eyes that stared accusingly and looked right through people. She was badly brought up and plain, thin in body and hair.

In the 1940s, an apartment block for pensioners was built in Kungsladugård and Johanna arranged for Hanna to have a modern one-roomer there. Hanna reckoned she had come to paradise, for she had a bathroom with a WC, hot water and central heating.

'What, in heaven's name, shall I do when I don't even have to light a fire?'

'Rest, Mother, rest.'

Hanna rested and, strangely enough, never disliked it. She could read, but had such difficulty with her letters that she never grasped what it was all about. Sometimes she listened to the radio, but both the talk and the music irritated her.

On the other hand, she loved going to films, what she called the cinematograph. Her sons often took her with them when they had time to go, her daughter more rarely. Johanna did not approve, and was ashamed of her mother's loud laughter at bad films. And it was really painful when men kissed women on the screen, for Hanna just covered her eyes and cried out loudly, 'Shame on you!'

The audience laughed at her. Didn't she notice? No, Johanna reckoned.

Over the years, Hanna grew very fat. After a long battle, Johanna got her to a doctor, who talked about a stomach ailment that was easy to operate on. His talk frightened Hanna to death: she was just as afraid of the knife as she was of the hospital. After the visit to the doctor, Johanna had to promise to look after her at home when the time came for her to die. 'I won't be any trouble to you.'

'I'm sure it'll be all right, Mother dear.'

When August committed suicide, her grief almost put paid to her and she aged ten years in a month.

But she was crystal clear in her head up until her death at over ninety. A week later, to the very day, Ragnar died on an elk hunt in Halland.

Accidentally shot, just like his father.

But there was no longer anyone who could remember Rickard Joelsson and his death in the days when the peasants of Trysil hunted bears in the forests of Dalsland.

Anna

INTERLUDE

CHAPTER 33

Anna was in her study with the fat blue notebook in front of her. On the front she had written JOHANNA, and on the fly-leaf, 'Try to chart what attitude to take to your mother without denying her riches or sacrificing yourself.'

She now thought that rather pretentious.

On the first page there were a few scattered, disconnected notes. The rest was empty, page after page of unwritten whiteness. I'm not there yet, she thought. Haven't arrived.

So she went back to the grey book, a hundred A4 pages, full, stuffed with loose notes, letters, newspaper cuttings. On the cover she had written HANNA.

Grandmother.

She had started in the parish registers in Dalsland, that alone an adventure, seeing the old family branching all over the landscape, into Norway, down to Göteborg, across to America. Then she had roamed along the shores of the long lake and attempted to make herself receptive to secrets in the unfathomably beautiful landscape.

Once back home, she had gone searching in libraries and second-hand bookshops. She had read ethnology and wept for Grandmother, the woman already a whore as a child. She had found the rune-master and his troll wife in an old newspaper cutting, astonished by how long heathendom had survived in distant border communities. She had looked at the economic history of the area and tried to grasp what the parish registers told her, that Grandmother's four older siblings had died of starvation during the famine.

She came across a number of local history books from the parishes round the lake. Old people wrote in them about Sundays and weekends, and weekdays that followed the seasons, not the clock. In them she read stories of ordinary people, but more often about unusual people, the kind long remembered in communities. There was a light serenity in the memories of bad times, and great melancholy over what had been lost for ever.

She sat by the big window in her study, ten floors up, looking out over the new world spread out below. It was autumn, grey light over a colourless world. Here and there a few pines had been left standing between the buildings, like toy trees carelessly flung there by children tired of playing with their building bricks.

Her view brought with it noise, for the motorway ran close to the high-rises.

Hanna first became flesh and blood after Anna had burgled a chest in the attic of her parents' home. There she had found what Grandmother had left, papers, inventories, copies of wills, announcements of births and deaths, and also whole bundles of yellowed letters from relatives in America, Norway and Göteborg.

Innocent letters, most of them, written in fine handwriting. Not a word about injustices, hunger or shame. The letter-writers kept themselves inside the limits of the world in which they had grown up and which they had never left, even if they had lived for decades in Minnesota.

Anna had taken out some of the letters and put them between the pages of her notebook. She took one out now, read it again and for the first time thought that the letters in their way were true. They reflected a reality in which bitterness and ingratitude were not admitted, so didn't exist.

Only the letters from Astrid in Halden and Oslo were different, written in large, meandering handwriting, full of ideas, thoughts and gossip. A gold mine, a personal testimony. Anna understood all too well that Astrid was no true witness, but more of a writer, and it was a writer's view and truth Anna needed.

Had her mother gone through Hanna's letters when she had inherited the collection? Anna didn't think so. She was like me, troubled by the family.

Anna had always known that Uncle Ragnar had had another father. The parish registers confirmed it in their crude language. 'Ill.', it said. 'Father unknown'. What it was like to be illegitimate, a bastard or, for that matter, a single mother and whore, her research in ethnology had taught her.

Hanna had been thirteen when she gave birth. When Anna had worked that out, she had wept with compassion and rage.

You must have been strong. As Mother said.

Anna had a great many memories of Uncle Ragnar. She thought of him as a king in a fairy-tale, handsome and huge right into old age, exotic and extravagant. She remembered his smile that began as a glint in his dark eyes, continued downwards and creased his brown face on its way to his mouth below the clipped moustache.

'He'd melt hearts of stone,' Mother said.

'You mean hearts of women,' said Father.

Now and again, and always surprisingly, Anna's amazing uncle would come tearing up in his great lorry, which was as overwhelming as he himself. 'Now, little sis, on with the coffee.' She remembered his great laugh rolling through the house, frightening and delighting. And she remembered what he smelt of, sweat, tobacco and beer.

And money, warm silver coins. She often sat on his knee and somehow or other he managed to slip a krona into her hand or pocket, always when Mother wasn't looking. Then he winked with his left eye as a sign that they had a secret together, he and the child.

It was magnificent.

He could also wiggle his ears.

The unknown father's name she had discovered in a letter from America. 'We heard that Rickard Joelsson at Lyckan had been accidentally shot. So he got his punishment in the end, that beast who ruined Hanna's life.'

She had seen a large exclamation mark by the name. Anna's children's father was also called Rickard, him, too. He was no rogue like the Joelsson boy, but had the same unfortunate tendency to become victim of his own power to charm.

Anna sighed.

Then she hunted out the envelope of photographs she'd stolen from the album at home. There he was, Ragnar, like his father Rickard, but so improbably unlike the others in the family. Perhaps Lovisa had allowed herself a wild love with a gypsy boy, perhaps lust had cracked her shell on nights in a deserted house in the forest.

It suddenly struck Anna that there was still a similarity between her own husband and the rapist in Dalsland. They had both had violated mothers, the kind to make their children share their bitterness. They often succeeded with the daughters, who identified themselves with the resentment of their mothers and carried the female anger on through the generations. But what about the sons? No, the strongest refused and became men constantly fleeing from all things emotional and difficult.

Signe, her husband Rickard's mother, was more sophisticated and much wilier than Lovisa at Lyckan. Her husband had found no real reason to kill her, and had chosen to die young. But it had been no easier for young Rickard Hård in the doll's-house apartment in Johanneberg than it had been for Rickard Joelsson at Lyckan.

CHAPTER 34

The clock struck twelve. Now they're feeding Mother.

She took a yoghurt out of the refrigerator and crumbled a slice of crispbread into it. As she ate, her thoughts about Rickard gnawed at her as if she'd opened an old wound that had refused to heal properly.

She thought about the time before their divorce, the worst years when she had cried as soon as she was alone. At first, she hadn't taken those daytime tears seriously, regarding them as self-pity. But when she started crying in her sleep, she was frightened and went to a psychiatrist. A fashionable man.

'You're one of these modern women who castrate their husbands,' he had said.

She had got up then and left.

That was stupid. He had had the last word and so she was to fight him for years.

She put her plate in the dishwasher and determinedly went back to her notes on Hanna. The differences between her and her grandmother were many, just as she'd expected. Hanna accepted, she defied. Hanna was spontaneous, Anna sought expression. Hanna belonged in her hard and unjust world. Anna felt she belonged only for short moments, when she could nod at a tree and say, I know you from somewhere.

They were not even as alike in appearance as Anna had thought. Hanna had been darker and heavier.

Once again she stopped at the description of the rape. Only twelve, it was crazy. How old was I when I was taken by Donald, the American exchange student lured here by rumours of Swedish sinfulness? I must have been over nineteen, my first year at university. And it wasn't rape – though it was, of course, mutual rape, if there is such a thing.

She hadn't given Donald a thought for many years. And yet they had had a long relationship. It had been hard, for they had had excellent opportunities to hurt each other's deepest feelings, even though they neither understood nor knew each other. It was a strange relationship, like kinship.

And, of course, I became pregnant, Grandmother, just like you. I had an abortion, easily arranged in university circles at the time. Nor did I have any second thoughts. My only fear concerned Mother, that she would find out in some way. But I was in Lund and she in Göteborg, so thank heavens she had no idea.

Naturally I thought it was love driving me into Donald's arms. In my generation, we were obsessed with a longing for a grand passion. Hanna, you would've understood nothing whatsoever about love of that kind. In your day, love hadn't penetrated from the upper classes to the depths of peasantry.

There was romantic influence, tragic stories told in country communities. But they had nothing to do with the basis and conditions of life. They were like penny dreadfuls. If Hanna ever

137

listened to cheap folksongs at all, she surely thought Lieutenant Sparre a conceited fool and the tightrope-walker a silly girl. The Älvsborg song would have upset her: 'I have killed a child for you …'

'Heavens, such rubbish! Why didn't you just slit the man's throat?' she would have said.

In the 1920s, great love had also held sway over ordinary people. Johanna considered young people's searching was largely about what she quite seriously called 'finding Mr Right'. That Mr Right in her case was a copy of her dead father, whom she had never known, reinforced the myth but didn't make her life any the less complicated.

And yet Johanna wasn't romantic and consequently not as demanding as the next generation of women were to be.

For Anna and her contemporaries, love was a fact that couldn't be discussed. Woe betide the poor creature not afflicted. Added to that was yet another demand: perfect sexuality. Being in love for life, and constant orgasms.

Then the dreams burst like bubbles in the wind. But change takes time. When people fail in love and the overwhelming desire for it to last a lifetime, they think something is wrong with them. Only now, when every other marriage ends in divorce, have people begun to understand that falling in love seldom grows into love, and that not even love can free a person from loneliness. And that sexual enjoyment does not make life meaningful.

'Jesus, how stupid,' said Anna. And then, a moment later, 'And yet?'

She almost swore when she saw the way she was heading. To Fjärås Bräcka, the ridge they escaped to every free day of that hot summer in the late 1950s. They had nuzzled each other, snuffled, bitten, licked and laughed. In front of them was the sea with its gulls and long salty breakers, behind them the enchanted landscape of lakes, the forest, with its birdsong, that ran steeply down towards it. The way he snuffled, tasted, laughed. The joy, his joy in her body. And his devotion and her gratitude, his gratitude.

He came from the sea, he said, and she believed him, could envisage him as he stepped out of the waves one bright morning with a wreath of seagrass in his hair, his trident carelessly on his shoulder. She came from the forest, he said, finely shaped by wind and rain, as light as the mist rising from the lake. An elf, hidden away in the forests for millions of years, forgetting the language of elves and now with great solemnity trying to learn the language of humans, he said. It was his task to give her substance, turn her into an earthly woman.

'And mine to hold on to the sea god so that he isn't dragged back by the next wave.'

She had laughed, but his eyes had darkened before he closed them, then clasped his hands. 'What are you doing?'

'Praying for the strength not to hurt you.'

Strangely enough, she hadn't asked him whether he was a believer. The moment had seemed too great for that.

Nor had she had the sense to feel uneasy, either.

CHAPTER 35

Hanna's relationship with the mirror had made a profound impression on Anna, who had always had a complicated attitude to her own appearance. She wondered when that had arisen. And how. Whose looks, whose words had given her a lifelong feeling that she was plain, clumsy, almost deformed?

Johanna was beautiful but had the same handicap. Anna had filmed the children when they were small and had plenty of sequences in which her mother had slunk away or covered her face with her hands whenever a camera had been directed at her.

To a thin, uncertain teenage daughter, Johanna had said, 'You're really pretty, my dear. Anyhow, what you look like doesn't matter at all.'

Divided attitude, double message.

When Anna was small, there had been much talk about who in the family a child resembled, though never any discussion about Anna. She was like her grandmother. The child detested the old woman, a wrinkled old witch with sharp features and watery blue eyes. And something gloomy and grandiose about her.

Johanna was afraid of her mother-in-law.

Everyone said her grandmother had been a beauty. Anna couldn't understand that until the old lady had died and photographs from her youth were brought out. Then, even Anna could see that they were right, she had been beautiful and there was a likeness.

But it was too late, the self-image of the plain girl was fixed for ever in her mind.

Of course, when she fell in love in that tempestuous way, Rickard Hård had made her – yes, actually made her – believe she was elf-like. He did that from the very first moment, miraculously, as if he'd touched her with a magic wand.

Though he used to wolf whistle.

In the summers, she went home from Lund, where she had worked hard but had never really liked it. She got a temporary job proof-reading at one of the newspapers in her home town.

She closed her eyes and saw the pleasant shabby premises, heard the clatter of printers and smelt paper, dust, printer's ink and tobacco smoke. On the very first day he was there in the doorway of her room, one of the young reporters, the most lively and the best-looking. He whistled with delight like a street boy, pulled himself together and said, 'Are you a woman or a dream?'

'Probably the latter,' she said, and laughed.

What had he looked like? Tall, craggy, dark, a sensitive face full of life, playful grey eyes. Anna again hunted out the photograph of Uncle Ragnar; perhaps there was a resemblance. In their smile, their kindness. She thought about Astrid, who used to call Ragnar a Sunday's child. Maybe gods were still born on earth, full of life and warmth, light-heartedness and charm. Faithless and sensual as Pan himself.

Anyhow, he at once fell in love, this young god in the grubby newspaper office. Naturally she was so flattered that she soon gave in, and was grateful to the American for what she had learned from him in bed. Everything went quickly, too quickly. Suddenly Rickard was there in their kitchen with Johanna, dispensing warmth, laughter and crazy stories.

When he had said goodbye that first evening, Father said, 'Now, there's a man for you.' Over at the sink, Mother had nodded silently, over and over again. Anna soon saw that she had found Mr Right.

Johanna never changed her mind. It took Anna only a month before she began to waver. 'Mother, everyone says he's a womaniser.'

There was a long silence on the phone before Johanna answered. 'That's a pity, Anna. But I don't think you'll escape.'

As she sat there in her study in Stockholm, remembering and taking notes, she felt annoyed. You should have told me to run away, quick as quick, from that man. Then she had to laugh. Then her mind went quite blank – in surprise.

For she had been thinking just as Hanna would have done.

It was fate.

For a long time she thought about Aunt Lisa, Ragnar's wife, who had found herself and was grateful. She was, after all, one of the first independent women, owner of a business with an income of her own.

But so tired, always tired.

The memory of her own grandmother led her to Rickard's, a frail, unreal old woman, transparent and clear. Anna had met her only once and that was in a nursing home where she was awaiting death. The words were her own.

To Anna, she'd said, 'I hope you're gentle and pliant. A hard woman could turn the boy into a monster.'

'Why is that?'

'I don't know. Perhaps it runs in the family. That's what ... his

141

mother's like. Sometimes boys have to be as hard as flint to survive. And, you know, flint's hard but breaks easily.'

Then she had fallen asleep in that abrupt way old people do, and she died only two weeks later.

How strange I'd forgotten her and what she'd said. How quickly I forgot. For I grew hard in the end.

'You're made of stone, so you'll always manage,' he had said, during a quarrel.

She hadn't been able to bring herself to answer, not then. She'd just screamed, 'You're a quitter.'

It's four o'clock now. They'll be tucking Mother up for the night.

CHAPTER 36

Oh, Mother, what a lot of guilt.

Like when an old sheet with a finely embroidered monogram on it turns up: A.H. in curly letters. Or those towels you made. You'd found such wonderful towelling, you said. It was true. I've still got them and no other towel dries so well or feels so pleasant.

You sewed all my 'bottom drawer' and I laughed at you. You could buy things like that whenever you needed them. I hope you didn't think I was defying or despising you. No doubt you just felt a vague sadness.

Your mirror. You brought it, proud and happy, a mirror for my hall. I was modern, had what was called good taste and liked the simplicity of the day. God, I hope you didn't notice my dismay as we stood there in the hall with that mirror and all its elaborate gilding. My children have it now, the generation that loves curlicues.

I must phone Father soon.

All her life, Hanna kept her faith in what had once been laid down, and she had a deep distrust of anything different, unknown or new. She despised those who sought out secret detours in a world in which everything was measured. An unusual thought, a new idea or an incomprehensible longing threatened her very foundations.

As this obstinate creature grew out of all those notes, Anna was annoyed. How impoverished she had been, how limited.

Then Anna thought that she was like most people, today as well. When our patterns are threatened by new facts, reason is seldom the victor: 'I know what I think, so don't go confusing me with new opinions.' She did that herself, automatically discarding knowledge that didn't match up with her own values. And finding with blind but unerring certainty the information that suited her and justified her actions.

Just as Hanna had done.

But the truths were different today, more substantial, equipped with evidence and supported by science.

Anna was aware, as it was called, of injustices towards women, for instance, which so much of her research was about, that led to bitterness, visible in so many women's faces and heard in their laughter.

'I want to believe in a just world,' she said aloud, to the framed photograph of Hanna on her desk. 'I need to, don't you see? The world must be the kind in which the good are rewarded and the wicked punished. So that everything has some meaning.'

God, how stupid!

Much stupider than your belief in a justice that makes the victims participants in the guilt. In a just world, little girls wouldn't be raped.

And yet, Grandmother, listen to me. It was the dream of the good being possible that built our new society. You were also given a share of it, a pension, hot water, a bathroom.

Human values?

I am always surprised by women's compassion. What use is it? There is a better word: empathy. If the psychologists are to be believed, the individual's ability to empathise depends on how much love the child was given, the way in which it was regarded and loved. But boy children were often loved more than girls, yet grew up into adults who never had to feel other people's torment. Or?

Mother had had endless compassion for the weak, the sick and the wronged. So there it fitted, for Johanna had been exceptionally loved and regarded for a child born around the turn of the century.

Suddenly a new thought, new notes. Was it her father's love that had made Johanna think she had some claims of her own? She had been politically active all her life. She and her generation had based the welfare state on the conviction that justice was possible. And they brought up a generation of disappointed men and women, badly equipped for sorrow and pain, and quite unprepared for death.

CHAPTER 37

Anna looked again at the photograph of Hanna.

You were jubilant when Rickard Joelsson died. I wept when I divorced Rickard Hård. You welcomed joy and became pregnant. I had just had a child when I found out that my husband had had a six-month relationship with a colleague. I wept floods of tears over the new baby's cot. My friends said it was good for me. It wasn't, either for me or the child.

You never cried, not until Grandfather died.

Anna turned back to the account of Hanna and her whore-cloth, something she hadn't been able to understand properly. She knew why. She could feel Hanna's shame on her own skin.

She remembered every single second.

They were at a party in Lidingö given by some newspaper people. She was eight months pregnant and enveloped in a silver lamé tent. White, stiff, wrong. As soon as they all rose from the table, Rickard vanished upstairs with his gypsy-like table partner. Remained absent. The others avoided looking at Anna. She didn't exist, only the shame. She couldn't remember how she managed to get out of the house, only that she had walked along slippery streets until a taxi had appeared and taken her home.

He wanted to talk about it the next day.

She didn't listen.

He always wanted to talk about it, his 'sidestepping', as he called it. She would understand.

But she never listened. She couldn't understand. He wanted forgiveness and she was unable to forgive.

They weren't able to talk to each other for several years after the divorce, and even when they did it was on the wrong day and at an inappropriate time – when he was just about to leave in an hour for Rome, where he had to cover an environmental conference. They must try again. For the sake of the children, he said.

'But you live in the same building as we do,' she said. 'Our children are much better off than children growing up in homes where their parents quarrel.'

'You're always right,' he said. 'That's what's so awful. I hate you for it. You're so damned practical. But I can't cope without you. Do you want me to go down on my knees?'

He never noticed she was crying.

'What you've never grasped is that my silly affairs were only a way of reaching you. But that didn't work, either. You didn't care about my infidelities.'

This raging man, her husband, went on, 'Women like you always give me a feeling of being seen through. That's why I'm frightened when I come near you. Not because of your intelligence, no, something much worse.'

The kind of woman who castrates her husband.

That broke her paralysis.

'But why is it so bad to be seen through and so important to come out on top?'

'I don't know.'

That was when she considered him a victim of the male pattern and not sufficiently stupid to fail to understand it. Unlike Father.

'Anna. There'll be no more of these silly affairs. I promise.'

Then she was able to cry, 'You're an idiot. Your faithlessness killed me, everything that was me, my confidence, my innocence. I died, don't you see? What's left of me is nothing but the witch, the one you're so afraid of.'

She could see that he understood, that at last he had understood. 'Oh, God, oh, God,' he said. Then finally, almost inaudibly, 'Why did you never say so?'

She wept, incapable of answering. Suddenly he was raging, 'You made me treat you badly. It made me hate myself. You just looked on when I failed at what I wanted most of all, and I thought it meant nothing to you.'

'That's not true.' And now he couldn't help seeing that she was weeping.

'Are you crying? You've never done that before.'

She laughed so hysterically that she frightened even herself.

'My dear,' he said.

But the terrible laughter went on. She was unable to stop herself. When at last she fell silent, he said, 'I probably didn't want to see things go wrong for you. I'd have gone mad if I'd understood. You were so intelligent and clear-headed, I was proud of you. Maybe I wanted you to be like that. Then got furious because you were. So damned strong.'

'I wasn't. I was going mad.'

Then the taxi horn sounded and he had to go.

Naturally she knew she would take him back. Her loneliness had already taken that decision. And the hunger for his body in hers?

Anna looked at her watch: past five, must phone Father! That was just as difficult every day. Reproaches.

'Oh, so you've suddenly remembered your poor old pappa, have you?'

'I phoned yesterday. How was Mother today?'

'All right. I got her to eat. I took one spoonful of the mince and one of the fruit fool. You know, she's just like a child, wanting second course first.'

'Clever of you.'

'When are you coming to see me?'

'I was with you last week. Have you forgotten?'

'I forget so easily.'

'I'll phone tomorrow as usual.'

It was over. It had gone unusually easily but the receiver was wet with sweat. Why the hell was it so difficult, this phone call she had to force herself to make every day?

I wish you were dead, both of you.

A few days after the quarrel with Rickard, she found a sentence in a book that made a great impression on her. 'A free man's love is never secure.'

That's true, she thought.

She was so taken with it that she bought a postcard, wrote the sentence on it and sent it to the hotel in Rome.

Then the letter came. She had to find it, rummaged in drawers for the key of her secret case, opened it, found the letter with the Rome postmark, and read it.

You've never wanted to listen to me. But you find it hard to resist the written word, so now I'm trying a letter.

You're naïve. A free man – that must be a man no one has any power over. He doesn't need revenge. My women are like me, they want revenge. At least, I started out from that. The first, Sonja, at the party, I'm sure of because her lover was at the dinner. He was a shit I'd known for a long time.

The one I wanted to humiliate, take my revenge on, there's no doubt about that. It was you. We, she and I, were suffering from the same kind of madness. We wanted to demonstrate what love is – not power, but desire in the encounter between an arbitrary male/female. It's perverse. But perversion doesn't reduce the desire. I think even you can understand that. On the other hand, what you probably can't understand is the excitement when two people deliberately behave badly, intending to hurt.

It was the same with all my women. Though I did make a mistake with Lilian. She fell in love with me and I was furious with her. As I saw it, that wasn't included in the agreement.

That was why it took so long to get rid of her. You were pregnant with Malin, more goddess-like than ever. Christ, what a shit I was.

That brings us to the main question. Why do I have to take revenge on you? You're honest and lovely – everything I've ever dreamed of.

I knew nothing about love until I met you. If I had, I would have run away. I didn't really want it, this consuming submission that makes a man a slave. So this 'free man's' answer is that you had unlimited power over me. If you were sulky at breakfast, my day was sheer hell. When you were happy, I was drunk with my victory. If you were ever angry and scolded me, I deserved it. It's still your power over me I'm afraid of. But I can't live without you. My position has no underlying base. I'm the one who's been whoring, lying, ratting on you. And yet I like to believe it could have been different if you'd just for once tried to listen. You're a very proud person. You've been brought up to that, so I'm not blaming you. It was beneath your dignity even to try to understand. Or what?

The letter wasn't signed. She had wondered why.

But she smiled when she thought about how she had spelt her way through her telegram to Rome.

'Meet you at Whitsun at Fjärås Bräcka.'

Then she thought, just as she had when she had received the letter; Rickard required attention in abundance. To maintain his hold on life, he needed to be able to choose and wreck, take and throw away. That was his weakness, his fundamental flaw.

Just as he had written, that was incompatible with love, with the dependence that lifelong fellowship entails.

Anna remembered Maria's teens, her rebellion, particularly a quarrel about Sandra, a schoolfriend, with whom Rickard had flirted. Maria was scarlet with shame, and shouted cruelly at her father.

'You're a silly fool, a damned tom-cat living in the belief you're

148

irresistible. There are some boys at school like you, but the girls with anything about them simply laugh at them. I've never understood how Mamma could stand you.'

Maria hadn't married, nor had Malin. They lived like men had in all times, in love sometimes, brief relationships. But they each had a child, free children who had escaped the game in that hellish triangle, father, mother, child.

Right from the beginning Anna had had an inkling that Rickard had little self-confidence. An autocratic mother? A weak father? But when she was young she hadn't wanted to understand. Constantly understanding was a danger to yourself. Her mother's life had taught her that. Johanna was one of those who always understood, so had had to endure a great deal.

Suddenly Anna remembered another quarrel, much later. The memory was knife-sharp. She could see the evening sun falling in through the big picture window in the living room in Minkgatan, dust whirling in the rays. Rickard had fallen into the habit of calling her Mother, even when they were alone.

'I'm not your mother,' she shrieked at him. 'Never have been and never will be.'

She saw he'd taken it badly, had stiffened.

'Of course not,' he said. 'It's only a manner of speech, a silly habit.'

At that moment, Anna knew it was neither a manner of speech nor a habit. But she couldn't bring herself to say so.

'Sorry I let fly,' she said, and the moment went by.

But Anna had seen her mother-in-law's face, lovely and self-absorbed, and had wondered how often and intensely the little boy had longed for her in vain. And she thought, That's why he's so furious with me. He's having his revenge on her.

She jotted notes, thinking she might find some answer, but then hesitated, put a question mark in the margin, thought for a while, then wrote: 'Rickard is always considerate towards his mother and defends her against the slightest criticism. But of his dead father he speaks only with contempt: "He was a fool."'

149

CHAPTER 38

She heard the key in the door.

'Got some plaice,' he called. 'Fresh.'

'Lovely. Coming.'

'I'll get us a drink.'

They raised their glasses and, slightly formally, he said as usual that it was great to be alive. Then he picked up the thick grey notebook, the Hanna book, and leafed through it.

'Read it while I peel the potatoes,' she said.

When he came out into the kitchen, he said, 'This'll be a book, Anna. It's damned powerful.'

She was pleased.

'Rather too much nostalgia, don't you think?'

'No. Anyhow, there's nothing wrong with nostalgia.'

He'd always helped her with her work. Right from the start. He was the one to come up with the idea of writing a popular version of her thesis.

'It's worth more than just collecting dust in a faculty.'

She wanted to reach a lot of people. 'Do you think I can?'

'We'll manage it,' he said. So she went to a school of journalism and learned to express complicated matters in a simple way, generalising and using examples. She was expecting a child, wrote at home in the daytime and he corrected the manuscript every evening.

It was fun. They were newly married, in their first two-roomed apartment in one of the new suburbs of Stockholm.

He was strict at first.

'For Christ's sake, that isn't Swedish. Listen to it yourself.'

She listened and took it in. A language entirely its own soon began to emerge, hers. It was like a miracle, almost as wonderful as the child growing inside her.

'I've met my match,' he said.

The book came out a few months after their daughter was born. Both were surprised by the attention it received.

Success. Happiness. Until that evening at the house in Lidingö.

They cleaned the fish and fried it. She sat at the kitchen table with her drink, watching how deftly he handled the knife and spatula, precisely and elegantly.

I know no one as sensuous as he is.

'Hello there, penny for your thoughts.'

She blushed, then told him, and she heard him laugh that dark laugh that came from down inside him and was always an introduction.

'I'm hungry,' she said. 'We must eat first.'

'I haven't made the slightest approach.'

'Just you dare.'

He wanted to have a house.

'Live on the ground, Anna. Before it's too late.'

The first time he'd said that, she'd thought it was already too late.

'Who plants apple trees after they're fifty?'

'Me,' he said calmly.

Then the idea had grown. Suddenly she dared feel how tired she was of high-rise apartment blocks, the anonymity and the motorway thundering through her days and nights. Not to mention those poor pine trees.

A garden!

'There were always rows about the garden at home,' she'd said. 'Mother had to do it all while Father went out sailing.'

Rickard had been angry. 'For Christ's sake, we can't have the whole of our life steered by what your parents got up to.'

'You're right.'

She knew what he meant by 'the whole of our life'. He was upset by her ties to her mother and furious about his relationship with his father. She reckoned he was right in principle, although his motives were dubious.

That day he had been to look at two places. One was too big and expensive, the other two smaller houses on one large rural site. Lovely situation, he said. Solid buildings. One house for work, hers and his as soon as he retired. And one to live in. 'There's an old croft there, too, derelict.'

'There must be a snag. Is it too expensive?'

'No, but it's a long way from town. Over twenty miles.'

'I've no objections. Better proper countryside than another suburb.'

'You're not afraid of being isolated?'

She suddenly felt that old unease. 'How would you get in and out of town?'

'There's a train,' he said. 'You'll have to be one of those wives who drive their husbands to the station. And fetch them in the evenings.'

Before she fell asleep, she lay there a long time thinking about those two little houses, about giving them apple trees and roses. He was going to talk to the vendor the next day and fix a meeting out there.

On Saturday, she thought. She'd already decided.

CHAPTER 39

As she tackled the notebooks, the next morning, it all seemed more serious, weightier, all because of Rickard saying, 'It'll be a book.'

How strange of me, she thought. I've actually known that all the time. But it was easier as long as I pretended it was just a journey, an outing into my own background. A little psychology, a little sociology, a little increased self-knowledge.

It had worked out like that, too. She had grown calmer in the course of the journey, made some discoveries and acquired new insights. She had stopped searching so desperately for childhood memories, out of 'the reality', as she used to say. She had realised there are only fragments, that 'memories' always consist of fragments the mind puts together into a pattern, adapts to a picture staked out early without the need for a connection with anything that really happened. A great deal is misunderstood by small children, then stored as images that attract similar images, confirming and reinforcing.

Then she thought that what hadn't happened might be more truthful than what had happened. Would have more to say.

She left her fragments lying there, scattered about, and found that that was the only way she could acquire information on the past, only briefly, of course, just moments.

She avoided the worst, what hurt. But that wouldn't do, if she was serious about it. Then she had to search more deeply. Into Hanna, for instance she could not just slide over her grandmother's grief when August drove through the bridge railing straight into the sea one dark night somewhere in Bohus County.

Anna had been in her teens when it happened and couldn't understand the old lady's despair. August was a grown man and made decisions about his own life for himself. He was divorced and had no children.

She asked Johanna, who looked at her with distance in her eyes. 'He was her child, Anna.'

I must find out why she mourned so terribly. And aged so cruelly in only a few weeks.

August had always had only a weak will to live, it was said. Had had all kinds of illnesses. For years, Hanna had walked the cottage floor at night with the boy in her arms.

Mother said, 'He was her child, Anna.'

Peter, she thought. Peter.

Like her grandmother and her mother, Anna had had difficult deliveries. Inherited that too? Genetic? Psychological? Peter was born after their divorce and reconciliation, six years after Malin. He arrived two months early, the wrong way round and as thin as a baby bird. The first time he was put to her breast, Anna knew there was something wrong with him, something ill-fated. He had no vitality.

The doctors laughed at her anxiety. The boy was healthy. She should be grateful he didn't have to go into an incubator.

Rickard was in some eastern state where there was a crisis on. He was to have been back in good time for the birth. If she had gone to full term …

Johanna came up and sat beside her at the maternity hospital, her eyes as uneasy as Anna's.

'The best help to me would be if you took the children back with you to Göteborg. Then I can devote all my time to this boy when I get home.'

Johanna hesitated, but talked to the doctor and grew calmer. They agreed not to tell Rickard, not to worry him.

Johanna took the two girls home with her, but telephoned twice a day. 'Haven't you got a friend, Anna? Where's Kristina?'

'In Åland. They're all away.'

It was high summer when Anna, alone with the baby, went into the darkened apartment. The child whimpered for light. He couldn't cry, but he whimpered the moment he was out of Anna's arms.

Oh, that lament, humble, hopeless.

A week, two, four then six. Forty days later, all carefully counted, he died one Wednesday afternoon. She looked at the clock. Three. A banality from the world of death announcements was turned into a profound truth: 'Little angel came today, smiled at us and turned away.'

But Peter had never given her a smile.

Anna did not put the child down as she drew back the curtains, the light slicing like lightning in her eyes. She looked out at the world with surprise, that it hadn't changed, people coming and going, children on swings down in the playground and squabbling in the sandpit. The telephone rang and she didn't answer it. She would never again respond to calls, she thought.

Then she fell asleep with the baby in her arms, going with him into the cold and death. Ten hours later she was woken by Rickard, who had had a telephone message from Johanna and had flown home via Berlin.

He dealt with all the practical matters, doctors, undertakers, telephoning parents and friends. He also looked after her, bathed her in warm water, made her drink, remade the bed, wrapped her in warm blankets.

She heard him crying at night.

She didn't cry for weeks. Weeks of unreality, as she was to call them later. Filled with peculiar experiences.

Like the day Rickard had to go in to the paper. 'Only two hours, Anna. Promise me to stay in bed.'

She promised.

When he got home, she had gone. He ran all round the district and was just about to give up and phone the police when she came walking along the street, straight at him, smiling. 'What luck I found you. You must help me.'

'But where've you been?'

'At the children's clinic, Rickard. That's where you take babies.'

'Which clinic?'

'The usual one, in the huts behind the market square.'

'But, Anna, that was pulled down years ago.'

'How peculiar,' she said. 'So that's why I couldn't find my way back. You see, I'd left Peter there. With the nurse.'

When she saw the look in his eyes, she misunderstood. 'Don't be angry with me, Rickard. He won't come to any harm. I mean, they're trained and all that ...'

'Let's go,' he said and, taking her arm, he steered her across the square with the pool and its idiotic sculpture, round the corner and down to the site where the children's clinic had been, and which was now a car park.

'But I don't understand. I was only here an hour or two ago. And where's Peter?'

'He's dead, and you know it.'

Their eyes met and he did not turn away. In the end, she nodded. 'I know.'

That evening her head cleared, but she was frightened. 'I was there, I remember, it's all so clear, the door they painted pale blue,

Sister Solveig who was tired but just as patient as usual. I was there, Rickard. And yet I can't have been there.'

'Sister Solveig died when Maria was quite small. Of cancer, don't you remember? We went to her funeral.'

'Dead? Like Peter, then?'

'Yes.'

She closed her eyes, her face smoothing out as if she had understood. But when at last she opened them again she was sensible. 'Rickard. I promise you I won't go mad.'

'You almost frightened the life out of me.'

Then she noticed how tired and pale he was and realised she must pull herself together. More experiences in unreality came, but never again did she involve him in them.

What helped her through the wall was her mother-in-law, who came to see her and said, 'But you mustn't grieve. It was almost only a foetus.'

'He was my child,' said Anna.

Then at last she was able to cry. She wept almost without stopping for two days.

Afterwards she cleaned her home, then put away her sleeping tablets and went with Rickard to the west coast, to her mother and the other children.

CHAPTER 40

By the time Rickard came home, she had put the memory of Peter on the computer. He looked at her uneasily.

'Anna, how pale you are.'

'You read it while I get dinner.'

She had already bought and cooked a piece of salted brisket of beef that afternoon. She peeled swedes, potatoes and carrots, cut them up into small pieces, boiled them and mashed in the stock.

He liked mashed swedes.

When he came out into the kitchen he was dark-eyed and pale. They hadn't the strength to talk as they ate, but afterwards, in the living room, he said, 'I often think about Peter, that it was as if he had a mission. For that was when things went ... as they did. Between us, I mean.'

She couldn't bring herself to reply.

CHAPTER 41

Did Mother ever tell Grandmother I was divorced?

Anna wrote down the question, then looked at it.

Then she wrote, I don't think so. She probably didn't want to worry her. Hanna was very fond of Rickard, too, and said he reminded her of Ragnar.

That was more true than Anna had realised.

After a while, she found yet another explanation. Mother had kept silent about the divorce because she had never really believed in it, and had said so occasionally over the lonely years. 'I don't think you two will ever get away from each other.'

Anna made the decision when she got back home from the maternity hospital with Malin. Rickard had been living for months with someone else, the smell of her on his clothes, in their living room and their bed.

When she told him she wanted to separate, he was desperate and refused to believe her. 'Anna, it was just stupid of me ... and then I couldn't get rid of her.'

'I haven't asked for an explanation.'

'But listen to me.'

'No, Rickard, I don't want to hear. It'll have to be as I said. You've got the spring to find somewhere else to live. Then we'll talk to Maria together.'

'You've thought everything out.'

'I've talked to a lawyer.'

'Maria will be very upset.'

'I know.'

Maria was the centre of the course of events now running relentlessly under its own volition. All anxiety and guilt were drawn towards her. She filled Anna's days with torment and her nights with nightmares. She appeared in a thousand guises, the abandoned child, the knifed child, a child lost in the forest, looking for her father.

Maria loved Rickard.

Rickard was a good father, amusing, enterprising and as inquisitive as the child. Safe.

Maria was a sensitive child, full of tenderness towards everything and everyone, quick-thinking and with an enquiring mind. Beautiful. 'Like you,' Richard used to say. But it wasn't true. Maria was a fair-haired copy of Johanna.

Malin was different. So far, she had been entirely Anna's baby.

He now said what she had most feared, that he would contest custody. 'May I give Maria a dog?' he said.

That was Friday evening, and he left. Didn't come back until Sunday, hung-over, scornful, almost crazy with despair. Anna took the children down one floor to Kristina. 'Please look after them.'

When she got back, he was in the shower.

'We must talk like grown people,' she said, as calmly as she could.

'What about?'

'About how this can be arranged so that it causes the least harm to the children and you. And me.'

'As you're made of stone, things are sure to be all right for you. I'm going to drink myself to death.'

'Rickard!'

But he went to bed.

The next morning he was calmer and she could talk to him. He took Maria to the kindergarten as usual, came back and phoned the office to say he was sick.

She was feeding Malin as she told him. He was to have the children every other weekend and for a month every summer.

'Magnificent.'

She needed maintenance for the children, a thousand kronor a month. 'To manage,' she said. She had already decided to move to a smaller apartment and take a lecturing job at the School of Sociology. She also made quite a decent income from freelance work.

'But you didn't want that job. And what about your book?'

'That was then,' she said.

He wept and found it difficult to get out the words when he appealed to her.

'Is there nothing, nothing on earth I can do to get you to change your mind?'

'No.'

That was all she could find to say.

It didn't work out as Anna had thought. Rickard got a job as foreign correspondent in Hong Kong. 'Covering the whole of the Far East.'

To blazes, thought Anna, and congratulated him.

Together they talked to Maria. He said he had to go. Anna said they were having a difficult time. They needed ... to be apart.

Maria said that was good. 'Then maybe you'll stop crying so much, Mamma.' She told Rickard she didn't want a dog.

Anna and Maria drove him to Arlanda airport. The five-year-old held out her hand. 'Goodbye, Pappa.' That was all.

He looked weighed down and old as he headed for the gate, and Anna almost cracked with pity. And doubts.

Those first lonely months ... heavens, how she missed him. She fumbled for him in her sleep, flung her arms round his pillow but couldn't sleep. Dry, parched, she looked for him on every street corner, in the square and in the shops.

That was when her desert dreams began. Night after night, Anna wandered in an endless desert, seeing his back disappearing among the dunes. It was heavy going, her feet sinking into the sand. She was exhausted and parched with thirst, searching for water, finding none, trying to rest but then she caught a glimpse of his back again and had to go on.

She borrowed some sleeping pills from Kristina and managed a few nights' rest.

Her last desert dream was the worst. The man walking ahead of her across the parched ground turned round and it wasn't Rickard but the doctor, the one who had said, 'You castrate your husband.'

She found a two-roomer right above the kindergarten. A man appeared and helped her move, an old friend, practical and handy. From gratitude – or loneliness or desire? – she went to bed with him and found sex much like her desert wanderings, sterile and meaningless. She woke with sand in her mouth, whispered that he had to go, that Maria might find him there. He obeyed, and she realised that the sex had been a disappointment to him as well.

She told Kristina. 'I'm a one-man woman.'

'Sounds fine,' said her friend. 'Pity Rickard's a many-woman man.'

They agreed that he was having a good time in the Far East, free to devote himself to geishas, diplomats' wives and sophisticated women reporters, the kind they saw on television.

But Anna knew it wasn't true, that Rickard was lonely and desperate. For the first time she asked herself whether that was so, whether it could possibly be true that what lay behind his womanising was to reach her.

Then she told herself she was being foolish. The next moment she was thinking that, if that was true, then it was even worse.

She was so deep in her notebook that she jumped when the telephone rang. It was Maria.

'Oh, darling,' said Anna.

'Were you asleep, Mamma?'

'No, no, just sitting here making notes and remembering.'

'I'm not sure it's good for you, all these memories,' said Maria in troubled tones. She had been to a conference in Oslo, of course, Anna remembered.

'I came back via Göteborg and went to see Grandfather.'

'How kind of you.'

But Maria said it was unbearable, both at the old man's house and at the hospital. Intolerable and impossible to do anything about it.

'I've been thinking a lot about you, how awful and lonely it must have been every damned month. I'll come with you next time.'

Anna's delight was so overwhelming she couldn't help herself, but when she heard the veiled touch in Maria's voice, she realised she had done what she most loathed. Showering guilt.

Half an hour later, Malin rang and said she'd been talking to Maria and they were going to take it in turns to go with her on the visits to Göteborg. As often as they could.

'I think you're mad,' said Anna.

Malin was unlike her sister — unlike her mother as well for that matter. More matter-of-fact, more open, less emotional, logical. Neither Rickard nor Anna could really grasp that they had a daughter reading theoretical physics.

'I was so pleased I made Maria feel guilty.'

'Me, too,' said Malin happily. 'Listen, Mum, you must know that only monsters manage to escape feeling guilty.'

'Salt-of-the-earth,' said Anna. That was one of her old nicknames for her remarkable younger daughter.

Johanna wasn't present during Anna's first lonely six months, nor when she moved, nor when she made arrangements for the children. That was the time when Hanna was living with Mother, and where she died. Mother needed a great deal of help. I managed to get there only once.

As Malin said, it's not possible to live without feeling guilty.

She had spent all day putting her notes into the third book, the red one with ANNA on the label on the cover. She turned back to the fly-leaf and wrote, 'On guilt and gratitude, and on having daughters.' Then she put a question mark against it.

CHAPTER 42

On the Friday morning Rickard was in a bad mood.

'Did you sleep badly?'

'Yes.'

As he stood in the hall before going to fetch the newspaper, he said: 'You quoted my letter from Rome.'

'But all that's still only notes, Rickard. We'll have to discuss it later ... when it's really clear it's going to be a book.'

'It's not that. What struck me was that you never answered my question.'

'What was it?' she said, although she knew.

'Why you never listened to me, never even tried.'

'That was just it,' she said.

She washed up and cleared away breakfast, her own words ringing in her ears. 'That was just it.'

Then she sat down to work and wrote.

I want to attempt a fairy-tale? Why a fairy-tale? I don't know, perhaps because it's true what some people say, that fairy-tales can say more than reports from what is called reality.

But it's probably mostly because you don't have to understand fairy-tales.

Once upon a time there was a little girl who grew up in a castle. It had three rooms full of secrets, cupboards with wonderful things in them, books with pictures, photographs of dead strangers, though they gazed at her with serious eyes. Round the castle was a large garden, roses and strawberries growing in it, a mountain in one corner, high, half-way to the clouds. One day she climbed up on to it and saw where the blue sea met the sky somewhere far away. After that she made the mountain hers, took herself up to the top and created her own world among the boulders and mountain ledges.

The mountain talked to the sea. She had heard that on the very first day. After a while, she realised that the mountain was also talking to her and to the lilacs flowering at its foot, and to the cat's foot, the house-leek and the meadow saxifrage growing in the cracks.

It was always summer, the weather always fine, and she was a happy little girl. Her mother loved her and her father was proud of her, for she was so wise and clever. Her mother also told her almost every day that she was just that, a happy girl. And life was good for her.

If life is good, then you mustn't be sad. That was a great worry to the child. For sometimes she was incomprehensibly sad. And sometimes she was terribly frightened.

What was she frightened of? Not that her mother would die? Well, yes, she probably was. But why?

She would never know.

Once, when she thought she would die of the fright making her heart beat so that it hurt in her chest, she found an invisible stairway leading right into the mountain. Inside was a cave, just big enough for her. She could sit down in it and feel all her terrors disappear.

She felt chosen.

How long did she play that game? Was it one summer or was it many? Anyhow, it took years before this happy little girl understood that the game was dangerous, this game that made her insensitive and invisible. When she finally grasped it, she was grown up and had left home.

What happened was that she took the mountain with her. It was always there, and, as soon as she was sad or frightened, she could escape into it. Now she didn't want to any longer. Now she was afraid of the cave that had such thick walls. But the mountain held her in its power.

When the prince came, and love made her more vulnerable than ever, she found a new use for her secret mountain cave.

The prince thought she was often cold and unreachable. And that was true. It's deathly cold in the mountain and anyone sitting in there is turned to stone. She cannot fight for her rights, or burn with jealousy, or scream, ask questions or accuse.

So, without wanting to, the girl went on escaping to her cave and hurting him. But guilt tormented her every time she came out and saw what she had done.

And so they married and lived ... ever after.

CHAPTER 43

Once Anna had her fairy-tale down in her notebook, she started striding around like a captive horse, back and forth, kicking at tables and chairs.

Then she filled a large glass with whisky and drank it in one draught. But stubborn and insane, as you are when you nearly find something you've lost and it's important, she went on. She picked up her pen and turned over to a new page.

Then she found it. When Peter died.

When she fell asleep with the dead child in her arms.

And when she found herself in the extreme unreality, when she lost her little boy at the children's clinic.

If you run away, you risk going mad.

She filled her glass again and took it with her into the bedroom. She didn't wake when the telephone rang, even when Rickard came home.

He woke her. 'Anna! Are you drunk?'

'Yes. Go away and read it.'

When she woke the next time, he was sitting on the edge of the bed with milk and sandwiches.

'I had an inkling,' he said.

He said nothing more for a while, then went on. 'I don't think you risk going mad. Nor do you have to feel guilty about me. You learn in time that people have their own characteristics. No, what's dangerous is when the person who has a cave to escape into never learns to fight.'

'And you have to do that?'

'Yes.'

CHAPTER 44

Saturday. Outing.

Anna woke early, packed some food, and watched out of the kitchen window the grey above the town giving way to the sun.

Of course, the weather had to be fine.

Rickard came out into the kitchen, sleepy, unshaven and in his awful old bathrobe.

'How are you feeling?' he said.

'As if I had fizzy lemonade in my veins. They're bubbling.'

'An amazing hangover.'

'Idiot. I'm happy, lighter in mind than for a long time.'

'Catharsis?'

'Precisely.'

From the kitchen she could hear him phoning the girls and inviting them out on Sunday, on an outing with a surprise, as he put it. He's so certain, she thought, certain they'll have the time. And that they'll want to. And certain the sale will come off.

When they got out on to the Roslag road and the traffic had thinned out, he said, 'I came across something last night. You've persisted in staying in these damned high-rises because you're afraid of gardens.'

'Good gracious!' He's right, she thought. Concrete suburbs have no secrets. There's no space for mystery under neon lights, no symbols, no relations to trees and flowers. Or to mountains.

'Good gracious!' she said again.

'What do you mean?'

'That it's all so sad, Rickard. That we've lived so ... dismally for all these years. And not really liked it.'

They were silent for a long time and then just as they were passing another vehicle, he said, 'There are lots of rocks out there.'

'Great!'

An elderly man met them at the turning and, as they bumped along the narrow gravel road, Anna reckoned it was going to be tougher than she'd thought. In the winter before the snowplough

165

came. In the spring when the snow was melting. But the forest was green round the road, real old-fashioned mixed woodlands with aspens, birches and maples between the pine trees.

Two squat houses crept along the ground, holiday houses from the 1960s. They had been linked together with a veranda-like glassed-in passage. They could just glimpse the water between the aspens, not the sea, but a large, calm inland lake.

'Gracious!' said Anna, then went on, when the man looked at her in surprise, 'I just meant I simply can't understand why anyone should want to sell this place.'

'My wife died last summer.'

There was nothing to say.

The two men started with the well. Anna heard them talking about pressure tanks and how they could be difficult in winter, then she set off on her own across the site. There were lots of rocks, as Rickard had said, flat, smooth rocks with polypody growing in the cracks. And plenty of roses, just as she had imagined. Down towards the lake was the old croft, tired and neglected and wonderful.

The garden was in the lee towards land. Two ancient trees were still there, laden with red apples. Anna stood with her back against one of the rough trunks and said hello. There was no doubt about it, they had known each other for a thousand years.

CHAPTER 45

The next weekend, Anna and Maria went to Göteborg. Maria spent most of the time with the old man in the house by the sea, talking, cleaning and cooking. Anna went to see her mother in the long-stay ward. She talked about Hanna. 'I've been with your mother a long time now. I think I'm just beginning to understand her.

'It's more difficult to get a picture of you and your life. That's because you're so close to me and I can't see you. It's probably true that we least understand those we love most.

'I've realised you were a secretive person. So I thought you ought to be allowed to speak for yourself. You're a good story-teller, Mother.'

In the car on the way back, she told Maria about Hanna and Dalsland. 'Your great-grandmother.'

Back at work, she moved from bookshelf to bookshelf, reading the titles, looking things up here and there, finding words that had once meant so much to her.

Was she looking for prototypes?

No, her thoughts were quite practical, on how everything should be packed and where they would find space in those small houses by the lake. Rickard had said to her what Ragnar had once said to Hanna. 'There's lots of old rubbish you can clear out.'

And, like Hanna, she wondered how on earth she had collected so much rubbish over the years.

She stopped at the poetry shelf and sat down with Ekelöf, Stagnelius, Martinson and Boyes. That was where it struck her that she was searching for a tone of voice, her mother's. She thought everyone had a tone of voice, unique to that person. Of course, she couldn't find it now, not like this. And she knew it was presumptuous to think she could get it to resound as it once did.

But if she was patient, if she waited, then perhaps she could find the right key.

Johanna
BORN 1902, DIED 1987

CHAPTER 46

My life has been divided into two halves. The first half lasted for eight years of childhood, so was the same length as the remaining seventy. When I look back on the second half, I find four stages that changed me.

The first was when I was stopped by an invisible hand from opening a door. That was a miracle and it gave me back the connection.

The next determining events were when I found work I liked, became self-sufficient and joined the Social Democrat Party.

Then there was love and marriage.

The fourth was when I gave birth to a daughter and named her after the old midwife in Norskvattnet. And when my daughter had children and I grandchildren.

What took place between all these events was the ordinary life of most women. A great deal of anxiety, hard work, great joy, many victories, more defeats. And, of course, the sorrow beneath it all.

I have thought a great deal about sorrow. After all, understanding is born from it, as well as reflection and the desire for change. We wouldn't be human if sorrow didn't exist, right down there in the depths of our being.

I ought to say one more thing before I start my story. I've always tried to tell the truth in the childish belief that it existed and was indivisible. I found it more and more difficult to think when truth fell apart into hundreds of different truths.

I have no words to contain my first eight years in Dalsland. Perhaps I put an end to them when Anna was small. I did that because it was fun, but also so that she could be at home in the world that comes between the child, stories and nature. Nowadays I don't know whether that was any use. Anna did not become a happy person.

Over the years I also lost the connection. That was so clear when Anna took me back to Dalsland that time. I recognised everything, the waterfall and the lakes, the trees and the paths. But they had forgotten me. That was bitter and I cried a lot.

But one should never return to sacred places.

I was Johanna, a city child, brought up in a corner haberdashery in Haga in the pleasant fragrance of new cloth, a place as cramped as a doll's house, which had hundreds of drawers full of secrets. Ribbons, elastic, laces – all kinds of wonderful things spread out before me on the polished darkbrown counter. Most of all, I loved the boxes of reels of silk.

'You must keep your fingers clean,' said Lisa, and I scrubbed my hands until they were sore.

I always started with the violet box, following the glowing range from pale pinkish blue to faint lilac up to the matt dark blue with the slightest touch of red in it.

'Queen colour?'

'I think you're right,' said Lisa, smiling.

Lisa rarely laughed, and never exclaimed in surprise or anger. She was quiet and unchanging, and that made me feel safe. When I first minded the shop, she was at her sewing machine in the little room behind and made me a cotton dress in small grey and white check.

'We have to be careful about colours. To consider your mother,' she said.

But she made cuffs, collar and pocket flaps out of green cotton with pink roses on it.

The moment she put that new dress on me was when I began life as someone else, far away from Father and the waterfall. It wasn't easy, and I've thought many a time that if Lisa hadn't existed, I would have gone into the Rosenlund canal.

At first there was the terrible business of words, the old words pouring out my mouth before I had time to think. I'd been good at school back home, and I was dressed in my best when I went to the city school for the first time.

Of course I was frightened, but all the same … I thought I was like everyone else. And perhaps it would have been all right if it hadn't been for the words. Lord, how they laughed at me.

I had to read a bit out of a book. But I never got to the end because of their horrible laughter. And the teacher said, 'Johanna, haven't you ever thought that you speak as you write? The words in your mouth are to be the same as in the book. Go home now and get that into your head.'

She wasn't nasty, but she knew nothing about what it was like for me when I got home to those unmade beds, piles of dirty clothes and stacks of unwashed dishes. And the boys' filthy shoes I had to clean. I had only half an hour before Mother came back from the bakery, bad-tempered as usual when she was exhausted. "Lazy trollop," she would scold, "spoilt by your father when you were little." Once she hit me so hard in the face, I couldn't go to school the next day.

After that day, I ran off to Lisa as soon as Mother came home. I could see that that saddened her, but she said nothing. Didn't dare, I suppose, in case I told Ragnar.

In the room behind Lisa's shop, I read aloud, day after day. I soon found that it wasn't at all true what the teacher had said: the words in books weren't at all the words you said, not even in those days. But, with Lisa's help, I learned to speak properly.

I thought it was proper Swedish, but many years later when I was at a political meeting, a woman said to me, 'Your Göteborg dialect is good to hear, but I think you ought to tidy it up a bit.'

Oh, how surprised I was.

At school I did well, in time, although I never had a friend and my classmates went on laughing at me. Things got worse and worse at home. My brothers gave up working, stayed at home and drank. While I tried to keep out of the way in the kitchen, I could hear them talking about women, about whores and fucking and pricks and cunts. I washed dishes and listened, and I hated them.

That was when I made my first decision. I would never get married, never in any way go with a man.

When it got so bad that Ragnar intervened and smashed the furniture and beat up the boys, I stood in a corner and was pleased. Mother screamed with terror but, heaven knows, she deserved it. Then I was allowed to live with Lisa and Ragnar, and a great calm descended on me. I still went back home after school and cleared up the worst, but I made quite sure I got away before I heard Mother's key in the door.

I had begun to despise her by then. "She behaves like a gypsy woman," I said to Lisa. Lisa reprimanded me and gave me a word I've never forgotten.

'Of course she's a little … primitive,' she said.

Primitive. Like the natives, I thought. At school I'd read about the savages in Africa, about the time when Stanley met Livingstone.

After that conversation with Lisa, I made my second resolution. I would become a civilised and educated person.

In Lisa's apartment immediately across the courtyard from ours, there were a great many books. At least ten, maybe fifteen. I read them all. They were love stories, and I found that strange. When I said so to Lisa, she was surprised and thought for a long time before she said anything.

'But that's what it's like, Johanna. For instance, I'm hopelessly in love with Ragnar. It wears me out all the time, but I can't get it out of me.'

I must have looked peculiar. I remember sitting down on a chair in the shop and opening my mouth without being able to get a word out. I wanted to tell her that Ragnar was kind, an unusually good man. I wanted to comfort her.

Comfort?

'So that's why you're so sad,' I said in the end, surprising even myself that I'd never thought of it before, what now seemed so obvious. That Lisa was sad.

I don't remember what she replied. It took me many years before I understood the connection between the talk about Ragnar as a womaniser and my brothers boasting about pricks in the cunts in Järntorget.

Lisa taught me three things of great importance. To understand other people, to endure with patience, and to work in a shop.

CHAPTER 47

Anna says I learned the first lesson far too well, the one about understanding people and feeling sorry for them.

My mother never understood. She issued judgements and repudiated anything with which she didn't agree, so evaded a lot of trouble.

But when Lisa started talking about my drunkard brothers, about how scared they'd been in the city and how the sense of alienation was hollowing them out, there was something in what she said that I recognised, like a tune I had once known. It was a long time before I realised what Father had taught me so long ago. I couldn't remember his words, only the feeling, which is always stronger than what is said.

Otherwise I shared Anna's opinion that anyone who understands a lot has to endure too much. That's true. What separates us is the basic attitude. I think life has to hurt. Anna considers it's to be enjoyed. It's difficult to think about this, because I know who taught her to expect a lot and only the best.

Lisa was an understanding person who had to endure far more than was reasonable. Her father had been an alcoholic and had treated his wife and children very badly. Two brothers had died, one had escaped to America and Lisa had run away to Göteborg when she was only twelve.

She preferred not to talk about how she made a living, but I realised, from the little she told me, that she'd begged her way and slept in entrance porches until she got work in the spinning factory, where she ruined her lungs in the dust. It was awful to hear her coughing in the long wet autumns. Ragnar couldn't stand it, and whenever her cough started up he would slip out through the door, as if pursued, and go down town. I knew what was tormenting him, but Lisa was miserable.

When her mother died, out in the country somewhere, her father took his own life. Lisa inherited the whole farm as there were no brothers and sisters to be found. That was when it turned out that she had a good business head. She sold the stock at auction, the fields to the neighbouring farmer, the forest to a company, and the house to a merchant wanting a summer place on the Halland coast.

Then she used the money to buy her haberdashery, which was situated on the boundary between working-class Haga and the gentry of Vasastan. She was certainly a free and independent person until the day she met Ragnar and fell hopelessly in love with him.

Was she happy before that? I don't know.

But she did seem happy when she married and became a respectable wife. She said that Ragnar had gone to the priest with her because of Hanna Broman, and she would be grateful to her for that for the rest of her life. I remember wondering what Mother had said to Ragnar. I had never ever seen him take anything she said seriously. He just laughed at her.

I didn't laugh at my mother. I hated her, scolded her and was ashamed of her.

In the middle of the war, when food was at its shortest, my breasts started growing and I had my period. Mother said that now all that wretched business was starting and the shame would afflict me at any moment. I remember it quite clearly because she turned as white as a sheet and her eyes looked terrified as she taught me how to fasten the towel. 'Promise me you'll be careful,' she said. 'And look out for yourself.'

I tried to ask her what I had to look out for, but she just snorted, flushed, and said nothing.

As so often, when things were difficult, I went to Lisa. But she didn't help me this time. She just looked peculiar and her voice was odd when she said she had to speak to Ragnar. Then I realised it wasn't just all that horrid blood running out of me. It was something much worse.

The next day Ragnar said rather abruptly, and in an embarrassed voice, that I must watch out for men. That was all I was told. The rest I put together on my own. I thought about those awful words I'd heard from my brothers, about pricks and cunts. Then I got some help from a childhood memory. I remembered when we were struggling through the forest with one of Mother's cows that was to go to the bull on Grandfather's farm. That was Erik and me, and when we at last got there we were given cakes and fruit juice by an aunt.

Then, as I watched the bull mounting the cow, I felt sorry for her. I knew how it was done, all right.

Lisa had her first child in the summer and I had to learn how to mind the shop in all seriousness. It went well. I calculated and measured, cut cloth and talked to customers. Lisa said I was amazingly clever for one so young. She brought the baby in at dinner-time, added up the till and was delighted. 'Goodness! If only I could afford to employ you.'

The grand ladies from Vasastan said I had good taste. That wasn't true. I laughed in secret at them, for they didn't realise I always agreed with them when they said the yellow ribbons suited them best and that blue suited Mrs Holm.

I soon learned a lot, more about people than materials and ribbons, but most of all, I learned the art of serving in a shop.

Mother was glad of the money I earned. But she didn't like my being alone in the shop.

'As soon as you leave school, you'll have to go into service,' she said. 'So I know where I have you. We'll find you a nice family, all right.'

'Never!'

I shouted at her. I went on saying no all through my last year at school, but it was no use. Mother was as stubborn as a mule. Lisa tried in vain to persuade her. Not even Ragnar could make her change her mind. Even Erik tried. 'You're stupid, Mum. The girl's much too clever to be a servant.'

'She's no cleverer than anyone else.'

I was sent to a family in Viktoriagatan. The master was especially grand, a doctor, and he wrote in the newspapers. Now, afterwards, I realise that it was there I became a Social Democrat. They were so colossally superior to me, just like that, as if that was quite self-evident. They simply didn't see me. I didn't exist. They farted, talked over my head, smelt of filth, had disgusting stains on their sheets and peculiar rubber things in bed.

At first I thought they had no shame at all. But then, when I found out what a fuss they made when they had company coming, I understood. I was no one. I was like the dog.

They used me like a beast of burden from six in the morning, when their children woke up, to late at night when I had to serve at table. They sent my miserable wages to my mother. I had one free afternoon a fortnight. Then I went to Lisa, not home. I was there for two years, and no one could ever have been lonelier.

Then there was that night when the doctor was in the dining room, writing an article and drinking cognac. I suddenly heard him staggering through the kitchen to the cubby-hole called the maid's room. He fumbled at the door and I'd just managed to get out of bed as he headed straight for me. I kicked him in the crotch. He yelled. The lady of the house came rushing in. While she was shouting and scolding, I grabbed my coat and rushed down the stairs. I thumped my way into Ragnar and Lisa's place and I don't think I've ever seen him so angry as when he rushed off to Viktoriagatan. In the middle of the night.

What he said to that lot, whether he threatened them with the police or to beat them up, I never knew. But he must have frightened them because when he came back he had all of fifty kronor for me. 'Hide it away from your mother,' he said.

Nor did I ever find out what he said the next morning to Mamma. But she fell ill and spent three days in bed with a high temperature. When she finally got up to go to the bakery, where you couldn't be ill for more than three days, she tried to say something to me. But she couldn't get the words out and I didn't care. I knew I had won over her.

'You're as thin as a rail,' she said, when she got back that afternoon.

'Don't go thinking I ever got anything inside me,' I said. 'Nothing but leftover scraps after they'd eaten. And there wasn't much left over, either.'

'There's a shortage of food with the gentry, too,' she said.

She'd made me a sandwich. I threw it straight in her face and went off to Lisa, where I ate as much as I wanted. Despite the war they had plenty of food. It was whispered that Ragnar did business on the black market, but I didn't know what that meant, and anyhow didn't care. I ate like a maniac, and when I wasn't eating, Lisa sent me off on long walks with the children.

They were good children, quiet and affectionate. With them, I discovered Slottsskogen, which made me feel at home but was grander, of course, with its grassy slopes and gentle mounds, and amazing trees I didn't recognise. And then, all those flowers!

In the evenings when I was alone in my sofa-bed in Lisa's kitchen, I kept thinking about what had happened that night when the doctor was drunk. At first, I thought most about how frightened I'd been. I really enjoyed the idea that I was a brave person. It took some time for me to realise that I hadn't had the wits to be afraid.

That was when I started thinking about that cunt I had, the one that ran with blood once a month.

I started investigating it. There was nothing odd about it. It was just a mouth that widened when you stuck a finger up it. What was peculiar was something else, that I liked it so much, got so excited by doing that. Once I'd started, it was hard to stop. I did it every night before I fell asleep.

For six months, I helped Lisa with the children and the shop. Then I got a job with Nisse Nilsson, who had a delicatessen in the market hall. He was a friend of Ragnar's. They did business together and used to go shooting together in the autumn. He was a kind, cheerful man, especially in the afternoons when his bottle of spirits was half empty.

'I need someone I can rely on then,' he said.

But he never drank more than he could hold. A bottle lasted for two days.

It was 1918 by then. The bread queues grew shorter and hunger slowly loosened its grip on the city. But then people started dying of the Spanish flu, which was only ordinary flu. So they really died of malnutrition, the children in the apartment below, the old woman across the hallway from Lisa, and lots of others. I was always frightened and kept a watchful eye on Lisa's children, and Mother, who was getting more and more exhausted every day.

But my worries faded away when I went to my new job at eight every morning, walking along the canal and across the bridge into the town centre where the market square and the great indoor markets were. For the first time, I noticed that the city was beautiful, with its glittering waterways and tall trees bowing over the quays. And I felt at home there. I was one of many plodding along on my way to work.

Spring eventually arrived and we thought that that would put an end to the Spanish flu. But the summer seemed to give it new strength and more and more people died in the wretched basements of Haga.

We called good morning to each other in the great indoor market as we took down the shutters and put out the delicacies of the day on our counters. Greta, who had a cheese booth, was nearly always the first to be ready and calling out that it was time for a coffee.

We drank it standing, munching on hard crispbread with cheese on top, and would just have time to swallow the last gulp of coffee before the great doors were opened and people started pouring in, at first wanting fresh bread for breakfast, newly churned butter and sometimes small cakes. I hadn't much to do for the first few hours, but later on in the morning, people began thinking about delicatessen and by the afternoon there was a queue.

I learned a lot, how to cut smoked salmon into paper-thin slices, how to distinguish between the many kinds of marinated herring, how to make delicious sauces, know just when the crabs were ready, how to boil shrimps and keep lobsters alive, as well as lots of other useful things such as weighing and calculating. And I got rid of my shyness and learned to talk. To give as good as I got, as Nisse Nilsson said. 'That's the most important of all, Johanna. And don't you forget it.'

Nisse was down at the harbour and the smokery in the mornings, and in the afternoon – well, that's what he was like. In the end I did almost everything, the till and the accounts, the invoices and dealings with the bank.

'Christ, what a girl,' he said, when Ragnar looked in occasionally. I grew up.

But best of all I had friends, some of them friends for life. Greta at the cheese booth, Aina at the pork butcher's and Lotta at the confectioner's.

And Stig, of course, the butcher's son. It was said that he was in love with me, but I pretended to ignore that so we were able to remain friends.

It was there in the market hall that I found out that I was pretty. The beauty of the market, Nisse said, though he was always exaggerating. But everywhere I went in the hall the boys whistled at me, however little that meant. It was a standing joke that they also sang, 'Can you whistle, Johanna?', that old song.

I'd learned to whistle like that back at the farm, two fingers in my mouth and then a shrill whistle that frightened the cats up into the trees.

I whistled like that in the market hall every time I heard that silly song. That was appreciated, but Nisse didn't like it. 'Stop that now,' he said. 'You'll spoil your lovely mouth.'

One day, quite early on, I caught sight of the doctor from Viktoriagatan. He was heading straight for my counter. My mouth turned dry and my heart started thumping, but the thought of Nisse sitting in the cubby-hole behind me calmed me.

Anyhow, I needn't have worried. The doctor didn't even recognise me. He wanted two lobsters, twenty thin slices of smoked salmon, a kilo of shrimps and half a kilo of smoked Baltic herrings.

I got them all ready for him and took his money. The total sum was, to a krona, double the wages he had paid me for a month's work.

He tried to haggle.

'Sorry, but we have fixed prices.'

Nisse had heard and came out and praised me. 'That's as it should be,' he said, friendly but firm. Then he said, 'How pale you are, girl. Go and have a cup of coffee.'

So I sat there in the café and tried to digest what seemed impossible. He hadn't even recognised me, the miserable wretch.

I said before that being in service had turned me into a Social Democrat. But I have a habit of making myself better than I am. It was the family in Viktoriagatan who taught me to hate the middle classes.

CHAPTER 48

It happened one stormy April day in 1920, just before the midday rush-hour.

I was alone in the stall. The counter was messy because I had just cut up an eel for a customer who'd told me there was a hurricane wind blowing outside and the canal had overflowed. After he'd gone, I was just about to wipe the counter clean when I found I hadn't any water.

We had no running water in the stalls. But in the middle of the hall below the glass cupola was a circular yard with a well and a pump. I asked Greta at the cheese stall to keep an eye on mine for me while I went off with the bucket.

'Hurry on back,' she said.

So I rushed. But just as I was about to open the heavy door to the glassed-in yard, I dropped the bucket and it fell to the stone floor with a clatter. Annoyed, I tried to bend down to pick it up again. But I couldn't.

Then I tried to lift my right hand to open the door. I couldn't do that, either, and I realised I was paralysed. For a moment, I thought about infantile paralysis. But I wasn't frightened. It was so quiet all round me. And inside me. Such peace, I could neither think nor feel any fear. It grew strangely light, too. It was somehow … solemn.

Several minutes passed and only momentarily did it occur to me that I was in a hurry.

Then there was a huge bang as the glass cupola gave way in the storm and fell in with a crash that would have woken the dead. The door flew open, struck my head and hurled me right across the passage into the wall. Splinters of glass flew all over the place and one stuck in my arm, but I covered my eyes with both hands, so my face wasn't affected. People came rushing in from all round, crying out, 'Thank heavens, Johanna's here. She'd gone out before … But she's bleeding. Telephone! Police! Ambulance.'

A nice doctor at the hospital took the glass splinter out of my arm and stitched up the wound.

'Your guardian angel was there with you,' he said.

Then men from the police and the chief of the fire brigade came to see me. No, I had neither seen nor heard anything unusual. 'I was in such a hurry,' I said.

They believed me.

The accident was much talked about, as the crash had been heard all over the city. It was in the newspaper, too, about the crash and me: 'The girl with the guardian angel'. They teased me at work.

'How's things with your angels today?'

One day it was all too much and I burst into tears. Stig comforted me and blew my nose. Then there was no more about guardian angels.

But Mother read about it in the paper and she said something strange. 'I hope you know it's true.'

I didn't answer, but for the first time in many years we looked at each other in agreement. Then she smiled slightly before speaking.

'Was it your father, Johanna?'

'I don't know, Mother.'

That was true. I didn't know. I don't know to this day. I didn't want an explanation. Neither then, nor later.

All I knew was that a miracle had occurred and after that I could remember Father and the forests, the roar of the falls, the diver calling at dusk, the stories he told me, the songs we sang. I hadn't dared do that before. Now the images came pouring over me, at first in dreams at night and then in broad daylight. I seemed to have opened a sluice gate.

I dreamed we were flying, Father and I, sailing in the upper currents by Wolf Mountain. Night had fallen by the time we got to the peak and had sat down to rest. He pointed at the stars and said they were distant, alien worlds. When I asked who lived there, he said the houses of the stars were empty and deserted.

We flew over lakes, too, the long lake and the Norwegian lakes and all the thousands of meres in the forest.

These dreams of flying filled me with an indescribable joy, a feeling of victory. Of power, yes, sheer power.

It was different in the daytime. It all came back to me. Everything, but everything, kept reminding me. A bird sang on my way home through the avenue and I stopped to listen. I knew. It's a chaffinch. I called in on Ernst at his stall and suddenly smelt flour from a barrel and saw the rays of sunlight dancing in the flour dust of the mill back at home. One Sunday, Greta and I walked up to Delsjön, sat down on the headland where the forest was reflected in the deep lake. On the shore were willows and birches with their perianths and catkins. Then I saw the maples back home, their pale green flowers falling into the Norwegian lakes.

'Can you smell honey?'

No, Greta didn't know that scent.

It was almost as strange with Mother. I'd thought I was free of her.

184

Now she came back with all the power a mother can have. Despite everything, she was the only one who had always been there.

I had long conversations with her, silent conversations, but they were real to me. We were sitting at the dinner table on May Day, after I'd joined the procession, heard the campaign songs and the rattle of the red flags in the wind.

'What's wrong with poor people claiming their rights?' I asked her.

'Things'll go wrong for folk who's no longer humble,' she said. 'Who's going to do what has to be done if the poor doesn't? Surely you doesn't believe the rich and powerful is going to clear up their own filth?'

'Mother, you must understand that times are different now.'

'I have understood. People hate.'

'There's something in that, Mother. The hatred is at last beginning to mature and will soon bear fruit.'

'And what does that taste like?'

'I think it'll be harsh, like sloes, Mother, that you've always said were so good for us.'

'No one can live on sloes.'

'No, but honest wages and safe jobs. There's something new, Mother, something you've never thought about.'

'And what would that be?'

'Justice, Mother.'

'There's no justice in this world. God rules just as He's always done.'

'Supposing God doesn't exist, that wicked God you believe in? Supposing it's we ourselves who rule?'

'You don't know what you're talking about, girl. Some folks are blind, sick and lame. Innocent children die. Lots have their life ruined long before they have time to think.'

'More would be alive and healthy if people had better food and housing.'

'True. But new masters always appear.'

'No. We're going to have a world in which people are their own

185

masters. I've just heard the speaker say that.'

She shook her head. 'Like Larsson in number three, then,' she said. 'He's rich, with his workshop, and he doesn't have to bow to anybody. But he beats the life out of his children and drinks like a fish. People don't get any better from having things better. What about that rich family you worked for? They weren't no better than the worst of 'em when I was a child.'

I thought about that conversation for a long time. Mother's misfortune was not that she was stupid. It was that she hadn't the words.

Then Ragnar had his fortieth birthday. We had a party with a long table under the big tree in the courtyard. The weather was fine, Lisa baked cakes and buns and Mother made little cakes. Nisse Nilsson filled a big box with herring and salmon and pâtés and all kinds of delicacies.

'Birthday present for your brother,' he said. 'But tell him he'll have to pay for the beer and spirits himself.'

A lot of people were coming, for Ragnar had friends all over town.

We women were proud when the table was ready. It looked beautiful with all the flowers and birch twigs and broad green ribbons. No one noticed that the tablecloths were sheets and the plates were of various kinds borrowed from the neighbours.

When Mother and I went back up to the apartment to put on our best clothes, we heard the accordion players begin practising. The Emperor Waltz.

Mother snorted. Then she took out her old long black woollen dress.

'Can't you put on something a bit more modern? The green one?'

But I knew she was implacable. She wanted to look respectable. Old and dignified.

The party was a success. People sang and ate, and as the bottles emptied, they grew more and more boisterous. Mother looked worried, but calmed down when Lisa whispered that Ragnar was sober and would make sure there was no fighting or anything unpleasant. Mother left early, saying quietly that she was tired and her back ached. I went up with her, helped her into bed and covered her with a blanket.

That annoyed her. She could never accept help or friendliness. 'The dancing's starting in the yard now. Go on down and enjoy yourself.'

I did a turn with Nisse Nilsson. But I didn't enjoy it at all. I was thinking about Mother all the time and was angry as well as miserable. Why couldn't she be happy like other people, like all the women sitting there in the evening sun, gossiping and laughing? Many of them were much older than she was. She was only fifty-three.

She was fifty-three!

Something incomprehensible was trying to come out, breaking through my head.

No.

Yes. She was fifty-three and her son was having his fortieth birthday.

She'd given birth at thirteen.

I counted nine months back and came to October.

When she was only twelve.

A child!

It wasn't possible. Perhaps he was a foster-son.

No, they're alike.

I had always known Ragnar had a different father from my brothers and me. Who? They said Mother had been in love with a cousin when she was young, but that couldn't be possible, either. A twelve-year-old doesn't fall so madly in love that she goes to bed with a man. Someone had said she had grieved almost to death when the cousin had been accidentally shot out hunting. Who? Must ask Lisa. But what would she know?

I left early, too, telling Lisa I must go up to Mother.

'Is she unwell?'

'I don't know. I'm worried.'

I ran up the stairs, knowing I must ask. 'Are you asleep, Mother?'
'No, just resting a bit.'

'I've just worked it out you were twelve when you got with child and hardly thirteen when you gave birth.'

She sat up, and despite the gathering dusk, I could see she was scarlet in the face. In the end she said, 'You've always been clever. Strange you didn't work it out before.'

'Yes, it is. But someone told me you were in love with Ragnar's father and you were terribly miserable when he died. So I didn't want to think about it, or ask you.'

She started to laugh, a terrible laugh, as if she'd gone out of her mind. When she saw that she was frightening me, she clapped her hand over her mouth and fell silent.

Then she said, 'Ragnar's father was a rapist and a rogue. When they shot him, it was the best thing to happen in my life. I was always afraid of him. Though there was no need to be, for when I married Broman, he had church papers for the boy.'

'How long were you on your own with Ragnar, before you met Father?'

'Four years it was, as a whore and in disgrace.'

I didn't dare look at her while I undressed. But I slipped in beside her on the kitchen sofa and cried myself to sleep, the accordions playing and the dancing going on round trees and table, privy and shed, down there in the courtyard.

CHAPTER 49

How I danced that summer when the city was three hundred years old and presented itself with Liseberg. Nowadays people only think of it as an amusement park with roundabouts and a roller-coaster. Though most have to admit it's lovely.

To us, living there when it was built, it was like a fairy-tale come true, buildings as beautiful as temples in the park, ponds and a water-lily pool, streams singing down the slopes, orchestras playing, theatre and ballet in the colonnades, and a thousand, no tens of thousands of flowers.

I wore out three pairs of shoes in a few weeks, and I remember the first half of the 1920s as the best in my life.

Though it wasn't just Liseberg.

We were given an eight-hour day. That was important to Mother, for her bad back got better. Then we were given holidays, and Aina and Greta and I took the train to Karlstad. From there, we went walking up Fryksdal to Sunne and Mårbacka. The journey alone was an adventure, not least for people in the villages along the lake. Three young women in long trousers, my goodness, walking on their own, yes, that really was astonishing at the time.

I now realise I've forgotten something important: Selma Lagerlöf. Aina had read about her in the newspaper and had borrowed *The Löwensköld Ring* from the library. All three of us read it, wearing it out just as we'd worn out our shoes over that jubilee summer. What an impression she made!

Perhaps most of all on me, who recognised it all. There it was, the enchantment of childhood. I read and reread it, and again felt the depths of the world. Here was someone telling me that nothing was what it appeared to be, that everything had a hidden meaning. I put away some of my wages every week and bought her books by paying in instalments at the bookshop. Handsome half-bound editions. How proud I was as I accumulated them on my little bookshelf.

I don't remember much about Mårbacka, and I think that's because it was a disappointment. Perhaps I'd imagined the whole place would glow, that the grounds would shimmer and Gösta Berling and Charlotte Löwensköld, Nils of Skrålycka and the girl from Stormyrtorpet could be glimpsed among the trees.

It was Selma Lagerlöf who taught me that love was a tremendous force, irresistible, more painful and more wonderful than I could ever have imagined. Now, so long afterwards, I wonder what Miss Lagerlöf did to those of us who were young and yearning, yet born into circumstances in which there was scarcely room for such grandiose emotions.

Anyhow, we started dreaming about the prince, Aina, Greta and I.

I mustn't just blame the books. When, one after another, we started aiming for 'Mr Right' and made marriage our goal, there were several other driving forces. Though we never saw the connection.

At the time, in the late 1920s, Göteborg was beginning to slow down. Money was tighter, two booths in the market hall went bankrupt and men without jobs began to roam the streets.

The great depression had begun, but at first we knew neither the word nor what it would mean.

It said in the papers that women were taking the men's jobs. New laws were demanded, prohibiting married women from working. All over town, girls were dismissed and owners themselves ran the shops. I had considered it obvious that I would always earn my living, so I became more and more worried.

It's almost impossible to explain to young women today how the longing for love became interwoven with fear, and eventually led to a desperate hunt. To us, it was a matter of life and death. We were back where Mother had once been, but with the difference that the peasant girl had had the support of her family in the search for a man who could keep her.

If anyone was receptive to great love, then I was when I met Arne. He was a foreman at one of the large shipyards, and surely the crisis would never reach them? But then I was ashamed of the thought, and later, when Mother said that he was a decent man and would always be able to support a family, I was angry.

'I'd marry him if he was a street-sweeper.'

I've said before that I have an unfortunate habit of making myself better than I am. Beautifying. The simple truth was that I felt I simply had to be in love, now that Nisse Nilsson sold scarcely enough salmon to cover my wages. Then Greta's cheese stall went bankrupt and she had to go into service.

But I was in love. Something happened to my body the first time

I saw Arne Karlberg. My hands grew sweaty, my heart thumped and I had a tickling feeling down below. For the first time, I realised there could be a hunger in that place I had, and a hot longing in my blood.

It was at a meeting of the local Social Democratic party. Man after man got up and said the usual things about injustices and that, despite the wretched times, we must stand firm with our demands. Towards the end a strapping great fellow went up and said that females were not only taking the work from the men, but they also contributed to keeping wages low by doing the same jobs as men, but not having the wits to ask for the same pay.

I was so angry, I forgot to be shy and asked to speak. I asked what they thought all the wives of drunken husbands, the unmarried women, all the widows and other lone mothers were to do to have a roof over their heads for themselves and their children.

There was a muttering in the audience.

But then Arne went up to the lectern and said that he agreed with the previous speaker, and that the trade unions ought to put all their energies into aligning themselves with the women and making sure they got the same working conditions.

Equal pay for equal work, he said, and that was the first time I'd ever heard those words.

There was a lot of derisive whistling in the hall.

But I looked at him and all those physical things happened, those I've just described. He was handsome. Tall and fair, his face both sensitive and forceful, blue eyes and a pugnacious chin.

At last!

After the meeting, he came over to me and asked if I'd like a cup of coffee. There was a café in Södra Allégatan and we went there, but found, after all, that we weren't that keen on coffee. So we walked on through the avenue and along the canals. We walked for half the night, taking in the quays as well as West and North and East Hamngatan. In the end we sat down on the plinth of the statue of the hero king in Gustav Adolf Square and Arne said the king was a rogue and a robber who could well listen to an honest conversation between two modern people.

I laughed. Then I stared at him, remembering what Father had said about King Karl XII – that the bullet that had put an end to that hero was a blessing.

But the night grew colder, and he walked me home. In our entrance, he said he'd never in his life seen anything prettier than the girl who'd stood up at the meeting and was so sparklingly angry.

He had a sailing boat he had built himself. On the Friday, just as we were shutting up the booth, he appeared in the market hall and asked me if I'd like to go sailing with him on Saturday. We could go north beyond the islands towards Marstrand and look at the fortress.

Then he said tentatively, 'Takes a bit of time, a trip like that. So you'll have to reckon on sleeping on the boat.'

I nodded. I understood. I was prepared.

He had a few instructions, too, warm clothes and cool clothes. He would bring eggs and bread and butter and sausage. If I wanted anything else, perhaps I could arrange it.

At midday on Saturday I cleared the booth of all the delicacies left, for I'd noticed his hungry eyes as he'd stood by the counter looking at all the good things we sold.

What did I say to Mother? I've forgotten.

What I remember most of all that weekend is neither Arne nor making love in that cramped boat. No, it's the sea. And the boat.

It's strange. I'd lived in Göteborg for many years. I'd known the city smelt of sea and salt when the wind came from the west. But I'd never seen the sea. All my outings had been to the forests and the mountains inland, not to the coast. Of course, I'd roamed round the harbour like everyone else, gazing at foreign ships and taking in the smell of spices and hemp and fruit. And like all Göteborgians, I'd stood on the quay as the *Kungsholm* had slipped in and moored.

But the American ship with its sloping funnels, so vast and handsome, did not belong in my world. That was for the rich.

Now I was in a boat dancing with full sails across infinity. Blue expanses to the end of the world, the murmur of the wind, the splash of waves, the glitter – so sparkling it hurt your eyes.

'Borrow my cap,' said Arne.

But I didn't want the peak shading my eyes. I wanted my eyes wide open to take in everything, the sea and the sky.

'Put a shirt over your shoulders, or you'll get burned,' said Arne.

But neither did I want a shirt. I wanted to receive all that magnificence with my entire body. But when it came to the shirt, Arne insisted and I had to obey. I was grateful later that evening, for I could feel the skin on my face and neck burning.

'That's Böttö lighthouse to port,' said Arne. 'And right out there is Vinga. When we get there, we'll turn and tack north in the channel between Invinga and Vinga. The boat'll list then, but that's nothing to worry about.'

I nodded, and when he tacked and the boat heeled over I screamed, not from fear but from sheer exhilaration.

'D'you think it's fun?'

Fun was not the word, and I laughed like a child. 'It's wonderful,' I cried.

We sailed close to the wind beyond the islands, heading north along the coast, the sails singing, the sea roaring and hissing salt water over us.

'I can take in sail if it frightens you.'

I didn't know what he meant, but I laughed again and cried out that I wasn't scared.

'I'll head for Stora Pölsan into the lee below Klåver Island,' he yelled. 'There's a good harbour called Utkäften.'

It all sounded as if he were reading poetry. The wind rose and Arne yelled again. 'We'll have to take down the foresail.'

I drew a great question mark in the air and he burst out laughing. 'You'll have to take the tiller while I go forward,' he yelled.

I took the tiller and he showed me the course. 'Due west over there, you see.' It took me only a couple of minutes to learn how to keep a straight course.

Once the foresail was down, the boat began to right and we slowed down. A moment later, we slipped into the lee behind the island and it was as calm as in the kingdom of heaven.

'You must take the tiller again while I take down the mainsail.'

The mainsail fluttered and flapped before it came down on deck. Then it was as quiet as quiet, nothing but a gentle murmur as the boat glided through the water. Then a gull screamed and after that the silence was even more intense. Then a huge splash as Arne flung the anchor into the sea before running forward and jumping ashore with a rope.

'This'll do fine,' he said, when he came back. 'Why are you crying?'

'It's all so marvellous.'

Then we stood on deck and kissed and hugged.

'God,' he said. 'You're the girl I've been waiting for all my life.'

Then he showed me the boat. Steps went down into the cabin, each step a big roomy drawer, in them a whole kitchen, glasses, porcelain, knives, cutlery, saucepans – everything. He had stowed the food under the floor of the cabin, in the keelson, he said. He showed me the paraffin stove and how to keep it out of the draught.

I cooked while he put the sails in order. It smelt divine, salt and seaweed and fried eggs and sausages. We ate as if starving.

'The sea gets you.'

'What do you mean?'

'The sea makes you hungry.'

I remember the island, flowers I'd never seen before, how warm the smooth rocks were to walk on and then the gulls diving down, screaming at us as if they'd gone mad.

'They've got eggs in their nests,' said Arne. 'We mustn't disturb them.'

That's just what Father said whenever we got too close to Wolf Mountain in the spring.

So we returned to the boat and went on kissing, and now I could feel the air between us tingling as if it had become electric, and I felt the blood rushing through my veins.

After that I remember that it hurt and then it was all over. Disappointing in a way. Not overwhelming.

194

CHAPTER 50

Mother and I were living on our own in the apartment now and could keep it clean and tidy. I had been given some leftover geraniums by the florist in the market hall and Mother tended them so that it was really lovely in our windows. Even in the middle of the week we used the embroidered tablecloths in the living room.

She was in a better mood these days, not just because we'd become intimate and got on so well together but mostly, perhaps, because things had gone better for my brothers. All three had work and were safely married.

She became quite talkative and in the evenings we often sat chatting about the old days, remembering together. I remembered the forest and the lakes, the peregrine falcons over Wolf Mountain and the birds singing in the evenings. Mother remembered people, the smith's wife and her evil eye, the smith who tempted Father into drinking. And old Anna, the midwife.

'Surely you remember her? She lived with us when you were little,' she said, and then I remembered the person who taught me everything about food and baking, herbs and medicines.

'She was a great person,' Mother said. 'And kind, too.'

She was an angel, I thought. Whatever had made me forget her?

'You've got her cleverness to thank for your life,' Mother said, and then I was to hear about that terrible birth 'of the babe that didn't want to come into the world. She hung on till Anna had to cut me.'

I was horrified. Didn't dare think about the Saturday on Arne's boat.

We mostly talked about Father and his stories.

'Do you remember the story about Death and the candle he had in his cave for every person?'

'Oh, yes. That was Johannes.'

She told me about the healer, about Grandmother's death and Johannes's prediction about Father.

'Turned out to be right in time.'

She talked about Ingegerd, the aunt who'd never married and was a free and independent person although she was a woman. In the middle of that story, she stopped and then said something very strange.

'She had a life that was her own. It's why she could always be true and honest.'

I said nothing for a long time. Then I told her about Arne.

She flushed as always when agitated.

'Can he keep you and the children?'

'Yes.'

She thought for a long time, then said, 'D'you like him?'

'I think so.'

'It's not so important at first. If he's a good man, you'll get fond of him with the years.'

This was as far from Selma Lagerlöf as anyone could get, but I didn't laugh, only hoped she was right.

Then the Saturday arrived when Arne was to visit us. By then I had told him about Dalsland and Father, and about my brothers who'd had such a bad time at first in the city, Ragnar who'd been a father to us, 'he's marvellous and a bit mad but now he's got three vehicles and, as always, things are going well for him.'

Arne looked rather dubious at the mention of Ragnar, but when I told him about Mother, that she was kind but let her tongue run away with her like a child, he brightened. 'I like people like that,' he said. 'They don't lie.'

'Gracious,' I said. It was true and I'd never thought of it before. Although we were walking along the street, I stopped and gave him a hug. People laughed and Arne was embarrassed.

At home everything was of the best, the most expensive cups on the very best cloth and seven different kinds of fancy biscuits with coffee. Mother was wearing her black dress, her jet necklace, a cross at her throat and a dazzling white apron.

'We've an apartment just like this only the other way round, if you understand,' said Arne.

Then he noticed the Värmland sofa. 'What a beauty. Such fine craftsmanship.'

He ran his hand over joints and corners, saying no one did that kind of carpentry these days, or such marquetry either.

Neither Mother nor I knew what marquetry was. I was surprised, but Mother almost fainted with delight.

'I'll have you know, Arne, they've all mocked me over the years on account of that sofa.'

Everything went smoothly that afternoon. Arne told us about his job at the Göta works and that he was responsible for the carpentry workshop where they made the interior equipment for the big ships.

Interior equipment, new words for both Mother and me.

'Do you mean the furniture?'

'Yes, but not ordinary furniture. Most of it's built in. Like on my little boat. But better quality, mahogany and walnut, that kind.'

'Oh, so grand,' said Mother.

Towards the afternoon, Ragnar dropped by and the two men looked each other up and down as if measuring each other's strength before a fight. But they shook hands like decent folk and in the middle of it all Ragnar started laughing. I've probably not mentioned it before, but somehow no one can ever resist his laughter. It shakes the whole room, the cups, too, and goes right to the heart, making everyone else laugh as well. At first Arne looked surprised, but then he laughed, and they laughed together so much that the petals started falling off the geraniums.

'Can't think what's so funny,' said Mother. 'But I'll brew some fresh coffee.'

Then Arne said, surprisingly, 'Maybe only a man can understand what's funny.'

I caught a glint of approval in Ragnar's eyes before the laughter started up again and rolled round the apartment. Then the two men started talking about motor vehicles, Ragnar showing off, though it was soon clear that Arne knew quite a bit about engines, too. After a while, they started on boats and Ragnar gave up. 'Know nothing about them. Landlubber, that's me.'

'Come on out for a spin some time.'

So it was decided we were to go out for a sail the next day, if wind and weather were right. But Mother didn't want to.

'Deadly afraid of the sea, I am.'

I had my period the next morning, so didn't go with them either. But when the men got back in the evening, I could see they'd had a good time. I was pleased, almost as pleased as I was about that blessed period.

Two things of importance were said that evening. First, when Ragnar said I'd always been a clever girl so, of course, I'd managed to get hold of a decent man.

Arne was glowing with pride after Ragnar left.

But when Mother heard that Arne still lived at home, although he was the eldest of the brothers, she said, 'So you're one of those chicks afraid to leave the nest, eh?'

He turned scarlet first, then white. I didn't know at the time that he changed colour like that when he was angry. But at the time he couldn't shout and bang his fist on the table. So he said nothing.

Many years later, he told me that it was Mother's words that evening that made him decide. For he did in the end. But not until I was with child. By then I had met his mother and had begun to understand a thing or two.

CHAPTER 51

She was seated in the middle of the sofa, alone, a small person demanding a great deal of space.

She was beautiful, too, rather like the kind of Chinese ivory statuette sold in grand shops in the Avenue. Straight back, long neck, finely drawn features, blue eyes. Like her son. But colder than him, much colder. I gave a little bob and held out my hand. She didn't take it.

Then I regretted the curtsy.

There was another woman there, younger and more friendly.

'This is Lotten. She's married to my brother,' said Arne.

'Gustav's coming soon,' she said. 'There was something he had to do.'

I liked her at once and she held my hand firmly for a long time, as if encouraging me.

It was quite a while before I noticed his father, a large man taking up no space at all. He was sitting in a corner behind the kitchen door, reading a newspaper. There was something timid about him and he didn't look at me as we shook hands. I could see he was afraid.

'So this is Johanna who wants to marry my boy. I suppose you're with child,' said the Ice Queen.

'No, not as far as I know,' I said. 'Anyhow, Arne's the one who most wants us to marry.'

The ivory yellow face flushed with anger, then turned white. Like her son's.

'Mother.' Arne's voice had appeal in it.

She offered me nothing, not even the simplest cup of coffee. They were all silent. It was ghostly. I looked around. The apartment was older and shabbier than ours. Dark brown wallpaper, walls covered with photographs and glossy religious prints. The moment I'd stepped over the threshold, I realised it smelt in there, that the people who lived there peed in the kitchen sink. Then Arne's brother came bouncing in and gave me a great hug.

'Lord, what a grand girl you've got hold of,' he said to his brother, then turned to me. 'Don't let Mother scare you. She's not as fierce as she looks.'

The ivory lady clutched at her heart. Lotten said, 'Let's go now. Gustav and Arne are going to try out the new sail.'

All four of us ran down the stairs. No one said goodbye, except me, and I shook the old man by the hand.

We didn't go to the boat, but home with Gustav and Lotten.

They had a fine two-roomer where the coffee was all ready on the table. There was even a cream gâteau to welcome me.

'You weren't scared, were you, girl?' said Gustav.

'A little. But surprised more than anything else.'

'So Arne hadn't told you?' Lotten asked the question, and there was ice in her voice.

'What the hell should I have said?' said Arne. 'You can't describe what Mamma's like.'

'Yes, you can,' said Lotten, her voice frosty. 'She's selfish and a megalomaniac.'

For the second time I saw him turn first white then red. Then he crashed his clenched fist down on the table and shouted, 'She has only one failing and that's that she's too fond of her children.'

'Calm down, now,' cried Lotten. 'You have to behave in our house.'

Gustav tried to mediate.

'It's not easy, Lotten. She was a kind mother until her heart started playing her up.'

'And that happened conveniently just when her sons started acquiring wives.'

'We're leaving, Johanna,' said Arne furiously.

'Not me,' I said. 'I'm not going to be the one to cause trouble between you. You must admit it wasn't nice of her, refusing to shake hands and not even offering us coffee. I've never been received like that before.'

I realised then how miserable I was. I swallowed the lump in my throat, but could do nothing about the tears.

Gustav and Lotten comforted me. Arne looked desperate.

'Can't you try to explain without quarrelling?'

They couldn't, so it turned quite silent.

'I'm sorry for your father,' I said. 'So shaming for him. Why didn't he say anything?'

'He got out of the habit of talking years ago,' said Gustav. 'It's awful.'

'But he could stand up to her,' said Arne loudly. 'Why the hell's he so cowardly, just creeping around saying nothing?'

'He's frightened of her,' said Lotten. 'So are you. And Gustav.'

'I'm bloody not frightened of her.'

'Show it, then. Don't go home until she's apologised. And marry Johanna.'

'I don't know whether I want to any longer,' I said, getting up, and after thanking them for coffee, I left. As I went out of the door I heard Lotten berating Arne, telling him he was letting his mother destroy his life. He ran after me down the stairs, but I turned round and said I wanted to be alone, that I needed to think.

But that didn't go well. My thoughts were whirling round in my head and were very confused.

When I look back at what I've written about that first strange meeting with Arne's mother, I wonder whether I'm telling lies. I can't remember word for word what was said. Memory selects and distorts, so perhaps I'm being untruthful without meaning to. What happened was that I detested my mother-in-law as long she lived. Over the years, I came to hate those sides of Arne that reminded me of her, his insistence on always being in the centre, on always getting his own way, his rage and fearful short temper.

When I got home to Mother, I told her I'd never met such a difficult person as my future mother-in-law. I cried as I told her about it.

'Is she religious, too?' she said

'I think so. There were crosses and pictures of Jesus on the walls.'

'Lord, it's bad,' said Mother. 'They're the ones who begrudge you your good name.'

Arne was waiting for me after work on Monday evening.

'I've left home,' he said.

'Where are you living?'

'On the boat. It's fine as long as the summer lasts.'

'What did you say to her?'

'Nothing. I just went home and packed my things. She'll have to give in now.'

Of course I was pleased. And yet?

'I need more time to think,' I said, and left him.

CHAPTER 52

But there was no time and I had no choice. Three weeks later, I was clearly with child. We exchanged rings, assuring each other that we belonged together and I convinced myself he was kind and safe.

'You don't have to marry,' said Mother. 'We can manage, you and me.'

That was magnificent.

Then I had to tell her how bad things were for Nisse Nilsson's shop and that we sold hardly any more than we bought in.

That night I found it hard to sleep. I lay there, twisting and turning, trying to get the pictures of Arne to fit together. The young man who'd bravely stood up at the meeting and been mocked for agreeing with justice for women. The sailor who was so bold at sea. Politically clear-sighted, intelligent and knowledgeable. Foreman. And then this feeble creature sneaking away from his mother.

I can't deny I thought a bit about Stig as well, the butcher's son in love with me, a man who would inherit the shop. I could keep my job with him, and all my friends, all my self-confidence. He was a nice person. Considerate. And both his parents liked me.

But he couldn't make my body tingle.

We were to be married in Copenhagen, to sail there. But first there was to be a betrothal party back at home with Mother. She took out her savings and equipped me as if I were gentry, sheets, pillow-cases, handwoven towels, the finest lace for curtains and two damask tablecloths.

There was a shortage of apartments, but we were relying on

Ragnar. He would fix that for us, with all his connections with builders in the city.

Then came that awful Monday. I was three months gone, but had peculiar period pains when I went to work in the morning. At Nisse Nilsson's, I collapsed and started bleeding heavily. Aina took me in a taxi to a private maternity clinic where they anaesthetised me. When I woke, it was achingly empty inside me.

Mother came in the afternoon. She was pale and went on and on about fate. Ragnar and Lisa sent flowers. I was sleepy and sick. I was also homesick, a strange longing for an unknown place I could call home.

They woke me with strong coffee and a sandwich. My head cleared. There were quite a few thoughts in it and plenty of time to brood on them.

When Arne appeared, I would tell him that he should go back to his mother. Calmly, not angrily or unpleasantly, I would say that that would be best for us both. He would have a clear conscience and wouldn't have to be torn between his mother and me. I would be free and feel good about it, because I was a very independent person.

But, when he came, he took both my hands in his and his eyes were moist, his voice wavering. 'Dear girl,' he said. 'Dear girl.'

That was all. It was enough. I knew at once he was a person to be trusted. And I wasn't wrong in my judgement. When things were difficult, when danger or illness arose, or fear threatened, he was the kind of man who became adult, strong and safe as Father had been.

'It was a little boy,' Arne said, and then I saw he was crying, too.

Before they pushed him out, he tried to say that it was an accident and we'd soon have another child. That gave me hope and when I fell asleep that night, I pressed my hands to the aching vacuum down below and whispered, 'Come back.'

Since then, I've often thought that that moment at the clinic sealed my fate. The question of just who he was came up again many times over the years. I gradually also learned to ask myself who I was. And then what he meant to me and I to him. What we had between us apart from our yearning. He was like me, after all, far away from home.

Now that I am old, I realise for the first time that yearning isn't a bad basis for fellowship. It can be both more secure and greater than the reality I desired so ardently when I was young. I don't believe in any reality now, and it is by chasing after it that we kill everything.

Mother gave the betrothal party one sunny summer Sunday, directly after morning service. Arne's mother sat alone on the Värmland sofa and at last it came into its own. They suited each other, the ivory lady and the uncomfortable but elegant piece of furniture. She didn't say much but she observed everything closely. She hadn't brought a wedding present with her and she spent a long time critically examining all Mother's fine linen. Dear kind Lisa devoted herself to Arne's father. They talked about farming, his eyes brightening and a ring coming into his voice.

He had something to say on that, indeed he had.

Then Gustav and Lotten came, bringing with them a coffee service, and both Mother and I noticed that Lotten did not speak to her mother-in-law. Ragnar came last and that was the end of worrying about keeping the conversation going. He brought bubbly white wine with him, opened it with a pop and proposed a toast to us.

'You've had better luck than you deserve,' he said to Arne. 'For Johanna isn't only the prettiest girl in town, she's also got the best mind and the kindest heart.'

Arne looked proud and his mother clutched at her heart. When Ragnar noticed, he burst out into his famous laughter. As it spread through the company, the old girl lost her certainty. Her gaze wandered and the hand holding the glass trembled. For one brief moment, I felt sorry for her.

Ragnar also had a taxi firm so he drove the old couple home while I helped Mother with the dishes. Arne kept hovering round us as if wanting to say something, then finally got it out. 'She's a bit peculiar, my mother.'

Hanna Broman was not a person ever to smooth things over, not this time either.

'To say the least of it. I'm sorry for your father.'

Then Ragnar was back wanting to talk about an idea he'd had. People were building their own houses out towards the sea, small houses round an old fishing village a few miles from town. One of the men had lost his job and gone bankrupt, and a timber yard Ragnar worked for had taken over the house the man was building. The roof was on and only the indoor carpentry and painting needed to be done. The timber-yard man wanted to sell, quickly and cheaply.

The colour had risen in Arne's face as Ragnar talked, and his eyes gleamed. 'How much?'

'About twelve thousand, but we can haggle.'

'I've only half that.'

The eagerness in Arne's blue eyes faded, but Ragnar went on. 'That's all right. You can borrow the rest from the bank. It'll work out all right. You've got a steady job and I'll stand guarantor.'

'But I promised Mother I'd never borrow.'

'Oh, for Christ's sake!' shouted Ragnar, and Arne realised he'd made a fool of himself.

'When can we look at the house?' he said.

'Now. I've a car outside. But maybe you ought to ask Johanna first.'

'At least we can go and take a look,' I said, but as we ran down the stairs I was dizzy with expectation and squeezed Arne's hand.

There was squelching mud, high hills and low, smooth granite rocks, there was goose-foot and couch-grass and a half-finished house, low and long, three rooms and kitchen, space for a nursery on the upper floor. We liked it straight away and I remembered those strange dreams of coming home.

'There's a lot of work to do,' said Ragnar.

'Who's afraid of work?' said Arne.

'I want a garden,' I said.

'It's windswept here, so that won't be easy,' said Arne. 'I'll have to build you a wall so it's sheltered.'

We took a ladder and climbed up to the floor above, and it was just as Arne had thought. We could see right out to sea, across the harbour where the fishing boats lay that Sunday.

Then we sat all evening in Mother's kitchen working out interest and the mortgage. It was going to be a tight squeeze, but we'd manage.

Nothing came of our plan to sail to Copenhagen. We had a simple wedding at the priest's in Haga, and then we set about it, me outside, Arne in the house. That was when I found that Arne had plenty of friends and a surprising ability to organise, lead and decide. He paid them with spirits to go with all the good food I cooked. Sunday evenings were cheerful and not much got done. He himself seldom took a drink.

All round us, young people were working on their half-finished houses. At once I had acquaintances, newly married women with the same expectations as I had.

We moved in in October. We hadn't decorated and we had practically no furniture. But it was fun. And we had a kitchen stove and two tiled stoves, so we didn't freeze.

CHAPTER 53

The bad times went on, and things got worse. The ball-bearing factory, where they had almost five thousand employees, now employed only three hundred. The others went hungry and froze. Cars were being made in an empty ball-bearing factory in Hisingen, cars called Volvo, and there were people who believed something would come of it.

Even the shipyards were threatened, Arne said. But so far they were getting by on repairs.

I was happy in all this. I had laid out a garden and I'm not boasting when I say it was wonderful. No one had such glorious apples as I had and nowhere, not even the Gardening Society, had such beautiful roses.

My garden had high mountains behind it, an open slope to the south-west and a wall facing the sea. And on the west coast it's amazing – if you have a piece of land in a sunny situation sheltered from the wind, your garden becomes almost as lovely as in the Mediterranean. You can grow grapes and peaches on espaliers. Not to mention roses.

I never told Arne things were going badly for Nisse Nilsson at his delicatessen. There was no need to, for Arne took it for granted that I would stay at home and he would support the family.

That also seemed natural to me at the time, that autumn when I had so much to do. All the sewing for our new home, just to mention one thing. Lisa gave me an old treadle machine. It was sluggish and kept jamming and I swore at and argued with the wretched thing. When Arne came home, he laughed at me, took it apart and oiled it here and there, while I stood admiringly beside him. When he put it together again, it was good and obedient, and over the years I've tramped a great many miles on it.

Our first bit of furniture was a huge second-hand workbench. In the basement! When Ragnar brought it out, I was angry – buying a workbench when we hadn't even got a table to eat at! But I didn't say anything, and I soon understood. Arne disappeared into the basement every evening. Table and chairs, cupboards and shelving soon appeared in a steady stream up the basement stairs.

Fine furniture, oak, mahogany and teak for the kitchen benches. 'Where do you get this fine timber from?'

He turned scarlet and said angrily I shouldn't ask so many questions. As usual, I didn't understand why he was so angry.

Most of my time that autumn was taken up with keeping an eye on the painter, Andersson. He was one of Arne's innumerable friends and I had been given definite instructions: a beer every other hour, no more, or the wallpaper would be crooked. A cooked meal and a drink before he went home in the evening. No more, or he wouldn't come back.

I kept Andersson going like that, and our home grew lighter as the evenings grew darker. We had green stripes in the bedroom and pale pink roses on a white background in the front room, where we put the new furniture of dark red mahogany. We did the kitchen ourselves, for one Saturday, Andersson had disappeared with a crate of beer I thought I'd managed to hide in the food store.

I reproached myself, but Arne laughed at the whole sorry tale.

Christmas came and we invited the family to dinner. Mother was awkward, for she found the new relatives difficult. But I went to Ragnar and said that if they didn't come, I'd kill him. So they all came, Mother, Lisa, Ragnar and the children. And two of my other brothers with their wives. We invited Gustav and Lotten as well, but they said they couldn't come.

The Ice Queen was quiet, not a single unpleasant remark crossing her lips.

'You see?' Arne whispered to me. 'She's softening.'

I couldn't see it. But before we all sat down to dinner, something significant happened. There was no snow, it was eight degrees above zero and a soft wind was blowing from the sea as my father-in-law and I walked round outside and I told him about the garden I'd dreamed of having.

The old man was transformed and his voice rang, his feet had a spring in them and he said he would help me. It could be a paradise here, he said. As long as we can fix a wall to the west ... Then the sun and the Gulf Stream will do the rest. A potato patch, he said, swedes, strawberries.

'Roses,' I said.

When he laughed, he was like Arne.

'Rely on me.'

Our guests had gone, I had done the dishes and Arne had taken the Christmas food down to the store. Then I told him what the old man had said. At first Arne smiled broadly, but then his face clouded.

'It won't work. Mamma won't let him.'

'Shall we take a bet?' I said. 'He'll come whatever she says.'

'You're an amazing person,' said Arne, and I flushed with pleasure, though also because I was not nearly as sure as I sounded. That evening we sat at the kitchen table for a long time, drawing sketches, one after another, of what the garden would be like, me talking about roses and violas, Arne about potatoes and vegetables.

'We'll have to save every penny.'

'I know, but I want roses along the wall and a big bed in front of the house. Phlox, pinks and mallows ...'

One morning in early January, I told Arne we had to go into town to see his parents that evening. 'We'll take the garden plans with us so we can discuss them with your father.' Arne was scared and pleased at the same time. I could see that, but pretended I hadn't. At this stage, I'd realised he was always feeling guilty about neglecting his mother. As we arrived at the apartment door in the old building they lived in, she was clearly pleased, and it took her several seconds to stiffen her features. 'Oh, but come on in. I'll make some coffee.'

We sat at the kitchen table and I extracted Father-in-Law from his corner and said come on now, we had things to discuss.

It worked. Life came back to the old man. He had objections. He'd been thinking. 'Arctic pines here by the end of the wall,' he said. 'The wind doesn't only come from the west. Storms also come from the south, so the wall should be at an angle,' he said. 'You want roses, Johanna, so you'll need a south wall.'

The Ice Queen was not the most surprised. Arne was.

And so pleased, so pleased. Then I took the next step.

'I'll try to get my brother to come too, then you could come out and go back by car.'

'I'll take the bus,' said the old man.

'If you get too tired, you could stay overnight,' said Arne.

My mother-in-law said nothing.

It was fun that spring when Father-in-Law and I laid out the garden. We borrowed a horse and harrow from a farm, and the old man went behind it as if he'd never done anything else. We dug the soil, got the potatoes in, dug beds and I sowed vegetables. We dug flower-beds and I sowed flowers. We dug deep holes and planted apple trees and red- and blackcurrant bushes. Once, when we were having a rest with coffee and a sandwich, he said, 'I've got old peasant blood in my veins.'

I felt that I had, too.

My father-in-law was not one for words, and yet he taught me such a lot. How to distinguish between fresh and matured manure. About the soil, how to crumble it in your fingers and feel if it needed sand or mulch, that the pretty wild pansies meant a lack of lime, and that I must always look out for the clay packing the soil solid.

It was knowledge born of experience and could be passed on with few words.

But he had ideas, too.

'Roses are all right in summer,' he said, 'but I should put in a forsythia by the wall up here by the window. With scillas and crocuses underneath.'

I nodded. I could see it in front of me. So we laid out a spring corner between the wall and the kitchen window. It gladdened me in March when the days were icy outside and you could hardly stick your nose out of the door for the cold wind. Then I sat with a cup of coffee by the window, looking out at the golden cloud on the spring bush. Father-in-law also tried to teach me patience. 'Growing things is waiting,' he said. 'You can't do anything about the weather.'

That's true, but I never learned patience. I got furious when it snowed on the tulips in May, and when treacherous February drew out the buds on bushes and trees only to kill them off with night frost.

I swore at the peonies, still doing nothing three years later, not flowering although I manured them and gave them mulch. In the fourth spring, I didn't even look at them, not until the day I took a spade and went to dig them up and throw them on the compost heap.

They were covered with big fat buds. Since then they've flowered every early summer for over twenty years.

At this time, only Father-in-Law and I worked in the garden. Arne's brother built the wall, stone by stone, at weekends. He was a mason, Gustav, happy as a lark when he and his father argued about frost-free depths and heights and breadths, and whether he should go to the expense of a sloping roof of tiles. Yes, he should, said the old man, and he made it sound like an order.

The wall had no sharp corners, but swung round in a curve to the south-west and joined the hill forming a gentle curve to the north. So my garden came to be like a round bowl with the house in the middle.

One day in the middle of all that hard work, Ragnar drove up with roses on the back, climbing roses, single roses, old-fashioned bush-roses. I jumped round him like a delighted child.

'Where did you buy all these? And what did they cost?'

'Nothing to do with you, little sis,' he said, looking just like Arne had when I'd asked what he'd paid for all that expensive timber for our furniture.

CHAPTER 54

I notice I have to be careful not to turn good memories from the past into the only truth. That's easy to do. It's probably a talent we've acquired in order to endure, this blessed ability to remember what was good and forget the bad. But a lot goes wrong if you build on such uncertain ground as Arne does, when he talks about his good mother and happy childhood.

Maybe I'm unjust. For what can anyone know, what does anyone really know, about what's a lie and what is truth? About what it was like, and how the child saw it. Nowadays, I'm always uncertain.

Anyhow, I'm sure that our first years out there by the sea were good years. I took the days as they came and accepted my husband for what he was. I don't think young love is as blind as young wives try to persuade themselves.

The first time I saw Arne in an explosion of rage, I was almost as angry as he was. I pointed at the door and shouted at him to get out! He'd smashed two plates, soup was all over the place and remains of food and bits of broken china were all over the kitchen floor.

I didn't wipe it up. I went straight into the bedroom and packed a suitcase. Then I sat on it in the hall and waited. When he came back, he was desperate and full of apologies. 'Johanna. Forgive me.'

That frightened me. For the first time I began to think there was something insane about these rapid changes of mood, something sick. I could see he enjoyed the contrition as much as the rage.

'I was going to go back to Mother,' I said. 'If it happens again, I shall.'

Then I walked up to the mountains, sat on a rocky ledge for a long time, wept a little and watched the sun sinking into the sea. When I got back home, the kitchen was clean and tidy, and afterwards he was unnaturally kind for a whole week.

The next time it happened, he hit me. It was summer. I ran, fled to the bus, to town and Mother. She didn't say much but bandaged me up and put me to bed. But she didn't take it seriously. She considered it the kind of thing women had to put up with.

'Do you mean Father hit you?'

'Indeed he did, several times.'

I was miserable. I didn't know if she was lying, yet felt as if she was slandering him.

Later on, I realised she had spoken to Ragnar, for when Arne appeared in Haga, all regrets and self-pity, he said my brother had threatened to report him to the police for maltreatment of his wife.

'Good,' I said. 'If he goes to the police, then a divorce will be easier.'

I spent two weeks looking for work in the market hall and got an hour or two here and there. A permanent job was out of the question, for booth after booth had closed down. Then I met Greta. She had trained as a hairdresser and had opened a little salon in

Vasastan, where people could still afford to get their hair done. I could start with her, learn the trade and gradually earn enough to live on. But I had only washed a couple of ladies' heads when I found I was with child again. Mother said it was, as she'd thought, fate.

When I went back to our house by the sea, the garden was overgrown with weeds and the currant bushes were almost collapsing with overripe fruits. Nevertheless, I was glad to see it all again. I had the courage to admit that I'd been longing to be there all the time ... longing for the apple trees, the flowers and the view over the sea.

Arne wept like a child when he came back and found me there. I told him what the situation was, that I'd come back because we were to have a child. He was pleased and his delight was genuine. But I no longer believed his assurances that he would never again give in to his fearful temper.

Things were a little warmer between us, although I was constantly on my guard. I was really only truly calm when Ragnar came out, and he often did. If Arne was at home he would ask, 'And how's things, little sis?'

It was insulting, and at first I was afraid Arne would be so furious that he would vent his anger on me. But he wasn't angry, and gradually I began to realise he liked being put in his place.

I would never understand my husband.

In September, I had another miscarriage. I can't bring myself to describe it.

What I want to remember is the garden, and our long summer sailing trips, just the two of us. They were wonderful. In the boat, Arne was a grown man, never unpredictable. We sailed to Copenhagen and enjoyed ourselves walking the alleys and parks, looking at all the sights.

The next summer we slipped into Oslo fjord to visit the relatives.

All the time I'd been growing up, I'd had fantasies about my aunt, my mother's sister, the beautiful Astrid. I had vague memories of something butterfly-like, exciting and wonderful. Then I had the letters. Hanna and Astrid corresponded all through the years. Astrid's letters were long, full of amusing things and unusual thoughts. As Mother was a poor hand at writing, I was always the one to write back. Astrid often asked after Ragnar, and I wrote eloquently about how well things were going for him in Göteborg and how happy he was with Lisa and their two sons.

She replied that she'd always known he would get on in life, and that he was a child of the gods with free access to their good gifts.

I loved the astonishing way she put things and the looping handwriting flowing over the pages.

When I wrote and told her that I was going to get married, she sent me a pearl necklace, genuine but cultured pearls that came right down to my waist.

In all honesty, I have to say that I wrote a lot more in those letters than Mother dictated to me and I never read them out to her.

Henriksen had taken his business to Oslo, and as far as we could make out, they were doing well there. So on this day in July, when Arne moored in the handsome guest harbour in the capital of Norway, I was ill at ease.

'I feel like the poor relation from the country.'

'Huh, if they're not nice, we'll have a cup of coffee and leave. But maybe you should phone first.'

So I telephoned, and the soft voice on the phone sounded so pleased that it seemed to warble.

'I'll come. I'll come at once and fetch you.'

She drove her own car and was just as beautiful as in my dreams. The years didn't seem to have left a trace on her figure or her character. Flowery organdie floated in clouds round her slim figure and she smelt like the peach blossom on the wall at home. She hugged me, pushed me away, clapped her hands and said, 'Lord, how pretty you've become, Johanna.' Then she hugged Arne, who blushed, delighted and appalled.

'Goodness, how alike you are,' he said.

'Aren't we? Yes!' said Astrid, laughing. 'It runs in the family. And I have a double dose of it, like Ragnar, but in another way.'

We didn't know what she meant, and she went on, her head on one side and the corners of her mouth turned down, 'My own sons all take after Henriksen and are as ugly as sin. Now, I want to see your boat.'

She jumped on board, as light as a fairy, admired everything, then kissed Arne when she was told that he'd built the boat and equipped it himself. 'Henriksen wants a sailing boat, too,' she said. 'When he sees this, he'll go mad.' She spoke quickly and I found it difficult to understand her Norwegian, although it sounded familiar.

We had dinner in their large apartment. She and I talked and talked, while Henriksen and Arne discussed Hitler. I suddenly heard Arne saying loudly, 'Is that true?'

Henriksen did business with Germany and this was the first time we'd heard about Jews disappearing and the killing of people in asylums.

Henriksen was sure of his facts. A silence fell round the table and it was hard to breathe. Then Astrid said, 'German boots will be tramping along Karl Johan in a few years.'

It sounded like a prediction. Arne protested, 'England would never allow that.'

Henriksen sighed. 'Astrid's been saying that for a long time now,' he said. 'And she's a great one for seeing into the future.'

Henriksen and Arne went out sailing, but the fish merchant was old and heavy, so slow to learn. 'He'll never be a sailor,' Arne said later. We had dinner with them again in their fine apartment. I met my cousins and for the first time felt like the poor relation from the country.

The most important thing that happened in Oslo was a long conversation when Astrid, Arne and I were in a café out by the museum with the *Oseberg* ship. We were talking about my father, and Astrid had a lot to say about him and many memories of him.

'He was the kind of person who was quite content simply to be himself,' she said. 'You know, that kind have no need to assert themselves.'

Then she told me how much he had loved me, the little daughter named after a child he'd had by his first marriage, how he'd looked after me when I was small, carrying me in a knapsack on his back and teaching me to listen to all the voices of the forest and to see the water, the skies and clouds.

'Hanna snorted, of course,' said Astrid. 'You were only an infant at the time.'

I had known all that, because the body and the senses have memories of their own. But no one in my family had ever said a word about it, only that he'd spoilt me. Now it was all confirmed.

She talked about the stories he'd told, and the songs he sang. Mother had done that, too, so I wasn't all that surprised.

'I've often thought about you, and what a loss it must have been when he died,' she said.

Then she said nothing for a while, as if hesitating before going on. 'And yet I didn't begrudge him dying. The last time we met, he said life had always been hard for him to bear. That he'd found it difficult to live, even as a child.'

In the winters, Arne and I went to Party meetings. I read a lot and learned a lot, and we had much to talk about.

Arne put a wireless together, a great monster that I loved for the music it broadcast. When he noticed my interest, he came with me to concerts, where almost at once he fell asleep while I enjoyed myself.

We bought a hand-wound gramophone.

They were good years.

We shared our anxiety about Hitler and the Nazis in Germany. Ragnar was a political idiot and he said that, anyhow, the bastard would get the wheels turning again, and Arne said that times would improve once rearmament got going. But then there would be war.

He sounded like Astrid, but I refused to let myself be frightened.

I was expecting again. This time it was to be born. I'd decided. The doctor who'd helped me through my miscarriages had assured me there was nothing wrong with me.

The district nurse came once a week. A good woman, who told

Arne he should be confident and take care of me. He did, too, reliable as always in a critical situation. She told me to be happy.

I did my best to obey. I thought about my garden and acquired new seed catalogues. I thought about Arne and how much gentler he'd become. I thought about Mother, soon to get a pension and be allowed to rest. Most of all I thought about all those lovely things Astrid had said about Father, and every night, before I fell asleep, I promised him I would give him a granddaughter. I was absolutely certain it was a girl. And, strangely enough, so was Arne.

CHAPTER 55

I mentioned in passing that we had new neighbours out there in the old fishing village, young families like ourselves. They were nice people, the kind you could make friends with, and I was friends with most of them, I think. We had coffee in each other's kitchens and talked and exchanged confidences in the way women do. I was wary of some, the kind to come too close. It was interesting and unpleasant to see the way we re-established the patterns that had governed life in the old villages where people all had their roots. We observed and were envious, helped and annoyed, soon creating a hierarchy, with the wretches at the bottom who were unemployed and drank, and the good people at the top.

Best of all was the schoolmaster's family. Then came the pilot, the police and the customs officer. No, Mrs Gren probably came after the schoolmaster. She kept the shop. Not that she did very well, but she had power. You had to ask her for credit when things were tight towards the end of the week.

The old people, the fishermen and their families lived in a world of their own and didn't mix with us. They were Pentecostalists, at least at weekends. Their boats came in on Saturday mornings. By then they had already been to the fish quay in town and sold their catch. As they moored their boats, the bachelors, in their best clothes, went in an assembled troop to the bars in Majorna and started drinking. They came back at night and there was much singing and jollification in the harbour. Sometimes they had women of a familiar kind on board. But on Sunday, once the fishermen had slept it off, their faces dark, they went to the Pentecostal church, where they confessed their sins and were forgiven.

Arne thought it disturbing. I thought it strange, but Mother, who often came to see us at weekends, found it quite natural, just as things had always been, she said.

Naturally we also had a gossip, the usual kind: her eyes, which saw no further than the length of her nose, noted a limited bit at a time, but very thoroughly, every tiny detail, and she always implied the worst when she put the details together into a somewhat dubious pattern.

Arne said Agneta Pettersson knew everything that was in every letter we ever received, even before they'd been written. He detested her.

'You may wonder how the Karlgrens can afford both a grand garden and a boat,' she said to Irene, who lived nearest to us and didn't hesitate to tell us.

I laughed. Arne was angry.

That was the spring we got a telephone. Even worse, Arne bought a second-hand car, a ramshackle DKW, from Ragnar. Then he neglected the boat, took the car's engine apart, put in new parts and was much praised by Ragnar. 'You could get a job as a mechanic at any time.'

But Arne wasn't interested. He was proud of his work at the shipyard, where times were good. 'We're making skis for aeroplanes,' he said. 'They've been ordered by the military and are to defend Norrland.'

'Good gracious!'

A Jewish family moved in among us in these colourful little red houses. Agneta Pettersson had a great deal to observe and much to talk about, racing excitedly round with her tongue wagging, as Mother put it.

Rakel Ginfarb looked like a bird and was just as timid. I thought about what I'd heard Henriksen telling us in Oslo. I went to the nursery to buy a flower and rang the newcomers' bell. 'Just to wish you welcome,' I said.

She probably saw how shy I was, for she slowly managed a smile, so I dared to go on. 'If you want any help, or have any questions, I live in the last house down towards the harbour.'

'Thank you,' she said. 'Thank you very much.'

That was how a friendship began that was to be of great importance to me.

On Sunday, we asked them to coffee in the garden. We actually asked them on the Saturday, but that wasn't possible, Rakel said, as it was the Sabbath.

'We have a few problems,' said Simon Ginfarb, after three cups of coffee and trying all my little cookies. 'I'm no good at putting up bookshelves.'

He didn't ask Arne directly for help, but Arne understood. He disappeared with Simon and was away all afternoon, while Rakel and I talked and her children played in the garden.

She had a son and two girls.

'And another on the way,' she said, running her hand over her stomach.

'So have I,' I said, surprising myself even. For some superstitious reason, I hadn't told anyone before. Only Arne and Mother knew. We quickly calculated that our children would be born at the same time and Rakel brightened.

'How wonderful for both to have someone the same age,' she said. 'Mine's a girl, I know.'

'So is mine.'

'It must be a sign,' she said, and I was suddenly afraid.

'What is it, Johanna?'

For the first time I was able to talk about my miscarriages, how much it had hurt to lose children and how ... inferior I felt. 'I sort of lost confidence,' I said.

She said nothing, but she could listen. Afterwards, we sat in silence for a long time, a silence that was of the sweeping kind, so profound that it had to change something. By the time the children's laughter, the screams of gulls and the chug of a fishing boat out at sea had broken the stillness, I had acquired new hope.

As she left, she whispered that she would pray for me, and I, who had no God to appeal to, was grateful.

Arne came back and said Simon was just what he'd thought, a man who's all thumbs. They'd laughed and while Arne had nailed, sawed and screwed, they'd talked politics.

'It's true what Henriksen told us. Both Rakel and Simon have relatives in Germany and they're damned worried. Always, every day.' Arne's eyes darkened, as always when he was frightened. 'I was thinking about Astrid's prediction,' he said. 'Do you think she can see into the future?'

'They say so. There've always been people with second sight in Mother's family.'

Arne snorted. 'Superstition!'

But then he said Astrid hadn't said that the Germans would march through Göteborg. 'Not a word about Sweden,' he said, looking relieved.

Before he fell asleep that night, he talked about the Ginfarbs. 'You wouldn't believe how many books they've got. He's a teacher at the college.'

That rather worried me. I thought about the new family being the best of all in the village, and about how uneducated I was, and also how much I hated the middle classes, the bourgeoisie.

But most of all I thought about that strange moment when we'd sat together in silence.

That autumn I helped Rakel plant roses in her garden. What she liked best was when we went with the children through the high pass in the mountains, or towards the inland meadow, along the shores, or up in the forest. One day I showed her my secret mountain ridge, warm, sheltered from the west wind and with the most beautiful view out over the sea.

'I'll soon be a real Swedish nature-lover,' she said.

She had persuaded her husband to buy the house out there in the country, she told me. She didn't like cities and regarded them as military defences.

'Huge buildings and neat street,' she said. 'As if people were trying to find safety by limiting their lives.'

I thought about the dirty alleys in Haga, and the vulnerable, constantly threatened life inside those huge apartment blocks. Her city wasn't my city. But I said nothing. I was cowardly, anxious that a chasm shouldn't appear between us.

She had a lot to give, primarily confidence, but also knowledge. About children, bringing them up, and how important it was to respect every single little child.

'They're all different, right from the beginning,' she said.

She once told me she always knew when a person was lying, and that she'd inherited that quality from her grandmother. When she said that she was less sure than usual when it came to me, I knew that was true. I had a habit of lying to myself, although I neither meant to nor even understood why I did.

'You're full of secrets,' she said.

Her husband was very elegant and smelt of well-being and cigars. He was religious and as an orthodox Jew regularly attended the synagogue. But his attitude was rational, more marked by respect for ancient rites than religious enthusiasm, he told us. Both Arne and I thought he was rather arrogant, but neither of us ever said so. The new neighbours were Jews, so above all criticism.

Simon took his evening walk in the direction of our kitchen in the evenings, to listen to the news from Berlin on the wireless Arne had put together.

Rakel was never there when we heard Hitler bawling away on the wireless.

'The women can be spared that,' said Simon.

But Arne objected. 'I don't think Johanna wants to be kept in ignorance,' he said.

Simon laughed. By this time we'd found out that he always laughed when he was unsure of himself.

The autumn storms came, then the winter, and Rakel and I grew in size together. I began to find it difficult to tie my shoelaces, and I thought, Now it's a child, a real child that's only got to grow a little more before it comes out.

CHAPTER 56

Then she came, one blue March day, and I would never have believed it could be so difficult. It was like walking a long way through unendurable pain, finally to reach a merciful death when the anaesthetic obliterated everything.

It went on for over twenty-four hours.

For many years afterwards, I looked at every mother with surprise. You! And you, too, and you, several times!

God, what women have to go through, and so rarely talk about it, so secret most women keep it to themselves.

But then it was the same for me as for others, an infinite joy, worth any suffering.

When I woke at the clinic, I was given some creamed fruit, then the baby was put into my arms. The next hours are harder to describe than the pain. We looked at each other. She looked steadily at me and I saw her only through a blur of tears. We were surrounded by light. I recognised it from my walks along the lakes that summer before Father died, and from the miracle in the market hall when I was prevented from opening a door.

There weren't many thoughts in my head that first day. I could only smile like an idiot when Arne came and tried to tell me how pleased he was.

When Mother came the next day, I remembered her description of when I was born. 'Mother,' I said, 'how strong you were.'

She was embarrassed and as usual warded off praise. It wasn't due to her that things had gone well that time, she said, it was the midwife.

Then I remember Anna, and without thinking I said I wanted to call the child Anna. Mother was pleased, I could see that, but she said I had to speak to Arne first.

He thought the name old-fashioned and good, and he was also pleased it wasn't already in the family.

'Have you noticed how intelligent she looks?' he said.

Of course, I laughed a little at him, but in secret I agreed. And he turned out to be right.

What a spring it was. And what a summer! As if life wanted to make up for things going so wrong for me before, this time seemed to be blessed. I had plenty of milk, and Anna was healthy, ate, slept, smiled and gurgled. I realised now that Arne had listened carefully when we were in Oslo and Astrid had talked about my father. For he did as Father had done, made a bark knapsack and roamed round the mountains with the child. And sang to her. He had a good singing voice. I could tell stories. Suddenly they were just there, all Father's rhymes and jingles.

My abundance was so great, I was even able to receive my mother-in-law with some warmth.

'Look, Anna, here's your grandmother.'

Anna was her first grandchild. She emerged from behind her stony exterior and smiled and prattled to the child. For the first time, I saw pleading behind the ivory mask. But when she said, and she was the first to say so, that the child resembled her, I was afraid.

And annoyed.

Maybe Arne was scared, too, for he laughed scornfully and said that all old women were crazy. 'Johanna's mother was here yesterday,' he said. 'And she thought Anna was like her and her family.'

I looked at him and smiled. We both knew Mother hadn't said a word about any family likeness. He's standing up for himself, I thought. He'd become a father and at last can oppose his mother.

My mother-in-law snorted.

A long time later, I realised she hadn't been entirely wrong. There's a fragile timidity in Anna, a pride and fear of letting anyone in or of relaxing. And she has her grandmother's ivory complexion and finely drawn features.

Only her mouth is mine, large and expressive.

Rakel returned from hospital a week after me. The little girls were very unalike, mine fair, strong and stubborn, hers dark, good and submissive.

But by then it was 1937, and Franco was dropping Hitler's bombs on the towns of Spain. You could no longer close your eyes to the fact that the world was darkening all round us.

CHAPTER 57

I've no intention of describing what the Second World War did to us, all of us crouching down like frightened rabbits behind a fragile neutrality.

I made a tremendous effort to build a wall between the world out there and my world with the child. I had seen early on that she sensed every shift of mood in me and I made myself not think about the war, not listen to the news, not be frightened, as long as the child was awake.

Then I sat by the radio in the evenings. I slept badly at night. I was alone for long periods, for Arne had been called up and was 'somewhere in Sweden'.

It wasn't easy trying to live in two worlds, but I did my best, and it took some time before I knew I'd failed. When Anna had her first birthday, Hitler marched into Austria. When she was two, he incorporated Czechoslovakia into the Third Reich, and in the autumn it was Poland's turn, and soon after it became world war.

So far, I'd managed to keep my fears at bay. But then came Anna's third birthday, and just after it the invasion of Denmark and Norway.

Swedish anti-aircraft guns rattled in the mountains round us and Anna's eyes darkened with questions. 'What are they shooting at?'

I lied and said they were only practising.

But one day a burning plane flew right over our heads, a plane with a swastika on it, flared up, spun round and disappeared to the west. I saw the German boy burning like a torch against the sky before being mercifully extinguished in the sea.

We were up on the mountain, Anna in my arms and me trying to hold her head against my shoulder. But she struggled free and stared as if bewitched. Then she turned her eyes to mine and I knew she could see right into my terror.

She didn't ask anything. I had nothing to say.

Arne came home on leave. Different. Harder. In uniform. He didn't avoid Anna's questions. He sat her on his knee and told her as it was, that there was great evil in the world and every decent person had to resist it. He was a soldier because we had to defend ourselves, and the anti-aircraft guns fired to keep the enemy outside our borders and that the good would be victorious in the end.

'But they kill ...' she said.

'Yes, Anna, they have to.'

He told me it was all appalling on the borders, that sometimes they had guns and no ammunition, sometimes ammunition and no guns.

'Are you frightened?'

'No, mostly angry.'

He wasn't lying. He was what he was, strong when things were difficult. The next day he phoned his parents. 'Hi, Mum. I'm in a hurry and want to talk to Dad.'

Then he spoke for a long time about evacuating us to the farm out in the forest where there was a cottage.

'You must come out here, Dad. Fix things up with Johanna. She'll help you phone up there and ask them to put the old croft in order.'

'But what about Mother?' I said, after he'd put down the receiver.

'If Ragnar doesn't arrange something for her, then you'll have to take her with you.'

But Ragnar had been called up as well, and all his vehicles had been requisitioned. I thought it would never work with Mother and Mother-in-Law in a cramped croft cottage. Then I was ashamed.

Before Arne left that evening, he stood for a long time with Anna in his arms.

'Now promise me you'll be a good little girl and look after your mother.'

The wrong thing to say. I felt in my whole being how wrong it was. But I had no desire to argue at that moment. Then things went as they went, and Anna's unease acquired a definite goal. 'Don't be frightened, Mummy.'

'I'm not frightened,' I said, then I cried and my three-year-old comforted me.

The war crept closer in other ways as well. Jewish refugees from Denmark and Norway poured through Rakel's house. They appeared in the dark, in the evenings or at night, slept there, ate, then disappeared. There was still a refugee route open from Torslanda to London.

Most of them were going on to America.

Some were Jews of the kind I'd only seen on Nazi posters and in Albert Engström's horrible comic magazine. Like caricatures. I realised now that they existed, men with peculiar hats and long curly side-locks. I can admit now, all this time later, that they frightened me.

One of them was a rabbi, and in contrast to the others, he came with his wife and sons one sunny afternoon. Anna was at the Ginfarbs' house. Things had worked out well with the two little girls, just as Rakel had predicted. They were inseparable.

She came running home, her eyes shining. 'Mummy, I've been blessed by God. He put his hand on my head and said lovely things I didn't understand.'

Thank God for that, I thought, smiling wryly at the way I'd put it.

Then came all the questions about God. Anna had a way of asking as if you were being cross-questioned in court. Why didn't we pray to God? Who was he? Was he invisible?

I answered as best I could, and at least I can take some credit for that. Seriously, as if to an adult. She was disappointed that the rabbi wasn't God himself, only his envoy on earth. But he had done something for the child, because she went on glowing long after that Jewish blessing.

'Simon's being very pressing,' said Rakel. 'He wants us to go, too.'

'Where?'

'To America. We have relatives there. I try to resist, but he keeps talking about all those blind and crazy Jews in Germany who stayed until it was too late.'

A week later, Swedish Nazis had drawn swastikas and Stars of David on the windows and doors of the Ginfarbs' house. I went to help her wash them off, crying, and that morning I was more ashamed than I'd ever been before. A fortnight later, the family was on its way to America. One of Arne's carpenters at the shipyard bought their house cheaply. I told Arne that was shameful.

The contents of the house were all put in store.

I was lonely.

In the terribly cold winter of 1941, on Christmas Eve itself, I counted the days and became aware I was pregnant again. I don't think I realised from the start that I would lose the child, but by February I had already arranged with Lisa that Anna should stay with her for a week or two in March. Should anything happen.

That was good. Anna never knew. On 15 March, the first creeping pains started, but I managed to get to Lisa's with Anna just before going into hospital. When I came round, I thought what a good time she was having, Anna, at the haberdashery with all those lovely reels of silk.

I probably mourned that child, too, but all over the world there were so many dead.

Arne got leave, came and fetched me from hospital. He was miserable. It had been a boy this time, too. We picked up Anna in Haga. She had gone quite pale and Arne said, 'You can't have become so city pale in only a week, girl.'

That was the first time I wondered whether she knew. In some way, she knows, though she can't know. I bled a lot and was often in bed. That was the spring Anna started playing up on the mountain, alone, secret games of her own.

'She's missing little Judith just as I miss Rakel,' I said to Arne.

Despite everything, he was in a better mood, the defences at last functioning, but then the Germans invaded Russia.

'Now they're for it,' said Arne, and began going on about King Karl XII and Napoleon.

And just in time for Christmas, the Japanese bombed Pearl Harbour and America was forced into the war.

'Now you'll see,' said Arne. 'Things'll be all right now.'

And they were.

In 1943, when the German Army surrendered at Stalingrad, I had my next and last miscarriage. It came suddenly, and I was already bleeding when I left Anna with Lisa.

I don't want to say anything more about that.

CHAPTER 58

I remember the spring when peace came, the shimmer over the days, a light that gave a sharpness to every detail.

The 1945 graduation day.

The bus to school was full of boys in white shirts, their hair plastered down, the girls in new light dresses, their hair curled, and the mothers in their best clothes with bunches of flowers in their hands. Anna had a seat opposite me and was as lovely as the apple blossom in our garden at home, although her hair was dead straight, the kind no curling tongs had any effect on.

I sat there thinking that the war had overshadowed her whole childhood, and peace had made it more difficult to hide anything from her. That spring she had once bought a newspaper on her way back from school, a foreign paper full of photographs from the recently opened concentration camps.

By the time she got home, her face had turned green. She flung the paper at me and disappeared into the bathroom to be sick.

I had no words with which to console her. I sat at the kitchen table and looked at the unfathomable photographs, quite incapable of crying.

The time of flowering was to come.

Did I imagine it, or was there some hope in those voices singing on that last day of school? No one had yet heard of the bomb or that city with its lovely name.

Hiroshima awaited us that autumn.

Soon the wheel began turning as never before, prosperity increased and the foundations of the 'people's home' were laid for the time being. The Social Democrats were in power and the reforms demanded but restrained by the war now lay before Parliament. Taxes on businesses and the rich rose and, oh, my goodness, what anger that caused among the bourgeoisie.

Arne and I were jubilant.

Things were good for me. Both Mother and my friends considered things were as good for me as a woman could ask for. Only one child to see to, a husband who brought in money every week and neither drank nor slept around. Mother didn't even lament my miscarriages. Unchanging, she considered every child not born was a plus. But I hadn't Mother's ability to accept without protest the role imposed on me. Arne's power increased and my ability to object did the opposite.

I wanted to believe it was the miscarriages that broke me, and it was obvious that the child I had increased my vulnerability. I evaded Arne, saying nothing in order to protect her. No disputes, no quarrels. All was to be sun, security and cosiness.

If I'd had four children, I'd probably have crawled humbly along the floor.

Or would I?

What did his power consist of?

Why was I so easily hurt and submissive? For I was. This was when I started appealing for pity. In vain, of course. I became a martyr, one of those martyrs, the woman who stayed at home, the housewife.

Detestable.

It was a long time before I found an answer to my questions and that was perhaps because I didn't want to see. It seemed so feeble, for it was all about money.

I don't think anyone who hasn't experienced it understands what it means to have to ask for every penny. He said his money ran through my fingers. That was true, and it wasn't my fault. I was not a bad housewife, but the value of money had gone down in the post-war period, now marked by a belief in the future and inflation.

I tried to think that my situation was just. I'd looked for security and had been given it.

I can see I have underestimated love. For it was there. I was fond of Arne. All through those years, I was in love with him in a way, a little. But I don't believe love would have produced the submissive-ness if I had kept on working and earned my own money.

One strange thing I shared with many women of my generation was that being in love had little to do with sex. Sex was inevitable, something that came with it. That you had to have. I did not find it repulsive – or, at any rate, not often. But nor did I enjoy it.

Maybe I hurt him? No, I don't think so. I think he would have been shocked and considered me lecherous if I'd liked it.

We were so ignorant. We didn't know how to show tenderness in sex. We closed our eyes and somehow let things go the usual way. We talked about emotions only when we quarrelled. He did, too, whenever he got so horribly sentimental in that way.

Once, in bed, afterwards, he said his grandparents had been lecherous. He flushed scarlet and I was surprised. I had never given a thought to what they were like, the ivory lady's mother and father.

'But they were religious,' I said.

'That's never stopped anyone being lecherous, has it?'

'Was your grandmother lecherous?' I was so surprised, I sat up.

'No, I don't suppose so. But Grandfather was an old goat and she liked it.'

'How do you know that?'

He shouted at me. 'Stop nagging!'

I was frightened, as usual, when he got angry. Said nothing. I soon heard he was asleep, and I lay awake thinking.

Long afterwards, I thought about that strange exchange, about whether what he'd said could be true and why he had said it. Now, so many years later, I wonder whether he had wanted to apologise for his own attitude to sex. And his mother's.

We hadn't enough words when it came to practical things, or politics.

Like me, when Anna was about eleven. One day she came in, white in the face and moving stiffly. She told me what a friend had said about that horrid thing a man has and how he pushes it in and pumps and pumps and how it hurts so you could die. I was ironing towels and was so frightened, I burned one. Then I said what Mother, Grandmother and Great-Grandmother had always said over the centuries, that it was something women had to put up with. 'And it doesn't hurt, Anna. A lot of people think it's wonderful.'

'Do you?'

'I've nothing against it.'

So feeble. But how was I to explain how infinitely complicated love and sex are, with falling in love and desire, how doubly complicated.

One day in the autumn when the sky and the sea had merged into a heavy greyness, Nisse Nilsson phoned to say that business was picking up again. Would I consider helping on Friday afternoons and Saturdays? For good wages?

I didn't even consider it. I said yes, just like that.

I sat by the telephone for a long time, realising there would be a tremendous to-do that evening. I prepared dinner with extra care, and Arne ate it and afterwards said, as so often, what a good cook I was.

Anna disappeared up into her room and Arne went down into the basement as usual, thank goodness. If we were to quarrel, Anna wouldn't hear.

So I went down to him and told him about my conversation with Nisse. He was surprised, then nodded. Then he said Anna was old enough to look after herself for a few hours. If I wanted to …

'I do.'

'I've often thought it must be lonely and boring for you here at home.'

I was surprised. 'It's not that, I've plenty to do, sewing and all that. But it's like being a servant, always doing things for others and having to ask for every penny.'

He wasn't angry, just dismayed. 'But why didn't you say so?'

It was a strange evening. I was the one to be furious, not him. For ten minutes at least it all poured out of me, the boat that cost so much, the rows over money for food, the fact that he simply expected freshly ironed shirts and perfect service at home, as well as lots of friends at work. 'I'm nothing but a servant!' I shouted at him. 'Nothing!' Then I rushed up the basement stairs.

When he came to bed, he was miserable. 'I didn't know,' he said. 'You could have said something.'

I thought for a long time, then decided he was right.

'You're rather a secretive person,' he said.

Just as Rakel had said.

I had to agree with that, too.

From that day onwards things were better. It wasn't just the joy of crossing the bridge with all the others on Saturday morning, or just the friends at work, or just the chat, the laughter and taking an interest in every customer, listening and answering back, as Nisse Nilsson said.

It was about self-image.

I told Nisse he had saved my life. I told Mother we needed the money, and that wasn't true. Finally I told Anna that I had to get outside our four walls.

She understood. She matured, cooked the dinner on Fridays, cleaned the house on Saturdays, and learned a lot about running a household, although she was only twelve. 'She has a sense of responsibility,' said Arne. He didn't complain when the meatballs were too salty and the fish not cooked right through. That was just a start. As always, Anna was ambitious and learned things from books, wore out my old cookery book and got a new and better one from Arne.

When I got home with my first wages, he said he had thought about what I'd said and admitted that he'd been mean and difficult about money.

'I was afraid of being like my father,' he said. 'She took every penny from him, then graciously gave him enough for his snuff. When he asked for it.'

I was, thank goodness, so surprised I said nothing about what I was thinking. Arne ran no risk of being like his father, but he had a lot in common with his mother.

He now wanted me to take over the family finances and said I was sure to be better at it than he was. From that day on, he handed his wages over to me and finally there was an end to all that talk of 'my money you keep spending'. And our finances were in much better shape. In the spring, he wanted to order new sails for the boat, but I reckoned we couldn't afford them. We needed our savings for a new oil-fired central-heating system.

At last I'd admitted something I'd always known. Women never get any respect until they can stand on their own two feet.

Now, so many years later, I'm not so sure.

Anna has always earned her own living and for her children. She managed better than I did. Over her divorce. But then. Is there something in women, something we don't want to see or admit?

CHAPTER 59

Just a few words about the old people.

With all the strength of my new self-confidence, I set about

Mother's housing problem. The apartment in Haga was too large for her, too difficult and old-fashioned to manage, draughty and heated by wood-burning stoves. Then there was the privy down in the courtyard and three floors to climb up and down. She wasn't happy there, either, now that so many of her neighbours had moved. And since Hulda Andersson across the landing had died.

They were building new blocks with apartments for pensioners, so I got her and Ragnar to come with me to look at a one-roomer, smaller than the one she had, but with central heating, bathroom and hot water.

She thought it was paradise.

Arne helped with all the paperwork. A great deal was required by the authorities, and the bureaucracy took even longer than building the place.

But we signed an agreement and she moved in with her Värmland sofa, which I covered in striped silk and put on it a lot of soft cushions. She sat on it and was happy.

An awful and unexpected thing happened to the two old people in Karl Johansgatan. The ivory lady's heart survived over the years, but one day she stepped straight out into the street in front of a tram.

She died in the ambulance on her way to hospital.

When the message came, I was alone at home. I had time for a lot of thinking before Arne came home, uneasy thoughts as to how I should tell him. And I can't deny feeling considerable relief.

As soon as I heard the car, I went out with my coat over my shoulders. 'Arne, something terrible has happened. We must go to Karl Johansgatan at once.'

I told him about the accident. As soon as I saw how relieved he was, I looked down, but he knew I'd noticed and would never forgive me.

'What shall we do about Dad?' he said, as we backed out.

'I suppose he'll have to move in with us.'

'But your job?'

I was frightened. 'He's sure to be able to manage for a few hours.'

He was. He was pleased to live with me, whom he'd always liked, but he wanted to be left to himself. So Anna gave up her room without complaint. She had always liked her grandfather.

Arne installed water and a WC up there.

I had a lot to do that summer and was very tired. I had to admit I was no longer young.

At first I thought that the old man would be relieved when his strange wife died, but I was wrong. He grieved for her, calling out for her when his cough woke him at night, and he wept like a child when she didn't come. He caught one cold after another and the doctor came and gave him antibiotics, but they were no help. Then he just grew worse and died that winter from the merciful pneumonia. I sat with him and held his hand. That was good for me. Afterwards I reckoned he cured me of the fear of death that had been with me ever since Father coughed his life away in the millhouse in Dalsland.

Anna was at high school now. She thinks she remembers some discussion about that, but she's wrong about that. Somehow it had always been obvious from the start to both Arne and me that she should have what we'd never had.

Education was most important of all.

But there were consequences we hadn't foreseen. Anna had one foot in another world, the world of education and the middle class.

She gave a lot of thought to it at first.

'I can't help liking some of my new friends,' she said.

'That's good,' I said, and I meant it.

But she looked at me suspiciously. 'They're childish in a lot of ways,' she said. 'Just think, they know practically nothing about the war and the extermination of the Jews.'

'That's understandable. In their homes, unpleasant things aren't talked about. I know that. I was once in service in that kind of household.'

As I said it, I remembered trying to protect Anna from the horrors of war. I noticed then that I'd become a little middle class myself.

'Were you? You never told me that,' Anna said.

So I did then, with all the awful details right up to the attempted rape.

Anna cried for me, so then I could cry too, over those two lost years of my youth.

But she saw things much more personally than I did, so she was suddenly angry with Mother.

'How could she?'

'Don't you understand? It was obvious to her, to everyone in those days. It was the social system.'

At first I found it difficult with all those middle-class children flitting in and out of my house and garden. Schoolfriends who, with all their self-confidence, reminded me of the horrid children in that doctor's family. But then I thought of Rakel, that lovely Jewish woman.

We wrote to each other. I remember the first letter I had with American stamps on it and me dancing round my roses as I read it.

Little Judith wrote, too, to Anna. She wrinkled her little nose and said Judith couldn't spell. Both Arne and I laughed at her and said Judith would certainly be able to spell in English, now she had another mother tongue. A few years later, Anna wrote back to her in English, at first with her teacher's help, then on her own.

In the 1960s, Judith emigrated to Israel and Anna and Rickard flew to Jerusalem to go to her wedding.

I don't know how Anna managed to juggle her school life with ours. She didn't say much. Like me, she was secretive about anything difficult. But I saw the distance increasing between her and Mother, the whole family, actually. She even distanced herself from Ragnar, whom she loved and admired.

She began correcting my speech.

Sometimes she was sharp to Arne, ironic and spiteful.

When she was to go on to university, Arne said he would somehow scrape up the money, though it wouldn't be easy. She said he needn't bother, she'd already got a student loan.

She pretended not to notice how hurt he was.

It was empty when she moved into a student apartment in Lund, but I can't deny that it was also a relief. I didn't have to see the gap between us widening every day, and I no longer had to act as intermediary in the quarrels that had become more and more frequent in recent years.

But I missed our closeness and confidences – heavens, how I missed them. Every day I said to myself that you can't hang on to your children, you must let them go. Perhaps it's true that confidence isn't possible between people so close to each other. The risk of hurting is too great. How could I tell her I knew all about her unhappy love affair with that foreigner in Lund? And the abortion?

The abortion.

How could I talk about that, I who'd said nothing to her about having had four miscarriages?

When she came back that summer, pale, thin and grave, I almost cracked with pity for her. We worked side by side in the garden, but she told me nothing and I didn't dare ask. Then she got a temporary job as proof-reader at the newspaper.

Rickard Hård.

I liked him from the very start.

That was due to many things, that his eyes were light grey with such long eyelashes they ought to have been a woman's, and then his mouth. Many people think eyes say most about a person. But I've never understood that. Gentle brown eyes lie just as well as blue. To me it's always been mouths that reveal character and attitudes. Not from the words pouring out of them, but the actual shape.

I've never seen a more sensitive mouth than Rickard's, large, generous, the corners curling up when he was amused or curious. Although so young, he already had plenty of laughter wrinkles.

He certainly could laugh.

And tell stories, one crazy story after another.

He reminded me of someone, but I couldn't think who, at the time, because he was so unlike him. A few weeks later, when he was having coffee with us and Ragnar came barging in, I knew. So I can't really say I was surprised when Anna phoned one day and said, with panic in her voice, 'They say he's a womaniser, Mother.'

I don't remember what I answered, just that I sat there by the phone for a long time afterwards, thinking Anna is not like Lisa, not in any way.

That year, when Anna was twenty-three and we had to write 1960, was when I learned that you can do nothing for your adult children.

Rickard had soon charmed the family, friends and neighbours. Mother was the worst. She literally melted as soon as she saw the boy. It was good to see, as he both liked and respected her. He never laughed at her as my brothers had. On the contrary, he listened with great interest. 'A book should be written about her,' he said to me.

'She hasn't that much to tell.'

'She has old ideas and values,' he said. 'Haven't you ever thought about her being one of the last of a dying breed?'

I was surprised, but he was right. Suddenly, and without really wanting to, I told him about Ragnar's birthday and what I'd discovered in the middle of the party.

'Raped at twelve and a mother at thirteen,' I said.

'Good God!'

I regretted telling him, of course, thinking I'd exposed her, and I made Rickard promise not to tell anyone. 'I don't want Anna to know.'

'I can't think why,' he said, but he promised.

They got engaged in August before Anna went back to university and Rickard went to Stockholm to work for a major newspaper.

'So you'll live in Stockholm?'

'I have to go with him. It's also easier for me to get a job there.'

She said she was sorry, but I knew that wasn't true. She was pleased to be going to a new life in a large, exciting city. Pleased also to get away from me and my eyes, which saw all too much.

'There are lots of trains, Mother. Fast ones, too. You'd be up to see me in a couple of hours.'

Arne and I had the fear all native Göteborgians have of that alien city on the wrong side of the country. And we thought Stockholmers were self-important and complaining, both when they spoke on the radio and when they spent their holidays on our islands.

But we had to learn. On our first visit we overcame our fears, and people in Stockholm turned out to be like most people, nice, and dressed much more simply and were less arrogant than lots of snotty Göteborgians. The city was beautiful. We'd heard about it, but all the same were much taken by it as we strolled along Stranden with Anna and watched the fishermen with their huge strange seine nets.

But now I've gone ahead of myself. First we had the wedding at our place by the sea. And that's where I met Signe, Rickard's mother, and began to understand one thing and another.

CHAPTER 60

We did push the boat out, we really did. As Arne said, we had only one daughter, so ... But I've forgotten most of it and have only a few scattered memories of cooking for a whole week and the house full of young people, dancing and music. What I do remember is Signe.

This time, I knew at once whom she was like although she was so dissimilar, smelling of scent, her face made up and talking about everything except what was important. She had the same blue, unseeing eyes as the ivory lady.

'Superficial and stupid,' Arne said afterwards.

Worse than that, I thought. Icy cold.

'The boy's like wax in her hands,' said Arne.

'I suppose he must have had a good dad.'

Arne looked relieved. Of course, that must be it. We knew the father had died when Rickard was twelve, but not that he had taken his own life.

Before they went off to Paris on their honeymoon, Anna and I had a brief conversation. We were stacking bottles in the dim light of the food store in the basement.

'What did you think, Mother?' said Anna. 'Of Signe?'

For once I spoke straight out. 'She's … she's like your father's mother, Anna.'

'Then I was right,' she said. 'Thanks for being so honest.'

But I hadn't been. I didn't say a word about Anna also being like her grandmother, not in her character, but in what she gave out. I thought about how incredibly in love Rickard was with her, and that love is often a reflection of an inner longing, a state in the one who loves.

After they'd left, I was uneasy and finally calmed down by telling myself I was seeing ghosts, that times were new and these two were new clear-sighted young people.

And that Signe from Johanneberg was not as mad as my mother-in-law.

I had given it a lot of thought during their engagement. Why didn't Rickard introduce us to his mother? Was he ashamed of us? No, he wasn't like that. His background was nothing special. His father had been a travelling salesman. In paper.

I realised now that it was his mother he was ashamed of. I'd seen it in his eyes at the wedding dinner. He was embarrassed and afraid of what we'd think about her boastful chatter. But I'd also realised he would never admit it. He'd do as Arne had, defend and gild her.

I knew better than most that men who've never managed to overcome their mothers take their revenge on their women, wives and daughters.

I tried to think about Rickard not being brutal, not like Arne. But I was worried. It was good they were moving to Stockholm.

But not even that consolation held, for a year or two later, Signe moved, exchanging her apartment in Johanneberg for a similar one in the same suburb in north Stockholm where Anna and Rickard had settled.

'He's all I've got,' she said, when she phoned to tell me her plans.

'Don't worry, Mother,' Anna said, over the phone. 'I can stand up for myself.'

A fortnight later, she phoned, jubilant. 'Just think, Rickard's found her a job in a newspaper office in Södertälje. So she's moving there.'

'That's good, Anna.'

'He understands much more than he cares to admit.'

'Don't you go letting on you know that,' I said, laughing in that way women have.

Over all the years, we kept contact, Greta, Aina and I. Not Lotta, unfortunately, as she married a policeman in England. We others met every other month, at Aina's apartment in Öregryte in winter, in my garden in summer. It was pleasant. We had open sandwiches and competed to find new and delicious combinations of ingredients.

Aina was also married and had stayed at home. Her husband was in the post office and didn't want her to work. She didn't say much about it, but it was clear she wasn't happy.

For a while she grew fat. Then she got terribly thin. One July day among the roses by the wall, she told me she had cancer and hadn't long to live. I'm ashamed when I think about how I could find no words to comfort her. All I could do was cry.

We went to see her in hospital twice that autumn and she just wasted away.

But Greta and I went on meeting, more often now as if we needed each other. We talked about getting older and how hard it was to take. Greta had given up her hairdressing salon and was back at the cheese stall in the market hall.

'I'm beginning to find the job hard,' she said once. 'Not physically, but mentally. I get muddled and can't calculate any longer.'

I hurried to tell her I was also getting forgetful. It didn't seem to console her. Then six months went by and I couldn't avoid noticing she was getting more and more ... incoherent. She couldn't even keep up the simplest chain of thought. Everything fell apart, and a month or so later she was admitted to a mental hospital.

In August, Anna and Rickard came to stay on holiday. It had been decided we were to sail to Skagen. They were happy and their happiness glowed from them.

'No wine for me, thanks,' said Anna, at dinner the first night. 'We're going to have a baby.'

I was so pleased I cried, and so frightened I almost fainted.

'Mother, dear, what a fuss!'

I looked at Arne and saw that he understood. He was as frightened as I was.

Anna had a temporary job lecturing at the university.

'I won't be able to keep that,' she said.

'Are you going to be a stay-at-home housewife?'

I tried to keep my voice steady, but don't know if I succeeded.

'Not on your life!' said Rickard. 'I don't want a stay-at-home housewife. Listen now.'

Then they both talked at once about the book Anna was going to write, a book people could understand based on her Lund thesis.

'Rickard's going to help me.'

'Oh, good,' I said, thinking they wouldn't earn much money from that kind of work.

The baby was due at the beginning of March. Anna made me promise I would be with them.

Maria arrived at the right time, and I'm sure it sounds strange when I say I was just as pleased as Rickard was. And Anna herself. The first time I held her in my arms, I seemed to have been given back something very dear I'd lost long ago.

She was a lovely baby, affectionate and sunny. She looked at me with Anna's clear blue eyes and smiled with Rickard's mouth. And yet she was most like … It was true, she was like my mother. A little Hanna, I thought, but I was careful not to say so. I knew how Anna had hated people saying she was like her grandmother.

They had moved into a three-roomer, a spacious, light apartment, beautifully appointed, cool and stylish as Anna liked it. But as soon as I arrived, I could see there was a shadow over both of them, bitter in her, and in him charged with anxiety.

I'd thought they would be jubilant over the success of Anna's book and filled with delight over the baby. But something had happened and I didn't like to ask. Actually, I didn't want to know.

'Things aren't easy,' was all she would say.

'I realise that. Do you want to talk about it?'

'Not now. I just want to think about the baby. And that things are good for her.'

So she became, as I had been, so preoccupied with the newborn babe that everything else fell away. I stayed until she had got the feeding going properly, then I left without asking what had happened.

'You know where I am,' I said, when I said goodbye.

'It's all about trust.'

'I realise that.'

In actual fact I'd understood all along. That first evening in Stockholm I'd thought about the telephone call she'd made a few years ago, when she'd said, 'They say he's a womaniser, Mother.'

All the way back on the train, I tried to concentrate on my delight over Maria. I knew we would be the best of friends. I imagined long summers with her by the sea and in my garden, all the things I'd teach her and show her, all the stories I would tell her and the songs I'd sing.

But I wasn't all that successful. The train thumped along the rails with its 'Devil take all men, devil take all men, devil take all bloody men'.

My own man was waiting at the central station in Göteborg, bad-tempered because I'd been away so long. 'I've been starving to death,' he said.

Devil take you, devil take you.

'So you couldn't find your way to the freezer?'

243

I had cooked ten dinners for him and all he had to do was to heat them up.

'No need to be sarcastic.'

I said nothing.

Then he said he really meant he'd been so lonely, and I had to clench my teeth not to feel sorry for him. At home the forsythia was in bud, a faint golden shimmer.

CHAPTER 61

Mother was often ill that spring. In the end, Ragnar and I had to be tough with her to get her to a doctor.

Heart, he said.

She was given drugs and that helped after a while.

One evening, when I'd been with her for so long I missed the last bus home, an unpleasant thing happened. I had phoned Arne and said I'd take the tram to Kungsten. He was to meet me there with the car.

It's true that I was tired as I sat there, right up at the front of the tram. Then I looked up and straight into the driver's rear mirror. In it was a woman so incredibly like my mother that I started, the same aged face and sorrowful eyes. I turned round to see who she was.

The tram was empty. I was the only passenger.

It took me a long time to realise that what I had seen was my own face. I was so miserable that tears started running down the old face in the mirror.

'You look tired,' Arne said, when I got into the car.

'Yes, more than I realised, I think. I'm getting old, Arne.'

'You're not,' said Arne. 'You're as young and pretty as ever.'

I looked searchingly at him, in the dim light from the dashboard, and he was just like himself, young and handsome.

The eyes of love tell lies. He was sixty-five and had only three years to go before retirement.

As usual, Arne fell asleep as soon as his head touched the pillow, but I lay awake trying to persuade myself that I hadn't seen what I'd seen, that it couldn't be true. Then I crept out to the mirror in the bathroom and stood there for a long time in the cold, revealing light.

What I'd seen was true. I had sharp perpendicular wrinkles on my long upper lip, so like Mother's. Flabby jawline, worry lines round my eyes, sorrowful eyes, grey streaks in my chestnut brown hair, my pride and joy. That wasn't really very strange. I would be sixty next year.

The strange thing was that I hadn't noticed, actually had had no idea. Nor felt it. I was as I'd always been, the same childish person. Inside.

But the body ages, and it didn't lie.

I held firmly on to the basin and the tears fell, making the face in the mirror older than ever. Can you whistle, Johanna? No, I no longer could.

In the end I crept into bed and cried myself to sleep.

The next morning Arne said I was to stay in bed that day. To rest. You've got books.

I always had books. I borrowed a pile every week from the library. But on this day I couldn't read. I lay in bed all morning, trying to comprehend all this about growing old, that I was old and I had to accept it.

Ageing with dignity.

What does that mean? How idiotic. At eleven o'clock I got up, phoned the hairdresser and fixed an appointment to have my hair cut and tinted. Bought an expensive 'miracle' cream and the first ever lipstick in my life. I finished off the day with a long walk up the steep mountains.

Exercise is supposed to be good for you.

When Arne came back, he said I was looking marvellous, and that was good because he'd been worried. He never even noticed the miracle cream, or that I now had dark red hair without a grey streak in it.

I hadn't dared use the lipstick.

And all my antics were useless.

You're old, Johanna.

I tried some joyful thoughts. Things were all right for me. I had a good husband who couldn't live without me, a lovely daughter, a new and beautiful grandchild. The garden, the sea, my mother still alive, friends, family.

But my heart kept objecting. My husband was becoming more like his mother over the years, complaining and demanding. My daughter was unhappy. Mother was sick.

Little Maria!

Yes.

And the garden?

I'd begun to find it rather hard, all the work it required. The sea?

Yes, it still had its strength.

Mother?

It was difficult thinking about her. She'd chosen old age early on, and had never really been young.

Later, when I'd got used to the idea of age, I wondered whether the shock that evening in the tram was some kind of fear of death. But I didn't think so. I'd never thought about ageing, but often about death. I'd always done that. Every day since I was a child.

I wasn't afraid of it any longer, not since my father-in-law had died. But I needed fundamentally to put myself into the position of what it meant not to exist. Almost a longing to be there sometimes.

Perhaps we learn not to age if we try to get used to death.

At the end of the week Anna phoned. Her voice sounded happier and she had news. Rickard was to go on a long assignment in America and she was asking whether she and Maria could spend the summer with us.

If she could!

I was so pleased I forgot about getting old.

'Maybe you ought to ask Pappa first?'

'But you know he'll be pleased.'

'I haven't been all that nice to him.'

'Anna, dear ...'

And he was pleased, Arne. I made him phone Anna and I could hear it when he said he was looking forward to seeing her and it would be great to see the little one.

'We'll go sailing. We'll make her into a real little sailor. It's never too early,' he said. 'You know, the earlier the better.'

I reckoned Anna had burst out laughing.

On the Saturday, he set about redecorating her old room upstairs. I bought a new bed for Anna. Arne made a pretty little cradle for Maria and also put together a baby-board. We also got a new rug and I made some airy white curtains.

'Darned good thing we put in water up there for Dad,' said Arne.

They flew down to Valborg. Arne didn't like the idea. He didn't trust aeroplanes, and on Walpurgis Night, the day before May Day, when we went to meet them, as usual, the weather was bad and stormy.

His fear was infectious, and I, too, stood holding firmly on to a railing at the terminal as the Stockholm plane danced down and slowed with a screech of tyres. It was just as Rickard had said on the phone, as safe as by train and much more comfortable for the baby.

I'd thought Arne would be pleased with the child, but hadn't expected him to be so over the moon about her. He stood there with the baby in his arms as if he were in heaven. When their luggage arrived, Anna and I had to carry everything to the car, because he refused to let go of Maria.

'Aren't you going to say hello to me?' said Anna.

'Haven't time.'

We laughed even more when we got to the car and Arne sat in the back with the baby and told Anna she could do the driving.

It took us longer than we had expected to get through town because of the carnival.

'Let's park somewhere,' said Anna. 'I'd like to watch the carnival as we used to when I was small. You can stay with the baby in the car, Mother.'

'I will,' said Arne. 'Go on, you two, off you go.'

That day was one long party. Anna and I laughed like children at the crazy Chalmer students, and when we got back home, the table was laid and all Anna's favourite dishes were in the oven.

Anna fed the baby while I heated up the food. The little girl sucked away, belched as she should, then abruptly fell asleep.

Arne asked after Rickard, and I saw a shadow cross Anna's face as she said he'd gone and was sorry to be away from Maria this first summer. But he hadn't been able to refuse the assignment. He was to do a whole series of reports on the racial scene in the USA, she said, smiling a sad little smile.

'A few months'll soon pass,' Arne said. 'Meanwhile, you two'll have to put up with us.'

'You can't imagine how much we'd like to.'

That was the first time she had even considered divorce.

She drank a glass of red wine in one draught. I must have looked worried because she said, 'There'll only be one, Mother.'

On May Day, Arne launched the boat, now scraped and freshly painted. We'd had a long, warm spring, so all the early work in the garden had also been done. Anna had no pram with her, so I went down into the basement and hunted out hers. It was old, but not ramshackle, I thought, and once I'd washed it clean, we put the child to sleep in it under the cherry blossom.

'I couldn't take everything on the plane,' Anna said. 'A friend of mine, Kristina Lundberg, is bringing everything we need by car next week. She's awfully nice, a social worker. Separated.'

She said nothing for a moment, then went on. 'She's bringing her two little boys with her. I hope they can stay overnight here.'

I was irritated by her humility. 'You know perfectly well your friends have always been welcome here.'

'I soon won't know anything, Mother. And I find it hard to accept all this kindness, my room which you've made so lovely for us … and …'

Then she was crying.

'Anna, dear,' I said, 'let's leave everything until tomorrow, when we're on our own.'

248

'Yes. Dad needn't know anything. Not yet, anyhow.'

'Exactly.'

Arne came home and almost had a stroke when he saw the pram.

'Johanna, for Christ's sake, the pins are all loose and the wheels aren't firm. Have you gone out of your mind?'

He mended it. It took almost an hour and he was really happy as he kept saying, 'Women!'

The kitchen was sunny. Warm. We undressed the baby and let her kick naked on a blanket on the kitchen table. When Arne came back, he sat on the kitchen sofa for ages, prattling and jogging the baby.

'What a miracle.'

Then she peed on him and smiled with relief.

'She's like Johanna. And Hanna. Have you noticed?'

'Yes,' said Anna. 'I'm glad she is.'

The good weather lasted all week. On the Monday, we were sitting under the cherry tree again, and at last I was told. It was worse than I'd thought.

There were no words to comfort her.

In the afternoon, we walked with Maria in the mountains and I told her about Ragnar. And Lisa.

Anna listened, wide-eyed. She hadn't known all that.

'They're two of a kind, those two men,' I said. 'The same warmth, humour and ... light-heartedness.'

Her eyes were large and dark blue when she answered. 'You're right. The worst of it is that I'm not like Lisa.'

I'd thought that myself.

It was all miserable.

But at the end of the week, the first letter from America came, and when I saw the eagerness with which she tore it open and how she glowed as she read it, I reckoned she'd never escape.

CHAPTER 62

That summer we talked a lot about men, how mysterious they were. I told her Arne had hit me when we were first married, and I'd gone back to Mother and she'd taken it all with a shrug.

'Then I found out that Father, my wonderful father, had hit her quite hard, several times.'

'That was in the old days,' said Anna. 'Why did you go back to Arne?'

'I liked him,' I said.

'Did it ever happen again?'

'No.'

I told her about Ragnar, how he'd watched over me like a hawk. 'I think he threatened Arne with the police, as well as a beating. You know, he's much bigger and stronger.'

We sat in silence for a long time, no doubt both of us thinking violence was a language men understood.

Then Anna said, 'I've seen, over the years, the way he slowly strangled you with his power games. I'd already noticed when I was only twelve, when you started working part-time.'

You can't hide things from children. I should have known that. And yet it still hurt.

'A lot was to do with money,' I said. I told her about the servant who was me, and how I'd had to ask for every penny. I didn't say I was heading back into the same situation because I didn't want to worry her. But maybe she understood. And she also realised what I meant with my story, because she said she managed her own finances, had a good income from her book and the publishers wanted another from her.

'I also write articles for various magazines and journals.'

We talked about our in-laws.

'Have you ever thought that Dad's mother was sick, mentally ill?'

I suppose I had occasionally. But reluctantly. I didn't like the modern way of explaining away evil as illness. As we walked back along the shore, I asked her if she thought illness of that kind could be inherited. No, she didn't.

'Otherwise I wouldn't have wanted to be a child of Grandmother's. Imagine a little thing like this exposed to grace and favour.'

She was carrying Maria in a pouch in front of her, the kangaroo bag, as Arne called it.

Then she said, slightly miserably, 'That applies to Rickard too, and his damned ice-cold mother.'

She was a more uncertain mother than I was, more afraid and clumsier. Not all that strange, considering I was thirty-five when I had a child and Anna was only twenty-four. It didn't trouble me, for she showered love and affection on the child. One afternoon, Maria had stomach-ache. Anna walked her to and fro, but she screamed as soon as we put her back to bed. I took her, while Anna hunted round for a children's doctor on the phone and finally got hold of one who said what I'd already said, that it was normal and nothing to worry about.

Anna was almost frantic with anxiety.

In the middle of it all, Arne came home, and with his large calm hands took over the child, put her against his shoulder and started walking to and fro as well. Now, now, just you calm down, little 'un. In two minutes, Maria was asleep, quite calm and sound asleep.

Anna wept in Arne's arms with relief and said she remembered, she'd suddenly remembered what it felt like when he'd held her when she was small and frightened.

Then she cried even more, until Arne said, 'That's just the way to frighten the baby. Just calm down.'

But I knew why she was crying and said nothing.

Kristina Lundberg came by car with all Anna's clothes, a large rather plain girl with a beaky, peasant nose, heavy eyelids and an ironic mouth. She had her two small boys with her and they raced round the house and garden like hooligans, and worst of all, along the quays in the harbour.

Wonderful kids.

We liked their mother too. She was the kind you can rely on. Politically, she was much more to the left than we were, a

Communist. In the evenings, she argued with Arne in the kitchen about social reforms and the dictatorship of the proletariat, often very loudly, and they both enjoyed themselves uninhibitedly. At the weekend, Arne and she went sailing with the little boys and calm descended on Anna, Maria and me.

When they came back on Sunday, Kristina packed. They were going on to relatives on some farm in Västergötland.

'It would've been nice if you could have stayed a little longer,' I said, and I meant it.

'I'd like to,' she said. 'But I mustn't rub the relations up the wrong way.' She looked downcast but decisive. 'And it'll be good for the boys,' she went on. 'They're such hard work. My mother's got lots of staff. She's already found a nursemaid, for the children are to stay all summer and my mother doesn't want the bother.'

She must have seen my surprise. 'Didn't Anna tell you?' she went on. 'My father's a count and has an estate, blue blood and all that, arrogant and generally somewhat limited.'

I remember that moment so clearly, for it was the first time I understood that we see only according to our own prejudices. The peasant girl in front of me was transformed, the long curved nose and the heavy eyelids becoming aristocratic.

How handsome she was!

The letters from America arrived in an even stream, answers were sent, Anna seemed in a better mood, and I felt things were improving. July came with rain, as usual. I was often alone with Maria, for Anna was working on her book. I sang to the child and listened to the even clatter of the typewriter upstairs. I went for long walks with the pram, in all weathers. That was good for me and I was fitter.

Anna didn't think I'd grown old.

Suddenly I have had another clear memory. It was a grey afternoon, rain streaming down the window-panes, and Anna said, 'Can't we have a look at the jewellery?'

I see I've omitted an awful lot in this description of my life. Such as my Norwegian relatives. Aunt Astrid died suddenly, without being ill, at the time when German boots were tramping at their worst down Karl Johan. And outside Møllergatan 19, from where Henriksen the fish merchant had vanished. Mother had a short letter from one of the sons, I a longer one from his wife Ninne, the only contact I had from our visit to Oslo. We were sad, but Mother wasn't surprised. She'd always known Astrid would leave life when it no longer suited her.

Some time after that, I had a telephone message from Oslo. A lawyer. He said there was a will and that Astrid Henriksen had left her jewellery to me. He also said that it was probably not worth much, but the Norwegian relatives wanted to keep it for sentimental reasons.

I was angry and said curtly that this concerned my mother's family jewellery and of course I should have it. Then I rushed off to Mother, who was still living in Haga at the time. She was so furious she screamed to high heaven, then got on the phone to Ragnar, who came and was just as angry. As he had acquaintances absolutely everywhere, it wasn't long before I was closeted in a lawyer's office with a nice elderly Jewish lawyer.

I'd written down the name of the Norwegian who had phoned me, and the lawyer in Göteborg had soon acquired a copy of the will and an inventory of the jewellery.

'The Norwegian lawyer was an honest man, thank goodness,' he said.

I went on sending food parcels to the Norwegian cousins, but I stopped writing to them.

I'd almost forgotten all about it, as it was a minor detail in comparison with everything that was happening during those years. But in the summer of 1945, my lawyer went to Oslo and came back with a large brown parcel, which Arne and I fetched from his office. And signed for. Arne hadn't taken the matter very seriously until that autumn evening when, in Mother's and Ragnar's presence, we took off the brown paper, found the blue jewel case and opened it with its gilt key.

There were brooches and rings, necklaces of sparkling red stones, bracelets and ear-rings. But most were old-fashioned buckles and clasps in various shapes. Grey. Pewter? Or could they be silver? Anna was dumbstruck and wide-eyed. Mother said there was much more than just the family jewellery there, some that Astrid had bought herself or been given by Henriksen over the years. Ragnar said we must get it all valued and Arne said, 'Where the hell shall we hide it?'

There were two heavy gold rings.

'Men's rings,' said Ragnar.

He told us about a farmer in the family who'd once found a gigantic gold coin when he'd been digging for new fencing posts. King Karl XII himself had dropped the ducat when he had stopped for a rest there at some time. That's what the farmer thought. He had had the coin melted down and there was enough gold for two wedding rings, which had then been passed down the family.

'Can I feel?'

Anna weighed the two royal rings in her hand, her eyes gleaming like the gold.

Ragnar smiled at her and told her about all the treasures that had been hidden in the soil of this poor country. When they'd finally built a road between Ed and Nössemark, they'd found a great hoard of silver with coins from the eighteenth century.

Anna looked at him in surprise and he went on to explain. 'There was unrest in the neighbouring area,' he said.

'Sometimes the land on the west of the long lake was Norwegian, sometimes Swedish. When King Karl XII lived in Ed and was planning his invasion of Norway, rich people buried their treasures.'

Mother picked up one of the finely worked buckles and told us the strange story about the Norwegian goldsmith who had fled from Bergen and been given a croft below Framgården. 'Nothing but wilderness,' Mother said.

But he'd lived there for many years with his wife and children, had his workshop in the front room, and made brooches, pendants and buckles out of silver. It was called royal silver.

'You can see for yourselves how he mixed it with cheap metals,' Mother said. 'It's quite grey.'

I remember I wanted to give one of the royal rings to Lisa. But Ragnar said no, the family jewellery shouldn't be dispersed and if Lisa wanted a gold ring he was man enough to get her one.

Arne pondered all weekend on how to solve the problem of where to keep the jewellery. Then he bought a fire-proof safe and made a secret compartment under the floor in the basement food store. We never bothered to get the jewellery valued, as if we didn't want to know. We wanted to think of the hidden treasure as an extra insurance, a security should something happen.

Now, sixteen years later, Anna wanted to see the jewellery and I said that that was no more than right as she would have it one day. 'But you must wait until your father comes back because I'm not going to burgle his secret compartment.'

'Where your jewellery is,' said Anna.

'I don't want to hurt him unnecessarily,' I said. 'Anyhow, I've no idea how to open it.'

'But, Mother ...'

It was a festive evening as we stood round Arne in the basement, Anna with Maria in her arms, and me, while Arne showed us the secret way to the safe with the jewel case.

'So now you know, should anything happen to me.'

Then we sat there as before, gaping at the glitter, Maria's eyes as wide as Anna's had been that time, though she was probably most affected by the solemn atmosphere. Anna took out a pendant in pale green enamel, partly gilded and richly decorated with small glittering stones.

'It's art nouveau,' she said. 'And I wouldn't be surprised if the stones weren't diamonds.'

'You're mad,' said Arne. 'She was only a fish-merchant's wife.'

'Take it, if you like it so much,' I said.

Then Anna said what Ragnar had once said. 'No, family jewellery shouldn't be split up.'

★

At the end of July, the sun came back, and at the end of August, Rickard returned from America. He had matured: deep lines of pain had appeared round his mouth and a dark sorrow in his eyes.

We spoke to each other on our own only once.

'You don't understand me, do you, Johanna?'

It was more of a statement than a question, so I had no need to answer.

He put his head on one side and then I saw for the first time that he was like a cat, a supple tom-cat, sure of his worth and his beauty. But also the kind that slinks round corners and howls for love on March nights.

I've always kept cats. Doctored tomcats.

I flushed and my heart thumped.

This man had all his sensuality intact, and I just touched on the thought that perhaps it was possible to understand him. Then I snorted at myself. Nonsense.

After they'd left, it was very empty everywhere. I missed Maria. I thought a lot about Anna and what she risked losing. Something I hadn't understood because I'd never had it. But which, perhaps, meant more than security.

CHAPTER 63

We did a lot to our house over those years. It was shabby and needed repairs. As usual, Arne did almost everything himself in the evenings and at weekends, with cheap assistance from friends of his, a metal worker and an electrician.

As soon as he retired, he made another room upstairs. In the daytime, I made curtains for our newly painted windows, now influenced by Anna and buying only white material.

But it is the dreams I had that I remember from this time, particularly the first one. In it, I found a door in the wall of the new upstairs room and opened it into a long corridor, narrow and scary. I

256

fumbled my way along it in the dark, and the passage grew narrower, but eventually I saw a strip of light far ahead where there was another door, just ajar. I hesitated for a long time before knocking.

The voice calling 'Come in' was familiar, as if I'd heard it every day for thousands of years. I went in and there was Father, sitting looking at a book. The whole room was full of books, bulging on shelves and in piles on the floor. He had a yellow pencil behind his ear and a large notebook beside him. A small girl was sitting in the corner looking at me with radiant brown eyes.

'Good that you came, Johanna. You can help me look.'

'What are you looking for, Father?'

I woke, so never heard the answer. When I sat up in bed, rather scared but mostly pleased, I remembered that the great library had no ceiling and was open to the sky. There was nothing surprising about the dream, nothing I hadn't always known.

The dream recurred, changing shape, but the message was the same and the feeling quite familiar. Once the corridor was a steep staircase and the room Father was in a laboratory. He lived there, he said, doing chemistry experiments. It smelt acrid and bracing. Again he was pleased I'd come, and asked me to help.

These dreams made me tidy up. On mornings when the dream seemed particularly vivid, I went so far as taking out the rugs and cleaning the windows.

My house was never just as I wanted it, never finished. The best of it was the roar of the sea beyond the wall. I was notorious in the village for my walks along the shore, every day and in all weathers. These roamings over the years taught me a great deal about the sea, what it sounded like and how it smelt in storms or calm, in dull weather, sun or mist. But I knew nothing of its intentions, or nothing I can put into words, though occasionally I thought it was all-embracing, like the presence of God.

Sofia Johansson was the person to induce such thoughts in me. She was a new friend, as unlike Rakel as anyone could be, a fisherman's wife from the old village.

As I said before, the original villagers didn't mix with us newcomers. But Sofia had a lovely garden and one day I'd stopped by her fence to look at her anemones, large deep blue flowers with black centres.

'I was just admiring them,' I'd said.

She'd smiled warmly. 'Yes, aren't they lovely? I could dig up a few tubers for you, if you like.'

I'd flushed with pleasure and said I'd look after them well.

'I know you will,' she said. 'I've seen your garden.'

She came the next morning with the knobbly brown tubers and helped me find a suitable place for them. We had coffee together and sat out of the wind below the wall. I had a low-growing, old-fashioned almost ground-cover rose she liked, and we agreed I'd dig it up and give it to her in the autumn.

'My name's Johanna,' I said.

She smiled again in that warm way and we agreed to use Christian names. From then on we often met in her garden or mine. As women do, we talked about many things. She had two sons on one of the fishing boats, but the sea had taken her husband many years ago.

'That was hard,' I said. 'How old were the children?'

The boys had left school and the boat lost with her husband had been their own. When they'd received the insurance, they'd bought another boat.

'They don't like life ashore,' she said.

She had a daughter, too. She sold fish in the market hall.

That interested me, so I told her I'd worked there for many years, indeed, right up to last year. 'Though only on Saturdays.'

She knew that. Her daughter had often seen me there and had been surprised.

'Why?'

'Your family's rather grand, aren't they,' said Sofia.

'No. Now, listen,' I said, and before I could think, I'd told her about growing up in Haga, about Mother and my brothers, and my father who'd died when I was a child. She liked the story, and told me her own, her childhood in the Bohuslän fishing village, where her father and brothers, cousins and neighbours laboured at sea for a living. A world of men, she said, dependent on the men, their strength and knowledge. But I realised she had never felt inferior, or female anger.

'Then I was saved,' she said, her eyes glowing.

I was embarrassed and didn't dare ask, thinking her too intelligent for the rather naïve Pentecostalist faith.

Talk about prejudices.

Now, I've forgotten which year it was when the spring storm grew into a hurricane and the sea came up over quays and houses, smashing boats and ripping loose moorings. Fortunately we hadn't launched our double-ender. It was propped up firmly in the shelter between the house and the mountain. But the tarpaulin broke loose and vanished inland like a gigantic bird.

The hurricane lasted for three days, and when it eventually moved on, I walked round the garden with some dismay. The old apple tree had snapped off and my roses were standing in the salt water the sea had poured over the wall. Then a neighbour appeared. 'Have you heard one of the boats from here has gone down?' she said. 'Crew and all.'

I was shaking all over as I switched on the radio, only to hear what I'd feared most. Sofia's sons were missing. I dug up my best Christmas roses, went down to the fishing village and knocked on Sofia's door.

There were lots of women there, all praying for the souls of the boys.

Sofia was very pale, white and fragile. She wasn't crying, but I was as I handed her the Christmas roses. 'Let me know if there's anything I can do,' I whispered.

'They're with God now,' she said.

As I walked home, I cried even more, thinking that God was just as cruel as Mother had always said. If he existed at all. But I was calm in some way.

I never was any help to Sofia. But if she hadn't been there that year when Mother was with me and lay dying, I don't think I would have coped.

Every summer, Arne and I looked after Maria, and between the child and me it became as I had dreamed. We had the same slow pace. We roamed about discovering new and amazing things in the mountains and along the shore. What a lot there was to stop and wonder at, driftwood, strange stones, flowers we'd not seen before. We picked them and looked them up in the flora back at home. And worms. And insects. And a tadpole we put in a bowl. It disappeared and I said nothing about the cat perhaps having eaten it.

Maria loved the cat.

We often spent Christmas in Stockholm. Things were better for Rickard and Anna, and they were both calmer. But I didn't dare ask any questions. Anna was expecting again.

'We're having another girl in May,' said Rickard.

'How do you know it's not a boy?' said Arne.

'Anna's sure. They've got that kind of mysterious gift, this Dalsland family.'

Arne shook his head. Then he told Rickard what Astrid had said about the Nazis marching in Oslo. In the mid-1930s!

We agreed Maria should come to us in the spring. I was to take the train up and fetch her.

But that didn't happen, for in March, Mother moved in with me and was dying.

'It won't be long now,' she said.

But it was. She wanted to die, but her body refused, and it was stronger than she was.

CHAPTER 64

It was difficult. My friend the district nurse came three times a week, tended Mother's bed-sores and helped me remake the bed. I borrowed a wheelchair and a bed-pan. The doctor came and we were given sleeping pills; it was easier when I could get some sleep at night. As usual when things were difficult, Arne was strong and patient. But there wasn't much he could do, for Mother was dreadfully embarrassed as soon as he appeared to help me lift her.

That was the worst, that she was so desperately ashamed and afraid of being a nuisance. 'You must wish me gone,' she said.

It wasn't true. Not even when things were at their worst was it true. I felt great tenderness for her, a tenderness I couldn't express and she couldn't accept. In me was also a dark and angry sorrow over her lonely poor life.

The only person to provide Mother with some joy in her last days was Sofia Johansson. She came every day, sat by Mother's bed and talked about her God. Mother had always been a believer, but her image of God was dark. She listened to this talk now about another God and found consolation.

'You have to believe her,' she said. 'God's taken husband and sons from her. She says He's called them home.'

Sofia said she hadn't come to save Hannah's soul. She wanted me to take a walk in the middle of the day, she said. And perhaps rest a bit after a bad night.

At the end of May, Anna came down with her new baby. Malin was different, not as affectionate as Maria, more serious, more observant. Like Anna, when she was little.

On the very first evening, Anna told us she was getting a divorce. Nothing could be hidden any longer from either Maria or Arne. He nearly went mad when she told us briefly about the other woman, a journalist Rickard had lived with when Anna was pregnant and in hospital. Anna had had albuminuria and a complicated delivery.

Arne wanted to go to Stockholm to teach Rickard a lesson.

'Then you'll have to go to Hong Kong. That's where he's working at the moment,' Anna said.

'Poor Pappa,' said Maria. My heart ached for her.

There was nothing we could do to help, not even obvious things like looking after Maria. When Anna went back with the children to move to a smaller apartment and find a permanent job, I phoned Kristina Lundberg and asked her to keep in contact with me.

'Anna's so proud. And introspective,' I said.

'I know. I'll phone you once a week and not tell her. But don't worry. She's strong as well.'

Arne went up in June and helped Anna move. She'd found a two-roomer and places at day nursery for both children.

He said the same as Kristina.

'She's strong. She'll manage.'

Mother died in October. It was difficult. She was in terrible pain to the last and cried out a lot.

I slept for two days. Arne arranged everything for the funeral and when I returned to everyday life again, I felt relieved. For her sake as well as for mine. She was buried on a Friday. Ragnar made a speech.

On the Sunday, he was dead, accidentally shot when out hunting. I fell ill and vomited all day and night. I had already been bleeding internally for some time and felt very weak. Now I couldn't even stand up. We had to get the doctor and a week or so later I was admitted to hospital.

Stomach ulcer. Operation.

Sometimes I think I was never the same again after that autumn.

But I'm exaggerating.

What I mean is that after Mother's and Ragnar's deaths, I grew old, finally old. And I didn't mind.

Nor does telling this story make things any better. That's because I can't bring myself to make it true. I've read a lot of memoirs in my day and always found them unbelievable. I seem to see quite quickly that the writers were selecting from among their memories, illuminating bits, but why just them? Once you discover that, you begin to have an inkling of what they had allowed to vanish into the darkness.

What was I doing? I don't think I've been selecting, not

consciously. Memory has struck me here and there as if it had a will of its own.

I think I have a lot of secrets left. But I don't really know which they are. Probably things that were so difficult I didn't dare look at them.

I remember now the day Lisa came to see me in hospital.

CHAPTER 65

It must have been about a week after the operation. The unpleasant sore in my stomach had begun to heal and I had less pain but was so tired I slept all day and night.

I had dreaded Lisa coming. I didn't want to see her grief. Now I'm letting the truth slide again. I didn't want to see the person with the right to such great grief over Ragnar.

She was pale but calm and ordinary. I wept.

'It was so unfair,' I said. 'Ragnar should've been immortal.'

She laughed at me, and when she said, 'That's childish, Johanna,' I hated her. But she went on. 'I don't think you ever grew up in relation to your big brother. You just closed your eyes and worshipped him.'

I closed my eyes quite literally then. She was right. I've never grown up when it comes to men. First Father, then Ragnar. Then Arne, who could treat me like a senseless child. Why had I allowed it? And then brooded on my humiliation as if on something bitter-sweet.

'But Ragnar was a wonderful person,' I said, in the end.

'Oh, yes,' said Lisa. 'He's left a big gap behind him, too. But that's being filled now. With relief.'

When she saw my horror, she became more voluble than usual. 'Don't you see? I need never again lie awake at night waiting for him, never wonder where he is or who he's with, never smell things on him. I've washed his damned stained long-johns for the last time.'

'Lisa, my dear ...'

'Yes, yes,' she said. 'We'll calm down.'

She spent half an hour talking about the future. She had bought a large apartment in a stone building diagonally across from her shop. She was going to move in there and use one of the rooms as a workshop.

'I'm going to expand,' she said. 'The boys and I will sell the transport firm and I'm thinking of buying the big shop on the corner, where Nilsson used to be. We'll do it up and make it smart. Anita is already designing new clothes. She and I are going to Paris next week to see the new fashions.'

I listened. This was a new, strong Lisa sitting by my bed. At that moment I detested her. She was spitting on my brother. But, worst of all, she was free and I was stuck.

'I remember when Anna phoned me and told me about her divorce,' she said. 'I congratulated her from my heart. Rickard Hård is a sorceror, he, too. Like Ragnar. Oh, Johanna, if only I'd had the strength to do the same when I was still young.'

That was the only time I ever saw her downhearted.

Just as she about to leave, she said, 'The police are investigating the accident. Most people say the friend who shot him is innocent. Ragnar had left his place and came out of the forest just behind the elk. That was careless.'

After she'd left, I tried to protect myself with horrible thoughts. About Anita, for instance, Lisa's daughter-in-law, whom I disliked. She had been properly trained at the Handcraft Association. She made pretty clothes and was pretty herself. She took from life without hesitation, almost insolently. I knew who would be mistress of Lisa's new business and I hoped it would go wrong.

Then I was ashamed and remembered what Ragnar had said. 'Anita reminds me of you, when you were young and ran Nisse Nilsson's shop.'

That afternoon, my temperature went up and I was given drugs. I slept through the evening meal and all night until four in the morning. When I woke I was cool and my head had cleared, so I had plenty of time to think about what Lisa had said. But mostly about myself, my dependence on men. About sorcerers like Ragnar and Rickard. About Arne who wasn't a sorcerer, and in many ways was more childlike than I was. I had always known that, and yet I had made him out to be a forceful man and had given him power.

About Ragnar again. Had he committed suicide?

Arne came in visiting hours. Pleased. He'd talked to the doctor and had been told I could go home next week.

'It's damned lonely without you,' he said.

Anna had phoned and asked him whether he thought I would be strong enough to have the children next summer.

'I'll do what I can to help,' he said, and I was able to smile at him and say what I felt, that of course we'd have them. And it would be nice.

I told him about Lisa's visit and what great plans she and her family had. And what she'd said about the police investigation. He knew all about it. There'd been something in the papers and wild rumours had gone round about Ragnar's firm being bankrupt. But then the gossip ceased, for the firm was solvent and his widow got a good price for it.

'Do you think Ragnar … killed himself?'

'No. If Ragnar had wanted to do himself in, he'd never choose a way that'd put a friend in a difficult position. I think he was tired, and confused with grief over Hanna.'

That was a great relief, for I saw at once that Arne was right. Afterwards I thought for a long time about how strong the ties were between him and Mother. And that no one had understood that.

CHAPTER 66

The years came and went, the children came and left. The worst of getting old is not tiredness and aches and pains, but that time rushes on, so quickly that in the end it doesn't seem to exist. It's Christmas and then it's Easter. It's a clear winter's day and then a hot summer's day. In between is a vacuum.

The girls grew and developed. The divorce didn't seem to have done them any harm and they didn't have to miss their father. He lived at the top of the same building as they did and took responsibility for them as well as taking part in their lives.

'What about your mother?'

'She seems all right. There are lots of children of divorced parents where we live, but our parents are different. They never speak ill of each other.'

Then Rickard came back, to Anna and to us. They married again. I grieved. I didn't understand. But Anna sounded like a lark in spring when she rang and told me they were coming at Whitsun, Rickard from Italy and the children and her from Stockholm. It was strange to see him again, older but more handsome than ever. Even more like a cat.

It was worse for Arne. They had a long talk down in the basement, he and Rickard, and afterwards Arne said he understood more now. Just what, I was never told, but I remember thinking the sorcerer had been waving his magic wand again.

Then Anna had another baby, a tiny boy who died. I could still help then.

The girls were grown up by the time illness crept up on me.

Perhaps you think it began with forgetfulness, with something like going out into the kitchen to fetch something and then forgetting what. That happened more and more often. I fought against it by acquiring definite routines for everyday tasks. First this, then that, then … They became rituals and worked quite well. I looked after the house and myself, keeping my fears at bay.

For a few years.

But my illness had begun earlier, when I no longer had any … any connections. When someone spoke to me, I didn't hear what was being said, just saw the mouth moving. And when I spoke, there was no longer anyone listening.

I was alone.

Arne explained and explained. Anna was busy running around.

266

Mother was dead. Ragnar was dead. Sofia was with God. Greta was in an asylum, and I didn't want to see Lisa.

The only people who had time and could listen were the grandchildren. I'll never understand why Anna had children who were so much nicer than my own.

But the conversations with Maria and Malin also ceased. By then I had been alone for so many years, no one could know where I was.

The last thing I remember is that they were suddenly all standing round me, all of them, their eyes large, dark with anxiety, and I wanted to comfort them with words that still existed but didn't get as far as my mouth. Then there was a hospital bed with high bars and a terrible fear of being shut in. I shook those bars all night, trying to break out and be free. At first, Anna sat beside me, all day long. She wept. She'd stopped running around. Now that a connection at last had become possible, I had lost any ability to do anything.

It was too late.

Anna
EPILOGUE

CHAPTER 67

Outside was raw, cold March, pop music and drunken young people shrieking in the square below, car tyres screeching on the wet asphalt by the kiosk. Not even the suburbs slept at night, these days.

As Anna drew the curtains, she stopped for a moment to look over at the city glittering on the horizon. Menacingly, she thought. A few weeks ago, someone over there had assassinated the prime minister.

She had no desire to think about Olof Palme.

She set about Johanna's manuscript once again. She had read it over and over again, gripped and grateful, and yet disappointed, as if she had wanted something else. I've always wanted something else, she thought. In my idiotic way, I wanted ... well, what?

To solve a mystery.

How naïve. A life can't be deciphered. You map it out as best you can and there you are, more uneasy than ever. So much has been stirred up and messed about. But I was always aware you were secretive. That comes through and was in your story. Only a brief glimpse, soon vanished. Like in a dream. Then you again take on the rôle of a caring person, orderly and comprehensible.

I have to start with what is simple. I think I know that, she thought. I'll write a letter.

She keyed in the date.

Stockholm, March 1986
Dear Mother,

I'm going to write you a letter tonight, say things I would never dare say if you were able to read it.

I have gone through your story, thoroughly. In a way you have come down from heaven and taken your place in an ordinary worldly existence.

There was nothing worldly in your life.

Naturally, nor were you the person I tried to trample on when I was young, scolding you for your lack of education and dead certainty. You say nothing about that time, as if it had passed without hurting you. Maybe you understood that I needed that idiotic academic defence to which insecure young people from the social-climbing generation take in order to overcome their parents and deny their origins.

For a while, I thought I had taken away your power with my education. But when I became a mother, you recaptured your place. Do you remember when Maria was crying with hunger in her cradle? It was awful, but I had learned, from a book, of course, that infants should be fed at definite times. And you said, 'But, Anna dear ...'

That was enough.

It's late at night, and I am writing in tumult. I am alone and upset. Oh, Mother, how healthy you were and how sick you became. So strong and so crushed.

I remember trying to protect you by drawing Father's rage on to me. As children do. You let it happen? Or you didn't see? He said I was like his mother, proud and fair-haired. Maybe that added to transferring the weight from you to me?

I challenged him. I was much angrier than you, too, more like him. And when I was in my teens and school had its effect, I was quicker to answer back and had many more words than he did.

Contemptuous? Yes. A class matter? Yes, that, too. Unendurable for him, who couldn't bear the slightest criticism. If he was offended, and that easily happened, he had to get it out of him. On to others. On to us.

He had had many a beating as a child and, like most of his generation, he talked with pride about beating. He had strange sadistic fantasies. As neither he nor anyone else understood they were sexual, he was able to give free rein to them.

Did he hate me? God, he's alive – does he hate me? Is all his furious rage directed at me now? Is that why it's so hard for me to phone? And go home to see him?

I'm simplifying. He had many good sides. He was security when things were difficult. Didn't let us down. Did you give Father the right to insult you because he reminded you of your own father? And what do you know about the miller from Värmland, about his dark spells and drinking? As far as I know, he was all you had. The child probably grows anxious in that kind of relationship. Was that the terror you passed on to Arne?

And me? I do as you did, submit, let things happen. Rickard is in London on a three-month job as correspondent. There's a woman there and he sleeps with her. He thinks that it's me he wants to reach, my 'untouchableness'. But it's always that banal ice-cold Signe from Johanneberg.

She's been dead for five years. But what does death mean to the person with no feet on the ground? And what happens to the child if the very first reality, the mother, lets it down?

Rickard flies, Mother, that's what makes him irresistible.

While I've been working, I've thought Hanna was the strongest of the three of us. She had sense and continuity. Was a realist. When I think of her, I am astonished at her boldness, stubbornly taking a stand of her own. And she lived as she believed. As your father says somewhere, she reckoned on injustices, so didn't collect them.

As you and I do.

She was angry because she couldn't cry. We've both cried as if we had oceans of tears to pour out.

Not that that helped.

I don't hesitate for one moment to say you're a better person than me, much better. But I am stronger. I have none the less not been bowed into total dependence. Of course, that's due to the spirit of the day, education, and I can support myself and the children. But also because I acquired my strength from a mother, not a father.

How surprised I was when I realised you envied me my divorce. I had no idea. As you say, it didn't become a victory. I fell back like a damned clinging vine.

Perhaps there is no independence.

When you tell me about sexuality, I am miserable on your behalf. Yet sensuality is so wonderful. So magnificent, in some way all-embracing.

That's why Rickard's infidelities are so unbearable.

Tomorrow I'll write a letter to London. 'I'm not going to take you back ...'

Shall I?

Mother, it's morning. I've slept for a few hours and am calmer. Less clear-sighted? I have something simple and important to tell you. What you got from your father, I got from you. To some extent, I have passed it on to Maria and Malin, and sometimes I dare to think they have more self-respect than you and I have. Perhaps they are not happy, whatever that is. But they have their children and their self-respect. You never met Stefan, Malin's fellow and Lena's father. But he was like Rickard. And Uncle Ragnar.

I'm reading your story again. In the sober light of dawn. How strange it is that a child can know without knowing. For in some way I knew there were, had been, siblings.

Dear Lord, how did you bear it? I know what it feels like. I've lost a child and I nearly went mad. Literally. I didn't tell you how far out into border country I was. Didn't want to frighten you.

The war is even more remarkable. I've never thought about how it left its mark on my childhood, how much of my fear has its origins there. And yet I remember the German pilot burning in the air above us, and Father coming and going, in uniform and talking about evil. And I'll never forget that foreign newspaper I bought at the kiosk with money Ragnar had given me.

There are things you've not seen, things about your brothers. You just see them as chauvinist pigs. But you had a need there for

274

revenge when you had to put up with their drunkenness, clean their shoes and listen to their foolish sexual boasts. They were jealous of the girl who was the best-looking and the most talented. And who got all their father's attention.

I know that, because Uncle August told me once. 'She was Father's doll. He would do anything for her. He never even looked at us.'

But they had their mother's interest, you may protest. I don't think that was worth much. Partly because she became an anachronism as soon as you all came to town, uneducated, a bumpkin. But also because her love for them was suffocating.

I don't know. I'm fumbling my way through a jungle of prejudice and psychological public property. This morning I woke in a dream about a train. I was alone in a carriage that was standing somewhere in a siding. It had been uncoupled by mistake. Forgotten. But it wasn't horrible, nothing to worry about. On the contrary. I'd been given time to think in a forgotten space.

It strikes me now that perhaps there's a main line we've missed. Love.

Perhaps we're prisoners of it, both you and I.

I suddenly remember an event some years ago. You were confused but hadn't entirely disappeared. You still had words and were pleased when I came to see you. You recognised me. Then Father fell ill and had to have an operation. I was alone in the house and went every day to see him in the hospital and then on to the long-stay hospital where you were. Every day, he said, 'You haven't time to sit here. Off you go now, to see Mother.'

I said, 'OK, I'll be off.' He smiled and waved as I left.

A week or two later he was discharged. I fetched him and drove him straight to you. When you caught sight of him, you flung out your arms like a bird about to fly away. You called out, 'Oh, there you are.' Then you turned to the girl pushing the wheelchair and said, 'Things'll be all right now, you'll see.'

I remember being jealous.

Why do men make it so difficult to love them?

Another thought: I said before that I was angrier than you. The strange thing is that I'm never angry with Rickard. It was the opposite for you. You directed all your aggression at Arne. Was that because you failed sexually? That your love was never given any outlet?

What did I want with this journey through the lives of three women? Was it to find my way home?

In that case, I've failed. There was no home. Or it couldn't be found again, anyhow not in the way I'd chosen. Everything was much more structured and full of contradictions, larger, darker than the child ever had an inkling of.

I don't even know whether I understand much more now. But I've learned a great deal and I'm damn well not going to do what you did, Mother, give up when the truth collapses into a thousand truths.

Anna was just about to finish off the letter when the telephone rang. She looked at the time in surprise: scarcely seven. Who would be phoning at this time on a Sunday morning?

As she reached out and picked up the receiver, she was frightened. So she wasn't surprised when the agitated home help at Father's in Göteborg cried out, 'We found him unconscious and an ambulance has just taken him to hospital.'

Anna dressed, packed a case with the barest necessities and phoned the hospital. It took a while to get through to Emergency in Göteborg, and a tired doctor said, 'Coronary. You'd better come at once. He hasn't long to go.'

She managed to get a call to Maria as well: 'So you know where I've gone.'

CHAPTER 68

She took a taxi, managed to get a stand-by ticket at Arlanda airport and another taxi at Landvetter.

Just before ten she was sitting at his bedside. He was in a general ward, unconscious, a drip in his hand.

'Isn't there a single ward?'

Yes, they were just getting one ready. They would give her a chair and a bunk to rest on.

The doctor with the tired voice came shortly afterwards and listened to his heart and lungs.

'Pneumonia has set in.'

There was a question in his voice and she understood.

'Can he get better?'

'No. His heart's giving out.'

'No antibiotics.'

He nodded, and told her they would see to it that the old man would not be in any pain.

So she sat there, the hours passing, her mind vacant. She was drained of emotion too, strangely unmoved. The ward sister came in during the afternoon and said they would send someone in so that she could go and get something to eat. There was a café in the entrance hall and would she stay there so that they knew where she was.

For the first time, Anna realised how hungry she was.

She had hash with two fried eggs and beetroot and had time to phone the long-stay hospital to tell them that she would be unable to visit Johanna today. Nothing had changed when she went back to the ward and took his old hand in hers again. A sister came in at around seven to say there was a call for her from London.

She was unreasonably relieved.

'How are things, Anna?'

'Strangely enough ... it's rather boring,' she said, then was ashamed.

'I'll get an early plane tomorrow. I'll be with you at about twelve.'

'Thanks.'

'I've spoken to Maria. She going to try to come tomorrow, but she's having trouble getting a sitter. We haven't got hold of Malin yet. She's in Denmark at some seminar.'

277

Once back with the old man, she started crying, the emptiness giving way and feeling returning. She took his hand again. 'You've been a good father,' she whispered.

It was true, she thought. He was always there and he always cared for me.

It was his rage that got in the way. Anger, not hatred.

At half past two in the morning, he moved uneasily. She was about to ring for the night sister when she saw he was trying to say something. His dry lips were moving but no words came.

She stroked his cheek and whispered that she understood.

His eyes were looking straight at her, then he heaved a great sigh and stopped breathing. It happened quickly, almost unnoticeably. As easily as if it had never happened.

She pressed the bell, and when the night sister came and looked grave, Anna knew he had died. A quiet, impotent pain filled her and she realised that it was grief, a grief she would long have to live with.

Some long, silent minutes later, the sister whispered that there was hot coffee in the office. Anna should go there while they made the necessary arrangements. She obeyed like a child, drank the coffee and ate half a sandwich. Then she was allowed back into the room, now neat and tidy. They had lit a candle each side of the old man and there was a bouquet of flowers on his chest.

She sat there for an hour, trying to fathom what had happened. At five in the morning, she phoned Maria and told her, saying she needn't come now. She would ring again when she had arranged for the funeral.

CHAPTER 69

Silvery mist lay over the town as she took a taxi to the house by the sea, the fog-horns sounding over rock and isle.

The home-helps had cleared away all traces of the night before when they had found him. She went from room to room, thinking, as so many times before, that the place had lost all personality since her mother had gone. No house-plants, no tablecloths or cushions. Only orderliness and the kind of bleak matter-of-factness with which men often surrounded themselves.

It was cold, too. She went down into the basement to adjust the oil heating, then went back upstairs to her room and took the quilt out of the cupboard. Once in bed, she thought about practical matters and found that that helped.

She woke at eleven. The heating was roaring away in the basement and it was almost unbearably hot. But she didn't turn it down, just opened all the windows and aired the rooms. Her back and arms ached with fatigue after the long vigil, but she stubbornly continued considering practicalities. Must phone Landvetter so Rickard knows to come here, not to the hospital. A hot bath. Was there any food in the house? Must go shopping.

She made the decision as she lay in the hot water, feeling the ache leave her body. She would stay. She would live here. In the spring, perhaps for always. She went out into the garden. My garden, she thought, for the first time, and was ashamed to see how neglected it was. The sun emerged through the mist and in the cold March light she saw the overgrown roses that hadn't flowered for many years, the lawn that was mostly moss and last year's tall weeds in the flower-beds.

She heard the car and it was him, then she was in his arms.

'Out in the cold in nothing but a bathrobe! And pretty well barefoot,' he said, as he let her go.

'It was so hot indoors,' she said.

'Have you had anything to eat?'

'No, there's no food here.'

'You crazy girl,' he said. Then without her understanding how it had come about, they were in the narrow bed upstairs and he was kissing her eyes and breasts, her grief obliterated, and she knew that this was where she belonged.

The main line?

A moment later, after he had found a jar of old coffee and given

279

her some, she thought that nothing was ever simple except just this, what Hanna called the bedding.

He didn't ask about the death and she was grateful.

'We must go to Mother,' she said.

He had hired a car at Landvetter, which was good. They made out a shopping list and she said he could go and get the things while she was at the hospital. They could have lunch in town before going to the undertaker's.

'You're busy arranging things, as you always do when you're scared,' he said, in a warm voice.

He was about to drop her off in front of the hospital, when she suddenly felt panic.

'What shall I say to her?'

'Tell her as it is.'

'Rickard, please come with me.'

'Of course,' he said, and went and parked the car.

He waited while she spoke to the ward nurse, who also told Anna she should tell her mother.

'We'll see if she understands.'

Johanna was far away as always, a long, long way away.

They sat looking at her for a while. Rickard took her hand and Anna leaned over her and said very clearly, 'Mother, listen to me. Arne died in the night.'

Did she start? Had she understood? No, I'm imagining things.

But when they left her, Rickard said he was sure she had. Her hand had reacted.

They had an early lunch in a new fish restaurant, then bought supplies and went to the undertaker's. Such a lot of decisions to be made. Anna said yes to an oak coffin, no to a cross in the newspaper announcement, yes to an urn. She suddenly realised what people meant when they said funeral arrangements kept grief at bay for the first week.

On their way home, she went shopping at Mother's old co-op. Then they went to the market garden and Anna bought flowers for the house. When at last they got home, they found Malin sitting on

280

the steps. Anna smiled and Rickard laughed with delight. Maria had got hold of her in Copenhagen the previous night and a friend had driven her to Helsingör, where she'd got a seat on the ferry.

'Mother, you've gone and shut yourself in again. What about having a good cry?'

'Can't.'

CHAPTER 70

Anna lay on her back in bed, holding Rickard's hand, a cold hand fumbling for a warm one. She was too tired to sleep.

He was worried, she could sense that.

'A sleeping pill?'

'No.'

'What about a whisky?'

'OK.'

She drank like a child drinking water and was surprised by how quickly it calmed her down. Just before she fell asleep, she said she could easily become an alcoholic. She woke to the smell of coffee coming up the stairs and heard Rickard and Malin talking in the kitchen. It was fine outside.

I must tell them, she thought, as she went downstairs. She was given a large cup of coffee at the kitchen table, added some milk and drank it.

'I've thought of staying here ... for a while. Someone has to visit Mother.'

'That suits me,' said Rickard. 'It's actually easier to get to Göteborg from here than from London.'

'It'll be lonely,' said Malin. 'But we'll come down as often as possible.'

'I thought I'd ring Maria and ask her to drive my car down. And bring the computer and printer and all my notes with her. And my clothes.'

Then she said, 'I might just as well be here and work.'

The words hung below the kitchen light. The same words as so many times before.

She lowered her head to the table, gave in and wept.

'I'll go back to bed for a while,' she said. 'I need to be alone.' She took a roll of household paper and went upstairs.

Then she lay in her old room until the tears finally dried and she began to shake with cold.

God, how cold she was. She woke again to a good smell. Food. Fried bacon, potatoes, onions. Her legs felt weak as she went to the bathroom, washed her face in cold water and thought she looked old and ravaged. But when she went into the kitchen, Rickard said, 'Wonderful, your eyes have come back again.'

'No longer empty wells,' said Malin, smiling at her. Anna felt her answering smile truly came from within her.

'It was good he was allowed to die,' she said.

'Yes, good for him and good for us. I think you should think about what an unusually long and full life he had.'

There was nothing remarkable about what he had said, but Anna . had found everything meaningless for so long; words had again acquired some weight. Every word.

'How long can you two stay?'

'Until after the funeral,' they both said.

'Do you think you could take on selling the boat, Rickard? It'd be good to get rid of it. And we need some cash.'

It didn't take him long to write out an advertisement and contact *Göteborg-Posten*. Then he disappeared down to the boatyard and came back with a man who tapped all round the hull, examined the interior and offered them a reasonable price.

'Talking about cash, oughtn't we perhaps to go through his accounts and bank books?'

'Yes. I'll show you his hiding-place.'

They found the secret box built into the wall behind the old man's underclothes in the wardrobe.

'Cunning,' said Rickard, with admiration. 'Why are you looking so strange?'

'I happened to think of something. Malin, where are my flowers?'

'In the basement. You took them down there yesterday after-noon.'

In the basement! Anna said to herself.

Malin and Anna cleaned all the windows, washed and ironed the curtains and bought some more geraniums for the empty window-sills. Rickard sold the boat, went to the bank and fetched the calm woman who came to do the inventory. She went through the whole house and put the lowest of prices on everything.

'Considering heritage tax,' she said.

On Thursday afternoon, Maria came with the car and the children. Anna nearly hugged the breath out of the little girls. After dinner, Rickard brought in the computer and printer.

'We'll have to fix up a proper place for you to work after the funeral.'

A lot of people came, many more than they had reckoned on, friends from work, Party members, sailing friends. And then the last remnants of the old family. The ceremony in the church and the reception afterwards both vanished into unreality for Anna.

CHAPTER 71

She was lonely. Days came and went.

She spent every morning on her book. It was going sluggishly, nothing but scattered thoughts. She could sit there for long spells thinking about Hanna's mother, who had seen four children die of starvation. Then she brooded over Johanna and her miscarriages, and over how strange it was that they, too, were four. She herself had lost only one child and that was quite enough.

Two children. The abortion. How had Mother found out about that? What kind of child was it that had not been allowed to be born? Boy? Girl?

'Pull yourself together,' she said aloud to herself. Not good to weep into the keyboard.

Then she wrote: 'To think that I've never known I grieved for the child.'

She thought about the ivory woman, Arne's mother, and her grandmother, and that Johanna's image of her made no attempt to understand her. That was unusual. Mother had always tried hard to understand and excuse. She must have hated her mother-in-law, blaming her for everything that had been difficult and incomprehensible in Father.

'He's getting more and more like his mother,' she used to say in her last years. 'I couldn't bring myself to listen. Anna just ran away.'

Was there a dark secret in Grandmother's life, a shame that had to be kept out of sight with all that suppressed pride?

She ate her yoghurt and corn flakes and went to the hospital to feed her mother. The old people in the ward no longer frightened her. Just like everything that becomes ordinary, there was something natural about them. She got to know other visitors, the tired little woman who came every day to feed her brother, the old man who made his way through town with his bad leg to visit his wife.

Daughters, many of her age.

They greeted each other, exchanged a few words about the sick relatives and the weather, this fine spring, sighing when they discussed how long the old one in number five had left.

Anna told Johanna about the garden, how she worked in it every afternoon to revive it. She no longer thought about whether Johanna understood.

'The lawn's the worst,' she would say. 'I've got all the moss out and bought some soil improver. As soon as it rains I'll sow some seed.'

Next day.

'The currant bushes are improving. I've cut them back fiercely, dug round them and manured them.'

One day she had some good news.

'The roses are in bud, just imagine! It helped to prune them and add some new soil and manure.

'Everything'll be as it was before, Mother,' she would say. 'I'm sowing annuals because only one perennial has survived. The peonies, those dark red ones, you know.'

In the end she was able to tell her more.

'It's almost done, Mother. And it'll look great.'

When the garden was ready, Johanna died, one night, in her sleep. Anna sat there as she had with her father, holding her hand.

When she got back home in the morning and walked round the garden, she felt no misery. Only a great melancholy.

The family came and helped her arrange the funeral and more people than they had reckoned on came this time as well.

'I'll stay on for a while,' said Anna.

'Anna!'

'Mother!'

Rickard's job in London was over and he was back at the office. He was miserable and she could see it.

'How long?'

'Until the dead are cold in their graves.'

He looked frightened and she realised that what she had said had been insanely put. Their bodies had been cremated. Rickard and she had together put the urns into Hanna's grave. Hanna was the only one to have prepared herself for death by buying a burial patch in Göteborg with the money from the mill.

'That was an odd expression,' said Rickard.

'Yes,' she said, nodding. 'But right in all its absurdity.'

She tried to explain.

'I had a vague idea I might learn ... not to worry. To get used to the idea that now things would be as they were, with everything.'

'With what, for instance?'

With your woman in London, to mention just one. I don't care who she is or what she looks like, or what she does in your life. She didn't say it, but laughed aloud with joy when she sensed it might be true.

'But we must be realistic. I've put down the deposit on the houses in Roslagen.'

She nodded, but was surprised. He hadn't mentioned the purchase since he'd gone to England. Perhaps there was no woman in London.

'You'll have to give me time.'

Malin settled the matter.

'I think that's sensible. You're not finished with this house yet. I don't think you will be until that book is finished.'

CHAPTER 72

There was a wordless joy in being alone.

After she had raked up the dead leaves and rubbish from last year into a pile and set light to it, she stood looking at the bonfire for a long time. Solemnly, far away in time. She roamed along the shores, sometimes running, climbing the steep hills, rolling small stones over the precipice down into the sea.

'You seem happy,' said Rickard, when she picked him up at the airport late on Friday evening. It was a question. She thought for quite a while.

'No,' she said finally, not really knowing what she meant. 'I have no expectations,' she said.

Happy? The question preoccupied her after he had left to go back to Stockholm. It annoyed her. No more happiness, she thought. No more of what was lovely, fragile and anguished, condemned to be crushed, the fragments always hurting. Bleeding, a plaster applied, an aspirin taken, hoping it will all heal.

But, as Mother says, everything leaves its traces.

And all old scars ache when there's bad weather ahead.

Maria came and went. She got nearer the truth when she said to Anna that she, Anna, had become childish.

'Yes.'

Malin came, too. 'Free at last, are you, Mother?'

There was something in that, yes. 'Maybe on my way,' said Anna with a slight laugh. 'At the moment I'm in limbo. You don't need words there. Best of all, there are no adjectives. I haven't seen for many years, neither the trees nor the sea, nor even you and Maria and the children. Those damned adjectives constantly get in the way.'

Eventually Anna was to find what existed in limbo. She hoped so. But she was in no hurry. She was cautious. Not inquisitive. She would take her time before asking any questions. For the time being, she was content to stop at interesting details.

Faces. Her own in the mirror. The post-mistress's, the postman's and the grave face of the child next door. And Birgir's, the only person to come to see her. His bright smile occupied her, the strange darkness in his eyes no longer frightening her. She paid a lot of attention to her whims. There weren't many. They came and went. But they surprised and pleased her, like the buds on the old rose bushes.

When the apple trees blossomed and were buzzing with bees, she made a new discovery. She could stop thinking and the eternal chatter in her mind fell silent. Suddenly she reached the place for which she had striven for years with her meditations.

Objects fascinated her. Driftwood along the shore. Stones. Again she found constant delight in stones. One day she found a polished stone with strange veins through it, softly shaped like a foetus. She sat still there for a long time, weeping. For a while she thought of taking it home with her, but she changed her mind and threw it back into the waves.

Nothing's ever comprehensible, she thought. But in small things, we can have an inkling.

CHAPTER 73

When she got home, a man and a woman were standing at her gate with some flowers, a heavy pot of Christmas roses, the flowers over. There was something familiar about the woman, with her broad face and open blue gaze.

'We met a long time ago,' she said. 'I'm Ingeborg, Sofia's daughter. We came to offer our condolences and return the Christmas roses your mother gave my mother when my brothers were lost at sea.

'This is my husband, Rune,' she went on, and Anna shook a strong male hand.

When Anna tried to thank her, she found herself crying. 'How kind of you,' she whispered, fumbling for a handkerchief, finding one, then stopping. 'I've become a real cry-baby,' she said. 'Do, please, come in and have a cup of coffee.'

They sat in the kitchen while Anna brewed coffee and thawed cinnamon buns.

'If anyone knows what grief is,' she said, 'then you must, Ingeborg.'

'Yes, that's true. Worst was when Father was lost. I was so small I couldn't understand.'

'Your mother was an angel. You know, she came here every day when Grandmother was dying.'

'Yes. She was pleased to be able to help.'

'When my mother grew old, she often listed all her dead. This one was dead, and this one, and Sofia was with God, she used to say.'

Then it was Ingeborg's turn to take out a handkerchief, and Rune began to look uneasy. He shifted on the kitchen sofa and cleared his throat.

'To tell the truth, we didn't just come to offer our condolences,' he said. 'We've something to ask you, too.'

'Rune!'

Ingeborg managed to stop him, and over their coffee, the two women spoke about how they'd never known each other.

'There were ten years between us, and that's a lot when you're a child,' said Ingeborg.

'I thought you were so big and good-looking. And you had a job in the market hall. Like Mother.'

'You were rather impressive with all your education.'

They could laugh now. Then they went out into the garden and planted the Christmas roses in their old patch of soil on the south slope.

'You've made a fine job of it here.'

'I managed to get the garden in order before Mother died.'

'Did she know that your father … had gone before her?'

'I think so.'

They went all over the house and Rune praised it, saying they must get down to what they wanted to say. 'The thing is, we'd like to buy it.'

Anna's head spun, round and round.

'And one day reality knocked at her door,' she whispered. Then she laughed with relief and said, 'I can't think of a better solution than that Sofia's daughter … and husband should take over Mother's house and garden.'

Rune talked about market prices and told her that they had the money. Anna shook her head and said that what was important to her was that they didn't alter the house with all those *nouveau-riche* tricksy things, and Rune said he was a carpenter and good at old houses, and Anna smiled and said, 'Now you remind me of my father and I think you'll be happy here,' and Ingeborg said she had always dreamed of this place ever since she was small, that it had been a kind of image of happiness with its young family and pretty little daughter.

I suppose it could have seemed like that, Anna thought, with surprise. Then she said she had to talk to her husband and children first. Rune looked worried.

Anna said that Rickard would be pleased and so would the girls.

'They want me back home. Rickard's coming at the weekend. Then we can meet again and settle the details. I'm worried about the furniture …'

'The fine mahogany furniture?'

'That Father made, yes. I don't want to throw it out …'

'Throw it out?' said Rune. 'That'd be mad.'

289

'Would you take over anything we haven't room for?'

'The lot,' said Rune, and Anna laughed.

'It belongs in this house, doesn't it?'

Then she said there was only one hitch and that was that she had to finish her book.

'Three weeks,' she said. 'I promise I'll get it done in three weeks.'

After they'd left, she sat and stared at the computer. She hadn't written a word since Mother had died.

'The time has come,' she said aloud to herself. 'What I've found out, I won't forget.'

She phoned Rickard. She'd expected him to be pleased but not that he would be so loud in his delight.

'My God, how I miss you.'

'See you on Saturday. You must settle things with this Rune.'

'I'll phone a Göteborg estate agent to find out what current prices are. How's the writing going?'

'It'll be all right now.'

She stood by the phone for a long time after putting down the receiver. At last she understood. There was no woman in London. If I hadn't had these weeks to myself, I might have become paranoid, she thought.

At seven the next morning she was at her computer, thinking with astonishment that it was all going to have a happy ending. Despite everything.

The decision to sell forced her into the long-postponed clearing of the house, sorting and arranging. She spent the afternoons doing it, starting on the top floor.

After a while she reckoned the house had more to reveal than Johanna's story. Like all those books in the north attic. They were in an old seaman's chest and were all tattered. Read to pieces. Had Mother saved them because she hadn't the heart to throw out books? Had she thought of mending them? Some of their spines had been taped.

All her life, Johanna had devoured books. All that reading must have left some traces, and yet she scarcely mentioned it, only Selma Lagerlöf at the beginning and then somewhere in passing that every week she borrowed a stack of books from the library.

Here was Strindberg, all his books as far as Anna could make out, in cheap unbound editions, some falling apart, some pages missing. Underlinings everywhere, angry exclamation marks here and there. The greatest impression made on Anna was Dostoevsky's *The Idiot*, a bundle with notes in the margins. At first Anna couldn't read what had been written, but when she took the book out into the daylight, she found that Johanna had written 'How true!' alongside every underlining.

Hjalmar Bergman's *Grandmother and Our Lord* was there, too, with Karin Boyes's *Kallocain* and the poems of Harald Foss, Moa Martinson, all unbound and tattered.

Strange!

The famous proletarian writers, Lo-Johansson, Harry Martinson and Vilhelm Moberg were all on the shelves in the living room in finely bound editions.

Why did we never talk about books? It had been a common interest, after all.

Because you didn't dare.

No, it can't be that.

Because I didn't listen? Yes.

I wasn't interested in you as a person, only as my mother. Not until you fell ill, disappeared and it was too late, had the questions come.

The next afternoon, she went through all her mother's clothes, good clothes, well cut and of good quality. Like Johanna herself. There was a jewellery case containing nothing but trash. She didn't like decking herself out, making herself visible, challenging.

Though you were so beautiful, Mother.

She found an unfamiliar box of old photographs. How pretty you were. That must be Astrid on a quay in Oslo. Anna's heart beat faster as she took the photographs down to the sofa in the living room. There was one of Astrid and Johanna together. Arne must have taken it. How alike they were.

So unlike Hanna, both of them. Here it was, in the break between the heavily earth-bound and the butterfly-light – this was where the secret lay. The … supernatural.

Anna hesitated for a long time over the word.

Found none better.

It was something you know, both of you.

Far in by the roof ridge was a huge parcel, gigantic, wrapped firmly in an old sail. Anna hauled and tugged at it. It was heavy but she finally managed to get it out and loosen the ropes.

There it was! Hanna's Värmland sofa!

CHAPTER 74

When Rickard came on Friday, he looked ten years younger. He raced through the house, exclaiming at all that had been done.

They hardly slept at all, the first night. For the first time, Anna thought, Here it is, the land without thoughts.

Then they became strictly practical, sorting, going to the tip, an impressive new installation, designed to accept most things, special cupboards for clothes, great boxes for books, paper here, metal there.

At midday Rune and Ingeborg appeared, as they had agreed. They were shyer now, as if Rickard frightened them. He was also uncertain.

'I'm no businessman,' he said. 'But I phoned an estate agent here in town and he gave me a price which seems to me a pure swindle. Round about a million, he said.'

'That's about right,' said Rune.

'No!' cried Anna. 'That's shameless, Rickard.'

'Yes, that's what I said.'

'It's the situation,' said Rune. 'View over the sea and large garden.'

'Eight hundred thousand at the most,' said Anna.

Rune's shyness vanished. 'I'm damned well not going to exploit the fact that we are dealing with financial idiots,' he said, and suddenly all four of them began to laugh.

'We have some capital, Anna,' said Ingeborg. 'You see, we saved the insurance money from the boat that went down.'

It was natural to Rune and Ingeborg and only Rickard and Anna lowered their eyes.

'Let's seal it with a drink,' said Rickard, unable to bear it any longer. 'We can settle the rest at the bank on Monday.'

'That's fine,' said Rune, and when Rickard brought the whisky, he added, 'Not bad at all.'

'Rickard!' said Anna, after their guests had left. 'Why didn't you tell me anything about values yesterday? Or last night. Or this morning.'

'Things were so great for us, Anna. I didn't want a row.'

'Are you afraid of me?'

'Yes, of your seriousness.'

Anna felt those idiotic tears coming again. But Rickard was angry and shouted, 'Why can't we ever be like other people? Why don't we cheer because we've suddenly become rich? Why don't we sit down and plan everything we can do to the houses by Lake Risjön?'

Anna started laughing and said he was absolutely right. Having money was wonderful. And there won't be any heritage tax because the house has been mine for years. But we still owe about a hundred thousand on it.

'As you're willing for once to discuss the realities of life, then I can tell you I got ninety thousand for the boat. And there's over fifty in his savings book.'

Anna gaped. 'And the way he complained about never having enough money. Why didn't you tell me?'

'Anna, my dear, why didn't you ask me?'

He's right, she thought. Any normal person would have been interested. I must get out into reality.

'There's another garden waiting for me,' she said.

'Exactly.'

They sat at the kitchen table all evening, sketching and planning. Anna realised at once that he had been thinking a great deal about it.

'We'll build a new large kitchen in the north angle. In a new house, you see? We'll have room for a bathroom and a laundry room there, too. And wardrobes and other storage space.'

'But what about water and drainage?'

'I've talked to a builder out there. They've got technical solutions to that kind of thing nowadays.'

'Then we've the glassed-in corridor between the houses. I'd like to widen it, here, in the middle. Then it could be like a conservatory, you see?'

Anna nodded eagerly.

'I'll put Grandmother's Värmland sofa in there,' she said.

They were so involved, they found it hard to sleep, which was just as well as at midnight the phone rang.

Anna went rigid with fear. Rickard leaped up to answer.

'Hi. Have you no shame? Do you know what the time is?'

Who is it? thought Anna, calm now. He sounded pleased.

'Yes, that'll be all right. But wait a moment while I talk to my wife.'

He called up the stairs that it was Sofie Rieslyn on her way home from London and she wanted to come and show him her photographs.

'She's welcome,' called Anna, as surprised as anyone could be.

'I've quite forgotten to ask about your book,' she said when he came back. 'It's dreadful how peculiar I've been.'

'It's over now, Anna. But I need your help with the arrangement and with … the language. I'd like to make it into something more than just reportage. But we can leave that until tomorrow.'

Thank goodness my manuscript's complete, Anna thought, as

Rickard fell asleep. But how odd that I forgot he'd taken time off to go to London to write a book about the city.

Together with Sofie Rieslyn.

On the borders of sleep, she realised it was the famous photographer she'd been afraid of. Paranoia, she thought. Watch your step, Anna.

CHAPTER 75

'She looks like a crow,' said Rickard at morning coffee. As usual when nervous, Anna was busy organising things.

'I'll clear up Father's room. Make up a bed for her. And pack away my papers. Then you can use the desk and the dining room to work in. Make a detour, will you, and get some fresh turbot?

'Shall do.'

She did not look like a crow, but more like a raven. Small, intense eyes, observant. Sharp lines in her face, white streaks in her dark hair.

'You're not a bit like the photographs Rickard showed me,' she said to Anna. 'I'll take some more.'

'Watch it,' said Rickard. 'Sofie's top speed when it comes to portraits is four hours.'

'But I'd like that,' said Anna. 'I'd like to know what I really look like. At last.'

'Whoever you are,' said the photographer, 'you get interesting when you're grieving.'

It became a long, lazy Sunday lunch and then Sofie said she needed to rest.

'Not surprised,' said Rickard. 'After being up so late last night.'

Anna usually found journalists' jargon difficult, their crude humour. But not today. She laughed and was able to share the joke.

In the afternoon, Sofie unpacked her photographs and Rickard whistled loudly with delight. And groaned: How the hell can I write captions to photos like these?

Anna walked round the tables and some time went by before they saw she had turned quite white and rigid.

Here's someone who knew, she thought. Who always stayed in the detail, in the little thing that could say everything.

'What's the matter, Anna?'

She didn't reply, but turned to Sofie.

'Have you always known?' she whispered.

'I think so.'

'I've just learned to. For three weeks here on the shore, I've learned.'

'Good, Anna. You won't lose it. You know, once seen …'

'I know.'

After a long silence, Rickard said he realised a simple hack like him shouldn't ask questions.

'Exactly,' Sofie and Anna agreed with a laugh.

'Horrible women,' said Rickard, and Anna hurried to say, as usual, in consolation, 'I'll explain later, Rickard.'

'Hello there,' said Sofie, and Anna flushed.

She left that same evening for her neglected studio in Stockholm, as she put it. 'We'll meet again,' she said, and Anna knew it was true, that the two of them would meet again.

On Monday they met Rune and Ingeborg as agreed at the bank.

On Tuesday the children came from Stockholm. Together they cleared the house and cleaned it. Malin wanted a bureau and two armchairs. Maria had never been able to resist books and packed the contents of the bookcases into her car. Both wanted the old porcelain and Rickard took some of the tools from Arne's basement.

'What about you, Mother? Don't you want anything?'

'Yes, I'm taking the Värmland sofa that's in the attic.'

'Heavens!'

'Out of affection?'

'You could say that.'

They had finished by the Wednesday. Early Thursday morning Ingeborg and Rune were coming to fetch the keys. Then the laden cars were to drive west and on the E4 northwards.

The long journey home, thought Anna.

After a light dinner of cold cuts and salmon, she said, 'Now listen to me, all of you. I'm going to tell you a fairy story.'

The little girls' eyes glowed. They loved Anna's stories, though Malin was uneasy.

'I can't bear it if you get sentimental, Mum.'

'Just sit still and listen,' said Anna.

She told them about the old place on the Norwegian border, the waterfall and the mill, and the miller who came from Värmland and proposed to Hanna. 'Your great-great-grandmother,' she said to the children.

She went on to tell them about the rich farm Hanna's ancestor had once been given by the king himself. Then she went on about the famine years, the children who had died of starvation and the farm, which had been divided up into smaller and smaller lots.

'When the last big farmer died, the home farm was still worth quite a lot,' she said. 'His daughter changed the inheritance. Hanna was given the deeds of the mill and all the stock on the farm, her brothers the smaller farms.

'But there was another sister, an elf-like girl who married in Norway. She was left all the family jewels. It was said they were just as valuable as the other shares.'

Anna showed them the photograph of Astrid, and the younger girl spoke.

'She's like Grandmother Johanna.'

'So, you saw that, did you?' said Anna.

According to tradition, the jewellery was to go from daughter to daughter in the family, she went on, and now they could all feel the tension. 'But Astrid had no daughters so she decided my mother should have it. Norway was at war when she died, but in the summer of 1945, a lawyer came here.

'I'll never forget that day.

297

'And now, Rickard, you must get yourself a suitable tool. For we're going to bring the treasure up from the basement.' The children were pale with excitement, Maria's eyes wide open and dark, and Malin had to make an effort to keep up her sceptical expression as they went down the basement stairs.

'You must count now, little one,' said Anna. 'Sixteen stones from the north wall.'

'Here,' said the girl.

'Good. Stay there now. Lena, you count four stones from the west wall.'

'There a beer crate there,' said the girl.

'Then we'll move it.'

The stone floor was clean and untouched under the crate, but Anna went on, 'Now, Rickard, get your chisel into the cracks just where Lena's standing.'

'It's mortar.'

'No, it's modelling clay.'

'Darn it, so it is.'

He raised the first stone, the second, then another.

'A safe!' he cried.

'Where's the key?' cried Malin.

'I've got it. Let's take the case up into the kitchen.'

They sat there staring at the glitter on the kitchen table and Malin gasped and said whatever was it all worth. Anna said it had never been valued, but she thought the big red stones in the necklace were probably rubies and the glittering stones in the brooches diamonds. 'The most valuable jewels don't really belong in the old inheritance. They're the ones Astrid was given or bought in Oslo. Her husband grew wealthy over the years.'

Then she lifted up the two heavy gold rings and told them the story of the warrior king who had dropped the gold coin and how the farmer who had found it had melted down the gold into rings for his daughters.

Then she started laughing and said the fairy-tale was over. Only one thing remained. 'I've had an extra key to the safe cut, so now I'm giving my daughters one each.'

They accepted the keys, but were quite incapable of thanking her.

'I think you've been struck dumb,' said Anna, still laughing.

Finally, Rickard said he wasn't surprised. He'd always known he'd married into a family full of secrets.

At dawn the next morning, they drove away from the house. Ingeborg said they were always welcome to come back to visit them, and Anna thanked her, but thought just as Hanna had that day when she had left the millhouse, I'll never return here again.